Fake D[...]

A Business
Deal

MERLINE LOVELACE

SARAH M. ANDERSON

MICHELLE CONDER

MILLS & BOON

First Published in Great Britain 2023
by Mills & Boon, an imprint of HarperCollins*Publishers* Ltd,
1 London Bridge Street, London, SE1 9GF

www.harpercollins.co.uk

HarperCollins*Publishers*
Macken House, 39/40 Mayor Street Upper,
Dublin 1, D01 C9W8, Ireland

ISBN: 978-0-263-31948-4

A BUSINESS ENGAGEMENT

MERLINE LOVELACE

To Susan and Monroe and Debbie and Scott and most
especially, le beau Monsieur Al. Thanks for those
magical days in Paris. Next time, I promise not to
break a foot – or anything else!

Prologue

Ah, the joys of having two such beautiful, loving granddaughters. And the worries! Eugenia, my joyful Eugenia, is like a playful kitten. She gets into such mischief but always seems to land on her feet. It's Sarah I worry about. So quiet, so elegant and so determined to shoulder the burdens of our small family. She's only two years older than her sister but has been Eugenia's champion and protector since the day those darling girls came to live with me.

Now Sarah worries about *me*. I admit to a touch of arthritis and have one annoying bout of angina, but she insists on fussing over me like a mother hen. I've told her repeatedly I won't have her putting her life on hold because of me, but she won't listen. It's time, I think, to take more direct action. I'm not quite certain at this point just what action, but something will come to me. It must.

From the diary of Charlotte,
Grand Duchess of Karlenburgh

One

Sarah heard the low buzz but didn't pay any attention to it. She was on deadline and only had until noon to finish the layout for *Beguile*'s feature on the best new ski resorts for the young and ultrastylish. She wanted to finish the mock-up in time for the senior staff's weekly working lunch. If she didn't have it ready, Alexis Danvers, the magazine's executive editor, would skewer her with one of the basilisk-like stares that had made her a legend in the world of glossy women's magazines.

Not that her boss's stony stares particularly bothered Sarah. They might put the rest of the staff in a flophouse sweat, but she and her sister had been raised by a grand-mother who could reduce pompous officials or supercilious headwaiters to a quivering bundle of nerves with the lift of a single brow. Charlotte St. Sebastian had once moved in the same circles as Princess Grace and Jackie O. Those days were long gone, Sarah acknowledged, as she switched the headline font from Futura to Trajan, but Grandmama still adhered to the unshakable belief that good breeding and quiet elegance could see a woman through anything life might throw at her.

Sarah agreed completely. Which was one of the reasons she'd refined her own understated style during her three years as layout editor for a magazine aimed at thirtysomethings determined to be chic to the death. Her vintage Chanel suits and Dior gowns might come from Grandmama's closet, but she teamed the gowns with funky costume jewelry and the suit jackets with slacks or jeans and boots. The result was a stylishly retro look that even Alexis approved of.

The primary reason Sarah stuck to her own style, of course, was that she couldn't afford the designer shoes and bags and clothing featured in *Beguile*. Not with Grandmama's medical bills. Some of her hand-me-downs were starting to show their wear, though, and...

The buzz cut into her thoughts. Gaining volume, it rolled in her direction. Sarah was used to frequent choruses of oohs and aahs. Alexis often had models parade through the art and production departments to field test their hair or makeup or outfits on *Beguile*'s predominantly female staff.

Whatever was causing this chorus had to be special. Excitement crackled in the air like summer lightning. Wondering what new Jimmy Choo beaded boots or Atelier Versace gown was creating such a stir, Sarah swung her chair around. To her utter astonishment, she found herself looking up into the face of Sexy Single Number Three.

"Ms. St. Sebastian?"

The voice was cold, but the electric-blue eyes, black hair and rugged features telegraphed hot, hot, hot. Alexis had missed the mark with last month's issue, Sarah thought wildly. This man should have *topped* the magazine's annual Ten Sexiest Single Men in the World list instead of taking third place.

The artist in her could appreciate six-feet-plus of hard, muscled masculinity cloaked in the civilized veneer of a hand-tailored suit and Italian-silk tie. The professional in her responded to the coldness in his voice with equally cool civility.

"Yes?"

"I want to talk to you." Those devastating blue eyes cut to the side. "Alone."

Sarah followed his searing gaze. An entire gallery of female faces peered over, around and between the production department's chin-high partitions. A few of those faces were merely curious. Most appeared a half breath away from drooling.

She turned back to Number Three. Too bad his manners didn't live up to his looks. The aggressiveness in both his tone and his stance were irritating and uncalled for, to say the least.

"What do you want to talk to me about, Mr. Hunter?"

He didn't appear surprised that she knew his name. She did, after all, work at the magazine that had made hunky Devon Hunter the object of desire by a good portion of the female population at home and abroad.

"Your sister, Ms. St. Sebastian."

Oh, no! A sinking sensation hit Sarah in the pit of her stomach. What had Gina gotten into now?

Her glance slid to the silver-framed photo on the credenza beside her workstation. There was Sarah, dark-haired, green-eyed, serious as always, protective as always. And Gina. Blonde, bubbly, affectionate, completely irresponsible.

Two years younger than Sarah, Gina tended to change careers with the same dizzying frequency she tumbled in and out of love. She'd texted just a few days ago, gushing about the studly tycoon she'd hooked up with. Omitting, Gina style, to mention such minor details as his name or how they'd met.

Sarah had no trouble filling in the blanks now. Devon Hunter was founder and CEO of a Fortune 500 aerospace corporation headquartered in Los Angeles. Gina was in

L.A. chasing yet another career opportunity, this time as a party planner for the rich and famous.

"I think it best if we make this discussion private, Ms. St. Sebastian."

Resigned to the inevitable, Sarah nodded. Her sister's flings tended to be short and intense. Most ended amicably, but on several occasions Sarah had been forced to soothe some distinctly ruffled male feathers. This, apparently, was one of those occasions.

"Come with me, Mr. Hunter."

She led the way to a glass-walled conference room with angled windows that gave a view of Times Square. Framed prominently in one of the windows was the towering Condé Nast Building, the center of the universe for fashion publications. The building was home to *Vogue, Vanity Fair, Glamour* and *Allure.* Alexis often brought advertisers to the conference room to impress them with *Beguile*'s proximity to those icons in the world of women's glossies.

The caterers hadn't begun setting up for the working lunch yet but the conference room was always kept ready for visitors. The fridge discreetly hidden behind oak panels held a half-dozen varieties of bottled water, sparkling and plain, as well as juices and energy drinks. The gleaming silver coffee urns were replenished several times a day.

Sarah gestured to the urns on their marble counter. "Would you care for some coffee? Or some sparkling water, perhaps?"

"No. Thanks."

The curt reply decided her against inviting the man to sit. Crossing her arms, she leaned a hip against the conference table and assumed a look of polite inquiry.

"You wanted to talk about Gina?"

He took his time responding. Sarah refused to bristle as his killer blue eyes made an assessing trip from her face to her Chanel suit jacket with its black-and-white checks and signature logo to her black boots and back up again.

"You don't look much like your sister."

"No, I don't."

She was comfortable with her slender build and what her grandmother insisted were classic features, but she knew she didn't come close to Gina's stunning looks.

"My sister's the only beauty in the family."

Politeness dictated that he at least make a show of disputing the calm assertion. Instead, he delivered a completely unexpected bombshell.

"Is she also the only thief?"

Her arms dropped. Her jaw dropped with them. "I beg your pardon?"

"You can do more than beg my pardon, Ms. St. Sebastian. You can contact your sister and tell her to return the artifact she stole from my house."

The charge took Sarah's breath away. It came back on a hot rush. "How dare you make such a ridiculous, slanderous accusation?"

"It's neither ridiculous nor slanderous. It's fact."

"You're crazy!"

She was in full tigress mode now. Years of rushing to her younger sibling's defense spurred both fury and passion.

"Gina may be flighty and a little careless at times, but she would never take anything that didn't belong to her!"

Not intentionally, that is. There was that nasty little Pomeranian she'd brought home when she was eight or nine. She'd found it leashed to a sign outside a restaurant in one-hundred-degree heat and "rescued" it. And it was true Gina and her teenaged friends used to borrow clothes from each other constantly, then could never remember what belonged to whom. And, yes, she'd been known to overdraw her checking account when she was strapped for cash, which happened a little too frequently for Sarah's peace of mind.

But she would never commit theft, as this…this boor was suggesting. Sarah was about to call security to have the man escorted from the building when he reached into his suit pocket and palmed an iPhone.

"Maybe this clip from my home surveillance system will change your mind."

He tapped the screen, then angled it for Sarah to view. She saw a still image of what looked like a library or study, with the focus of the camera on an arrangement of glass shelves. The objects on the shelves were spaced and spotlighted for maximum dramatic effect. They appeared to be an eclectic mix. Sarah noted an African buffalo mask, a small cloisonné disk on a black lacquer stand and what looked like a statue of a pre-Columbian fertility goddess.

Hunter tapped the screen again and the still segued into a video. While Sarah watched, a tumble of platinum-blond curls came into view. Her heart began to thump painfully even before the owner of those curls moved toward the shelving. It picked up more speed when the owner showed her profile. That was her sister. Sarah couldn't even pretend to deny it.

Gina glanced over her shoulder, all casual nonchalance, all smiling innocence. When she moved out of view again, the cloisonné medallion no longer sat on its stand. Hunter froze the frame again, and Sarah stared at the empty stand as though it was a bad dream.

"It's Byzantine," he said drily. "Early twelfth century, in case you're interested. One very similar to it sold recently at Sotheby's in London for just over a hundred thousand."

She swallowed. Hard. "Dollars?"

"Pounds."

"Oh, God."

She'd rescued Gina from more scrapes than she could count. But this… She almost yanked out one of the chairs and collapsed in a boneless heap. The iron will she'd inherited from Grandmama kept her spine straight and her chin up.

"There's obviously a logical explanation for this, Mr. Hunter."

"I very much hope so, Ms. St. Sebastian."

She wanted to smack him. Calm, refined, always polite Sarah had to curl her hands into fists to keep from slapping that sneer off his too-handsome face.

He must have guessed her savagely suppressed urge. His jaw squared and his blue eyes took on a challenging glint, as if daring her to give it her best shot. When she didn't, he picked up where they'd left off.

"I'm very interested in hearing that explanation before I refer the matter to the police."

The police! Sarah felt a chill wash through her. Whatever predicament Gina had landed herself in suddenly assumed a very ominous tone. She struggled to keep the shock and worry out of her voice.

"Let me get in touch with my sister, Mr. Hunter. It may… it may take a while. She's not always prompt about returning calls or answering emails right away."

"Yeah, I found that out. I've been trying to reach her for several days."

He shot back a cuff and glanced at his watch.

"I've got meetings scheduled that will keep me tied up for the rest of this afternoon and well into the night. I'll make dinner reservations for tomorrow evening. Seven o'clock. Avery's, Upper West Side." He turned that hard blue gaze on her. "I assume you know the address. It's only a few blocks from the Dakota."

Still stunned by what she'd seen in the surveillance clip, Sarah almost missed his last comment. When it penetrated, her eyes widened in shock. "You know where I live?"

"Yes, Lady Sarah, I do." He tipped two fingers to his brow in a mock salute and strode for the door. "I'll see you tomorrow."

* * *

Lady Sarah.

Coming on top of everything else, the use of her empty title shouldn't have bothered her. Her boss trotted it out frequently at cocktail parties and business meetings. Sarah had stopped being embarrassed by Alexis's shameless peddling of a royal title that had long since ceased to have any relevance.

Unfortunately, Alexis wanted to do more than peddle the heritage associated with the St. Sebastian name. Sarah had threatened to quit—twice!—if her boss went ahead with the feature she wanted to on *Beguile*'s own Lady Sarah Elizabeth Marie-Adele St. Sebastian, granddaughter to Charlotte, the Destitute Duchess.

God! Sarah shuddered every time she remembered the slant Alexis had wanted to give the story. That destitute tag, as accurate as it was, would have shattered Grandmama's pride.

Having her younger granddaughter arrested for grand larceny wouldn't do a whole lot for it, either.

Jolted back to the issue at hand, Sarah rushed out of the conference room. She had to get hold of Gina. Find out if she'd really lifted that medallion. She was making a dash for her workstation when she saw her boss striding toward her.

"What's this I just heard?"

Alexis's deep, guttural smoker's rasp was always a shock to people meeting her for the first time. *Beguile*'s executive editor was paper-clip thin and always gorgeously dressed. But she would rather take her chances with cancer than quit smoking and risk ballooning up to a size four.

"Is it true?" she growled. "Devon Hunter was here?"

"Yes, he…"

"Why didn't you buzz me?"

"I didn't have time."

"What did he want? He's not going to sue us, is he?

Dammit, I told you to crop that locker-room shot above the waist."

"No, Alexis. You told me to make sure it showed his butt crack. And I told *you* I didn't think we should pay some smarmy gym employee to sneak pictures of the man without his knowledge or consent."

The executive editor waved that minor difference of editorial opinion aside. "So what did he want?"

"He's, uh, a friend of Gina's."

Or was, Sarah thought grimly, until the small matter of a twelfth-century medallion had come between them. She had to get to a phone. Had to call Gina.

"Another one of your sister's trophies?" Alexis asked sarcastically.

"I didn't have time to get all the details. Just that he's in town for some business meetings and wants to get together for dinner tomorrow."

The executive editor cocked her head. An all-too-familiar gleam entered her eyes, one that made Sarah swallow a groan. Pit bulls had nothing on Alexis when she locked her jaws on a story.

"We could do a follow-up," she said. "How making *Beguile*'s Top Ten list has impacted our sexy single's life. Hunter's pretty much a workaholic, isn't he?"

Frantic to get to the phone, Sarah gave a distracted nod. "That's how we portrayed him."

"I'm guessing he can't take a step now without tripping over a half-dozen panting females. Gina certainly smoked him out fast enough. I want details, Sarah. Details!"

She did her best to hide her agitation behind her usual calm facade. "Let me talk to my sister first. See what's going on."

"Do that. And get me details!"

Alexis strode off and Sarah barely reached the chair at her worktable before her knees gave out. She snatched up her iPhone and hit the speed-dial number for her sister. Of course, the call went to voice mail.

"Gina! I need to talk to you! Call me."

She also tapped out a text message and zinged off an email. None of which would do any good if her sister had forgotten to turn on her phone. Again. Knowing the odds of that were better than fifty-fifty, she tried Gina's current place of employment. She was put through to her sister's distinctly irate boss, who informed her that Gina hadn't shown up for work. Again.

"She called in yesterday morning. We'd catered a business dinner at the home of one our most important clients the night before. She said she was tired and was taking the day off. I haven't heard from her since."

Sarah had to ask. "Was that client Devon Hunter, by any chance?"

"Yes, it was. Look, Ms. St. Sebastian, your sister has a flair for presentation but she's completely unreliable. If you speak to her before I do, tell her not to bother coming in at all."

Despite the other, far more pressing problem that needed to be dealt with, Sarah hated that Gina had lost yet another job. She'd really seemed to enjoy this one.

"I'll tell her," she promised the irate supervisor. "And if she contacts you first, please tell her to call me."

She got through the working lunch somehow. Alexis, of course, demanded a laundry list of changes to the ski-resort layout. Drop shadows on the headline font. Less white space between the photos. Ascenders, not descenders, for the first letter of each lead paragraph.

Sarah made the fixes and shot the new layout from her computer to Alexis's for review. She then tried to frame another article describing the latest body-toning techniques. In between, she made repeated calls to Gina. They went unanswered, as did her emails and text messages.

Her concentration in shreds, she quit earlier than usual and hurried out into the April evening. A half block away, Times Square glowed in a rainbow of white, blue and brilliant-red lights. Tourists were out in full force, crowding the sidewalks and snapping pictures. Ordinarily Sarah took the subway to and from work, but a driving sense of urgency made her decide to splurge on a cab. Unbelievably, one cruised up just when she hit the curb. She slid in as soon as the previous passenger climbed out.

"The Dakota, please."

The turbaned driver nodded and gave her an assessing glance in the rearview mirror. Whatever their nationality, New York cabbies were every bit as savvy as any of *Beguile*'s fashion-conscious editors. This one might not get the label on Sarah's suit jacket exactly right but he knew quality when he saw it. He also knew a drop-off at one of New York City's most famous landmarks spelled big tips.

Usually. Sarah tried not to think how little of this month's check would be left after paying the utilities and maintenance fees for the seven-room apartment she shared with her grandmother. She also tried not to cringe when the cabbie scowled at the tip she gave him. Muttering something in his native language, he shoved his cab in gear.

Sarah hurried toward the entrance to the domed and turreted apartment building constructed in the 1880s and nodded to the doorman who stepped out of his niche to greet her.

"Good evening, Jerome."

"Good evening, Lady Sarah."

She'd long ago given up trying to get him to drop the empty title. Jerome felt it added to the luster of "his" building.

Not that the Dakota needed additional burnishing. Now a National Historic Landmark, its ornate exterior had been featured in dozens of films. Fictional characters in a host of novels claimed the Dakota as home. Real-life celebri-

ties like Judy Garland, Lauren Bacall and Leonard Bern-
stein had lived there. And, sadly, John Lennon. He'd been
shot just a short distance away. His widow, Yoko Ono, still
owned several apartments in the building.

"The Duchess returned from her afternoon constitutional about an hour ago," Jerome volunteered. The merest
hint of a shadow crossed his lean face. "She was leaning
rather heavily on her cane."

Sharp, swift fear pushed aside Sarah's worry about her
sister. "She didn't overdo it, did she?"

"She said not. But then, she wouldn't say otherwise,
would she?"

"No," Sarah agreed in a hollow voice, "she wouldn't.

Charlotte St. Sebastian had witnessed the brutal execution of her husband and endured near-starvation before
she'd escaped her war-ravaged country with her baby in
her arms and a king's ransom in jewels hidden inside her
daughter's teddy bear. She'd fled first to Vienna, then New
York, where she'd slipped easily into the city's intellectual
and social elite. The discreet, carefully timed sale of her
jewels had allowed her to purchase an apartment at the Dakota and maintain a gracious lifestyle.

Tragedy struck again when she lost both her daughter
and son-in-law in a boating accident. Sarah was just four
and Gina still in diapers at the time. Not long after that, an
unscrupulous Wall Street type sank the savings the duchess had managed to accrue into a Ponzi scheme that blew
up in his and his clients' faces.

Those horrific events might have crushed a lesser
woman. With two small girls to raise, Charlotte St. Sebastian wasted little time on self-pity. Once again she was
forced to sell her heritage. The remaining jewels were discreetly disposed of over the years to provide her granddaughters with the education and lifestyle she insisted was
their birthright. Private schools. Music tutors. Coming-out

balls at the Waldorf. Smith College and a year at the Sorbonne for Sarah, Barnard for Gina.

Neither sister had a clue how desperate the financial situation had become, however, until Grandmama's heart attack. It was a mild one, quickly dismissed by the iron-spined duchess as a trifling bout of angina. The hospital charges weren't trifling, though. Nor was the stack of bills Sarah had found stuffed in Grandmama's desk when she sat down to pay what she'd thought were merely recurring monthly expenses. She'd nearly had a heart attack herself when she'd totaled up the amount.

Sarah had depleted her own savings account to pay that daunting stack of bills. Most of them, anyway. She still had to settle the charges for Grandmama's last echocardiogram. In the meantime, her single most important goal in life was to avoid stressing out the woman she loved with all her heart.

She let herself into their fifth-floor apartment, as shaken by Jerome's disclosure as by her earlier meeting with Devon Hunter. The comfortably padded Ecuadoran who served as maid, companion to Charlotte and friend to both Sarah and her sister for more than a decade was just preparing to leave.

"*Hola,* Sarah."

"*Hola,* Maria. How was your day?"

"Good. We walked, *la duquesa* and me, and shopped a little." She shouldered her hefty tote bag. "I go to catch my bus now. I'll see you tomorrow."

"Good night."

When the door closed behind her, a rich soprano voice only slightly dimmed by age called out, "Sarah? Is that you?"

"Yes, Grandmama."

She deposited her purse on the gilt-edged rococo sideboard gracing the entryway and made her way down a hall tiled in pale pink Carrara marble. The duchess hadn't been reduced to selling the furniture and artwork she'd acquired when she'd first arrived in New York, although Sarah now knew how desperately close she'd come to it.

"You're home early."

Charlotte sat in her favorite chair, the single aperitif she allowed herself despite the doctor's warning close at hand. The sight of her faded blue eyes and aristocratic nose brought a rush of emotion so strong Sarah had to swallow before she could a reply past the lump in her throat.

"Yes, I am."

She should have known Charlotte would pick up on the slightest nuance in her granddaughter's voice.

"You sound upset," she said with a small frown. "Did something happen at work?"

"Nothing more than the usual." Sarah forced a wry smile and went to pour herself a glass of white wine. "Alexis was on a tear about the ski-resort mock-up. I had to rework everything but the page count."

The duchess sniffed. "I don't know why you work for that woman."

"Mostly because she was the only one who would hire me."

"She didn't hire you. She hired your title."

Sarah winced, knowing it was true, and her grandmother instantly shifted gears.

"Lucky for Alexis the title came with an unerring eye for form, shape and spatial dimension," she huffed.

"Lucky for *me*," Sarah countered with a laugh. "Not everyone can parlay a degree in Renaissance-era art into a job at one of the country's leading fashion magazines."

"Or work her way from junior assistant to senior editor in just three years," Charlotte retorted. Her face softened into an expression that played on Sarah's heartstrings like a finely tuned Stradivarius. "Have I told you how proud I am of you?"

"Only about a thousand times, Grandmama."

They spent another half hour together before Charlotte decided she would rest a little before dinner. Sarah knew better than to offer to help her out of her chair, but she wanted to. God, she wanted to! When her grandmother's cane had thumped slowly down the hall to her bedroom, Sarah fixed a spinach salad and added a bit more liquid to the chicken Maria had begun baking in the oven. Then she washed her hands, detoured into the cavernous sitting room that served as a study and booted up her laptop.

She remembered the basics from the article *Beguile* had run on Devon Hunter. She wanted to dig deeper, uncover every minute detail she could about the man before she crossed swords with him again tomorrow evening.

Two

Seated at a linen-draped table by the window, Dev watched Sarah St. Sebastian approach the restaurant's entrance. Tall and slender, she moved with restrained grace. No swinging hips, no ground-eating strides, just a smooth symmetry of motion and dignity.

She wore her hair down tonight. He liked the way the mink-dark waves framed her face and brushed the shoulders of her suit jacket. The boxy jacket was a sort of pale purple. His sisters would probably call that color lilac or heliotrope or something equally girlie. The skirt was black and just swished her boot tops as she walked.

Despite growing up with four sisters, Dev's fashion sense could be summed up in a single word. A woman either looked good, or she didn't. This one looked good. *Very* good.

He wasn't the only one who thought so. When she entered the restaurant and the greeter escorted her to the table by the window, every head in the room turned. Males without female companions were openly admiring. Those with women at their tables were more discreet but no less appreciative. Many of the women, too, slanted those seemingly casual, careless glances that instantly catalogued every detail of hair, dress, jewelry and shoes.

How the hell did they do that? Dev could walk into the belly of a plane and tell in a single glance if the struts were buckling or the rivets starting to rust. As he'd discovered since that damned magazine article came out, however, his powers of observation paled beside those of the female of the species.

He'd treated the Ten Sexiest Singles list as a joke at first. He could hardly do otherwise, with his sisters, brothers-in-law and assorted nieces and nephews ragging him about it nonstop. And okay, being named one of the world's top ten hunks did kind of puff up his ego.

That was before women began stopping him on the street to let him know they were available. Before waitresses started hustling over to take his order and make the same pronouncement. Before the cocktail parties he was forced to attend as the price of doing business became a total embarrassment.

Dev had been able to shrug off most of it. He couldn't shrug off the wife of the French CEO he was trying to close a multibillion dollar deal with. The last time Dev was in Paris, Elise Girault had draped herself all over him. He knew then he had to put a stop to what had become more than just a nuisance.

He'd thought he'd found the perfect tool in Lady Eugenia Amalia Therése St. Sebastian. The blonde was gorgeous, vivacious and so photogenic that the vultures otherwise known as paparazzi wouldn't even glance at Dev if she was anywhere in the vicinity.

Thirty minutes in Gina St. Sebastian's company had deep-sixed that idea. Despite her pedigree, the woman was as bubbleheaded as she was sumptuous. Then she'd lifted the Byzantine medallion and the game plan had changed completely. For the better, Dev decided as he rose to greet the slender brunette being escorted to his table.

Chin high, shoulders back, Sarah St. Sebastian carried herself like the royalty she was. Or would have been, if her grandmother's small Eastern European country hadn't dispensed with royal titles about the same time Soviet tanks had rumbled across its border. The tanks had rumbled out again four decades later. By that time the borders of Eastern Europe had been redrawn several times and the duchy that had been home to the St. Sebastians for several centuries had completely disappeared.

Bad break for Charlotte St. Sebastian and her granddaughters. Lucky break for Dev. Lady Sarah didn't know it yet, but she was going to extract him from the mess she and her magazine had created.

"Good evening, Mr. Hunter."

The voice was cool, the green eyes cold.

"Good evening, Ms. St. Sebastian."

Dev stood patiently while the greeter seated her. A server materialized instantly.

"A cocktail or glass of wine before dinner, madam?"

"No, thank you. And no dinner." She waved aside the gilt-edged menu he offered and locked those forest-glade eyes on Dev. "I'll just be here a few minutes, then I'll leave Mr. Hunter to enjoy his meal."

The server departed, and Dev reclaimed his seat. "Are you sure you don't want dinner?"

"I'm sure." She placed loosely clasped hands on the table and launched an immediate offensive. "We're not here to exchange pleasantries, Mr. Hunter."

Dev sat back against his chair, his long legs outstretched beneath the starched tablecloth and his gaze steady on her face. Framed by those dark, glossy waves, her features fascinated him. The slight widow's peak, the high cheekbones, the aquiline nose—all refined and remote and in seeming contrast to those full, sensual lips. She might have modeled for some famous fifteenth- or sixteen-century sculptor. Dev was damned if he knew which.

"No, we're not," he agreed, still intrigued by that face. "Have you talked to your sister?"

The clasped hands tightened. Only a fraction, but that small jerk was a dead giveaway.

"I haven't been able to reach her."

"Neither have I. So what do you propose we do now?"

"I propose you wait." She drew in a breath and forced a small smile. "Give me more time to track Gina down before you report your medallion missing or...or..."

"Or stolen?"

The smile evaporated. "Gina didn't steal that piece, Mr. Hunter. I admit it appears she took it for some reason, but I'm sure...I *know* she'll return it. Eventually."

Dev played with the tumbler containing his scotch, circling it almost a full turn before baiting the trap.

"The longer I wait to file a police report, Ms. St. Sebastian, the more my insurance company is going to question why. A delay reporting the loss could void the coverage."

"Give me another twenty-four hours, Mr. Hunter. Please."

She hated to beg. He heard it in her voice, saw it in the way her hands were knotted together now, the knuckles white.

"All right, Ms. St. Sebastian. Twenty-four hours. If your sister hasn't returned the medallion by then, however, I..."

"She will. I'm sure she will."

"And if she doesn't?"

She drew in another breath: longer, shakier. "I'll pay you the appraised value."

"How?"

Her chin came up. Her jaws went tight. "It will take some time," she admitted. "We'll have to work out a payment schedule."

Dev didn't like himself much at the moment. If he didn't have a multibillion-dollar deal hanging fire, he'd call this farce off right now. Setting aside the crystal tumbler, he leaned forward.

"Let's cut to the chase here, Ms. St. Sebastian. I had my people run an in-depth background check on your feather-headed sister. On you, too. I know you've bailed Gina out of one mess after another. I know you're currently providing your grandmother's sole support. I also know you barely make enough to cover her medical co-pays, let alone re-imburse me for a near-priceless artifact."

Every vestige of color had drained from her face, but pride sparked in those mesmerizing eyes. Before she could tell him where to go and how to get there, Dev sprang the trap.

"I have an alternate proposal, Ms. St. Sebastian."

Her brows snapped together. "What kind of a proposal?"

"I need a fiancée."

For the second time in as many days Dev saw her composure crumble. Her jaw dropping, she treated him to a disbelieving stare.

"Excuse me?"

"I need a fiancée," he repeated. "I was considering Gina for the position. I axed that idea after thirty minutes in her company. Becoming engaged to your sister," he drawled, "is not for the faint of heart."

He might have stunned her with his proposition. That didn't prevent her from leaping to the defense. Dev suspected it came as natural to her as breathing.

"My sister, Mr. Hunter, is warm and generous and open-hearted and..."

"Gone to ground." He drove the point home with the same swift lethality he brought to the negotiating table. "You, on the other hand, are available. And you owe me."

"*I* owe you?"

"You and that magazine you work for." Despite his best efforts to keep his irritation contained, it leaked into his voice. "Do you have any idea how many women have accosted me since that damned article came out? I can't even grab a meatball sub at my favorite deli without some female writing her number on a napkin and trying to stuff it into my pants pocket."

Her shock faded. Derision replaced it. She sat back in her chair with her lips pooched in false sympathy.

"Ooh. You poor, poor sex object."

"You may think it's funny," he growled. "I don't. Not with a multibillion-dollar deal hanging in the balance."

That wiped the smirk off her face. "Putting you on our Ten Sexiest Singles list has impacted your business? How?"

Enlightenment dawned in almost the next breath. The smirk returned. "Oh! Wait! I've got it. You have so many women throwing themselves at you that you can't concentrate."

"You're partially correct. But it's not a matter of not being able to concentrate. It's more that I don't want to jeopardize the deal by telling the wife of the man I'm negotiating with to keep her hands to herself."

"So instead of confronting the woman, you want to hide behind a fiancée."

The disdain was cool and well-bred, but it was there. Dev was feeling the sting when he caught a flutter of movement from the corner of one eye. A second later the flutter evolved into a tall, sleek redhead being shown to an empty table a little way from theirs. She caught Dev's glance, arched a penciled brow and came to a full stop beside their table.

"I know you." She tilted her head and put a finger to her chin. "Remind me. Where have we met?"

"We haven't," Dev replied, courteous outside, bracing inside.

"Are you sure? I never forget a face. Or," she added as her lips curved in a slow, feline smile, "a truly excellent butt."

The grimace that crossed Hunter's face gave Sarah a jolt

of fierce satisfaction. Let him squirm, she thought glee-fully. Let him writhe like a specimen under a microscope. He deserved the embarrassment.

Except...

He didn't. Not really. *Beguile* had put him under the mi-croscope. *Beguile* had also run a locker-room photo with the face angled away from the camera just enough to keep them from getting sued. And as much as Sarah hated to admit it, the man had shown a remarkable degree of re-straint by not reporting his missing artifact to the police immediately.

Still, she didn't want to come to his rescue. She *really* didn't. It was an innate and very grudging sense of fair play that compelled her to mimic her grandmother in one of Charlotte's more imperial moods.

"I beg your pardon," she said with icy hauteur. "I be-lieve my fiancé has already stated he doesn't know you. Now, if you don't mind, we would like to continue our conversation."

The woman's cheeks flushed almost the same color as her hair. "Yes, of course. Sorry for interrupting."

She hurried to her table, leaving Hunter staring after her while Sarah took an unhurried sip from her water goblet.

"That's it." He turned back to her, amusement slashing across his face. "That's exactly what I want from you."

Whoa! Sarah gripped the goblet's stem and tried to blunt the impact of the grin aimed in her direction. Devon Hunter all cold and intimidating she could handle. Devon Hunter with crinkly squint lines at the corners of those killer blue eyes and his mouth tipped into a rakish smile was some-thing else again.

The smile made him look so different. That, and the more casual attire he wore tonight. He was in a suit again, but he'd dispensed with a tie and his pale blue shirt was open at the neck. This late in the evening, a five-o'clock shadow darkened his cheeks and chin, giving him the sophisticated bad-boy look so many of *Beguile*'s male models tried for but could never quite pull off.

The research Sarah had done on the man put him in a different light, too. She'd had to dig hard for details. Hunter was notorious about protecting his privacy, which was why *Beguile* had been forced to go with a fluff piece instead of the in-depth interview Alexis had wanted. And no doubt why he resented the article so much, Sarah acknowledged with a twinge of guilt.

The few additional details she'd managed to dig up had contributed to an intriguing picture. She'd already known that Devon Hunter had enlisted in the Air Force right out of high school and trained as a loadmaster on big cargo jets. She hadn't known he'd completed a bachelor's *and* a master's during his eight years in uniform, despite spending most of those years flying into combat zones or disaster areas.

On one of those combat missions his aircraft had come under intense enemy fire. Hunter had jerry-rigged some kind of emergency fix to its damaged cargo ramp that had allowed them to take on hundreds of frantic Somalian refugees attempting to escape certain death. He'd left the Air Force a short time later and patented the modification he'd devised. From what Sarah could gather, it was now used on military and civilian aircraft worldwide.

That enterprise had earned Hunter his first million. The rest, as they say, was history. She hadn't found a precise estimate of the man's net worth, but it was obviously enough to allow him to collect hundred-thousand-pound museum pieces. Which brought her back to the problem at hand.

"Look, Mr. Hunter, this whole…"

"Dev," he interrupted, the grin still in place. "Now that we're engaged, we should dispense with the formalities. I know you have a half-dozen names. Do you go by Sarah or Elizabeth or Marie-Adele?"

"Sarah," she conceded, "but we are *not* engaged."

He tipped his chin toward the woman several tables away, her nose now buried in a menu. "Red there thinks we are."

"I simply didn't care for her attitude."

"Me, either." The amusement left his eyes. "That's why I offered you a choice. Let me spell out the basic terms so there's no misunderstanding. You agree to an engagement. Six months max. Less, if I close the deal currently on the table. In return, I destroy the surveillance tape and don't report the loss."

"But the medallion! You said it was worth a hundred thousand pounds or more."

"I'm willing to accept your assurances that Gina will return it. Eventually. In the meantime..." He lifted his tumbler in a mock salute. "To us, Sarah."

Feeling much like the proverbial mouse backed into a corner, she snatched at her last lifeline. "You promised me another twenty-four hours. The deal doesn't go into effect until then. Agreed?"

He hesitated, then lifted his shoulders in a shrug. "Agreed."

Surely Gina would return her calls before then and this whole, ridiculous situation would be resolved. Sarah clung to that hope as she pushed away from the table.

"Until tomorrow, Mr. Hunter."

"Dev," he corrected, rising, as well.

"No need for you to walk me out. Please stay and enjoy your dinner."

"Actually, I got hungry earlier and grabbed a Korean taco from a street stand. Funny," he commented as he tossed some bills on the table, "I've been in and out of Korea a dozen times. Don't remember ever having tacos there."

He took her elbow in a courteous gesture Grandmama would approve of. Very correct, very polite, not really possessive but edging too close to it for Sarah's comfort. Walking beside him only reinforced the impression she'd gained yesterday of his height and strength.

They passed the redhead's table on the way to the door. She glanced up, caught Sarah's dismissive stare and stuck her nose back in the menu.

"I'll hail you a cab," Hunter said as they exited the restaurant.

"It's only a few blocks."

"It's also getting dark. I know this is your town, but I'll feel better sending you home in a cab."

Sarah didn't argue further, mostly because dusk had started to descend and the air had taken on a distinct chill. Across the street, the lanterns in Central Park shed their golden glow. She turned in a half circle, her artist's eye delighting in the dots of gold punctuating the deep purple of the park.

Unfortunately, the turn brought the redhead into view again. The picture there wasn't as delightful. She was squinting at them through the restaurant's window, a phone jammed to her ear. Whoever she was talking to was obviously getting an earful.

Sarah guessed instantly she was spreading the word about Sexy Single Number Three and his fiancée. The realization gave her a sudden, queasy feeling. New York City lived and breathed celebrities. They were the stuff of life on *Good Morning America,* were courted by Tyra Banks and the women of *The View,* appeared regularly on *Late Show with David Letterman.* The tabloids, the glossies, even the so-called "literary" publications paid major bucks for inside scoops.

And Sarah had just handed them one. Thoroughly disgusted with herself for yielding to impulse, she smothered a curse that would have earned a sharp reprimand from Grandmama. Hunter followed her line of sight and spotted the woman staring at them through the restaurant window, the phone still jammed to her ear. He shared Sarah's pessimistic view of the matter but didn't bother to swallow his curse. It singed the night air.

"This is going turn up in another rag like *Beguile,* isn't it?"

Sarah stiffened. True, she'd privately cringed at some of the articles Alexis had insisted on putting in print. But that didn't mean she would stand by and let an outsider disparage her magazine.

"*Beguile* is hardly a rag. We're one of the leading fashion publications for women in the twenty to thirty-five age range, here and abroad."

"If you say so."

"I do," she ground out.

The misguided sympathy she'd felt for the man earlier had gone as dry and stale as yesterday's bagel. It went even staler when he turned to face her. Devon Hunter of the crinkly squint lines and heart-stuttering grin was gone. His intimidating alter ego was back.

"I guess if we're going to show up in some pulp press, we might as well give the story a little juice."

She saw the intent in his face and put up a warning palm. "Let's not do anything rash here, Mr. Hunter."

"Dev," he corrected, his eyes drilling into hers. "Say it, Sarah. Dev."

"All right! Dev. Are you satisfied?"

"Not quite."

His arm went around her waist. One swift tug brought them hip to hip. His hold was an iron band, but he gave her a second, maybe two, to protest.

Afterward Sarah could list in precise order the reasons she should have done exactly that. She didn't like the man. He was flat-out blackmailing her with Gina's rash act. He was too arrogant, and too damned sexy, for his own good.

But right then, right there, she looked up into those

dangerous blue eyes and gave in to the combustible mix of guilt, nagging worry and Devon Hunter's potent masculinity.

Three

Sarah had been kissed before. A decent number of times, as a matter of fact. She hadn't racked up as many admirers as Gina, certainly, but she'd dated steadily all through high school and college. She'd also teetered dangerously close to falling in love at least twice. Once with the sexy Italian she'd met at the famed Uffizi Gallery and spent a dizzying week exploring Florence with. Most recently with a charismatic young lawyer who had his eye set on a career in politics. That relationship had died a rather painful death when she discovered he was more in love with her background and empty title than he was with her.

Even with the Italian, however, she'd never indulged in embarrassingly public displays of affection. In addition to Grandmama's black-and-white views of correct behavior, Sarah's inbred reserve shied away from the kind of exuberant joie de vivre that characterized her sister. Yet here she was, locked in the arms of a near stranger on the sidewalk of one of New York's busiest avenues. Her oh-so-proper self shouted that she was providing a sideshow for everyone in and outside the restaurant. Her other self, the one she let off its leash only on rare occasions, leaped to life.

If *Beguile* ever ran a list of the World's Ten Best Kissers, she thought wildly, she would personally nominate Devon Hunter for the top slot. His mouth fit over hers as though it was made to. His lips demanded a response.

Sarah gave it. Angling her head, she planted both palms on his chest. The hard muscles under his shirt and suit coat provided a feast of tactile sensations. The fine bristles scraping her chin added more. She could taste the faint, smoky hint of scotch on his lips, feel the heat that rose in his skin.

There was nothing hidden in Hunter's kiss. No attempt to impress or connect or score a victory in the battle of the sexes. His mouth moved easily over hers. Confidently. Hungrily.

Her breath came hard and fast when he raised his head. So did his. Sarah took immense satisfaction in that—and the fact that he looked as surprised and disconcerted as she felt at the moment. When his expression switched to a frown, though, she half expected a cutting remark. What she got was a curt apology.

"I'm sorry." He dropped his hold on her waist and stepped back a pace. "That was uncalled for."

Sarah wasn't about to point out that she hadn't exactly resisted. While she struggled to right her rioting senses, she caught a glimpse of a very interested audience backlit inside the restaurant. Among them was the redhead, still watching avidly, only this time she had her phone aimed in their direction.

"Uncalled for or not," Sarah said with a small groan, "be prepared for the possibility that kiss might make its way into print. I suspect your friend's phone is camera equipped."

He shot a glance over his shoulder and blew out a disgusted breath. "I'm sure it is."

"What a mess," she murmured half under her breath. "My boss will *not* be happy."

Hunter picked up on the ramifications of the comment instantly. "Is this going to cause a problem for you at work? You and me, our engagement, getting scooped by some other rag, uh, magazine?"

"First, we're not engaged. Yet. Second, you don't need to worry about my work."

Mostly because he wouldn't be on scene when the storm hit. If *Beguile*'s executive editor learned from another source that Sarah had locked lips with Number Three on busy Central Park West, she'd make a force-five hurricane seem like a spring shower.

Then there was the duchess.

"I'm more concerned about my grandmother," Sarah admitted reluctantly. "If she should see or hear something before I get this mess straightened out…"

She gnawed on her lower lip, trying to find a way out of what was looking more and more like the kind of dark, tangly thing you find at the bottom of a pond. To her surprise, Hunter offered a solution to at least one of her problems.

"Tell you what," he said slowly. "Why don't I take you home tonight? You can introduce me to your grandmother. That way, whatever happens next won't come as such a bolt from the blue."

It was a measure of how desperate Sarah was feeling that she actually considered the idea.

"I don't think so," she said after a moment. "I don't want to complicate the situation any more at this point."

"All right. I'm staying at the Waldorf. Call me when you've had time to consider my proposal. If I don't hear from you within twenty-four hours, I'll assume your tacit agreement."

With that parting shot, he stepped to the curb and flagged down a cab for her. Sarah slid inside, collapsed against the seat and spent the short ride to the Dakota alternately feeling the aftereffects of that kiss, worrying about her sister and cursing the mess Gina had landed her in.

When she let herself in to the apartment, Maria was emptying the dishwasher just prior to leaving.

"*Hola,* Sarah."

"*Hola,* Maria. How did it go today?"

"Well. We walk in the park this afternoon."

She tucked the last plate in the cupboard and let the dishwasher close with a quiet whoosh. The marble counter got a final swipe.

"We didn't expect you home until late," the housekeeper commented as she reached for the coat she'd draped over a kitchen chair. "*La duquesa* ate an early dinner and retired to her room. She dozed when I checked a few minutes ago."

"Okay, Maria. Thanks."

"You're welcome, *chica.*" The Ecuadoran shrugged into her coat and hefted her suitcase-size purse. Halfway to the hall, she turned back. "I almost forgot. Gina called."

"When!"

"About a half hour ago. She said you texted her a couple times."

"A couple? Try ten or twenty."

"Ah, well." A fond smile creased the maid's plump cheeks. "That's Gina."

"Yes, it is," Sarah agreed grimly. "Did she mention where she was?"

"At the airport in Los Angeles. She said she just wanted to make sure everything was all right before she got on the plane."

"What plane? Where was she going?"

Maria's face screwed up in concentration. "Switzerland, I think she said. Or maybe…Swaziland?"

Knowing Gina, it could be either. Although, Sarah thought on a sudden choke of panic, Europe probably boasted better markets for twelfth-century Byzantine artifacts.

She said a hurried good-night to Maria and rummaged

frantically in her purse for her phone. She had to catch her sister before her plane took off.

When she got the phone out, the little green text icon indicated she had a text message. And she'd missed hearing the alert. Probably because she was too busy letting Devon Hunter kiss her all the way into next week.

The message was brief and typical Gina.

Met the cuddliest ski instructor.
Off to Switzerland. Later.

Hoping against hope it wasn't too late, Sarah hit speed dial. The call went immediately to voice mail. She tried texting and stood beside the massive marble counter, scowling at the screen, willing the little icon to pop back a response.

No luck. Gina had obviously powered down her phone. If she ran true to form, she would forget to power the damned thing back up for hours—maybe days—after she landed in Switzerland.

Sarah could almost hear a loud, obnoxious clock ticking inside her head as she went to check on her grandmother. Hunter had given her an additional twenty-four hours. Twenty-three now, and counting.

She knocked lightly on the door, then opened it as quietly as she could. The duchess sat propped against a bank of pillows. Her eyes were closed and an open book lay in her lap.

The anxiety gnawing at Sarah's insides receded for a moment, edged aside by the love that filled her like liquid warmth. She didn't see her grandmother's thin, creased cheeks or the liver spots sprinkled across the back of her hands. She saw the woman who'd opened her heart and her arms to two scared little girls. Charlotte St. Sebastian had nourished and educated them. She'd also shielded them from as much of the world's ugliness as she could. Now it was Sarah's turn to do the same.

She tried to ease the book out of the duchess's lax fingers without waking her. She didn't succeed. Charlotte's papery eyelids fluttered up. She blinked a couple of times to focus and smiled.

"How was your dinner?"

Sarah couldn't lie, but she could dodge a bit. "The restaurant was definitely up to your standards. We'll have to go there for your birthday."

"Never mind my birthday." She patted the side of the bed. "Sit down and tell me about this friend of Eugenia's. Do you think there's anything serious between them?"

Hunter was serious, all right. Just not in any way Charlotte would approve of.

"They're not more than casual acquaintances. In fact, Gina sent me a text earlier this evening. She's off to Switzerland with the cuddliest ski instructor. Her words, not mine."

"That girl," Charlotte huffed. "She'll be the death of me yet."

Not if Sarah could help it. The clock was pounding away inside her head, though. In desperation, she took Hunter's advice and decided to lay some tentative groundwork for whatever might come tomorrow.

"I actually know him better than Gina does, Grandmama."

"The ski instructor?"

"The man I met at the restaurant this evening. Devon Hunter." Despite everything, she had to smile. "You know him, too. He came in at Number Three on our Ten Sexiest Singles list."

"Oh, for heaven's sake, Sarah. You know I only peruse *Beguile* to gain an appreciation for your work. I don't pay any attention to the content."

"I guess it must have been Maria who dog-eared that particular section," she teased.

Charlotte tipped her aristocratic nose. The gesture was

instinctive and inbred and usually preceded a withering set-down. To Sarah's relief, the nose lowered a moment later and a smile tugged at her grandmother's lips.

"Is he as hot in real life as he is in print?"

"Hotter." She drew a deep mental breath. "Which is why I kissed him outside the restaurant."

"You kissed him? In public?" Charlotte *tch-tched,* but it was a halfhearted effort. Her face had come alive with interest. "That's so déclassé, dearest."

"Yes, I know. Even worse, there was a totally obnoxious woman inside the restaurant. She recognized Devon and made a rather rude comment. I suspect she may have snapped a picture or two. The kiss may well show up in some tabloid."

"I should hope not!"

Her lips thinning, the duchess contemplated that distasteful prospect for a moment before making a shrewd observation.

"Alexis will throw a world-class tantrum if something like this appears in any magazine but hers. You'd best forewarn her."

"I intend to." She glanced at the pillbox and crystal water decanter on the marble-topped nightstand. "Did you take your medicine?"

"Yes, I did."

"Are you sure? Sometimes you doze off and forget."

"I took it, Sarah. Don't fuss at me."

"It's my job to fuss." She leaned forward and kissed a soft, lily-of-the-valley-scented cheek. "Good night, Grandmama."

"Good night."

She got as far as the bedroom door. Close, so close, to making an escape. She had one hand on the latch when the duchess issued an imperial edict.

"Bring this Mr. Hunter by for drinks tomorrow evening, Sarah. I would like to meet him."

"I'm not certain what his plans are."

"Whatever they are," Charlotte said loftily, "I'm sure he can work in a brief visit."

Sarah went to sleep trying to decide which would be worse: entering into a fake engagement, informing Alexis that a tabloid might beat *Beguile* to a juicy story involving one of its own editors or continuing to feed her grandmother half-truths.

The first thing she did when she woke up the next morning was grab her cell phone. No text from Gina. No email. No voice message.

"You're a dead woman," she snarled at her absent sibling. "Dead!"

Throwing back the covers, she stomped to the bathroom. Like the rest of the rooms in the apartment, it was high ceilinged and trimmed with elaborate crown molding. Most of the fixtures had been updated over the years, but the tub was big and claw-footed and original. Sarah indulged in long, decadent soaks whenever she could. This morning she was too keyed up and in too much of a hurry for anything more than a quick shower.

Showered and blow-dried, she chose one of her grandmama's former favorites—a slate-gray Pierre Balmain minidress in a classic A-line. According to Charlotte, some women used to pair these thigh-skimming dresses with white plastic go-go boots. *She* never did, of course. Far too gauche. She'd gone with tasteful white stockings and Ferragamo pumps. Sarah opted for black tights, a pair of Giuseppi Zanottis she'd snatched up at a secondhand shoe store and multiple strands of fat faux pearls.

Thankfully, the duchess preferred a late, leisurely breakfast with Maria, so Sarah downed her usual bagel and black coffee and left for work with only a quick goodbye.

She got another reprieve at work. Alexis had called in to say she was hopping an early shuttle to Chicago for a short-notice meeting with the head of their publishing group. And to Sarah's infinite relief, a computer search of stories in print for the day didn't pop with either her name or a lurid blowup of her wrapped in Devon Hunter's arms.

That left the rest of the day to try to rationalize her un-expected reaction to his kiss and make a half-dozen futile attempts to reach Gina. All the while the clock marched steadily, inexorably toward her deadline.

Dev shot a glance at the bank of clocks lining one wall of the conference room. Four-fifteen. A little less than four hours to the go/no-go point.

He tuned out the tanned-and-toned executive at the head of the gleaming mahogany conference table. The man had been droning on for almost forty minutes now. His equally slick associates had nodded and ahemed and interjected several editorial asides about the fat military contract they were confident their company would win.

Dev knew better. They'd understated their start-up costs so blatantly the Pentagon procurement folks would laugh these guys out of the competition. Dev might have chalked this trip to NYC as a total waste of time if not for his meet-ing with Sarah St. Sebastian.

Based on the profile he'd had compiled on her, he'd ex-pected someone cool, confident, levelheaded and fiercely loyal to both the woman who'd raised her and the sibling who gave her such grief. What he hadn't expected was her inbred elegance. Or the kick to his gut when she'd walked into the restaurant last night. Or the hours he'd spent af-terward remembering her taste and her scent and the press of her body against his.

His visceral reaction to the woman could be a potential glitch in his plan. He needed a decoy. A temporary fian-cée to blunt the effect of that ridiculous article. Someone to act as a buffer between him and the total strangers hitting on him everywhere he went—and the French CEO's wife who'd whispered such suggestive obscenities in his ear.

Sarah St. Sebastian was the perfect solution to those embarrassments. She'd proved as much last night when she'd cut Red off at the knees. Problem was the feel of her, the taste of her, had damned near done the same to Dev. The delectable Sarah could well prove more of a distraction than the rest of the bunch rolled up together.

So what the hell should he do now? Call her and tell her the deal he'd offered was no longer on the table? Write off the loss of the medallion? Track Gina down and recover the piece himself?

The artifact itself wasn't the issue, of course. Dev had lost more in the stock market in a single day than that bit of gold and enamel was worth. The only reason he'd pursued it this far was that he didn't like getting ripped off any more than the next guy. That, and the damned Ten Sexiest Singles article. He'd figured he could leverage the theft of the medallion into a temporary fiancée.

Which brought him full circle. What should he do about Sarah? His conscience had pinged at him last night. It was lobbing 50mm mortar shells now.

Dev had gained a rep in the multibillion-dollar world of aerospace manufacturing for being as tough as boot leather, but honest. He'd never lied to a competitor or grossly underestimated a bid like these jokers were doing now. Nor had he ever resorted to blackmail. Dev shifted uncomfortably, feeling as prickly about the one-sided deal he'd offered Sarah as by the patently false estimates Mr. Smooth kept flashing up on the screen.

To hell with it. He could take care of at least one of those itches right now.

"Excuse me, Jim."

Tanned-and-toned broke off in midspiel. He and his associates turned eager faces to Dev.

"We'll have to cut this short," he said without a trace of

apology. "I've got something hanging fire that I thought could wait. I need to take care of it now."

Jim and company concealed their disappointment behind shark-toothed smiles. Professional courtesy dictated that Devon offer a palliative.

"Why don't you email me the rest of your presentation? I'll study it on the flight home."

Tanned-and-toned picked up an in-house line and murmured an order to his AV folks. When he replaced the receiver, his smile sat just a few degrees off center.

"It's done, Dev."

"Thanks, Jimmy. I'll get back to you when I've had a chance to review your numbers in a little more depth."

Ole Jim's smile slipped another couple of degrees but he managed to hang on to its remnants as he came around the table to pump Devon's hand.

"I'll look forward to hearing from you. Soon, I hope."

"By the end of the week," Devon promised, although he knew Mr. Smooth wouldn't like what he had to say.

He decided to wait until he was in the limo and headed back to his hotel to contact Sarah. As the elevator whisked him down fifty stories, he tried to formulate exactly what he'd say to her.

His cell phone buzzed about twenty stories into the descent. Dev answered with his customary curt response, blissfully unaware a certain green-eyed brunette was just seconds away from knocking his world off its axis.

"Hunter."

"Mr. Hunter… Dev… It's Sarah St. Sebastian."

"Hello, Sarah. Have you heard from Gina?"

"Yes. Well, sort of."

Hell! So much for his nagging guilt over coercing this woman into a fake engagement. All Devon felt now was a searing disappointment that it might not take place. The feeling was so sharp and surprisingly painful he almost missed her next comment.

"Gina's on her way to Switzerland. Or she was when she texted me last night."

"What's in…?"

He broke off, knowing the answer before he asked the question. Bankers in Switzerland would commit hara-kiri before violating the confidentiality of deals brokered under their auspices. What better place to sell—and deposit the proceeds of—a near-priceless piece of antiquity?

"So where does that leave us?"

It came out stiffer than he'd intended. She responded in the same vein.

"I'm still trying to reach Gina. If I can't…"

The elevator reached the lobby. Dev stepped out, the phone to his ear and his adrenaline pumping the way it did when his engineers were close to some innovative new concept or major modification to the business of hauling cargo.

"If you can't?" he echoed.

"I don't see I have any choice but to agree to your preposterous offer."

She spelled it out. Slowly. Tightly. As if he'd forgotten the conditions he'd laid down last night.

"Six months as your fiancée. Less if you complete the negotiations you're working on. In return, you don't press charges against my sister. Correct?"

"Correct." Crushing his earlier doubts, he pounced. "So we have a deal?"

"On one condition."

A dozen different contingency clauses flashed through his mind. "And that is?" he said cautiously.

"You have to come for cocktails this evening. Seven o'clock. My grandmother wants to meet you."

Four

Dev frowned at his image in the elevator's ornate mirror and adjusted his tie. He was damned if he knew why he was so nervous about meeting Charlotte St. Sebastian.

He'd flown into combat zones more times than he could count, for God's sake. He'd also participated in relief missions to countries devastated by fires, tsunamis, earthquakes, horrific droughts and bloody civil wars. More than once his aircraft had come under enemy fire. And he still carried the scar from the hit he'd taken while racing through a barrage of bullets to get a sobbing, desperate mother and her wounded child aboard before murderous rebels overran the airport.

Those experiences had certainly shaped Dev's sense of self. Building an aerospace design-and-manufacturing empire from the ground up only solidified that self-confidence. He now rubbed elbows with top-level executives and power brokers around the world. Charlotte St. Sebastian wouldn't be the first royal he'd met, or even the highest ranking.

Yet the facts Dev had gathered about the St. Sebastian family painted one hell of an intimidating picture of its matriarch. The woman had once stood next in line to rule a duchy with a history that spanned some seven hundred years. She'd been forced to witness her husband's execution by firing squad. Most of her remaining family had disappeared forever in the notorious gulags. Charlotte herself had gone into hiding with her infant daughter and endured untold hardships before escaping to the West.

That would be heartbreak enough for anyone. Yet the duchess had also been slammed with the tragic death of her daughter and son-in-law, then had raised her two young granddaughters alone. Few, if any, of her friends and acquaintances were aware that she maintained only the facade of what appeared to be a luxurious lifestyle. Dev knew because he'd made it his business to learn everything he could about the St. Sebastians after beautiful, bubbly Lady Eugenia had lifted the Byzantine medallion.

He could have tracked Gina down. Hell, anyone with a modicum of computer smarts could track a GPS-equipped cell phone these days. Dev had considered doing just that until he'd realized her elder sister was better suited for his purposes. Plus, there was the bonus factor of where Sarah St. Sebastian worked. It had seemed only fair that he get a little revenge for the annoyance caused by that article.

Except, he thought as he exited the elevator, revenge had a way of coming back to bite you in the ass. What had seemed like a solid plan when he'd first devised it was now generating some serious doubts. Could he keep his hands off the elegant elder sister and stick to the strict terms of their agreement? Did he want to?

The doubts dogged him right up until he pressed the button for the doorbell. He heard a set of melodic chimes, and his soon-to-be fiancée opened the door to him.

"Hello, Mr.… Dev."

She was wearing chunky pearls, a thigh-skimming little dress and black tights tonight. The pearls and gray dress gave her a personal brand of sophistication, but the tights showcased her legs in a way that made Dev's throat go bone-dry. He managed to untangle his tongue long enough to return her greeting.

"Hello, Sarah."

"Please, come in."

She stood aside to give him access to a foyer longer than the belly of a C-17 and almost as cavernous. Marble tiles, ornate wall sconces, a gilt-edged side table and a crystal bowl filled with something orange blossomy. Dev absorbed the details along with the warning in Sarah's green eyes.

"I've told my grandmother that you and Gina are no more than casual acquaintances," she confided in a low voice.

"That's true enough."

"Yes, well…" She drew in a breath and squared shoulders molded by gray silk. "Let's get this over with."

She led the way down the hall. Dev followed and decided the rear view was as great as the front. The dress hem swayed just enough to tease and tantalize. The tights clung faithfully to the curve of her calves.

He was still appreciating the view when she showed him into a high-ceilinged room furnished with a mix of antiques and a few pieces of modern technology. The floor here was parquet; the wood was beautifully inlaid, but cried for the cushioning of a soft, handwoven carpet to blunt some of its echo. Windows curtained in pale blue velvet took up most of two walls and gave what Dev guessed was one hell of a view of Central Park. Flames danced in the massive fireplace fronted in black marble that dominated a third wall.

A sofa was angled to catch the glow from the fire. Two high-backed armchairs faced the sofa across a monster coffee table inset with more marble. The woman on one of those chairs sat ramrod straight, with both palms resting on the handle of an ebony cane. Her gray hair was swept up into a curly crown and anchored by ivory combs. Lace wrapped her throat like a muffler and was anchored by a cameo brooch. Her hawk's eyes skewered Dev as he crossed the room.

Sarah summoned a bright smile and performed the introductions. "Grandmama, this is Devon Hunter."

"How do you do, Mr. Hunter?"

The duchess held out a veined hand. Dev suspected that courtiers had once dropped to a knee and kissed it reverently. He settled for taking it gently in his.

"It's a pleasure to meet you, ma'am. Gina told me she'd inherited her stunning looks from her grandmother. She obviously had that right."

"Indeed?" Her chin lifted. Her nose angled up a few degrees. "You know Eugenia well, then?"

"She coordinated a party for me. We spoke on a number of occasions."

"Do sit down, Mr. Hunter." She waved him to the chair across from hers. "Sarah, dearest, please pour Mr. Hunter a drink."

"Certainly. What would you like, Dev?"

"Whatever you and your grandmother are having is fine."

"I'm having white wine." Her smile tipped into one of genuine affection as she moved to a side table containing an opened bottle of wine nested in a crystal ice bucket and an array of decanters. "Grandmama, however, is ignoring her doctor's orders and sipping an abominable brew concocted by our ancestors back in the sixteenth century."

"*Žuta Osa* is hardly abominable, Sarah," the duchess countered. She lifted a tiny liqueur glass and swirled its amber-colored contents before treating her guest to a bland look. "It simply requires a strong constitution."

Dev recognized a challenge when one smacked him in the face. "I'll give it a try."

"Are you sure?" Sarah shot him a warning glance from behind the drinks table. "The name translates roughly to yellow wasp. That might give you an idea of what it tastes like."

"Really, Sarah! You must allow Mr. Hunter to form his own opinion of what was once our national drink."

Dev was already regretting his choice but concealed it behind a polite request. "Please call me Dev, ma'am."

He didn't presume to address the duchess by name or by rank. Mostly because he wasn't sure which came first. European titles were a mystery wrapped up in an enigma to most Americans. Defunct Eastern European titles were even harder to decipher. Dev had read somewhere that the form of address depended on whether the rank was inherited or bestowed, but that didn't help him a whole lot in this instance.

The duchess solved his dilemma when she responded to his request with a gracious nod. "Very well. And you may call me Charlotte."

Sarah paused with the stopper to one of the decanters in hand. Her look of surprise told Dev he'd just been granted a major concession. She recovered a moment later and filled one of the thimble-size liqueur glasses. Passing it to Dev, she refilled her wineglass and took a seat beside her grandmother.

As he lifted the glass in salute to his hostess, he told himself a half ounce of yellow wasp couldn't do much damage. One sip showed just how wrong he was. The fiery, plum-based liquid exploded in his mouth and damned near burned a hole in his esophagus.

"Holy sh…!"

He caught himself in time. Eyes watering, he held the glass at arm's length and gave the liqueur the respect it deserved. When he could breathe again, he met the duchess's amused eyes.

"This puts the stuff we used to brew in our helmets in Iraq to shame."

"You were in Iraq?" With an impatient shake of her

head, Charlotte answered her own question. "Yes, of course you were. Afghanistan, too, if I remember correctly from the article in *Beguile*."

Okay, now he was embarrassed. The idea of this gray-haired matriarch reading all that nonsense—and perusing the picture of his butt crack!—went down even rougher than the liqueur.

To cover his embarrassment, Dev took another sip. The second was a little easier than the first but still left scorch marks all the way to his gullet.

"So tell me," Charlotte was saying politely, "how long will you be in New York?"

"That depends," he got out.

"Indeed?"

The duchess did the nose-up thing again. She was good at it, Dev thought as he waited for the fire in his stomach to subside.

"On what, if I may be so bold to ask?"

"On whether you and your granddaughter will have dinner with me this evening. Or tomorrow evening."

His glance shifted to Sarah. The memory of how she'd fit against him, how her mouth had opened under his, hit with almost the same sucker punch as the *Žuta Osa*.

"Or any evening," he added, holding her gaze.

Sarah gripped her wineglass. She didn't have any trouble reading the message in his eyes. It was a personal challenge. A not-so-private caress. Her grandmother would have to be blind to miss either.

Okay. All right. She'd hoped this meeting would blunt the surprise of a sudden engagement. Dev had done his part. The ball was now in her court.

"I can't speak for Grandmama, but I'm free tomorrow evening. Or any evening," she added with what felt like a silly, simpering smile.

She thought she'd overplayed her hand. Was sure of it when the duchess speared her with a sharp glance.

The question in her grandmother's eyes ballooned Sarah's guilt and worry to epic proportions. She couldn't do this. She couldn't deceive the woman who'd sold every precious family heirloom she owned to provide for her granddaughters. A confession trembled on her lips. The duchess forestalled it by turning back Devon Hunter.

"I'm afraid I have another engagement tomorrow evening."

Both women knew that to be a blatant lie. Too caught up in her own web of deceit to challenge her grandmother, Sarah tried not to squirm as the duchess slipped into the role of royal matchmaker.

"But I insist you take my granddaughter to dinner tomorrow. Or any evening," she added drily. "Right now, however, I'd like to know a little more about you."

Sarah braced herself. The duchess didn't attack with the same snarling belligerence as Alexis, but she was every bit as skilled and tenacious when it came to extracting information. Dev didn't stand a chance.

She had to admit he took the interrogation with good grace. Still, her nerves were stretched taut when she went to bed some hours later. At least she'd mitigated the fallout from one potentially disastrous situation. If—*when*—she and Devon broke the news of their engagement, it wouldn't come as a complete shock to Grandmama.

She woke up the next morning knowing she had to defuse another potentially explosive situation. A quick scan of her phone showed no return call or text from Gina. An equally quick scan of electronic, TV and print media showed the story hadn't broken yet about Sarah and Number Three. It would, though. She sensed it with every instinct she'd developed after three years in the dog-eat-dog publishing business.

Alexis. She had to tell Alexis some version of her involvement with Devon Hunter. She tried out different slants as she hung from a handrail on the subway. Several more in the elevator that zoomed her up to *Beguile*'s offices. Every possible construction but one crumbled when Alexis summoned her into her corner office. Pacing like a caged tiger, the executive editor unleashed her claws.

"Jesus, Sarah!" Anger lowered Alexis's smoker's rasp to a frog-like croak. "You want to tell me why I have to hear secondhand that one of my editors swapped saliva with Sexy Single Number Three? On the street. In full view of every cabbie with a camera phone and an itch to sell a sensational story."

"Come on, Alexis. How many New York cabbies read *Beguile* enough to recognize Number Three?"

"At least one, apparently."

She flung the sheet of paper she was holding onto the slab of Lucite that was her desk. Sarah's heart tripped as she skimmed the contents. It was a printed email, and below the printed message was a grainy color photo of a couple locked in each other's arms. Sarah barely had time for a mental apology to Red for thinking she'd be the one to peddle the story before Alexis pounced.

"This joker wants five thousand for the picture."

"You're kidding!"

"See this face?" The executive editor stabbed a finger at her nose. "Does it look like I'm kidding?"

"This…this isn't what you think, Alexis."

"So maybe you'll tell me what the hell it is, Lady Sarah."

It might have been the biting sarcasm. Or the deliberate reference to her title. Or the worry about Gina or the guilt over lying to her grandmother or the pressure Devon Hunter had laid on her. Whatever caused Sarah's sudden meltdown, the sudden burst of tears shocked her as much as it did Alexis.

"Oh, Christ!" Her boss flapped her hands like a PMS-ing

hen. "I'm sorry. I didn't mean to come at you so hard. Well, maybe I did. But you don't have to cry about it."

"Yes," Sarah sobbed, "I do!"

The truth was she couldn't have stopped if she wanted to. All the stress, all the strain, seemed to boil out of her. Not just the problems that had piled up in the past few days. The months of worrying about Grandmama's health. The years of standing between Gina and the rest of the world. Everything just seemed to come to a head. Dropping into a chair, she crossed her arms on the half acre of unblemished Lucite and buried her face.

"Hey! It's okay." Alexis hovered over her, patting her shoulder, sounding more desperate and bullfroggish by the moment. "I'll sit on this email. Do what I can to kill the story before it leaks."

Sarah raised her head. She'd struck a deal. She'd stand by it. "You don't have to kill it. Hunter... He and I..."

"You and Hunter...?"

She dropped her head back onto her arms and gave a muffled groan. "We're engaged."

"What! When? Where? How?"

Reverting to her natural self, Alexis was relentless. Within moments she'd wormed out every succulent detail. Hunter's shocking accusation. The video with its incontrovertible proof. The outrageous proposal. The call from Gina stating that she was on her way to Switzerland.

"Your sister is a selfish little bitch," Alexis pronounced in disgust. "When are you going to stop protecting her?"

"Never!" Blinking away her tears, Sarah fired back with both barrels. "Gina's all I have. Gina and Grandmama. I'll do whatever's necessary to protect them."

"That's all well and good, but your sister..."

"*Is* my sister."

"Okay, okay." Alexis held up both palms. "She's your sister. And Devon Hunter's your fiancé for the next six months. Unless..."

Her face took on a calculating expression. One Sarah knew all too well. She almost didn't want to ask, but the faint hope that her boss might see a way out of the mess prompted a tentative query.

"Unless what?"

"What if you keep a journal for the next few weeks? Better yet, a photo journal?"

Deep in thought, Alexis tapped a bloodred nail against her lips. Sarah could almost see the layout taking shape in her boss's fertile mind.

"You and Hunter. The whirlwind romance. The surprise proposal. The romantic dinners for two. The long walks in Central Park. Our readers would eat it up."

"Forget it, Alexis. I'm not churning out more juicy gossip for our readers."

"Why not?"

The counter came as swift and as deadly as an adder. In full pursuit of a feature now, Alexis dropped into the chair next to Sarah and pressed her point.

"You and I both know celebrity gossip sells. And this batch comes with great bonus elements. Hunter's not only rich, but handsome as hell. You're a smart, savvy career woman with a connection to royalty."

"A connection to a royal house that doesn't exist anymore!"

"So? We resurrect it. Embellish it. Maybe send a photographer over to shoot some local color from your grandmother's homeland. Didn't you say you still had some cousins there?"

"Three or four times removed, maybe, but Grandmama hasn't heard from anyone there in decades."

"No problem. We'll make it work."

She saw the doubt on Sarah's face and pressed her point with ruthless determination.

"If what you give me is as full of glam and romance as I think it could be, it'll send our circulation through the roof. And that, my sweet, will provide you with enough of a bonus to reimburse Hunter for his lost artifact. *And* pay off the last of your grandmother's medical bills. *And* put a little extra in your bank account for a rainy day or two."

The dazzling prospect hung before Sarah's eyes for a brief, shining moment. She could extricate Gina from her latest mess. Become debt-free for the first time in longer than she could remember. Splurge on some totally unnecessary luxury for the duchess. Buy a new suit instead of retrofitting old classics.

She came within a breath of promising Alexis all the photos and R-rated copy she could print. Then her irritating sense of fair play raised its head.

"I can't do it," she said after a bitter internal struggle. "Hunter promised he wouldn't file charges against Gina if I play the role of adoring fiancée. I'll try to get him to agree to a photo shoot focusing on our—" she stopped, took a breath, continued "—on our engagement. I'm pretty sure he'll agree to that."

Primarily because it would serve his purpose. Once the word hit the street that he was taken, all those women shoving their phone numbers at him would just have to live with their disappointment. So would Alexis.

"That's as far as I'll go," Sarah said firmly.

Her boss frowned and was priming her guns for another salvo when her intercom buzzed. Scowling, she stabbed at the instrument on her desk.

"Didn't I tell you to hold all calls?"

"Yes, but…"

"What part of 'hold' don't you understand?"

"It's…"

"It's what, dammit?"

"Number Three," came the whispered reply. "He's here."

Five

If Dev hadn't just run past a gauntlet of snickering females, he might have been amused by the almost identical expressions of surprise on the faces of his fiancée and her boss. But he had, so he wasn't.

Alexis Danvers didn't help matters by looking him up and down with the same scrutiny an auctioneer might give a prize bull. As thin as baling wire, she sized him up with narrowed, calculating eyes before thrusting out a hand tipped with scarlet talons.

"Mr. Hunter. Good to meet you. Sarah says you and she are engaged."

"Wish I could say the same, Ms. Danvers. And yes, we are."

He shifted his gaze to Sarah, frowning when he noted her reddened eyes and tearstained cheeks. He didn't have to search far for the reason behind them. The grainy color photo on Danvers's desk said it all.

Hell! Sarah had hinted the crap would hit the fan if some magazine other than hers scooped the story. Looked as if it had just hit. He turned back to the senior editor and vectored the woman's anger in his direction.

"I'm guessing you might be a little piqued that Sarah didn't clue you in to our relationship before it became public knowledge."

Danvers dipped her chin in a curt nod. "You guessed right."

"I'm also guessing you understand why I wasn't real anxious for another avalanche of obnoxious publicity."

"If you're referring to the Ten Sexiest Singles article…"

"I am."

"Since you declined to let us interview you for that article, Mr. Hunter, everything we printed was in the public domain. Your military service. That cargo thingamajig you patented. Your corporation's profits last quarter. Your marital status. All we did was collate the facts, glam them up a little, toss in a few pictures and offer you to an admiring audience."

"Any more admiration from that audience and I'll have to hire a bodyguard."

"Or a fiancée?"

She slipped that in with the precision of a surgeon. Dev had to admire her skill even as he acknowledged the hit.

"Or a fiancée," he agreed. "Luckily I found the perfect one right here at *Beguile*."

Which reminded him of why he'd made a second trek to the magazine's offices.

"Something's come up," he told Sarah. "I was going to explain it to you privately, but…"

"You heard from Gina?"

Her breathless relief had Dev swearing silently. Little Miss Gina deserved a swift kick in the behind for putting her sister through all this worry. And he might just be the one to deliver it.

"No, I haven't."

The relief evaporated. Sarah's shoulders slumped. Only for a moment, though. The St. Sebastian steel reasserted itself almost immediately. Good thing, as she'd need every ounce of it for the sucker punch Dev was about to deliver.

"But I did hear from the CEO I've been negotiating with for the past few months. He's ready to hammer out the final details and asked me to fly over to Paris."

She sensed what was coming. He saw it in the widening of her green eyes, the instinctive shake of her head. Dev ignored both and pressed ahead.

"I told him I would. I also told him I might bring my fiancée. I explained we just got engaged, and that I'm thinking of taking some extra time so we can celebrate the occasion in his beautiful city."

"Excuse me!" Danvers butted in, her expression frigid. "Sarah has an important job here at *Beguile,* with deadlines to meet. She can't just flit off to Paris on your whim."

"I appreciate that. It would only be for a few days. Maybe a week."

Dev turned back to Sarah, holding her gaze, holding her to their bargain at the same time.

"We've been working this deal for months. I need to wrap it up. Monsieur Girault said his wife would be delighted to entertain you while we're tied up in negotiations."

He slipped in that veiled reminder of one of his touchiest problems deliberately. He'd been up front with her. He wanted her to provide cover from Elise Girault. In exchange, he'd let her light-fingered sister off the hook.

Sarah got the message. Her chin inched up. Her shoulders squared. The knowledge she would stick to her side of the bargain gave him a fiercer sense of satisfaction than he had time to analyze right now.

"When are you thinking of going?" she asked.

"My executive assistant has booked us seats on a seven-ten flight out of JFK."

"Tonight?"

"Tonight. You have a current passport, don't you?"

"Yes, but I can't just jet off and leave Grandmama!"

"Not a problem. I also had my assistant check with the top home health-care agencies in the city. A licensed, bonded RN can report for duty this afternoon and stay with your grandmother until you get back."

"Dear God, no!" A shudder shook her. "Grandmama would absolutely hate that invasion of her privacy. I'll ask our housekeeper, Maria, to stay with her."

"You sure?"

"I'm sure."

"Since I'm springing this trip on you with such short notice, please tell your housekeeper I'll recompense her for her time."

"That's not necessary," she said stiffly.

"Of course it is."

She started to protest, but Dev suggested a daily payment for Maria's services that made Sarah blink and her boss hastily intervene.

"The man's right, kiddo. This is his gig. Let him cover the associated costs."

She left unsaid the fact that Dev could well afford the generous compensation. It was right there, though, like the proverbial elephant in the room, and convinced Sarah to reluctantly agree.

"We're good to go, then."

"I…I suppose." She chewed on her lower lip for a moment. "I need to finish the Sizzling Summer Sea-escapes layout, Alexis."

"And the ad for that new lip gloss," her boss put in urgently. "I want it in the June edition."

"I'll take my laptop. I can do both layouts on the plane." She pushed out of her chair and faced Dev. "You understand that my accompanying you on this little jaunt is contingent on Maria's availability."

"I understand. Assuming she's available, can you be ready by three o'clock?"

"Isn't that a little early for a seven-ten flight?"

"It is, but we need to make a stop on the way out to JFK. Or would you rather go to Cartier now?"

"Cartier? Why do we...? Oh." She gave a low groan. "An engagement ring, right?"

"Right."

She shook her head in dismay. "This just keeps getting better and better."

Her boss took an entirely different view. With a hoarse whoop, she reached for the phone on her desk.

"Perfect! We'll send a camera crew to Cartier with you." She paused with the phone halfway to her ear and raked her subordinate with a critical glance. "Swing by makeup on your way out, Sarah. Have them ramp up your color. Wouldn't hurt to hit wardrobe, too. That's one of your grandmother's Dior suits, right? It's great, but it needs something. A belt, maybe. Or..."

Sarah cut in, alarm coloring her voice. "Hold on a minute, Alexis."

"What's to hold? This is exactly what we were talking about before Hunter arrived."

Sarah shot Dev a swift, guilty glance. It didn't take a genius for him to fill in the blanks. Obviously, her boss had been pressing to exploit the supposed whirlwind romance between one of her own and Number Three.

As much as it grated, Dev had to admit a splashy announcement of his engagement to Sarah St. Sebastian fell in with his own plans. If nothing else, it would get the word out that he was off the market and, hopefully, keep Madame Girault's claws sheathed.

"I'll consent to a few pictures, if that's what Sarah wants."

"A few pictures," she agreed with obvious reluctance, leveling a pointed look at her boss. "Just this *one* time."

"Come on, Sarah. How much more romantic can you get than April in Paris? The city of light and love. You and Hunter here strolling hand in hand along the Quai de Conti…"

"No, Alexis."

"Just think about it."

"No, Alexis."

There was something in the brief exchange Dev couldn't quite get a handle on. The communication between the two women was too emphatic, too terse. He didn't have time to decipher it now, however.

"Your people get this one shoot," he told Danvers, putting an end to the discussion. "They can do it at Cartier." He checked his watch. "Why don't you call your housekeeper now, Sarah? Make sure she's available. If she is, we'll put a ring on your finger and get you home to pack."

Sarah battled a headache as the limo cut through the Fifth Avenue traffic. Devon sat beside her on the cloud-soft leather, relaxed and seemingly unperturbed about throwing her life into total chaos. Seething, she threw a resentful glance at his profile.

Was it only two days ago he'd stormed into her life? Three? She felt as though she'd been broadsided by a semi. Okay, so maybe she couldn't lay all the blame for the situation she now found herself in on Dev. Gina had certainly contributed her share. Still…

When the limo pulled up at the front entrance to Cartier's iconic flagship store, the dull throb in her temples took on a sharper edge. With its red awnings and four stories of ultra high-end merchandise, the store was a New York City landmark.

Sarah hadn't discovered until after her grandmother's heart attack that Charlotte had sold a good portion of her jewels to Cartier over the years. According to a recent invoice, the last piece she'd parted with was still on display in their Estate Jewelry room.

Dev had called ahead, so they were greeted at the door

by the manager himself. "Good afternoon, Mr. Hunter. I'm Charles Tipton."

Gray-haired and impeccably attired, he shook Dev's hand before bowing over Sarah's with Old World courtesy.

"It's a pleasure to meet you, Ms. St. Sebastian. I've had the honor of doing business with your grandmother several times in the past."

She smiled her gratitude for his discretion. "Doing business with" stung so much less than "helping her dispose of her heritage."

"May I congratulate you on your engagement?"

She managed not to wince, but couldn't help thinking this lie was fast taking on a life of its own.

"Thank you."

"I'm thrilled, of course, that you came to Cartier to shop for your ring. I've gathered a selection of our finest settings and stones. I'm sure we'll find something exactly to your…"

He broke off as a cab screeched over to the curb and the crew from *Beguile* jumped out. Zach Zimmerman—nicknamed ZZ, of course—hefted his camera bags while his assistant wrestled with lights and reflectors.

"Hey, Sarah!" Dark eyed and completely irreverent about everything except his work, ZZ stomped toward them in his high-top sneakers. "You really engaged to Number Three or has Alexis been hitting the sauce again?"

She hid another wince. "I'm really engaged. ZZ, this is my fiancé, Devon…"

"Hunter. Yeah, I recognize the, uh, face."

He smirked but thankfully refrained from referring to any other part of Dev's anatomy.

"If you'll all please come with me."

Mr. Tipton escorted them through the first-floor show-room with its crystal chandeliers and alcoves framed with white marble arches. Faint strains of classical music floated on the air. The seductive scent of gardenia wafted from strategically positioned bowls of potpourri.

A short elevator ride took them to a private consultation room. Chairs padded in gold velvet were grouped on either side of a gateleg, gilt-trimmed escritoire. Several cases sparkling with diamond engagement sets sat on the desk's burled wood surface.

The manager gestured them to the chairs facing the desk but before taking his own he detoured to a sideboard holding a silver bucket and several Baccarat flutes.

"May I offer you some champagne? To toast your engagement, perhaps?"

Sarah glanced at Dev, saw he'd left the choice up to her, and surrendered to the inevitable.

"Thank you. That would be delightful."

The cork had already been popped. Tipton filled flutes and passed them to Sarah and Dev. She took the delicate crystal, feeling like the biggest fraud on earth. Feeling as well the stupidest urge to indulge in another bout of loud, sloppy tears.

Like many of *Beguile*'s readers, Sarah occasionally got caught up in the whole idea of romance. You could hardly sweat over layouts depicting the perfect engagement or wedding or honeymoon without constructing a few private fantasies. But this was about as far from those fantasies as she could get. A phony engagement. A pretend fiancé. A ring she would return as soon as she fulfilled the terms of her contract.

Then she looked up from the pale gold liquid bubbling in her flute and met Dev's steady gaze. His eyes had gone deep blue, almost cobalt, and something in their depths made her breath snag. When he lifted his flute and tipped it to hers, the fantasies begin to take on vague form and shape.

"To my…" he began.

"Wait!" ZZ pawed through his camera bag. "I need to catch this."

The moment splintered. Like a skater on too-thin ice,

Sarah felt the cracks spidering out beneath her feet. Panic replaced the odd sensation of a moment ago. She had to fight the urge to slam down the flute and get off the ice before she sank below the surface.

She conquered the impulse, but couldn't summon more than a strained smile once ZZ framed the shot.

"Okay," the photographer said from behind a foot-long lens, "go for it!"

Dev's gesture with his flute was the same. So was the caress in his voice. But whatever Sarah had glimpsed in his blue eyes a moment ago was gone.

"To us," he said as crystal clinked delicately against crystal.

"To us," she echoed.

She took one sip, just one, and nixed ZZ's request to repeat the toast so he could shoot it from another angle. She couldn't ignore him or his assistant, however, while she tried on a selection of rings. Between them, they made the process of choosing a diamond feel like torture.

According to Tipton, Dev had requested a sampling of rings as refined and elegant as his fiancée. Unfortunately, none of the glittering solitaires he lifted from the cases appealed to Sarah. With an understanding nod, he sent for cases filled with more elaborate settings.

Once again Sarah could almost hear a clock ticking inside her head. She needed to make a decision, zip home, break the startling news of her engagement to Grandmama, get packed and catch that seven-ten flight. Yet none of the rings showcased on black velvet triggered more than a tepid response.

Like it mattered. Just get this over with, she told herself grimly.

She picked up a square cut surrounded by glittering baguettes. Abruptly, she returned it to the black velvet pad.

"I think I would prefer something unique." She looked Tipton square in the eye. "Something from your estate sales, perhaps. An emerald, for my birth month. Mounted in gold."

Her birthday was in November, and the stone for that month was topaz. She hoped Hunter hadn't assimilated that bit of trivia. The jeweler had, of course, but he once again proved himself the soul of discretion.

"I believe we might have just the ring for you."

He lifted a house phone and issued a brief instruction. Moments later, an assistant appeared and deposited an intricately wrought ring on the display pad.

Thin ropes of gold were interwoven to form a wide band. An opaque Russian emerald nested in the center of the band. The milky green stone was the size and shape of a small gumball. When Sarah turned the ring over, she spotted a rose carved into the stone's flat bottom.

Someone with no knowledge of antique jewelry might scrunch their noses at the overly fussy setting and occluded gemstone. All Sarah knew was that she had to wear Grandmama's last and most precious jewel, if only for a week or so. Her heart aching, she turned to Dev.

"This is the one."

He tried to look pleased with her choice but didn't quite get there. The price the manager quoted only increased his doubts. Even fifteen-karat Russian emeralds didn't come anywhere close to the market value of a flawless three- or four-karat diamond.

"Are you sure this is the ring you want?"

"Yes."

Shrugging, he extracted an American Express card from his wallet. When Tipton disappeared to process the card, he picked up the ring and started to slip it on Sarah's finger.

ZZ stopped him cold. "Hold it!"

Dev's blue eyes went glacial. "Let us know when you're ready."

"Yeah, yeah, just hang on a sec."

ZZ thrust out a light meter, scowled at the reading and

barked orders to his assistant. After a good five minutes spent adjusting reflectors and falloff lights, they were finally ready.

"Go," the photographer ordered.

Dev slipped the ring on Sarah's finger. It slid over her knuckle easily, and the band came to rest at the base of her finger as though it had been sized especially for her.

"Good. Good." ZZ clicked a dozen fast shots. "Look up at him, Sarah. Give him some eye sex."

Heat rushed into her cheeks but she lifted her gaze. Dev wore a cynical expression for a second or two before exchanging it for one more lover-like.

Lights heated the room. Reflectors flashed. The camera shutter snapped and spit.

"Good. Good. Now let's have the big smooch. Make it hot, you two."

Tight lines appeared at the corners of Dev's mouth. For a moment he looked as though he intended to tell ZZ to take his zoom lens and shove it. Then he rose to his feet with lazy grace and held out a hand to Sarah.

"We'll have to try this without an audience sometime," he murmured as she joined him. "For now, though…"

She was better prepared this time. She didn't stiffen when he slid an arm around her waist. Didn't object when he curled his other hand under her chin and tipped her face to his. Yet the feel of his mouth, the taste and the scent of him, sent tiny shock waves rippling through her entire body.

A lyric from an old song darted into her mind. Something about getting lost in his kiss. That was exactly how she felt as his mouth moved over hers.

"Good. Good."

More rapid-fire clicks, more flashes. Finally ZZ was done. He squinted at the digital screen and ran through the entire sequence of images before he gave a thumbs-up.

"Got some great shots here. I'll edit 'em and email you

the best, Sarah. Just be sure to credit me if you use 'em on your bridal website."

Right. Like that was going to happen. Still trying to recover from her second session in Devon Hunter's arms, Sarah merely nodded.

While ZZ and his assistant packed up, Dev checked his watch. "Do you want to grab lunch before I take you home to pack?"

Sarah thought for a moment. Her number-one priority right now was finding some way to break the news to the duchess that her eldest granddaughter had become engaged to a man she'd met only a few days ago. She needed a plausible explanation. One that wouldn't trigger Charlotte's instant suspicion. Or worse, so much worse, make her heart stutter.

Sarah's glance dropped to the emerald. The stone's cloudy beauty gave her the bravado to respond to Dev's question with a completely false sense of confidence.

"Let's have lunch with Grandmama and Maria. We'll make it a small celebration in honor of the occasion, then I'll pack."

Six

Dev had employed a cautious, scope-out-the-territory approach for his first encounter with the duchess. For the second, he decided on a preemptive strike. As soon as he and Sarah were in the limo and headed uptown, he initiated his plan of attack.

"Do you need to call your grandmother and let her know we're coming?"

"Yes, I should." She slipped her phone out of her purse. "And I'll ask Maria to put together a quick lunch."

"No need. I'll take care of that. Does the duchess like caviar?"

"Yes," Sarah replied, a question in her eyes as he palmed his own phone, "but only Caspian Sea osetra. She thinks beluga is too salty and sevruga too fishy."

"What about Maria? Does she have a favorite delicacy?"

She had to think for a moment. "Well, on All Saints Day she always makes *fiambre*."

"What's that?"

"A chilled salad with fifty or so ingredients. Why?" she asked as he hit a speed-dial key. "What are you...?"

He held up a hand, signaling her to wait, and issued a

quick order. "I need a champagne brunch for four, delivered to Ms. St. Sebastian's home address in a half hour. Start with osetra caviar and whatever you can find that's close to... Hang on." He looked to Sarah. "What was that again?"

"Fiambre."

"Fiambre. It's a salad...Hell, I don't know...Right. Right. Half an hour."

Sarah was staring at him when he cut the connection. "Who was that?"

"My executive assistant."

"She's here, in New York?"

"It's a he. Patrick Donovan. We used to fly together. He's back in L.A."

"And he's going to have champagne and caviar delivered to our apartment in half an hour?"

"That's why he gets paid the big bucks." He nodded to the phone she clutched in her hand. "You better call the duchess. With all this traffic, lunch will probably get there before we do."

Despite his advance preparations, Dev had to shake off a serious case of nerves when he and Sarah stepped out of the elevator at the Dakota. His introduction to Charlotte St. Sebastian last night had given him a keen appreciation of both her intellect and her fierce devotion to her grand-daughters. He had no idea how she'd react to this sudden engagement, but he suspected she'd make him sweat.

Sarah obviously suspected the same thing. She paused at the door to their apartment, key in hand, and gave him a look that was half challenge, half anxious appeal.

"She...she has a heart condition. We need to be careful how we orchestrate this."

"I'll follow your lead."

Pulling in a deep breath, she squared her shoulders. The key rattled in the lock, and the door opened on a parade of white-jacketed waiters just about to exit the apartment. Their arms full of empty cartons, they stepped aside.

"Your grandmother told us to set up in the dining room," the waiter in charge informed Sarah. "And may I say, ma'am, she has exquisite taste in crystal. Bohemian, isn't it?"

"Yes, it is."

"I thought so. No other lead crystal has that thin, liquid sheen."

Nodding, Sarah hurried down the hall. Dev lingered to add a hefty tip to the service fee he knew Patrick would have already taken care of. Gushing their thanks, the team departed and Dev made his way to the duchess's high-ceilinged dining room.

He paused on the threshold to survey the scene. The mahogany table could easily seat twelve, probably twenty or more with leaves in, but had been set with four places at the far end. Bone-white china gleamed. An impressive array of ruby-red goblets sparkled at each place setting. A sideboard held a row of domed silver serving dishes, and an opened bottle of champagne sat in a silver ice bucket.

Damn! Patrick would insist Dev add another zero to his already astronomical salary for pulling this one off.

"I presume this is your doing, Devon."

His glance zinged to the duchess. She stood ramrod straight at the head of the table, her hands folded one atop the other on the ivory handle of her cane. The housekeeper, Maria, hovered just behind her.

"Yes, ma'am."

"I also presume you're going to tell me the reason for this impromptu celebration."

Having agreed to let Sarah take the lead, Dev merely moved to her side and eased an arm around her waist. She stiffened, caught herself almost instantly and relaxed.

"We have two reasons to celebrate, Grandmama. Dev's asked me to go to Paris with him."

"So I understand. Maria informed me you asked her to stay with me while you're gone."

Her arctic tone left no doubt as to her feelings about the matter.

"It's just for a short while, and more for me than for you. This way I won't feel so bad about rushing off and leaving you on such short notice."

The duchess didn't unbend. If anything, her arthritic fingers clutched the head of her cane more tightly.

"And the second reason for this celebration?"

Sarah braced herself. Dev could feel her body go taut against his while she struggled to frame their agreement in terms her grandmother would accept. It was time for him to step in and draw the duchess's fire.

"My sisters will tell you I'm seriously deficient in the romance department, ma'am. They'll also tell you I tend to bulldoze over any and all obstacles when I set my sights on something. Sarah put up a good fight, but I convinced her we should get engaged before we take off for Paris."

"Madre de Dios!" The exclamation burst from Maria, who gaped at Sarah. "You are *engaged?* To this man?"

When she nodded, the duchess's chin shot up. Her glance skewered Dev where he stood. In contrast to her stark silence, Maria gave quick, joyous thanks to the Virgin Mary while making the sign of the cross three times in rapid succession.

"How I prayed for this, *chica!*"

Tears sparkling in her brown eyes, she rushed over to crush Sarah against her generous bosom. Dev didn't get a hug, but he was hauled down by his lapels and treated to a hearty kiss on both cheeks.

The duchess remained standing where she was. Dev was damned if he could read her expression. When Sarah approached, Charlotte's narrow-eyed stare shifted to her granddaughter.

"We stopped by Cartier on our way here, Grandmama. Dev wanted to buy me an engagement ring."

She raised her left hand, and the effect on the duchess was instant and electric.

"Dear God! Is that...? Is that the Russian Rose?"

"Yes," Sarah said gently.

Charlotte reached out a veined hand and stroked the emerald's rounded surface with a shaking fingertip. Dev felt uncomfortably like a voyeur as he watched a succession of naked emotions cross the older woman's face. For a long moment, she was in another time, another place, reliving memories that obviously brought both great joy and infinite sadness.

With an effort that was almost painful to observe, she returned to the present and smiled at Sarah.

"Your grandfather gave me the Rose for my eighteenth birthday. I always intended you to have it."

Her glance shifted once again to Dev. Something passed between them, but before he could figure out just what the hell it was, the duchess became all brisk efficiency.

"Well, Sarah, since you're traipsing off to Paris on such short notice, I think we should sample this sumptuous feast your...your fiancé has so generously arranged. Then you'll have to pack. Devon, will you pour the champagne?"

"Yes, ma'am."

Dev's misguided belief that he'd escaped unscathed lasted only until they'd finished brunch and Sarah went to pack. He got up to help Maria clear the table. She waved him back to his seat.

"I will do this. You sit and keep *la duquesa* company."

The moment Maria bustled through the door to the kitchen, *la duquesa* let loose with both barrels. Her pale eyes dangerous, she unhooked her cane from her chair arm and stabbed it at Dev like a sword.

"Let's be sure we understand each other, Mr. Hunter. I

may have been forced to sell the Russian Rose, but if you've purchased it with the mistaken idea you can also purchase my granddaughter, you'd best think again. One can't buy class or good genes. One either has both—" she jabbed his chest with the cane for emphasis "—or one doesn't."

Geesh! Good thing he was facing this woman over three feet of ebony and not down the barrel of an M16. Dev didn't doubt she'd pull the trigger if he answered wrong.

"First," he replied, "I had no idea that emerald once belonged to you. Second, I'm perfectly satisfied with my genes. Third…"

He stopped to think about that one. His feelings for Sarah St. Sebastian had become too confused, too fast. The way she moved…. The smile in her green eyes when she let down her guard for a few moments…. Her fierce loyalty to her grandmother and ditz of a sister…. Everything about her seemed to trigger both heat and hunger.

"Third," he finally admitted, "there's no way I'll ever match Sarah's style or elegance. All I can do is appreciate it, which I most certainly do."

The duchess kept her thoughts hidden behind her narrowed eyes for several moments. Then she dropped the tip of the cane and thumped the floor.

"Very well. I'll wait to see how matters develop."

She eased back against her chair and Dev started to breathe again.

"I'm sure you're aware," she said into the tentative truce, "that Paris is one of Sarah's favorite cities?"

"We haven't gotten around to sharing all our favorites yet," he replied with perfect truthfulness. "I do know she attended the Sorbonne for a year as an undergraduate."

That much was in the background dossier, as was the fact she'd majored in art history. Dev planned to use whatever spare time they might have in Paris to hit a few museums with her. He looked forward to exploring the Louvre or the Cluny with someone who shared his burgeoning interest in art. He was certainly no expert, but his appreciation of art in its various forms had grown with each incremental increase in his personal income...as evidenced by the Byzantine medallion.

The belated reminder of why he was here, being poked in the chest by this imperious, indomitable woman, hit with a belated punch. He'd let the side details of his "engagement" momentarily obscure the fact that he'd arm-twisted Sarah into it. He was using her, ruthlessly and with cold deliberation, as a tool to help close an important deal. Once that deal was closed...

To borrow the duchess's own words, Dev decided, they'd just have to wait and see how matters develop. He wouldn't employ the same ruthlessness and calculation to seduce the eminently seductive Lady Sarah as he had to get a ring on her finger. But neither would he pass up the chance to finesse her into bed if the opportunity offered.

The possibility sent a spear of heat into his belly. With a sheer effort of will, he gave the indomitable Charlotte St. Sebastian no sign of the knee-jerk reaction. But he had to admit he was now looking forward to this trip with considerably more anticipation than when Jean-Jacques Girault first requested it.

Seven

Three hours out over the Atlantic Sarah had yet to get past her surprise.

"I still can't believe Grandmama took it so well," she said, her fingers poised over the keyboard of her laptop. "Not just the engagement. This trip to Paris. The hefty bonus you're paying Maria. Everything!"

Dev looked up from the text message he'd just received. Their first-class seat pods were separated by a serving console holding his scotch, her wine and a tray of appetizers, but they were seated close enough for him to see the lingering disbelief in her jade-green eyes.

"Why shouldn't she take it well?" he countered. "She grilled me last night about my parents, my grandparents, my siblings, my education, my health, my club memberships and my bank account. She squeezed everything else she wanted to know out of me today at lunch. It was a close call, but evidently I passed muster."

"I think it was the ring," Sarah murmured, her gaze on the milky stone that crowned her finger. "Her whole attitude changed when she spotted it."

Dev knew damn well it was the ring, and noted with

interest the guilt and embarrassment tinging his fiancée's cheeks.

"I supposed I should have told you at Cartier that the Russian Rose once belonged to Grandmama."

"Not a problem. I'm just glad it was available."

She was quiet for a moment, still pondering the luncheon.

"Do you know what I find so strange? Grandmama didn't once ask how we could have fallen in love so quickly."

"Maybe because she comes from a different era. Plus, she went through some really rough times. Could be your security weighs as heavily in her mind as your happiness."

"That can't be it. She's always told Gina and me that her marriage was a love match. She had to defy her parents to make it happen."

"Yes, but look what came next," Dev said gently. "From what I've read, the Soviet takeover of her country was brutal. She witnessed your grandfather's execution. She barely escaped the same fate and had to make a new life for herself and her baby in a different country."

Sarah fingered the emerald, her profile etched with sadness. "Then she lost my parents and got stuck with Gina and me."

"Why do I think she didn't regard it as getting stuck? I suspect you and your sister went a long way to filling the hole in her heart."

"Gina more than me."

"I doubt that," Dev drawled.

As he'd anticipated, she jumped instantly to her sister's defense.

"I know you think Gina's a total airhead..."

"I do."

"...but she's so full of joy and life that no one—I repeat, *no one*—can be in her company for more than three minutes without cracking a smile."

Her eyes fired lethal darts, daring him to disagree. He didn't have to. He'd achieved his objective and erased the sad memories. Rather than risk alienating her, he changed the subject.

"I just got a text from Monsieur Girault. He says he's delighted you were able to get away and accompany me."

"Really?" Sarah hiked a politely skeptical brow. "What does his wife say?"

To Dev's chagrin, heat crawled up his neck. He'd flown in and out of a dozen different combat zones, for God's sake! Could stare down union presidents and corporate sharks with equal skill. Yet Elise Girault had thrown him completely off stride when he'd bent to give her the obligatory kiss on both cheeks. Her whispered suggestion was so startling—and so erotic—he'd damned near gotten whiplash when he'd jerked his head back. Then she'd let loose with a booming, raucous laugh that invited him to share in their private joke.

"He didn't say," Dev said in answer to Sarah's question, "but he did ask what you would like to do while we're locked up in a conference room. He indicated his wife is a world-class shopper. Apparently she's well-known at most of the high-end boutiques."

He realized his mistake the moment the words were out. He'd run Sarah St. Sebastian's financials. He knew how strapped she was.

"That reminds me," he said with deliberate nonchalance. "I don't intend for you to incur any out-of-pocket expenses as part of our deal. There'll be a credit card waiting for you at the hotel."

"Please tell me you're kidding."

Her reaction shouldn't have surprised him. Regal elegance was only one of the traits Lady Sarah had inherited from her grandmother. Stiff-necked pride had to rank right up near the top of the list.

"Be reasonable, Sarah. You're providing me a personal service."

Which was becoming more personal by the hour. Dev was getting used to her stimulating company. The heat she ignited in him still took him by surprise, though. He hadn't figured that into his plan.

"Of course I'll cover your expenses."

Her expression turned glacial. "The hotel, yes. Any meals we take with Madame and Monsieur Girault, yes. A shopping spree on the rue du Faubourg Saint-Honoré, no."

"Fine. It's your call."

He tried to recover with an admiring survey of her petal-pink dress. The fabric was thick and satiny, the cut sleek. A coat in the same style hung in their cabin's private closet.

"The rue du Whatever has nothing on Fifth Avenue. That classy New York look will have Elise Girault demanding an immediate trip to the States."

She stared at him blankly for a moment, then burst into laughter. "You're not real up on haute couture, are you?"

"Any of my sisters would tell you I don't know haute from hamburger."

"I wouldn't go that far," she said, still chuckling. "Unless I miss my guess, your shoes are Moroccan leather, the suit's hand-tailored and the tie comes from a little shop just off the Grand Canal in Venice."

"Damn, you're good! Although Patrick tells me he orders the ties from Milan, not Venice. So where did that dress come from?"

"It's vintage Balenciaga. Grandmama bought it in Madrid decades ago."

The smile remained, but Dev thought it dimmed a few degrees.

"She disposed of most of her designer originals when… when they went out of style, but she kept enough to provide a treasure trove for me. Thank goodness! Retro is the new 'new,' you know. I'm the envy of everyone at *Beguile*."

Dev could read behind the lines. The duchess must have sold off her wardrobe as well as her jewelry over the years. It was miracle she'd managed to hang on to the apartment at the Dakota. The thought of what the duchess and Sarah had gone through kicked Dev's admiration for them both up another notch. Also, his determination to treat Sarah to something new and obscenely expensive. He knew better than to step on her pride again, though, and said merely, "Retro looks good on you."

"Thank you."

After what passed for the airline's gourmet meal, Dev used his in-flight wireless connection to crunch numbers for his meetings with Girault and company while Sarah went back to work on her laptop. She'd promised Alexis she would finish the layout for the Summer Sea-escapes but the perspectives just wouldn't gel. After juggling Martha's Vineyard with Catalina Island and South Padre Island with South Georgia Island, she decided she would have to swing by *Beguile*'s Paris offices to see how the layout looked on a twenty-five-inch monitor before shooting it off to Alexis for review.

Dev was still crunching numbers when she folded down the lid of her computer. With a polite good-night, she tugged up the airline's fleecy blue blanket and curled into her pod.

A gentle nudge brought her awake some hours later. She blinked gritty eyes and decided reality was more of a fantasy than her dreams. Dev had that bad-boy look again. Tie loosened. Shirt collar open. Dark circles below his blue eyes.

"We'll be landing in less than an hour," he told her.

As if to emphasize the point, a flight attendant appeared with a pot of fresh-brewed coffee. Sarah gulped down a half cup before she took the amenity kit provided to all business- and first-class passengers to the lavatory. She emerged with her face washed, teeth brushed, hair combed and her soul ready for the magic that was springtime in Paris.

Or the magic that might have been.

Spring hadn't yet made it to northern France. The temperature hovered around fifty, and a cold rain was coming down in sheets when Sarah and Dev emerged from the terminal and ducked into a waiting limo. The trees lining the roads from the airport showed only a hint of new green and the fields were brown and sere.

Once inside the city, Paris's customary snarl of traffic engulfed them. Neither the traffic nor the nasty weather could dim the glory of the 7th arrondissement, however. The townhomes and ministries, once the residences of France's wealthiest nobility, displayed their mansard roofs and wrought-iron balconies with haughty disregard for the pelting rain. Sarah caught glimpses of the Eiffel Tower's iron symmetry before the limo rolled to a stop on a quiet side street in the heart of Saint-Germain. Surprise brought her around in her seat to face Dev.

"We're staying at the Hôtel Verneuil?"

"We are."

"Gina and I and Grandmama stayed here years ago, on our last trip abroad together."

"So the duchess informed me." His mouth curved. "She also informed me that I'm to take you to Café Michaud to properly celebrate our engagement," he said with a smile.

Sarah fell a little bit in love with him at that moment. Not because he'd booked them into this small gem of a palace instead of a suite at the much larger and far more expensive Crillon or George V. Because he'd made such an effort with her grandmother.

Surprised and shaken by the warmth that curled around her heart, she tried to recover as they exited the limo. "From what I remember, the Verneuil only has twenty-five or twenty-six rooms. The hotel's usually full. I'm surprised you could get us in with such short notice."

"I didn't. Patrick did. After which he informed me that I'd just doubled his Christmas bonus."

"I have to meet this man."

"That can be arranged."

He said it with a casualness that almost hid the implication behind his promise. Sarah caught it, however. The careless words implied a future beyond Paris.

She wasn't ready to think about that. Instead she looked around the lobby while Dev went to the reception desk. The exposed beams, rich tapestries and heavy furniture covered in red velvet hadn't changed since her last visit ten or twelve years ago. Apparently the management hadn't, either. The receptionist must have buzzed her boss. He emerged from the back office, his shoulders stooped beneath his formal morning coat and a wide smile on his face.

"*Bonjour,* Lady Sarah!"

A quick glance at his name tag provided his name. "*Bonjour,* Monsieur LeBon."

"What a delight to have you stay with us again," he exclaimed in French, the Parisian accent so different from that of the provinces. "How is the duchess?"

"She's very well, thank you."

"I'm told this trip is in honor of a special occasion," the manager beamed. "May I offer you my most sincere congratulations?"

"Thank you," she said again, trying not to cringe at the continuation of their deception.

LeBon switched to English to offer his felicitations to Dev. "If I may be so bold to say it, Monsieur Hunter, you are a very lucky man to have captured the heart of one such as Lady Sarah."

"Extremely lucky," Dev agreed.

"Allow me to show you to your floor."

He pushed the button to summon the elevator, then stood aside for them to enter the brass-bedecked cage. While it lifted them to the upper floors, he apologized profusely for not being able to give them adjoining rooms as had been requested.

"We moved several of our guests as your so very capable assistant suggested, Monsieur Hunter, and have put you and Lady Sarah in chambers only a short distance apart. I hope they will be satisfactory."

Sarah's was more than satisfactory. A mix of antique, marble and modern, it offered a four-poster bed and a lovely sitting area with a working fireplace and a tiny balcony. But it was the view from the balcony that delighted her artist's soul.

The rain had softened to a drizzle. It glistened on the slate-gray rooftops of Paris. Endless rows of chimneys rose from the roofs like sentries standing guard over their city. And in the distance were the twin Gothic towers and flying buttresses of Notre Dame.

"I don't have anything scheduled until three this afternoon," Dev said while Monsieur LeBon waited to escort him to his own room. "Would you like to rest awhile, then go out for lunch?"

The city beckoned, and Sarah ached to answer its call. "I'm not tired. I think I'd like to take a walk."

"In the rain?"

"That's when Paris is at its best. The streets, the cafés, seem to steal the light. Everything shimmers."

"Okay," Dev said, laughing, "you've convinced me. I'll change and rap on your door in, say, fifteen minutes?"

"Oh, but…"

She stopped just short of blurting out that she hadn't intended that as an invitation. She could hardly say she didn't want her fiancé's company with Monsieur LeBon beaming his approval of a romantic stroll.

"…I'll need a bit more time than that," she finished. "Let's say thirty minutes."

"A half hour it is."

As she changed into lightweight wool slacks and a hip-length, cherry-red sweater coat that belted at the waist, Sarah tried to analyze her reluctance to share these first hours in Paris with Dev. She suspected it stemmed from the emotion that had welled up when they'd first pulled up at the Hôtel Verneuil. She knew then that she could fall for him, and fall hard. What worried her was that it wouldn't take very much to push her over the precipice.

True, he'd blackmailed her into this uncomfortable charade. Also true, he'd put a ring on her finger and hustled her onto a plane before she could formulate a coherent protest. In the midst of those autocratic acts, though, he'd shown incredible forbearance and generosity.

Then there were the touches, the kisses, the ridiculous whoosh every time he smiled at her. Devon Hunter had made *Beguile*'s list based on raw sex appeal. Sarah now realized he possessed something far more potent…and more dangerous to her peace of mind.

She had to remember this was a short-term assignment. Dev had stipulated it would last only until he wrapped up negotiations on his big deal. It looked now as though that might happen within the next few days. Then this would all be over.

The thought didn't depress her. Sarah wouldn't let it. But worked hard to keep the thought at bay.

She was ready when Dev knocked. Wrapping on a biscuit-colored rain cape, she tossed one of its flaps over a shoulder on her way to the door. With her hair tucked up under a flat-brimmed Dutch-boy cap, she was rainproof and windproof.

"Nice hat," Dev said when she stepped into the hall.

"Thanks."

"Nice everything, actually."

She could have said the same. This was the first time she'd seen him in anything other than a suit. The man was made for jeans. Or vice versa. Their snug fit emphasized his flat belly and lean flanks. And, she added with a gulp when he turned to press the button for the elevator, his tight, trim butt.

He'd added a cashmere scarf in gray-and-blue plaid to his leather bomber jacket, but hadn't bothered with a hat. Sarah worried that it would be too cold for him, but when they exited the hotel, they found the rain was down to a fine mist and the temperature had climbed a few degrees.

Dev took her arm as they crossed the street, then tucked it in his as they started down the boulevard. Sarah felt awkward with that arrangement at first. Elbow to elbow, shoulder to shoulder, strolling along the rain-washed boulevard, they looked like the couple they weren't.

Gradually, Sarah got used to the feel of him beside her, to the way he matched his stride to hers. And bit by bit, the magic of Paris eased her nagging sense that this was all just a charade.

Even this late in the morning the *boulangeries* still emitted their seductive, tantalizing scent of fresh-baked bread. Baguettes sprouted from tall baskets and the racks were crammed with braided loaves. The pastry shops, too, had set out their day's wares. The exquisitely crafted sweets, tarts, chocolate éclairs, gâteaux, caramel mousse, napoleons, macaroons—all were true works of art, and completely impossible to resist.

"God, these look good," Dev murmured, his gaze on the colorful display. "Are you up for a coffee and an éclair?"

"Always. But my favorite patisserie in all Paris is just a couple of blocks away. Can you hold out a little longer?"

"I'll try," he said, assuming an expression of heroic resolution.

Laughing, Sarah pressed his arm closer to her side and guided him the few blocks. The tiny patisserie was nested between a bookstore and a bank. Three dime-size wrought-iron tables sat under the striped awning out front; three more were wedged inside. Luckily two women were getting up from one of the tables when Dev and Sarah entered.

Sarah ordered an espresso and *tart au citron* for herself, and a café au lait for Dev, then left him debating his choice of pastries while she claimed the table. She loosed the flaps of her cape and let it drift over the back of her chair while she observed the drama taking place at the pastry case.

With no other customers waiting, the young woman behind the counter inspected Dev with wide eyes while he checked out the colorful offerings. When he made his selection, she slid the pastry onto a plate and offered it with a question.

"You are American?"

He flashed her a friendly smile. "I am."

Sarah guessed what was coming even before the woman's face lit up with eager recognition.

"Aah, I knew it. You are Number Three, yes?"

Dev's smile tipped into a groan, but he held his cool as she called excitedly to her coworkers.

"C'est lui! C'est lui! Monsieur Hunter. Numéro trois."

Sarah bit her lip as a small bevy of females in white aprons converged at the counter. Dev took the fuss with good grace and even autographed a couple of paper napkins before retreating to the table with his chocolate éclair.

Sarah felt the urge to apologize but merely nodded when he asked grimly if *Beguile* had a wide circulation in France.

"It's our third-largest market."

"Great."

He stabbed his éclair and had to dig deep for a smile when the server delivered their coffees.

"In fact," Sarah said after the girl giggled and departed,

"*Beguile* has an office here in the city. I was going to swing by there when you go for your meeting."

"I'll arrange a car for you."

The reply was polite, but perfunctory. The enchantment of their stroll through Paris's rain-washed streets had dissipated with the mist.

"No need. I'll take the subway."

"Your call," Dev replied. "I'll contact you later and let you know what time we're meeting the Giraults for dinner tonight."

Eight

The French offices of *Beguile* were located only a few blocks from the Arc de Triomphe, on rue Balzac. Sarah always wondered what that famed French novelist and keen observer of human absurdities would think of a glossy publication that pandered to so many of those absurdities.

The receptionist charged with keeping the masses at bay glanced up from her desk with a polite expression that morphed into a welcoming smile when she spotted Sarah.

"*Bonjour,* Sarah! So good to see you again!"

"*Bonjour,* Madeline. Good to see you, too. How are the twins?"

"Horrors," the receptionist replied with a half laugh, half groan. "Absolute horrors. Here are their latest pictures."

After duly admiring the impish-looking three-year-olds, Sarah rounded the receptionist's desk and walked a corridor lined with framed, poster-size copies of *Beguile* covers. Paul Vincent, the senior editor, was pacing his glass cage of an office and using both hands to emphasize whatever point he was trying to make to the person on the speakerphone. Sarah tipped him a wave and would have proceeded to the production unit, but Paul gestured her inside and abruptly terminated his call.

"Sarah!"

Grasping her hands, he kissed her on both cheeks. She bent just a bit so he could hit the mark. At five-four, Paul tended to be as sensitive about his height as he was about the kidney-shaped birthmark discoloring a good portion of his jaw. Yet despite what he called his little imperfections, his unerring eye for color and style had propelled him from the designers' cutting rooms to his present exalted position.

"Alexis emailed to say you would be in Paris," he informed Sarah. "She's instructed me to put François and his crew at your complete disposal."

"For what?"

"To take photos of you and your fiancé. She wants all candids, no posed shots and plenty of romantic backdrop in both shallow and distant depth of field. François says he'll use wide aperture at the Eiffel Tower, perhaps F2.8 to…"

"No, Paul."

"No F2.8? Well, you'll have to speak with François about that."

"No, Paul. No wide aperture, no candids, no Eiffel Tower, no François!"

"But Alexis…."

"Wants to capitalize on my engagement to Number Three. Yes, I know. My fiancé agreed to a photo shoot in New York, but that's as far as either he or I will go. We told Alexis that before we left."

"Then you had better tell her again."

"I will," she said grimly. "In the meantime, I need to use Production's monitors to take a last look at the layout I've been working on. When I zap it to Alexis, I'll remind her of our agreement."

She turned to leave, but Paul stopped her. "What can you tell me of the Chicago meeting?"

The odd inflection in his voice gave Sarah pause. Won-

dering what was behind it, she searched her mind. So much
had happened in the past few days that she'd forgotten about
the shuttle Alexis had jumped for an unscheduled meeting
with the head of their publishing group. All she'd thought
about her boss's unscheduled absence at the time was that it
had provided a short reprieve. Paul's question now brought
the Chicago meeting forcibly to mind.

"I can't tell you anything," she said honestly. "I didn't
have a chance to talk to Alexis about it before I left. Why,
what have you heard?"

He folded his arms, bent an elbow and tapped two fingers against the birthmark on his chin. It was a nervous
gesture, one he rarely allowed. That he would give in to it
now generated a distinct unease in Sarah.

"I've heard rumors," he admitted. "Only rumors, you
understand."

"What rumors?"

The fingers picked up speed, machine-gunning his chin.

"Some say... Not me, I assure you! But some say that
Alexis is too old. Too out of touch with our target reader-
ship. Some say the romance has gone out of her, and out
of our magazine. Before, we used to beguile, to tantalize.
Now we titillate."

Much to her chagrin, Sarah couldn't argue the point.
The butt shot of Dev that Alexis had insisted on was case
in point. In the most secret corners of her heart, she agreed
with the ambiguous, unnamed "some" Paul referenced.

Despite her frequent differences of opinion with her
boss, however, she owed Alexis her loyalty and support.
She'd hired Sarah right out of college, sans experience, sans
credentials. Grandmama might insist Sarah's title had in-
fluenced that decision. Maybe so, but the title hadn't done
more than get a neophyte's foot in the door. She'd sweated
blood to work her way up to layout editor. And now, apparently, it was payback time.

Alexis confirmed that some time later in her response to Sarah's email.

Sea-escapes layout looks good. We'll go with it. Please rethink the Paris photo shoot. Chicago feels we need more romance in our mag. You and Hunter personify that, at least as far as our readers are concerned.

The email nagged at Sarah all afternoon. She used the remainder of her private time to wander through her favorite museum, but not even the Musée d'Orsay could resolve her moral dilemma. Questions came at her, dive-bombing like suicidal mosquitoes as she strolled through the converted railroad station that now housed some of the world's most celebrated works of art.

All but oblivious to the Matisses and Rodins, she weighed her options. Should she support her boss or accede to Dev's demand for privacy? What about the mess with Gina? Would Alexis exploit that, too, if pushed to the wall? Would she play up the elder sister's engagement as a desperate attempt to save the younger from a charge of larceny?

She would. Sarah knew damned well she would. The certainty curdled like sour milk in the pit of her stomach. Whom did she most owe her loyalty to? Gina? Dev? Alexis? Herself?

The last thought was so heretical it gnawed at Sarah's insides while she prepped for her first meeting with the Giraults early that evening. Dev had told her this would be an informal dinner at the couple's Paris town house.

"Ha!" she muttered as she added a touch of mascara. "I'll bet it's informal."

Going with instinct, she opted for a hip-length tuxedo jacket that had been one of Grandmama's favorite pieces. Sarah had extracted the jacket from the to-be-sold pile on at least three separate occasions. Vintage was vintage, but

Louis Féraud was art. He'd opened his first house of fashion in Cannes 1950, became one of Brigitte Bardot's favorite designers and grew into a legend in his own lifetime.

This jacket was quintessential Féraud. The contour-hugging design featured wide satin lapels and a double-breasted, two-button front fastening. Sarah paired it with a black, lace-edged chemise and wide-pegged black satin pants. A honey-colored silk handkerchief peeked from the breast pocket. A thin gold bangle circled her wrist. With her hair swept up in a smooth twist, she looked restrained and refined.

For some reason, though, restrained just didn't hack it tonight. Not while she was playing tug-of-war between fiercely conflicting loyalties. She wanted to do right by Dev. And Alexis. And Gina. And herself. Elise Girault could take a flying leap.

Frowning, she unclipped her hair and let the dark mass swirl to her shoulders. Then she slipped out of the jacket and tugged off the chemise. When she pulled the jacket on again, the two-button front dipped dangerously low. Grandmama would have a cow if she saw how much shadowy cleavage her Sarah now displayed. Dev, she suspected, would approve.

He did. Instantly and enthusiastically. Bending an arm against the doorjamb, he gave a long, low whistle.

"You look fantastic."

"Thanks." Honesty compelled her to add, "So do you."

If the afternoon negotiating session with Monsieur Girault had produced any stress, it didn't show in his face. He was clean shaven, clear eyed and smelled so darned good Sarah almost leaned in for a deeper whiff. His black hair still gleamed with damp. From a shower, she wondered as she fought the urged to feather her fingers through it, or the foggy drizzle that had kept up all day?

His suit certainly wasn't vintage, but had obviously been

tailored with the same loving skill as Grandmama's jacket. With it he wore a crisp blue shirt topped by a blue-and-silver-striped tie.

"What was it Oscar Wilde said about ties?" Sarah murmured, eyeing the expensive neckwear.

"Beats me."

"Something about a well-tied tie being the first serious step in a man's life. Of course, that was back when it took them hours to achieve the perfect crease in their cravat."

"Glad those days are gone. Speaking of gone… The car's waiting." He bowed and swept a hand toward the door. "Shall we go, *ma chérie?*"

Her look of surprise brought a smug grin.

"I had some time after my meeting so I pulled up a few phrases on Google Translate. How's the accent?"

"Well…"

"That bad, huh?"

"I've heard worse."

But not much worse. Hiding a smile, she picked up her clutch and led the way to the door.

"How did the meeting go, by the way?"

"We're making progress. Enough that my chief of production and a team of our corporate attorneys are in the air as we speak. We still need to hammer out a few details, but we're close."

"You *must* be making progress if you're bringing in a whole team."

Sarah refused to acknowledge the twinge that gave her. She hadn't really expected to share much of Paris with Dev. He was here on business. And she was here to make sure that business didn't get derailed by the wife of his prospective partner. She reminded herself of that fact as the limo glided through the lamp-lit streets.

Jean-Jacques Girault and his wife greeted them at the door to their magnificent town house. Once inside the palatial foyer, the two couples engaged in the obligatory cheek-kissing. Madame Girault behaved herself as she congratulated her guests on their engagement, but Dev stuck close to his fiancée just in case.

The exchange gave Sarah time to assess her hostess. The blonde had to be in her mid-fifties, but she had the lithe build and graceful carriage of a ballerina...which she used to be, she informed Sarah with a nod toward the portrait holding place of honor in the palatial foyer. The larger-than-life-size oil depicted a much younger Elise Girault costumed as Odile, the evil black swan in Tchaikovsky's *Swan Lake.*

"I loved dancing that part." With a smile as wicked as the one she wore in the portrait, Madame Girault hooked an arm in Sarah's and led her through a set of open double doors into a high-ceilinged salon. "Being bad is so much more fun than being good, yes?"

"Unless, as happens to Odile in some versions of *Swan Lake,* being bad gets you an arrow through the heart."

The older woman's laugh burst out, as loud and booming as a cannon. "Aha! You are warning me, I think, to keep my hands off your so-handsome Devon."

"If the ballet slipper fits..."

Her laugh foghorned again, noisy and raucous and totally infectious. Sarah found herself grinning as Madame Girault spoke over her shoulder.

"I like her, Devon."

She pronounced it Dee-vón, with the accent on the last syllable.

"I was prepared not to, you understand, as I want you for myself. Perhaps we can arrange a ménage à trois, yes?"

With her back to Dev, Sarah missed his reaction to the suggestion. She would have bet it wasn't as benign as Monsieur Girault's.

"Elise, my pet. You'll shock our guests with these little jokes of yours."

The look his wife gave Sarah brimmed with mischief and the unmistakable message that she was *not* joking.

Much to Sarah's surprise, she enjoyed the evening. Elise Girault didn't try to be anything but herself. She was at times sophisticated, at other times outrageous, but she didn't cross the line Sarah had drawn in the sand. Or in this case, in the near-priceless nineteenth-century Aubusson carpet woven in green-and-gold florals.

The Giraults and their guests took cocktails in the salon and dinner in an exquisitely paneled dining room with windows overlooking the Seine. The lively conversation ranged from their hostess's years at the Ballet de l'Opéra de Paris to Sarah's work at *Beguile* to, inevitably, the megabusiness of aircraft manufacturing. The glimpse into a world she'd had no previous exposure to fascinated Sarah, but Elise tolerated it only until the last course was cleared.

"Enough, Jean-Jacques!"

Pushing away from the table, she rose. Her husband and guests followed suit.

"We will take coffee and dessert in the petite salon. And you," she said, claiming Dev's arm, "will tell me what convinced this delightful woman to marry you. It was the story in *Beguile,* yes?" Her wicked smile returning, she threw Sarah an arch look. "The truth, now. Is his derriere as delicious as it looked in your magazine?"

Her husband shook his head. "Be good, Elise."

"I am, *mon cher.* Sooo good."

"I'm good, Dee-vón." Grinning, Sarah batted her lashes as the Hôtel Verneuil's elevator whisked them upward. "Sooo good."

Amused, Dev folded his arms and leaned his shoulders against the cage. She wasn't tipsy—she'd restricted her alcoholic intake to one aperitif, a single glass of wine and a few sips of brandy—but she was looser than he'd yet seen her.

He liked her this way. Her green eyes sparkling. Her hair windblown and brushing her shoulders. Her tuxedo jacket providing intermittent and thoroughly tantalizing glimpses of creamy breasts.

Liked, hell. He wanted to devour her whole.

"You were certainly good tonight," he agreed. "Especially when Elise tried to pump you for details about our sex life. I still don't know how you managed to give the impression of torrid heat when all you did was arch a brow."

"Ah, yes. The regal lift. It's one of Grandmama's best weapons, along with the chin tilt and the small sniff."

She demonstrated all three and had him grinning while he walked her to her door.

"Elise may be harder to fend off when she and I have lunch tomorrow," Sarah warned as she extracted the key card from her purse. "I may need to improvise."

His pulse jumping, Dev took the key and slid it into the electronic lock. The lock snicked, the door opened and he made his move.

"No reason you should have to improvise."

She turned, her expression at once wary and disbelieving. "Are you suggesting we go to bed together to satisfy Elise Girault's prurient curiosity?"

"No, ma'am." He bent and brushed his lips across hers. "I'm suggesting we go to bed together to satisfy ours."

Her jaw sagged. "You're kidding, right?"

"No, ma'am," he said again, half laughing, wholly serious.

She snapped her mouth shut, but the fact that she didn't stalk inside and slam the door in his face set Dev's pulse jumping again.

"Maybe," she said slowly, her eyes locked with his, "we could go a little way down that road. Just far enough to provide Elise with a few juicy details."

That was all the invitation he needed. Scooping her into his arms, he strode into the room and kicked the door shut. The maid had left the lamps on and turned down the duvet on the bed. Much as Dev ached to vector in that direction, he aimed for the sofa instead. He settled on its plush cushions with Sarah in his lap.

Exerting fierce control, he slid a palm under the silky splash of her hair. Her nape was warm, her lips parted, her gaze steady. The thought flashed into Dev's mind that he was already pretty far down the road.

Rock hard and hurting, he bent his head again. No mere brush of lips this time. No tentative exploration. No show for the cameras. This was hunger, raw and hot. He tried to throttle it back, but Sarah sabotaged that effort by matching him kiss for kiss, touch for touch. His fingers speared through her hair. Hers traced the line of his jaw, slipped inside his collar, found the knot of his tie.

"To hell with Oscar Wilde," she muttered after a moment. "The tie has to go."

The tie went. So did the suit coat. When she popped the top two buttons of his dress shirt, he reached for the ones on her jacket. The first one slid through its opening and Dev saw she wasn't wearing a bra. With a fervent prayer of thanks, he fingered the second button.

"I've been fantasizing about doing this from the moment you opened the door to me this evening," he admitted, his voice rough.

"I fantasized about it, too. Must be why I discarded the chemise I usually wear with this outfit."

Her honesty shot straight to his heart. She didn't play games. Didn't tease or go all pouty and coy. She was as hungry as Dev and not ashamed to show it.

Aching with need, he slid the second button through its opening. The satin lapels gaped open, baring her breasts. They were small and proud and tipped with dark rose nipples that Dev couldn't even begin to resist. Hefting her a little higher, he trailed a line of kisses down one slope and caught a nipple between his lips.

Her neck arched. Her head tipped back. With a small groan, Sarah reveled in the sensations that streaked from her breast to her belly. They were so deep, so intense, she purred with pleasure.

It took her a few moments to realize she wasn't actually emitting that low, humming sound. It was coming from the clutch purse she'd dropped on the sofa table.

"That's my cell phone," she panted through waves of pleasure. "I put it on vibrate at the Giraults."

"Ignore it."

Dev turned his attention to her other breast and Sarah was tempted, so tempted, to follow his gruff instruction.

"I can't," she groaned. "It could be Grandmama. Or Maria," she added with a little clutch of panic.

She scrambled upright and grabbed her bag. A glance at the face associated in her address book with the incoming number made her sag with relief.

Only for a moment, however. What could Alexis want, calling this late? Remembering her conversation with Paul Vincent at *Beguile*'s Paris office this afternoon, Sarah once again felt the tug of conflicting loyalties.

"Sarah? Are you there?" Alexis's hoarse rasp rattled through voice mail. "Pick up if you are."

Sarah sent Dev an apologetic glance and hit Answer. "I'm here, Alexis."

"Sorry, kiddo, I didn't think about the time difference. Were you in bed?"

"Almost," Dev muttered.

Sarah made a shushing motion with her free hand but it was too late. Alexis picked up the scent like a bloodhound.

"Is that Hunter? He's with you?"

"Yes. We just got in from a late dinner."

Not a lie, exactly. Not the whole truth, either. There were some things her boss simply didn't need to know.

"Good," Alexis was saying. "He can look over the JPEGs I just emailed you from the photo shoot at Cartier. I marked the one we're going to use with the blurb about your engagement."

"We'll take a look at them and get back to you."

"Tonight, kiddo. I want the story in this month's issue."

"Okay." Sighing, Sarah closed the flaps of her jacket and fastened the top button one-handed. "Shoot me the blurb, too."

"Don't worry about it. It's only a few lines."

The too-bland assurance set off an internal alarm.

"Send it, Alexis."

"All right, all right. But I want it back tonight, too."

She cut the connection, and Sarah sank back onto the cushions. Dev sat in his corner, one arm stretched across the sofa back. His shirttails hung open and his belt had somehow come unbuckled. He looked more than willing to pick up where they'd left off, but Sarah's common sense had kicked in. Or rather her sense of self-preservation.

"Saved by the bell," she said with an attempt at lightness. "At least now I won't have to improvise when Elise starts digging for details."

The phone pinged in her hand, signaling the arrival of a text message.

"That's the blurb Alexis wants to run with the pictures from Cartier. I'll pull it up with the photos so you can review them."

"No need." Dev pushed off the sofa, stuffed in his shirt and buckled his belt. "I trust you on this one."

"I'll make sure there are no naked body parts showing," she promised solemnly.

"You do that, and I'll make sure we're not interrupted next time."

"Next time?"

He dropped a quick kiss on her nose and grabbed his discarded suit coat.

"Oui, ma chérie," he said in his truly execrable French. "Next time."

Nine

Dev had a breakfast meeting with his people, who'd flown in the night before. That gave Sarah the morning to herself. A shame, really, because the day promised glorious sunshine and much warmer temperatures. Perfect for strolling the Left Bank with that special someone.

Which is what most of Paris seemed to be doing, she saw after coffee and a croissant at her favorite patisserie. The sight of so many couples, young, old and in between, rekindled some of the raw emotions Dev had generated last night.

In the bright light of day, Sarah couldn't believe she'd invited him to make love to her. Okay, she'd practically demanded it. Even now, as she meandered over the Pont de l'Archevêché, she felt her breasts tingle at the memory of his hands and mouth on them.

She stopped midway across the bridge. Pont de l'Archevêché translated to the Archbishop's Bridge in English, most likely because it formed a main means of transit for the clerics of Notre Dame. The cathedral's square towers rose on the right. Bookseller stalls and cafés crowded the broad avenue on the left. The Seine flowed dark and silky below. What intrigued her, though, were the padlocks of all shapes and sizes hooked through the bridge's waist-high, iron-mesh scrollwork. Some locks had tags attached, some were decorated with bright ribbons, some included small charms.

She'd noticed other bridges sporting locks, although none as heavily adorned as this one. They'd puzzled her but she hadn't really wondered about their significance. It became apparent a few moments after she spotted a pair of tourists purchasing a padlock from an enterprising lock seller at the far end of the bridge. The couple searched for an empty spot on the fancy grillwork to attach their purchase. Then they threw the key into the Seine and shared a long, passionate kiss.

When they walked off arm in arm, Sarah approached the lock seller. He was perched on an upturned wooden crate beside a pegboard displaying his wares. His hair sprouted like milky-white dandelion tufts from under his rusty-black beret. A cigarette hung from his lower lip.

"I've been away for a while," she said in her fluent Parisian. "When did this business with the locks begin?"

"Three years? Five? Who can remember?" His shoulders lifted in the quintessential Gallic shrug. "At first the locks appeared only at night, and they would be cut off each day. Now they are everywhere."

"So it seems."

Mistaking her for a native, he winked and shared his personal opinion of his enterprise. "The tourists, they eat this silly stuff up. As if they can lock in the feelings they have right now, today, and throw away the key. We French know better, yes?"

His cigarette bobbed. His gestures grew extravagant as he expounded his philosophy.

"To love is to take risks. To be free, not caged. To walk away if what you feel brings hurt to you or to your lover. Who would stay, or want to stay, where there is pain?"

The question was obviously rhetorical, so Sarah merely spread her hands and answered with a shrug.

She was still thinking about the encounter when she met Madame Girault for lunch later that day. She related the lock seller's philosophy to Elise, who belted out a raucous laugh that turned heads throughout the restaurant.

"My darling Sarah, I must beg to disagree!"

With her blond hair drawn into a tight bun that emphasized her high cheekbones and angular chin, Elise looked more like the Black Swan of her portrait. Her sly smile only heightened the resemblance.

"Locks and, yes, a little pain can add a delicious touch to an affair," she said, her eyes dancing. "And speaking of which…"

Her mouth took a sardonic tilt as a dark-haired man some twenty-five or thirty years her junior rose from his table and approached theirs.

"Ah, Elise, only one woman in all Paris has a laugh like yours. How are you, my love?"

"Very well. And you, Henri? Are you still dancing attendance on that rich widow I saw you with at the theater?"

"Sadly, she returned to Argentina before I extracted full payment for services rendered." His dark eyes drifted to Sarah. "But enough of such mundane matters. You must introduce me to your so-lovely companion."

"No, I must not. She's in Paris with her fiancé and has no need of your special skills." Elise flapped a hand and shooed him off. "Be a good boy and go away."

"If you insist…"

He gave a mocking half bow and returned to his table, only to sign the check and leave a few moments later. A fleeting look of regret crossed Elise's face as he wove his way toward the exit. Sighing, she fingered her glass.

"He was so inventive in bed, that one. So *very* inventive. But always in need of money. When I tired of emptying my purse for him, he threatened to sell pictures of me in certain, shall we say, exotic positions."

Sarah winced, but couldn't say anything. Any mention of the paparazzi and sensational photographs struck too close to home.

"Jean-Jacques sent men to convince him that would not be wise," Elise confided. "The poor boy was in a cast for weeks afterward."

The offhand comment doused the enjoyment Sarah had taken in Elise's company up to that point. Madame Girault's concept of love suddenly seemed more tawdry than amusing. Deliberately, Sarah changed the subject.

"I wonder how the negotiations are going? Dev said he thought they were close to a deal."

Clearly disinterested, Elise shrugged and snapped her fingers to summon their waiter.

Halfway across Paris, Dev had to force himself to focus on the columns of figures in the newly restructured agreement. It didn't help that his seat at the conference table offered a panoramic view of the pedestrians-only esplanade and iconic Grande Arche that dominated Paris's financial district. Workers by the hundreds were seated on the steps below the Grande Arche, their faces lifted to the sun while they enjoyed their lunch break.

One couple appeared to be enjoying more than the sun. Dev watched them share a touch, a laugh, a kiss. Abruptly, he pushed away from the table.

"Sorry," he said to the dozen or so startled faces that turned in his direction. "I need to make a call."

Jean-Jacques Girault scooted his chair away from the table, as well. "Let's all take a break. We'll reconvene in thirty minutes, yes? There'll be a catered lunch waiting when we return."

Dev barely waited for Girault to finish his little speech. The urge to talk to Sarah, to hear her voice, drove him through the maze of outer offices and into the elevator. A short while later he'd joined the throng on the steps below the Grande Arche.

It took him a moment to acknowledge the unfamiliar sensation that knifed through him as he dialed Sarah's number. It wasn't just the lust that had damned near choked him last night. It was that amorphous, indefinable feeling immortalized in so many sappy songs. Grimacing, he admitted the inescapable truth. He was in love, or close enough to it to make no difference.

Sarah answered on the second ring. "Hello, Dev. This must be mental telepathy. I was just talking about you."

"You were, huh?"

"How are the negotiations going?"

"They're going."

The sound of her voice did something stupid to his insides. To his head, too. With barely a second thought, he abandoned Girault and company to the team of sharks he'd flown in last night.

"We've been crunching numbers all morning. I'm thinking of letting my people handle the afternoon session. What do you have planned?"

"Nothing special."

"How about I meet you back at the hotel and we'll do nothing special together?"

He didn't intend to say what came next. Didn't have any control over the words. They just happened.

"Or maybe," he said, his voice going husky, "we can work on our next time."

A long silence followed his suggestion. When it stretched for several seconds, Dev kicked himself for his lack of finesse. Then she came back with a low, breathless response that damned near stopped his heart.

"I'll catch a cab and meet you at the hotel."

* * *

Sarah snapped her phone shut and sent Madame Girault a glance that was only a shade apologetic. "That was Dev. I'm sorry, but I have to go."

Elise looked startled for a moment. But only a moment. Then her face folded into envious lines.

"Go," she ordered with a wave of one hand. "Paris is the city of love, after all. And I think yours, *ma petite,* is one that deserves a lock on the Archbishop's Bridge."

Sarah wanted to believe that was what sent her rushing out of the restaurant. Despite the lock seller's philosophical musings, despite hearing the details of Elise's sordid little affair, she wanted desperately to believe that what she felt for Dev could stand the test of time.

That hope took a temporary hit when she caught up with the dark-haired, dark-eyed Henri on the pavement outside of the restaurant. He'd just hailed a cab, but generously offered it to her instead.

Or not so generously. His offer to escort her to her hotel and fill her afternoon hours with unparalleled delight left an unpleasant taste in Sarah's mouth. Unconsciously, she channeled Grandmama.

"I think not, monsieur."

The haughty reply sent him back a pace. The blank surprise on his face allowed Sarah more than enough time to slide into the cab and tell the driver her destination. Then she slammed the door and forgot Henri, forgot Elise, forgot everything but the instant hunger Dev's call had sparked in her.

She wrestled with that hunger all the way back to the hotel. Her cool, rational, practical-by-necessity self kept asserting that her arrangement with Dev Hunter was just that, an arrangement. A negotiated contract that would soon conclude. If she made love with him, as she desperately wanted to do, she'd simply be satisfying a short-term physical need while possibly setting herself up for long-term regrets.

The other side of her, the side she usually kept so sternly repressed, echoed Gina at her giddiest. Why not grab a little pleasure? Taste delight here, now, and let tomorrow take care of itself?

As was happening all too frequently with Dev, giddy and greedy vanquished cool and rational. By the time Sarah burst out of the elevator and headed down the hall toward her room, heat coursed through her, hot and urgent. The sight of Dev leaning against the wall beside the door to her room sent her body temperature soaring up another ten degrees.

"What took you so long?" he demanded.

Snatching the key card from her hand, he shoved it into the lock. Two seconds after the door opened, he had her against the entryway wall.

"I hope you had a good lunch. We won't be coming up for food or drink anytime soon."

The bruising kiss spiked every one of Sarah's senses. She tasted him, drank in his scent, felt his hips slam hers against the wall.

He kicked the door shut. Or did she? She didn't know, didn't care. Dev's hands were all over her at that point. Unbuttoning her blouse. Hiking up her skirt. Shoving down her bikini briefs.

Panting, greedy, wanting him so much she ached with it, she struggled out of her blouse. Kicked her shoes off and the panties free of her ankles. Hooked one leg around his thighs.

"Sarah." It was a groan and a plea. "Let's take this to the bedroom."

Mere moments later she was naked and stretched out on the king-size bed. Her avid gaze devoured Dev as he stood beside the bed and shed his clothing.

She'd seen portions of him last night. Enough to confirm that he ranked much higher than number three on her personal top ten list. Those glimpses didn't even begin to compare with the way he looked now with his black hair catching the afternoon light and his blue eyes fired with need. Every muscle in his long, lean body looked taut and eager. He was hard for her, and hungry, and so ready that Sarah almost yelped when he turned away.

"What are you doing?"

"Making sure you don't regret this."

Her dismay became a wave of relief when she saw him extract a condom from the wallet in his discarded pants. She wasn't on the pill. She'd stopped months ago. Or was it years? Sarah couldn't remember. She suspected her decision to quit birth control had a lot to do with the realization that taking care of Grandmama and keeping a roof over their heads were more important to her than casual sex.

Showed what she knew. There was nothing casual about this sex, however. The need for it, the gnawing hunger for it, consumed her.

No! Her mind screamed the denial even as she opened her arms to Dev. This wasn't just sex. This wasn't just raw need. This was so elemental. So…so French. Making love in the afternoon. With a man who filled her, physically, emotionally, every way that mattered.

His hips braced against hers. His knees pried hers apart. Eagerly, Sarah opened her legs and her arms and her heart to him. When he eased into her, she hooked her calves around his and rose up to meet his first, slow thrusts. Then the pace picked up. In. Out. In again.

Soon, *too* soon, dammit, her vaginal muscles began to quiver and her belly contracted. She tried to suppress the spasms. Tried to force her muscles to ease their greedy grip. She wanted to build to a steady peak, spin the pleasure as long as she could.

Her body refused to listen to her mind. The tight, spiraling sensation built to a wild crescendo. Panting, Sarah arched her neck. A moment later, she was flying, sailing, soaring. Dev surged into her, went taut and rode to the crest with her. Then he gave a strangled grunt and collapsed on top of her.

* * *

Sarah was still shuddering with the aftershocks when he whispered a French phrase into her ear. Her eyes flew open. Her jaw dropped.

"What did you say?"

He levered up on one elbow. A flush rode high in his cheeks and his blue eyes were still fever bright, but he managed a semicoherent reply.

"I was trying to tell you I adore you."

Sarah started giggling and couldn't stop. No easy feat with 180 plus pounds of naked male pinning her to the sheets.

A rueful grin sketched across Dev's face. "Okay, what did I really say?"

"It sounded…it sounded…" Helpless with laughter, she gasped for breath. "It sounded like you want to hang an ornament on me."

"Yeah, well, that, too." His grin widening, he leaned down and dropped a kiss on her left breast. "Here. And here…"

He grazed her right breast, eased down to her belly.

"And here, and…"

"Dev!"

Pleasure rippled in waves across the flat plane of her stomach. She wouldn't have believed she could become so aroused so fast. Particularly after that shattering orgasm. Dev, on the other hand, was lazy and loose and still flaccid.

"Don't you need to, uh, take a little time to recharge?"

"I do." His voice was muffled, his breath hot against her skin. "Doesn't mean you have to. Unless you want to?"

He raised his head and must have seen the answer in her face. Waggling his brows, he lowered his head again. Sarah gasped again when his tongue found her now super-sensitized center.

The climax hit this time without warning. She'd just reached up to grip the headboard and bent a knee to avoid a cramp when everything seemed to shrink to a single, white-hot nova. The next second, the star exploded. Pleasure pulsed through her body. Groaning, she let it flow before it slowly, exquisitely ebbed.

When she opened her eyes again, Dev looked smug and pretty damn pleased with himself. With good reason, she thought, drifting on the last eddies. She sincerely hoped he still needed some time to recharge. She certainly did!

To her relief, he stretched out beside her and seemed content to just laze. She nestled her head on his arm and let her thoughts drift back to his mangled French. He said he'd been trying to tell her that he adored her. What did that mean, exactly?

She was trying to find a way to reintroduce the subject when the phone buzzed. His this time, not hers. With a muffled grunt, Dev reached across her and checked his phone's display.

"Sorry," he said with a grimace. "I told them not to call unless they were about to slam up against our own version of a fiscal cliff. I'd better take this."

"Go ahead. I'll hit the bathroom."

She scooped up the handiest article of clothing, which happened to be Dev's shirt, and padded into the bathroom. The tiles felt cool and smooth against her bare feet. The apparition that appeared in the gilt-edged mirrors made her gasp.

"Good grief!"

Her hair could have provided a home for an entire flock of sparrows. Whatever makeup she'd started out with this morning had long since disappeared. She was also sporting one whisker burn on her chin and another on her neck. Shuddering at the thought of what Elise Girault would say if she saw the telltale marks, Sarah ran the taps and splashed cold water on her face and throat.

That done, she eyed the bidet. So practical for Europeans, so awkward for most Americans. Practical won hands down in this instance. Clean and refreshed, Sarah reentered the bedroom just as Dev was zipping up his pants.

"Uh-oh. Looks like your negotiators ran into that cliff."

"Ran into it, hell. According to my chief of production, they soared right over the damned thing and are now in a free fall."

"That doesn't sound good."

Detouring to her closet, she exchanged Dev's shirt for the thigh-length, peony-decorated silk robe Gina had given her for her birthday last year.

"It's all part of the game," he said as she handed him back his shirt. "Girault's just a little better at it than I gave him credit for."

The comment tripped a reminder of Elise's disclosures at lunch. Sarah debated for a moment over whether she should share them with Dev, then decided he needed to know the kind of man he would be doing business with.

"Elise said something today about her husband that surprised me."

Dev looked up from buttoning his shirt. "What was that?"

"Supposedly, Jean-Jacques sent some goons to rough up one of her former lovers. The guy had threatened to sell pictures of her to the tabloids."

"Interesting. I would have thought Girault man enough to do the job himself. I certainly would have." He scooped up his tie and jacket and gave her a quick kiss. "I'll call as soon as I have a fix on when we'll break for dinner."

Sarah nodded, but his careless remark about going after Elise's lover for trying to sell pictures of her had struck home. The comment underscored his contempt for certain members of her profession. How much would it take, she wondered uneasily, for him to lump her in with the sleaziest among them?

Ten

Still troubled by Dev's parting comment, Sarah knotted the sash to her robe and stepped out onto her little balcony. She'd lost herself in the view before, but this time the seemingly endless vista of chimneys and gray slate roofs didn't hold as much interest as her bird's-eye view of the street four stories below.

The limo Dev had called for idled a few yards from the hotel's entrance. When he strode out of the hotel, the sight of him once again outfitted in his business attire gave Sarah's heart a crazy bump. She couldn't help contrasting that with the image of his sleek, naked body still vivid in her mind.

The uniformed driver jumped out to open the rear passenger door. Dev smiled and said a few words to him, inaudible from Sarah's height, and ducked to enter the car. At the last moment he paused and glanced up. When he spotted her, the friendly smile he'd given the driver warmed into something so private and so sensual that she responded without thinking.

Touching her fingers lightly to her lips, she blew him a kiss—and was immediately embarrassed by the gesture. It was so schmaltzy, and so out of character for her. More like something Gina might do. Yet she remained on the balcony like some lovelorn Juliet long after Dev had driven off.

Even worse, she couldn't summon the least desire to get dressed and meander through the streets. Peering into shop windows or people watching at a café didn't hold as much allure as it had before. She would rather wait until Dev finished with his meeting and they could meander together.

She'd take a long, bubbly bath instead, she decided. But first she had catch up on her email. And call Grandmama. And try Gina again. Maybe this time her sister would answer the damned phone.

Gina didn't, but Sarah caught the duchess before she went out for her morning constitutional. She tried to temper her habitual concern with a teasing note.

"You won't overdo it, will you?"

"My darling Sarah," Charlotte huffed. "If I could walk almost forty miles through a war-torn country with an infant in my arms, I can certainly stroll a few city blocks."

Wisely, Sarah refrained from pointing out that the duchess had made the first walk more than fifty years ago.

"Have you heard from Gina?" she asked instead.

"No, have you?"

"Not since she texted me that she was flitting off to Switzerland."

She'd tried to keep her the response casual, but the duchess knew her too well.

"Listen to me, Sarah Elizabeth Marie-Adele. Your sister may act rashly on occasion, but she's a St. Sebastian. Whatever you think she may be up to, she won't bring shame on her family or her name."

The urge to tell her grandmother about the missing medallion was so strong that Sarah had to bite her lip to keep from blurting it out. That would only lead to a discussion of how she'd become involved with Dev, and she wasn't ready to explain that, either. Thankfully, her grandmother was content to let the subject drop.

"Now tell me about Paris," she commanded. "Has Devon taken you to Café Michaud yet?"

"Not yet, but he said you'd given him strict orders to do so. Oh, and he had his people work minor miracles to get us into the Hôtel Verneuil on such short notice."

"He did? How very interesting."

She sounded so thoughtful—and so much like a cat that had just lapped up a bowl of cream—that Sarah became instantly suspicious.

"What other instructions did you give him?"

"None."

"Come on. Fess up. What other surprises do I have in store?"

A soft sigh came through the phone. "You're in Paris, with a handsome, virile man. One whom I suspect is more than capable of delivering surprises of his own."

Sarah gave a fervent prayer of thanks that the duchess hadn't yet mastered the FaceTime app on her phone. If she had, she would have seen her elder granddaughter's cheeks flame at the thought of how much she'd *already* enjoyed her handsome, virile fiancé.

"I'll talk to you tomorrow, Grandmama. Give Maria my love."

She hung up, marveling again at how readily everyone seemed to have accepted Dev Hunter's sudden appearance in their lives. Grandmama. Maria. Alexis. Sarah herself. Would they accept his abrupt departure as readily?

Would they have to?

Sarah was no fool. Nor was she blind. She could tell Dev felt at least some of the same jumbled emotions she did. Mixed in with the greedy hunger there was the shared laughter, the seduction of this trip, the growing delight in each other's company. Maybe, just maybe, there could be love, too.

She refused to even speculate about anything beyond that. Their evolving relationship was too new, too fragile, to project vary far ahead. Still, she couldn't help humming the melody from Edith Piaf's classic, "La Vie En Rose," as she started for the bathroom and a long, hot soak.

The house phone caught her halfway there. She detoured to the desk and answered. The caller identified himself as Monsieur LeBon, the hotel's manager, and apologized profusely for disturbing her.

"You're not disturbing me, monsieur."

"Good, good." He hesitated, then seemed to be choosing his words carefully. "I saw Monsieur Hunter leave a few moments ago and thought perhaps I might catch you alone."

"Why? Is there a problem?"

"I'm not sure. Do you by chance know a gentleman by the name of Henri Lefèvre?"

"I don't recognize the name."

"Aha! I thought as much." LeBon gave a small sniff. "There was something in his manner…"

"What has this Monsieur Lefèvre to do with me?"

"He approached our receptionist earlier this afternoon and claimed you and he were introduced by a mutual acquaintance. He couldn't remember your name, however. Only that you were a tall, slender American who spoke excellent French. And that you mentioned you were staying at the Hôtel Verneuil."

The light dawned. It had to be Elise's former lover. He must have heard her give the cabdriver instructions to the hotel.

"The receptionist didn't tell him my name, did she?"

"You may rest assured she did not! Our staff is too well trained to disclose information on any of our guests. She referred the man to me, and I sent him on his way."

"Thank you, Monsieur LeBon. Please let me know immediately if anyone else inquires about me."

"Of course, Lady Sarah."

The call from the hotel manager dimmed a good bit of Sarah's enjoyment in her long, bubbly soak. She didn't particularly like the fact that Elise's smarmy ex-lover had tracked her to the hotel.

Dev called just moments after she emerged from the tub. Sounding totally disgusted, he told her he intended to lock everyone in the conference room until they reached a final agreement.

"The way it looks now that might be midnight or later. Sorry, Sarah. I won't be able to keep our dinner date."

"Don't worry about that."

"Yeah, well, I'd much rather be with you than these clowns. I'm about ready to tell Girault and company to shove it."

Sarah didn't comment. She couldn't, given the staggering sums involved in his negotiations. But she thought privately he was taking a risk doing business with someone who hired thugs to pound on his wife's lover.

Briefly, she considered telling Dev that same lover had shown up at the hotel this afternoon but decided against it. He had enough on his mind at the moment and Monsieur LeBon appeared to have taken care of the matter.

She spent what remained of the afternoon and most of the evening on her laptop, with only a short break for soup and a salad ordered from room service. She had plenty of work to keep her busy and was satisfied with the two layouts she'd mocked up when she finally quit. She'd go in to the offices on rue Balzac tomorrow to view the layouts on the twenty-five-inch monitor.

Unless Dev finished negotiations tonight as he swore he would do. Then maybe they'd spend the day together. And the night. And…

Her belly tightening at the possibilities, she curled up in bed with the ebook she'd downloaded. She got through only a few pages before she dozed off.

* * *

The phone jerked her from sleep. She fumbled among the covers, finally found it and came more fully awake when she recognized Dev's number.

"Did you let them all out of the conference room?" she asked with a smile.

"I did. They're printing the modified contracts as we speak. They'll be ready to sign tomorrow morning."

"Congratulations!"

She was happy for him, she really was, even if it meant the termination of their arrangement.

"I'm on my way back to the hotel. Is it too late for a celebration?"

"I don't know. What time is it?"

"Almost one."

"No problem. Just give me a few minutes to get dressed. Do you have someplace special in mind? If not, I know several great cafés that stay open until 2:00 a.m."

"Actually, I was hoping for a private celebration. No dressing required."

She could hear the smile in his voice, and something more. Something that brought Gina forcefully to mind. Her sister always claimed she felt as though she was tumbling through time and space whenever she fell in love. Sarah hadn't scoffed but she *had* chalked the hyperbole up to another Gina-ism.

How wrong she was. And how right Gina was. That was exactly how Sarah felt now. As though Dev had kicked her feet out from under her and she was on some wild, uncontrollable slide.

"A private celebration sounds good to me," she got out breathlessly.

She didn't change out of the teddy and bikini briefs she'd worn to bed, but she did throw on the peony robe and make a dash to the bathroom before she answered Dev's knock.

As charged up as he'd sounded on the phone, she half expected him to kick the door shut and pin her against the wall again. Okay, she kind of hoped he would.

He didn't, but Sarah certainly couldn't complain about his altered approach. The energy was there, and the exultation from having closed his big deal. Yet the hands that cupped her face were incredibly gentle, and the kiss he brushed across her mouth was so tender she almost melted from the inside out.

"Jean-Jacques told me to thank you," he murmured against her lips.

"For what?"

"He thinks I finally agreed to his company's design for the pneumatic turbine assembly because I was so damned anxious to get back to you."

"Oh, no!"

She pulled back in dismay. She had no idea what a pneumatic turbine assembly was, but it sounded important.

"You didn't concede anything critical, did you?"

"Nah. I always intended to accept their design. I just used it as my ace in the hole to close the deal. *And* to get back to you."

He bent and brushed her mouth again. When he raised his head, the look in his eyes started Sarah on another wild spin through time and space.

"I don't want to risk any more mangled verbs," he said with a slow smile, "so I'll stick to English this time. I love you, Sarah St. Sebastian."

"Since…? Since when?"

He appeared to give the matter some consideration. "Hard to say. I have to admit it started with a severe case of lust."

She would have to admit the same thing. Later. Right now she could only try to keep breathing as he raised her hand and angled it so the emerald caught the light.

"By the time I put this on your finger, though, I was

already strategizing ways to keep it there. I know I black-mailed you into this fake engagement, Sarah, but if I ask very politely and promise to be nice to your ditz of a sister, would you consider making it real?"

Although it went against a lifetime of ingrained habit, she didn't fire up in Gina's defense. Instead she drew her brows together.

"I need a minute to think about it."

Surprise and amusement and just a touch of uncertainty colored Dev's reply. "Take all the time you need."

She pursed her lips and gave the matter three or four seconds of fierce concentration.

"Okay."

"Okay you'll consider it, or okay you'll make it real?"

Laughing, Sarah hooked her arms around his neck. "I'm going with option B."

Dev hadn't made a habit of going on the prowl like so many crew dogs he'd flown with, but he'd racked up more than a few quality hours with women in half a dozen countries. Not until *this* woman, however, did he really appreciate the difference between having sex and making love. It wasn't her smooth, sleek curves or soft flesh or breathless little pants. It was the sum of all parts, the whole of her, the elegance that was Sarah.

And the fact that she was his.

He'd intended to make this loving slow and sweet, a sort of unspoken acknowledgment of the months and years of nights like this they had ahead. She blew those plans out of the water mere moments after Dev positioned her under him. Her body welcomed him, her heat fired his. The primitive need to possess her completely soon had him pinning her wrists to the sheets, his thrusts hard and deep. Her head went back. Her belly quivered. A moan rose from deep in her throat, and Dev took everything she had to give.

* * *

She was still half-asleep when he leaned over her early the next morning. "I've got to shower and change and get with Girault to sign the contracts. How about we meet for lunch at your grandmother's favorite café?"

"Mmm."

"Tell me the name of it again."

"Café Michaud," she muttered sleepily, "rue de Monttessuy."

"Got it. Café Michaud. Rue de Monttessuy. Twelve noon?"

"Mmm."

He took his time in the shower, answered several dozen emails, reviewed a bid solicitation on a new government contract and still made the ten o'clock signing session at Girault's office with time to spare.

The French industrialist was in a jovial mood, convinced he'd won a grudging, last-minute concession. Dev didn't disabuse him. After initialing sixteen pages and signing three, the two chief executives posed for pictures while their respective staffs breathed sighs of relief that the months of intense negotiations were finally done.

"How long do you remain in Paris?" Girault asked after pictures and another round of handshakes.

"I had planned to fly home as soon as we closed this deal, but I think now I'll take some downtime and stay over a few more days."

"A very wise decision," Girault said with a wink. "Paris is a different city entirely when explored with one you love. Especially when that one is as delightful as your Sarah."

"I won't argue with that. And speaking of my Sarah, we're meeting for lunch. I'll say goodbye now, Jean-Jacques."

"But no! Not goodbye. You must have dinner with Elise and me again before you leave. Now that we are partners, yes?"

"I'll see what Sarah has planned and get back to you."

* * *

The rue de Monttessuy was in the heart of Paris's 7th arrondissement. Tall, stately buildings topped with slate roofs
crowded the sidewalks and offered a glimpse of the Eiffel
Tower spearing into the sky at the far end of the street.
Café Michaud sat midway down a long block, a beacon of
color with its bright red awnings and window boxes filled
with geraniums.

Since he was almost a half hour early, Dev had his driver
drop him off at the intersection. He needed to stretch his
legs, and he preferred to walk the half block rather than
wait for Sarah at one of the café's outside tables. Maybe
he could find something for her in one of the shops lining
the narrow, cobbled street. Unlike the high-end boutiques
and jeweler's showrooms on some of the more fashion-
able boulevards, these were smaller but no less intriguing.

He strolled past a tiny grocery with fresh produce displayed in wooden crates on either side of the front door, a
chocolatier, a wine shop and several antique shops. One
in particular caught his attention. Its display of military
and aviation memorabilia drew him into the dim, musty
interior.

His eyes went instantly to an original lithograph depicting Charles Lindbergh's 1927 landing at a Paris airfield
after his historic solo transatlantic flight. The photographer
had captured the shadowy images of the hundreds of Model
As and Ts lined up at the airfield, their headlamps illumi-
nating the grassy strip as the *Spirit of St. Louis* swooped
out of the darkness.

"I'll take that," he told the shopkeeper.

The man's brows soared with surprise and just a touch
of disdain for this naive American who made no attempt
to bargain. Dev didn't care. He would have paid twice the
price. He'd never thought of himself as particularly sentimental, but the key elements in the print—aviation and
Paris—were what had brought him and Sarah together.

As if to compensate for his customer's foolishness, the shopkeeper threw in at no cost the thick cardboard tube the print had been rolled in when he himself had discovered it at a flea market.

Tube in hand, Dev exited the shop and started for the café. His pulse kicked when he spotted Sarah approaching from the opposite direction. She was on the other side of the street, some distance from the café, but he recognized her graceful walk and the silky brown hair topped by a jaunty red beret.

He picked up his pace, intending to cross at the next corner, when a figure half-hidden amid a grocer's produce display brought him to a dead stop. The man had stringy brown hair that straggled over the shoulders and a camera propped on the top crate. Its monster zoom lens was aimed directly at Sarah. While Dev stood there, his jaw torquing, the greaseball clicked off a half-dozen shots.

"What the hell are you doing?"

The photographer whipped around. He said something in French, but it was the careless shrug that fanned Dev's anger into fury.

"Bloodsucking parasites," he ground out.

The hand gripping the cardboard tube went white at the knuckles. His other hand bunched into a fist. Screw the lawsuits. He'd flatten the guy. The photographer read his intent and jumped back, knocking over several crates of produce in the process.

"Non, non!" He stumbled back, his face white with alarm under the greasy hair. "You don't...you don't understand, Monsieur Hunter. I am François. With *Beguile.* I shoot the photos for the story."

For the second time in as many moments, Dev froze. "The story?"

"Oui. We get the instructions from New York."

He thrust out the camera and angled the digital display.

His thumb beat a rapid tattoo as he clicked through picture after picture.

"But look! Here are you and Sarah having coffee. And here you walk along the Seine. And here she blows you a kiss from the balcony of her hotel room."

Pride overrode the photographer's alarm. A few clicks of the zoom button enlarged the shot on the screen.

"Do you see how perfectly she is framed? And the expression on her face after you drive away. Like one lost in a dream, yes? She stays like that long enough for me to shoot from three different angles."

The anger still hot in Dev's gut chilled. Ice formed in his veins.

"She posed for you?" he asked softly, dangerously.

The photographer glanced up, nervous again. He stuttered something about New York, but Dev wasn't listening. His gaze was locked on Sarah as she approached the café.

She'd posed for this guy. After making all those noises about allowing only that one photo shoot at Cartier, she'd caved to her boss's demands. He might have forgiven that. He had a harder time with the fact that she'd set this all up without telling him.

Dev left the photographer amid the produce. Jaw tight, he stalked toward the café. Sarah was still a block away on the other side of the street. He was about to cross when a white delivery van slowed to a rolling stop and blocked her from view. A few seconds later, Dev heard the thud of its rear doors slam. When the van cut a sharp left and turned down a narrow side street, the sidewalk Sarah had been walking along was empty.

Eleven

Dev broke into a run even before he fully processed what had just happened. All he knew for sure was that Sarah had been strolling toward him one moment and was gone the next. His brain scrambled for a rational explanation of her sudden disappearance. She could have ducked into a shop. Could have stopped to check something in a store window. His gut went with the delivery van.

Dev hit the corner in a full-out sprint and charged down the side street. He dodged a woman pushing a baby carriage, earned a curse from two men he almost bowled over. He could see the van up ahead, see its taillights flashing red as it braked for a stop sign.

He was within twenty yards when the red lights blinked off. Less than ten yards away when the van began another turn. The front window was halfway down. Through it Dev could see the driver, his gaze intent on the pedestrians streaming across the intersection and his thin black cigarillo sending spirals of smoke through the half-open window.

Dev calculated the odds on the fly. Go for the double rear doors or aim for the driver? He risked losing the van if the rear doors were locked and the vehicle picked up speed after completing the turn. He also risked causing an accident if he jumped into traffic in the middle of a busy intersection and planted himself in front of the van.

He couldn't take that chance on losing it. With a desperate burst of speed, he cut the corner and ran into the street right ahead of an oncoming taxi. Brakes squealing, horn blaring, the cab fishtailed. Dev slapped a hand on its hood, pushed off and landed in a few yards ahead of the now-rolling van. He put up both hands and shouted a fierce command.

"Stop!"

He got a glimpse, just a glimpse, of the driver's face through the windshield. Surprise, fear, desperation all flashed across it in the half second before he hit the gas.

Well, hell! The son of a bitch was gunning straight for him.

Dev jumped out of the way at the last second and leaped for the van's door as the vehicle tried to zoom past. The door was unlocked, thank God, although he'd been prepared to hook an arm inside the open window and pop the lock if necessary. Wrenching the panel open, he got a bulldog grip on the driver's leather jacket.

"Pull over, dammit."

The man jerked the wheel, cursing and shouting and trying frantically to dislodge him. The van swerved. More horns blasted.

"Dev!"

The shout came from the back of the van. From Sarah. He didn't wait to hear more. His fist locked on the driver's leather jacket, he put all his muscle into a swift yank. The bastard's face slammed into the steering wheel. Bone crunched. Blood fountained. The driver slumped.

Reaching past him, Dev tore the keys from the ignition. The engine died, but the van continued to roll toward a car that swerved wildly but couldn't avoid a collision. Metal crunched metal as both vehicles came to an abrupt stop, and Dev fumbled for the release for the driver's seat belt. He dragged the unconscious man out and let him drop to the pavement. Scrambling into the front seat, he had one leg over the console to climb into the rear compartment when the back doors flew open and someone jumped out.

It wasn't Sarah. She was on her knees in the back. A livid red welt marred one cheek. A roll of silver electrical tape dangled from a wide strip wrapped around one wrist. Climbing over the console, Dev stooped beside her.

"Are you okay?"

"Yes."

Her eyes were wide and frightened, but the distant wail of a siren eased some of their panic. Dev tore his glance from her to the open rear doors and the man running like hell back down the side street.

"Stay here and wait for the police. I'm going after that bastard."

"Wait!" She grabbed his arm. "You don't need to chase him! I know who he is."

He swung back. "You *know* him?"

When she nodded, suspicion knifed into him like a serrated blade. His fists bunched, and a distant corner of his mind registered the fact that he'd lost the lithograph sometime during the chase. The rest of him staggered under a sudden realization.

"This is part of it, isn't it? This big abduction scene?"

"Scene?"

She sounded so surprised he almost believed her. Worse, dammit, he wanted to believe her!

"It's okay," he ground out. "You can drop the act. I bumped into the photographer from *Beguile* back there on rue de Monttessuy. We had quite a conversation."

Her color drained, making the red welt across her cheek look almost obscene by contrast. "You...you talked to a photographer from my magazine?"

"Yeah, Lady Sarah, I did. François told me about the shoot. Showed me some of the pictures he's already taken. I'll have to ask him to send me the one of you on the balcony. You make a helluva Juliet."

The sirens were louder now. Their harsh, up-and-down bleat almost drowned out her whisper.

"And you think we...me, this photographer, my magazine...you think we staged an abduction?"

"I'm a little slow. It took me a while to understand the angle. I'm betting your barracuda of a boss dreamed it up. Big, brave Number Three rescues his beautiful fiancée from would-be kidnappers."

She looked away, and her silence cut even deeper than Dev's suspicion. He'd hoped she would go all huffy, deny at least some of her part in this farce. Apparently, she couldn't.

Well, Sarah and her magazine could damned well live with the consequences of their idiotic scheme. At the least, they were looking at thousands of dollars in vehicle damage. At the worst, reconstructive surgery for the driver whose face Dev had rearranged.

Thoroughly disgusted, he took Sarah's arm to help her out of the van. She shook off his hold without a word, climbed down and walked toward the squad car now screeching to a halt. Two officers exited. One went to kneel beside the moaning van driver. The other soon centered on Sarah as the other major participant in the incident. She communicated with him in swift, idiomatic French. He took notes the entire time, shooting the occasional glance at Dev that said his turn would come.

It did, but not until an ambulance had screamed up and two EMTs went to work on the driver. At the insistence of the officer who'd interviewed Sarah, a third medical tech examined her. The tech was shining a penlight into her pupils when the police officer turned his attention to Dev. Switching to English, he took down Dev's name, address while in Paris and cell-phone number before asking for his account of the incident.

He'd had time to think about it. Rather than lay out his suspicion that the whole thing was a publicity stunt, he stuck to the bare facts. He'd spotted Sarah walking toward him. Saw the van pull up. Saw she was gone. Gave chase.

The police officer made more notes, then flipped back a few pages. "So, Monsieur Hunter, are you also acquainted with Henri Lefèvre?"

"Who?"

"The man your fiancée says snatched her off the street and threw her into the back of this van."

"No, I'm not acquainted with him."

"But you know Monsieur Girault and his wife?"

Dev's eyes narrowed as he remembered Sarah telling him about the goons Girault had employed to do his dirty work. Was Lefèvre one of those goons? Was Jean-Jacques somehow mixed up in all this?

"Yes," he replied, frowning, "I know Monsieur Girault and his wife. How are they involved in this incident?"

"Mademoiselle St. Sebastian says Lefèvre is Madame Girault's former lover. He came to their table while they were at lunch yesterday. She claims Madame Girault identified him as a gigolo, one who tried to extort a large sum of money from her. We'll verify that with madame herself, of course."

Dev's stomach took a slow dive. Christ! Had he misread the situation? The kidnapping portion of it, anyway?

"Your fiancée also says that the manager of your hotel told her Lefèvre made inquiries as to her identity." The officer glanced up from his notes. "Are you aware of these inquiries, Monsieur Hunter?"

"No."

The police officer's expression remained carefully neutral, but he had to be thinking the same thing Dev was.

What kind of a man didn't know a second- or third-class gigolo was sniffing after his woman?

"Do you have any additional information you can provide at this time, Monsieur Hunter?"

"No."

"Very well. Mademoiselle St. Sebastian insists she sustained no serious injury. If the EMTs agree, I will release her to return to your hotel. I must ask you both not to leave Paris, however, until you have spoken with detectives from our *Brigade criminelle*. They will be in touch with you."

Dev and Sarah took a taxi back to the hotel. She stared out the window in stony silence while he searched for a way to reconcile his confrontation with the photographer and his apparently faulty assumption about the attempted kidnapping. He finally decided on a simple apology.

"I'm sorry, Sarah. I jumped too fast to the wrong conclusion."

She turned her head. Her distant expression matched her coolly polite tone. "No need to apologize. I can understand how you reached that conclusion."

Dev reached for her hand, trying to bridge the gap. She slid it away and continued in the same, distant tone.

"Just for the record, I didn't know the magazine had put a photographer on us."

"I believe you."

It was too little, too late. He realized that when she shrugged his comment aside.

"I am aware, however, that Alexis wanted to exploit the story, so I take full responsibility for this invasion of your privacy."

"*Our* privacy, Sarah."

"Your privacy," she countered quietly. "There is no us. It was all just a facade, wasn't it?"

"That's not what you said last night," Dev reminded her, starting to get a little pissed.

How the hell did he end up as the bad guy here? Okay, he'd blackmailed Sarah into posing as his fiancée. And, yes, he'd done his damnedest to finesse her into bed. Now that he had her there, though, he wanted more. Much more!

So did she. She'd admitted that last night. Dev wasn't about to let her just toss what they had together out the window.

"What happened to option B?" he pressed. "Making it real?"

She looked at him for a long moment before turning her face to the window again. "I have a headache starting. I'd rather not talk anymore, if you don't mind."

He minded. Big time. But the angry bruise rising on her cheek shut him up until they were back at the hotel.

"We didn't have lunch," he said in an effort to reestablish a common ground. "Do you want to try the restaurant here or order something from room service?"

"I'm not hungry." Still so cool, still so distant. "I'm going to lie down."

"You need ice to keep the swelling down on your cheek. I'll bring some to your room after I talk to Monsieur LeBon."

"There's ice in the minifridge in my room."

She left him standing in the lobby. Frustrated and angry and not sure precisely where he should target his ire, he stalked to the reception desk and asked to speak to the manager.

Sarah's first act when she reached her room was to call *Beguile*'s Paris offices. Although she didn't doubt Dev's account, she couldn't help hoping the photographer he'd spoken to was a freelancer or worked for some other publication. In her heart of hearts, she didn't want to believe *her* magazine had, in fact, assigned François to shoot pictures of her and Dev. Paul Vincent, the senior editor, provided the corroboration reluctantly.

"Alexis insisted, Sarah."

"I see."

She disconnected and stared blankly at the wall for several moments. How naive of her to trust Alexis to hold to her word. How stupid to feel so hurt that Dev would jump to the conclusion he had. Her throat tight, she tapped out a text message. It was brief and to the point.

I quit, effective immediately.

Then she filled the ice bucket, wrapped some cubes in a hand towel and shed her clothes. Crawling into bed, she put the ice on her aching cheek and pulled the covers over her head.

The jangle of the house phone dragged her from a stew of weariness and misery some hours later.

"I'm sorry to disturb you, Lady Sarah."

Grimacing, she edged away from the wet spot on the pillow left by the soggy hand towel. "What is it, Monsieur LeBon?"

"You have a call from *Brigade criminelle*. Shall we put it through?"

"Yes."

The caller identified herself as Marie-Renee Delacroix, an inspector in the division charged with investigating homicides, kidnappings, bomb attacks and incidents involving personalities. Sarah wanted to ask what category this investigation fell into but refrained. Instead she agreed to an appointment at police headquarters the next morning at nine.

"I've already spoken to Monsieur Hunter," the inspector said. "He'll accompany you."

"Fine."

"Just so you know, Mademoiselle St. Sebastian, this

meeting is a mere formality, simply to review and sign the official copy of your statement."

"That's all you need from me?"

"It is. We already had the van driver in custody, and we arrested Henri Lefèvre an hour ago. They've both confessed to attempting to kidnap you and hold you for ransom. Not that they could deny it," the inspector added drily. "Their fingerprints were all over the van, and no fewer than five witnesses saw Lefèvre jump out of it after the crash. We've also uncovered evidence that he's more than fifty thousand Euros in debt, much of which we believe he owes to a drug dealer not known for his patience."

A shudder rippled down Sarah's spine. She couldn't believe how close she'd come to being dragged into such a dark, ugly morass.

"Am I free to return to the United States after I sign my statement?"

"I'll have to check with the prosecutor's office, but I see no reason for them to impede your return given that Lefèvre and his accomplice have confessed. I'll confirm that when you come in tomorrow, yes?"

"Thank you."

She hung up and was contemplating going back to bed when there was a knock on her door.

"It's Dev, Sarah."

She wanted to take the coward's way out and tell him she didn't feel up to company, but she couldn't keep putting him off.

"Just a minute," she called through the door.

She detoured into the bedroom and threw on the clothes she'd dropped to the floor earlier. She couldn't do much about the bruise on her cheek, but she did rake a hand through her hair. Still, she felt messy and off center when she opened the door.

Dev had abandoned his suit coat but still wore the pleated pants and pale yellow dress shirt he'd had on earlier. The shirt was open at the neck, the cuffs rolled up. Sarah had to drag her reluctant gaze up to meet the deep blue of his eyes. They were locked on her cheek.

"Did you ice that?"

"Yes, I did. Come in."

He followed her into the sitting room. Neither of them sat. She gravitated to the window. He shoved his hands into his pants pockets and stood beside the sofa.

"Have you heard from Inspector Delacroix?"

"She just called. I understand we have an appointment with her at nine tomorrow morning."

"Did she tell you they've already obtained confessions?"

Sarah nodded and forced a small smile. "She also told me I could fly home after I signed the official statement. I was just about to call and make a reservation when you knocked."

"Without talking to me first?"

"I think we've said everything we needed to."

"I don't agree."

She scrubbed a hand down the side of her face. Her cheek ached. Her heart hurt worse. "Please, Dev. I don't want to beat this into the ground."

Poor verb choice, she realized when he ignored her and crossed the room to cup her chin. The ice hadn't helped much, Sarah knew. The bruise had progressed from red to a nasty purple and green.

"Did Lefèvre do this to you?"

The underlying savagery in the question had her pulling hastily away from his touch.

"No, he didn't. I hit something when he pushed me into the van."

The savagery didn't abate. If anything, it flared hotter and fiercer. "Good thing the bastard's in police custody."

Sarah struggled to get the discussion back on track. "Lefèvre doesn't matter, Dev."

"The hell he doesn't."

"Listen to me. What matters is that I didn't know Alexis had sicced a photographer on us. But even if she hadn't, some other magazine or tabloid would have picked up the story sooner or later. I'm afraid that kind of public scrutiny is something you and whoever you *do* finally get engaged to will have to live with."

"I'm engaged to you, Sarah."

"Not any longer."

Shoving her misery aside, she slid the emerald off her finger and held it out. He refused to take it.

"It's yours," he said curtly. "Part of your heritage. Whatever happens from here on out between us, you keep the Russian Rose."

The tight-jawed response only added to her aching unhappiness. "Our arrangement lasted only until you and Girault signed your precious contracts. That's done now. So are we."

She hadn't intended to sound so bitter. Dev had held to his end of their bargain. Every part of it. She was the one who'd almost defaulted. If not personally, then by proxy through Alexis.

But would Dev continue to hold to his end? The sudden worry that he might take his anger out on Gina pushed her into a rash demand for an assurance.

"I've fulfilled the conditions of our agreement, right? You won't go after my sister?"

She'd forgotten how daunting he could look when his eyes went hard and ice blue.

"No, Lady Sarah, I won't. And I think we'd better table this discussion until we've had more time to think things through."

"I've thought them through," she said desperately. "I'm going home tomorrow, Dev."

He leaned in, all the more intimidating because he didn't touch her, didn't raise his voice, didn't so much as blink.

"Think again, sweetheart."

Twelve

Left alone in her misery, Sarah opened her hand and stared at the emerald-and-gold ring. No matter what Dev said, she couldn't keep it.

Nor could she just leave it lying around. She toyed briefly with the thought of taking it downstairs and asking Monsieur LeBon to secure it in the hotel safe, but didn't feel up to explaining either her bruised cheek or the call from *Brigade criminelle*.

With an aching sense of regret for what might have been, she slipped the ring back on her finger. It would have to stay there until she returned it to Dev.

She was trying to make herself go into the bedroom and pack when a loud rumble from the vicinity of her middle reminded her she hadn't eaten since her breakfast croissant and coffee. She considered room service but decided she needed to get out of her room and clear her head. She also needed, as Dev had grimly instructed, to think more.

After a fierce internal debate, she picked up the house phone. A lifetime of etiquette hammered in by the duchess demanded she advise Dev of her intention to grab a bite at a local café. Fiancé or not, furious or not, he deserved the courtesy of a call.

Relief rolled through her in waves when he didn't answer. She left a quick message, then took the elevator to the lobby. Slipping out one of the hotel's side exits, she hiked up the collar of her sweater coat. It wasn't dusk yet, but the temperature was skidding rapidly from cool to cold.

As expected this time of day, the sidewalks and streets were crowded. Parisians returning from work made last-minute stops at grocers and patisseries. Taxis wove their erratic path through cars and bicycles. Sarah barely noticed the throng. Her last meeting with Dev still filled her mind. Their tense confrontation had shaken her almost as much as being snatched off the street and tossed into a delivery van like a sack of potatoes.

He had every right to be angry about the photographer, she conceded. She was furious, too. What had hurt most, though, was Dev's assumption that *Beguile* had staged the kidnapping. And that Sarah was part of the deception. How could he love her, yet believe she would participate in a scam like that?

The short answer? He couldn't.

As much as she wanted to, Sarah couldn't escape that brutal truth. She'd let Paris seduce her into thinking she and Dev shared something special. Come so close to believing that what they felt for each other would merit a padlock on the Archbishop's Bridge. Aching all over again for what might have been, she ducked into the first café she encountered.

A waiter with three rings piercing his left earlobe and a white napkin folded over his right forearm met her at the door. His gaze flickered to the ugly bruise on her cheek and away again.

"Good evening, madame."

"Good evening. A table for one, please."

Once settled at a table in a back corner, she ordered

without glancing at the menu. A glass of red table wine and a croque-monsieur—the classic French version of a grilled ham and cheese topped with béchamel sauce—was all she wanted. All she could handle right now. That became apparent after the first few sips of wine.

Her sandwich arrived in a remarkably short time given this was Paris, where even the humblest café aimed for gastronomic excellence. Accompanied by a small salad and thin, crisp fries, it should have satisfied her hunger. Unfortunately, she never got to enjoy it. She took a few forkfuls of salad and nibbled a fry, but just when she was about to bite into her sandwich she heard her name.

"Lady Sarah, granddaughter to Charlotte St. Sebastian, grand duchess of the tiny duchy once known as Karlenburgh."

Startled, she glanced up at the flat screen TV above the café's bar. While Sarah sat frozen with the sandwich halfway to her mouth, one of a team of two newscasters gestured to an image that came up on the display beside her. It was a photo of her and Gina and Grandmama, one of the rare publicity shots the duchess had allowed. It'd been taken at a charity event a number of years ago, before the duchess had sold her famous pearls. The perfectly matched strands circled her neck multiple times before draping almost to her waist.

"The victim of an apparent kidnapping attempt," the announcer intoned, "Lady Sarah escaped injury this afternoon during a dramatic rescue by her fiancé, American industrialist Devon Hunter."

Dread churned in the pit of Sarah's stomach as the still image gave way to what looked like an amateur video captured on someone's phone camera. It showed traffic swerving wildly as Dev charged across two lanes and planted himself in front of oncoming traffic.

Good God! The white van! It wasn't going to stop!

Her heart shot into her throat. Unable to breathe, she saw

Dev dodge aside at the last moment, then leap for the van door. When he smashed the driver's face into the wheel, Sarah gasped. Blobs of béchamel sauce oozed from the sandwich hanging from her fork and plopped unnoticed onto her plate. She'd been in the back of the van. She hadn't known how Dev had stopped it, only that he had.

Stunned by his reckless courage, she watched as the street scene gave way to another video. This one was shot on the steps of the Palais de Justice. Henri Lefèvre was being led down the steps to a waiting police transport. Uniformed officers gripped his arms. Steel cuffs shackled his wrists. A crowd of reporters waited at the bottom of the steps, shouting questions that Lefèvre refused to answer.

When the news shifted to another story, Sarah lowered her now-mangled sandwich. Her mind whirled as she tried to sort through her chaotic thoughts. One arrowed through all the others. She knew she had to call her grandmother. Now. Before the story got picked up by the news at home, if it hadn't already. Furious with herself for not thinking of that possibility sooner, she hit speed dial.

To her infinite relief, the duchess had heard nothing about the incident. Sarah tried to downplay it by making the kidnappers sound like bungling amateurs. Charlotte was neither amused nor fooled.

"Were you the target," she asked sharply, "or Devon?"

"Devon, of course. Or rather his billions."

"Are you sure? There may still be some fanatics left in the old country. Not many after all this time, I would guess. But your grandfather… Those murderous death squads…" Her voice fluttered. "They hated everything our family stood for."

"These men wanted money," Sarah said gently, "and Dev made them extremely sorry they went after it the way they did. One of them is going to need a whole new face."

"Good!"

The duchess had regained her bite, and her granddaughter breathed a sigh of relief. Too soon, it turned out.

"Bring Devon home with you, Sarah. I want to thank him personally. And tell him I see no need for a long engagement," Charlotte added briskly. "Too many brides today spend months, even years, planning their weddings. I thank God neither of my granddaughters are prone to such dithering."

"Grandmama…"

"Gina tends to leap before she looks. You, my darling, are more cautious. More deliberate. But when you choose, you choose wisely. In this instance, I believe you made an excellent choice."

Sarah couldn't confess that she hadn't precisely chosen Dev. Nor was she up to explaining that their relationship was based on a lie. All she could do was try to rein in the duchess.

"I'm not to the point of even thinking about wedding plans, Grandmama. I just got engaged."

And unengaged, although Dev appeared to have a different take on the matter.

"You don't have to concern yourself with the details, dearest. I'll call the Plaza and have Andrew take care of everything."

"Good grief!" Momentarily distracted, Sarah gasped. "Is Andrew still at the Plaza?"

Her exclamation earned an icy retort. "The younger generation may choose to consign seniors to the dustbin," the duchess returned frigidly. "Some of us are not quite ready to be swept out with the garbage."

Uh-oh. Before Sarah could apologize for the unintended slight, Charlotte abandoned her lofty perch and got down to business.

"How about the first weekend in May? That's such a lovely month for a wedding."

"Grandmama! It's mid-April now!"

"Didn't you hear me a moment ago? Long engagements are a bore."

"But...but..." Scrambling, Sarah grabbed at the most likely out. "I'm sure the Plaza is booked every weekend in May for the next three years."

Her grandmother heaved a long-suffering sigh. "Sarah, dearest, did I never tell you about the reception I hosted for the Sultan of Oman?"

"I don't think so."

"It was in July...no, August of 1962. Quite magnificent, if I do say so myself. President Kennedy and his wife attended, of course, as did the Rockefellers. Andrew was a very new, very junior waiter at the time. But the letter I sent to his supervisor commending his handling of an embarrassingly inebriated presidential aide helped catapult him to his present exalted position."

How could Sarah possibly respond to that? Swept along on a relentless tidal wave, she gripped the phone as the duchess issued final instructions. "Talk to Devon, dearest. Make sure the first weekend in May is satisfactory for him. And tell him I'll take care of everything."

Feeling almost as dazed as she had when Elise Girault's smarmy ex-lover manhandled her into that white van, Sarah said goodbye. Her meal forgotten, she sat with her phone in hand for long moments. The call to her grandmother had left her more confused, more torn.

Dev had risked his life for her. And that was after he'd confronted the photographer from *Beguile*. As angry as he'd been about her magazine stalking him, he'd still raced to her rescue. Then, of course, he'd accused her of being party to the ruse. As much as she wanted to, Sarah couldn't quite get past the disgust she'd seen in his face at that moment.

Yet he'd also shown her moments of incredible tenderness in their short time together. Moments of thoughtfulness and laughter and incredible passion. She couldn't get past those, either.

Or the fact that she'd responded to him so eagerly. So damned joyously. However they'd met, whatever odd circumstances had thrown them together, Dev Hunter stirred—and satisfied—a deep, almost primal feminine hunger she'd never experienced before.

The problem, Sarah mused as she paid her check and walked out into the deepening dusk, was that everything had happened so quickly. Dev's surprise appearance at her office. His bold-faced offer of a deal. Their fake engagement. This trip to Paris. She'd been caught up in the whirlwind since the day Dev had showed up at her office and tilted her world off its axis. The speed of it, the intensity of it, had magnified emotions and minimized any chance to catch her breath.

What they needed, she decided as she keyed the door to her room, was time and some distance from each other. A cooling-off period, after which they could start over. Assuming Dev wanted to start over, of course. Bracing herself for what she suspected would be an uncomfortable discussion, she picked up the house phone and called his room.

He answered on the second ring. "Hunter."

"It's Sarah."

"I got your message. Did you have a good dinner?"

She couldn't miss the steel under the too-polite query. He wasn't happy that she'd gone to eat without him.

"I did, thank you. Can you come down to my room? Or I'll come to yours, if that's more convenient."

"More convenient for what?"

All right. She understood he was still angry. As Grandmama would say, however, that was no excuse for boorishness.

"We need to finish the conversation we started earlier," she said coolly.

He answered with a brief silence, followed by a terse agreement. "I'll come to your room."

Dev thought he'd done a damned good job of conquering his fury over that business with the photographer. Yes, he'd let it get the better of him when he'd accused Sarah's magazine of staging her own abduction. And yes, he'd come on a little strong earlier this evening when she'd questioned whether he'd hold to his end of their agreement.

He'd had plenty of time to regret both lapses. She'd seen to that by slipping out of the hotel without him. The brief message she'd left while he was in the shower had pissed him off all over again.

Now she'd issued a summons in that aristocratic lady-of-the-manor tone. She'd better not try to shove the emerald at him again. Or deliver any more crap about their "arrangement" being over. They were long past the arrangement stage, and she knew it. She was just too stubborn to admit it.

She'd just have to accept that he wasn't perfect. He'd screwed up this afternoon by throwing that accusation at her. He'd apologize again. Crawl if he had to. Whatever it took, he intended to make it clear she wasn't rid of him. Not by a long shot.

That was the plan, anyway, right up until she opened the door. The mottled purple on her cheek tore the heart and the heat right out of him. Curling a knuckle, he brushed it gently across the skin below the bruise.

"Does this hurt as bad as it looks?"

"Not even close."

She didn't shy away from his touch. Dev took that as a hopeful sign. That, and the fact that some of the stiffness went out of her spine as she led him into the sitting area.

Nor did it escape his attention that she'd cut off the view that had so enchanted her before. The heavy, room-darkening drapes were drawn tight, blocking anyone from seeing out…or in.

"Would you like a drink?" she asked politely, gesturing to the well-stocked minibar.

"No, thanks, I'm good."

As he spoke, an image on the TV snagged his glance. The sound was muted but he didn't need it to recognize the amateur video playing across the screen. He'd already seen it several times.

Sarah noticed what had caught his attention and picked up the remote. "Have you seen the news coverage?"

"Yeah."

Clicking off the TV, she sank into an easy chair and raised a stockinged foot. Her arms locked around her bent knee and her green eyes regarded him steadily.

"I took your advice and thought more about our…our situation."

"That's one way to describe it," he acknowledged. "You come to any different conclusions about how we should handle it?"

"As a matter of fact, I did."

Dev waited, wanting to hear her thoughts.

"I feel as though I jumped on a speeding train. Everything happened so fast. You, me, Paris. Now Grandmama is insisting on…" She broke off, a flush rising, and took a moment to recover. "I was afraid the news services might pick up the kidnapping story, so I called her and tried to shrug off the incident as the work of bumbling amateurs."

"Did she buy that?"

"No."

"Smart woman, your grandmother."

"You might not agree when I tell you she segued immediately from that to insisting on a May wedding."

Well, what do you know? Dev was pretty sure he'd passed inspection with the duchess. Good to have it confirmed, especially since he apparently had a number of hurdles to overcome before he regained her granddaughter's trust.

"I repeat, your grandmother's a smart woman."

"She is, but then she doesn't know the facts behind our manufactured engagement."

"Do you think she needs to?"

"What I think," Sarah said slowly, "is that we need to put the brakes on this runaway train."

Putting the brakes on was a long step from her earlier insistence they call things off. Maybe he didn't face as many hurdles as he'd thought.

His tension easing by imperceptible degrees, Dev cocked his head. "How do you propose we do that?"

"We step back. Take some time to assess this attraction we both seem to…"

"Attraction?" He shook his head. "Sorry, sweetheart, I can't let you get away with that one. You and I both know we've left attraction in the dust."

"You're right."

She rested her chin on her knee, obviously searching for the right word. Impatience bit at him, but he reined it in. If he hadn't learned anything else today, he'd discovered Sarah could only be pushed so far.

"I won't lie," she said slowly. "What I feel for you is so different from anything I've ever experienced before. I think it's love. No, I'm pretty sure it's love."

That was all he needed to hear. He started toward her, but she stopped him with a quick palms-up gesture.

"What I'm *not* sure of, Dev, is whether love's enough to overcome the fact that we barely know each other."

"I know all I need to know about you."

"Oh. Right." She made a wry face. "I forgot about the background investigation."

He wouldn't apologize. He'd been up front with her about that. But he did attempt to put it in perspective.

"The investigation provided the externals, Sarah. The

time we've spent together, as brief as it's been, provided the essentials."

"Really?" She lifted a brow. "What's my favorite color? Am I a dog or a cat person? What kind of music do I like?"

"You consider those essentials?" he asked, genuinely curious.

"They're some of the bits and pieces that constitute the whole. Don't you think we should see how those pieces fit together before getting in any deeper?"

"I don't, but you obviously do."

If this was a business decision, he would ruthlessly override what he privately considered trivial objections. He'd made up his mind. He knew what he wanted.

Sarah did, too, apparently. With a flash of extremely belated insight, Dev realized she wanted to be courted. More to the point, she *deserved* to be courted.

Lady Sarah St. Sebastian might work at a magazine that promoted flashy and modern and ultrachic, but she held to old-fashioned values that he'd come to appreciate as much as her innate elegance and surprising sensuality. Her fierce loyalty to her sister, for instance. Her bone-deep love for the duchess. Her refusal to accept anything from him except her grandmother's emerald ring, and then only on a temporary basis.

He could do old-fashioned. He could do slow and courtly. Maybe. Admittedly, he didn't have a whole lot of experience in either. Moving out and taking charge came as natural to him as breathing. But if throttling back on his more aggressive instincts was what she wanted, that was what she'd get.

"Okay, we'll do it your way."

He started toward her again. Surprised and more than a little wary of his relatively easy capitulation, Sarah let her raised foot slip to the floor and pushed out of her chair.

He stopped less than a yard away. Close enough to kiss,

which she had to admit she wouldn't have minded all that much at this point. He settled for a touch instead. He kept it light, just a brush of his fingertips along the underside of her chin.

"We'll kick off phase two," he promised in a tone that edged toward deep and husky. "No negotiated contracts this time, no self-imposed deadlines. Just you and me, learning each other's little idiosyncrasies. If that's what you really want…?"

She nodded, although the soft dance of his fingers under her chin and the proximity of his mouth made it tough to stay focused.

"It's what I really want."

"All right, I'll call Patrick."

"Who? Oh, right. Your executive assistant. Excuse me for asking, but what does he have to do with this?"

"He's going to clear my calendar. Indefinitely. He'll blow every one of his fuses, but he'll get it done."

His fingers made another pass. Sarah's thoughts zinged wildly between the little pinpricks of pleasure he was generating and that "indefinitely."

"What about your schedule?" he asked. "How much time can you devote to phase two?"

"My calendar's wide-open, too. I quit my job."

"You didn't have to do that. I'm already past the business with the photographer."

"You may be," she retorted. "I'm not."

He absorbed that for a moment. "All right. Here's what we'll do, then. We give our statements to the *Brigade criminelle* at nine tomorrow morning and initiate phase two immediately after. Agreed?"

"Agreed."

"Good. I'll have a car waiting at eight-thirty to take us downtown. See you down in the lobby then."

He leaned in and brushed his lips over hers.

"Good night, Sarah."

She'd never really understood that old saying about being hoisted with your own petard. It had something to do with getting caught up in a medieval catapult, she thought. Or maybe hanging by one foot in a tangle of ropes from the mast of a fourteenth-century frigate.

Either situation would pretty much describe her feelings when Dev crossed the room and let himself out.

Thirteen

Sarah spent hours tossing and turning and kicking herself for her self-imposed celibacy. As a result, she didn't fall asleep until almost one and woke late the next morning.

The first thing she did was roll over in bed and grab her cell phone from the nightstand to check for messages. Still nothing from Gina, dammit, but Alexis had left two voice mails apologizing for what she termed an unfortunate misunderstanding and emphatically refusing to accept her senior layout editor's resignation.

"Misunderstanding, my ass."

Her mouth set, Sarah deleted the voice mails and threw back the covers. She'd have to hustle to be ready for the car Dev had said would be waiting at eight-thirty. A quick shower eliminated most of the cobwebs from her restless night. An equally quick cup of strong brew from the little coffeemaker in her room helped with the remainder.

Before she dressed, she stuck her nose through the balcony doors to assess the weather. No fog or drizzle, but still chilly enough to make her opt for her gray wool slacks and cherry-red sweater coat. She topped them with a scarf doubled around her throat European-style and a black beret tilted to a decidedly French angle.

She rushed down to the lobby with two minutes to spare and saw Dev had also prepared for the chill. But in jeans, a black turtleneck and a tan cashmere coat this morning instead of his usual business suit. He greeted her with a smile and a quick kiss.

"*Bonjour, ma chérie.* Sleep well?"

She managed not to wince at his accent. "Fairly well."

"Did you have time for breakfast?"

"No."

"I was running a little late, too, so I had the driver pick up some chocolate croissants and coffees. Shall we go?"

He offered his arm in a gesture she was beginning to realize was as instinctive as it was courteous. When she tucked her hand in the crook of his elbow, she could feel his warmth through the soft wool. Feel, too, the ripple of hard muscle as he leaned past her to push open the hotel door.

Traffic was its usual snarling beast, but the coffee and chocolate croissants mitigated the frustration. They were right on time when they pulled up at the block-long building overlooking the Seine that housed the headquarters of the *Brigade criminelle*. A lengthy sequence of security checkpoints, body scans and ID verification made them late for their appointment, however.

Detective Inspector Marie-Renée Delacroix waved aside their apologies as unnecessary and signed them in. Short and barrel-shaped, she wore a white blouse, black slacks and rubber-soled granny shoes. The semiautomatic nested in her shoulder holster belied her otherwise unprepossessing exterior.

"Thank you for coming in," she said in fluent English. "I'll try to make this as swift and painless as possible. Please, come with me."

She led them up a flight of stairs and down a long corridor interspersed with heavy oak doors. When Delacroix pushed through the door to her bureau, Sarah looked about with interest. The inspector's habitat didn't resemble the bull pens depicted on American TV police dramas. American bull pens probably didn't, either, she acknowledged wryly.

There were no dented metal file cabinets or half-empty cartons of doughnuts. No foam cups littering back-to-back desks or squawking phones. The area was spacious and well lit and smoke free. Soundproofing dividers offered at least the illusion of privacy, while monitors mounted high on the front wall flashed what looked like real-time updates on hot spots around Paris.

"Would you like coffee?" Delacroix asked as she waved them to seats in front of her desk.

Sarah looked to Dev before answering for them both. "No, thank you."

The inspector dropped into the chair behind the desk. Shoulders hunched, brows straight-lined, she dragged a wireless keyboard into reach and attacked it with two stubby forefingers. The assault was merciless, but for reasons known only to French computer gods, the typed versions of the statements Sarah and Dev had given to the responding officers wouldn't spit out of the printer.

"Merde!"

Muttering under her breath, she jabbed at the keyboard yet again. She looked as though she'd like to whip out her weapon and deliver a lethal shot when she finally admitted defeat and slammed away from her desk.

"Please wait. I need to find someone who can kick a report out of this piece of sh— Er, crap."

She returned a few moments later with a colleague in a blue-striped shirt and red suspenders. Without a word, he pressed a single key. When the printer began coughing up papers, he rolled his eyes and departed.

"I hate these things," Delacroix muttered as she dropped into her chair again.

Sarah and Dev exchanged a quick look but refrained from comment. Just as well, since the inspector became all brisk efficiency once the printer had disgorged the documents she wanted. She pushed two ink pens and the printed statements in their direction.

"Review these, please, and make any changes you feel necessary."

The reports were lengthy and correct. Delacroix was relieved that neither Sarah nor Dev had any changes, but consciously did her duty.

"Are you sure, mademoiselle? With that nasty bruise, we could add assault to the kidnapping charge."

Sarah fingered her cheek. Much as she'd like to double the case against Lefèvre, he hadn't directly caused the injury.

"I'm sure."

"Very well. Sign here, please, and here."

She did as instructed and laid down her pen. "You said you were going to talk to the prosecuting attorney about whether we need to remain in Paris for the arraignment," she reminded Delacroix.

"Ah, yes. He feels your statements, the evidence we've collected and the confessions from Lefèvre and his associate are more than sufficient for the case against them. As long as we know how to contact you and Monsieur Hunter if necessary, you may depart Paris whenever you wish."

Oddly, the knowledge that she could fly home at any time produced a contradictory desire in Sarah to remain in Paris for the initiation of phase two. That, and the way Dev once again tucked her arm in his as they descended the broad staircase leading to the main exit. There was still so much of the city—*her* city—she wanted to share with him.

The moment they stepped out into the weak sunshine, a blinding barrage of flashes sent Sarah stumbling back. Dismayed, she eyed the wolf pack crowding the front steps, their news vans parked at the curb behind them. While sound handlers thrust their boom mikes over the reporters' heads, the questions flew at Sarah like bullets. She heard her name and Dev's and Lefèvre's and Elise Girault's all seemingly in the same sentences.

She ducked her chin into her scarf and started to scramble back into police headquarters to search out a side exit. Dev stood his ground, though, and with her arm tucked tight against his side, Sarah had no choice but to do the same.

"Might as well give them what they want now," he told her. "Maybe it'll satisfy their appetites and send them chasing after their next victim."

Since most of the questions zinged at them were in French, Sarah found herself doing the translating and leaving the responding to Dev. He'd obviously fielded these kinds of rapid-fire questions before. He deftly avoided any that might impact the case against the kidnappers and confirmed only that he and Sarah were satisfied with the way the police were handling the matter.

The questions soon veered from the official to the personal. To Sarah's surprise, Dev shelved his instinctive dislike of the media and didn't cut them off at the knees. His responses were concise and to the point.

Yes, he and Lady Sarah had only recently become engaged. Yes, they'd known each other only a short time. No, they hadn't yet set a date for the wedding.

"Although," he added with a sideways glance at Sarah, "her grandmother has voiced some thoughts in that regard."

"Speaking of the duchess," a sharp-featured reporter commented as she thrust her mike almost in Sarah's face, "Charlotte St. Sebastian was once the toast of Paris and New York. From all reports, she's now penniless. Have you insisted Monsieur Hunter include provisions for her maintenance in your prenup agreement?"

Distaste curled Sarah's lip but she refused to give the

vulture any flesh to feed on. "As my fiancé has just stated," she said with a dismissive smile, "we've only recently become engaged. And what better place to celebrate that engagement than Paris, the City of Lights and Love? So now you must excuse us, as that's what we intend to do."

She tugged on Dev's arm and he took the hint. When they cleared the mob and started for the limo waiting a half block away, he gave her a curious look.

"What was that all about?"

She hadn't translated the last question and would prefer not to now. Their engagement had been tumultuous enough. Despite her grandmother's insistence on booking the Plaza, Sarah hadn't really thought as far ahead as marriage. Certainly not as far as a prenup.

They stopped beside the limo. The driver had the door open and waiting but Dev waved him back inside the car.

"Give us a minute here, Andre."

"*Oui*, monsieur."

While the driver slid into the front seat, Dev angled Sarah to face him. Her shoulders rested against the rear door frame. Reluctantly, she tipped up her gaze to meet his.

"You might as well tell me," he said. "I'd rather not be blindsided by hearing whatever it was play on the five-o'clock news."

"The reporter wanted details on our prenup." She hunched her shoulders, feeling awkward and embarrassed. "I told her to get stuffed."

His grin broke out, quick and slashing. "In your usual elegant manner, of course."

"Of course."

Still grinning, he studied her face. It must have reflected her acute discomfort because he stooped to speak to the driver.

"We've decided to walk, Andre. We won't need you anymore today."

When the limo eased away from the curb, he hooked

Sarah's arm through his again and steered her into the stream of pedestrians.

"I know how prickly you are about the subject of finances, so we won't go there until we've settled more important matters, like whether you're a dog or cat person. Which are you, by the way?"

"Dog," she replied, relaxing for the first time that morning. "The bigger the better, although the only one we've ever owned was the Pomeranian that Gina brought home one day. She was eight or nine at the time and all indignant because someone had left it leashed outside a coffee shop in one-hundred-degree heat."

Too late she realized she might have opened the door for Dev to suggest Gina had developed kleptomaniac tendencies early. She glanced up, met his carefully neutral look and hurried on with her tale.

"We went back and tried to find the owner, but no one would claim it. We soon found out why. Talk about biting the hand that feeds you! The nasty little beast snapped and snarled and wouldn't let anyone pet him except Grandmama."

"No surprise there. The duchess has a way about her. She certainly cowed me."

"Right," Sarah scoffed. "I saw how you positively quaked in her presence."

"I'm still quaking. Finish the story. What happened to the beast?"

"Grandmama finally palmed him off on an acquaintance of hers. What about you?" she asked, glancing up at him again. "Do you prefer dogs or cats?"

"Bluetick coonhounds," he answered without hesitation. "Best hunters in the world. We had a slew of barn cats, though. My sisters were always trying to palm their litters off on friends, too."

Intrigued, Sarah pumped him for more details about

his family. "I know you grew up on a ranch. In Nebraska, wasn't it?"

"New Mexico, but it was more like a hardscrabble farm than a ranch."

"Do your parents still work the farm?"

"They do. They like the old place and have no desire to leave it, although they did let me make a few improvements."

More than a few, Sarah guessed.

"What about your sisters?"

He had four, she remembered, none of whom had agreed to be interviewed for the *Beguile* article. The feeling that their business was nobody else's ran deep in the Hunter clan.

"All married, all comfortable, all happy. You hungry?"

The abrupt change of subject threw Sarah off until she saw what had captured his attention. They'd reached the Pont de l'Alma, which gave a bird's-eye view of the glass-roofed barges docked on the north side of the Seine. One boat was obviously set for a lunch cruise. Its linen-draped tables were set with gleaming silver and crystal.

"Have you ever taken one of these Seine river cruises?" Dev asked.

"No."

"Why not?"

"They're, uh, a little touristy."

"This is Paris. Everyone's a tourist, even the Parisians."

"Good God, don't let a native hear you say that!"

"What do you say? Want to mingle with the masses for a few hours?"

She threw a glance at a tour bus disgorging its load of passengers and swallowed her doubts.

"I'm game if you are."

He steered her to the steps that led down to the quay. Sarah fully expected them to be turned away at the ticket office. While a good number of boats cruised the Seine, picking up or letting off passengers at various stops, tour agencies tended to book these lunch and dinner cruises for large groups months in advance.

Whatever Dev said—or paid—at the ticket booth not only got them on the boat, it garnered a prime table for two beside the window. Their server introduced herself and filled their aperitif glasses with kir. A smile in his eyes, Dev raised his glass.

"To us."

"To us," Sarah echoed softly.

The cocktail went down with velvet smoothness. She savored the intertwined flavors while Dev gave his glass a respectful glance.

"What's in this?"

"*Crème de cassis*—black-currant liqueur—topped with white wine. It's named for Félix Kir, the mayor of Dijon, who popularized the drink after World War II."

"Well, it doesn't have the same wallop as your grandmother's *Žuta Osa* but it's good."

"'Scuse me."

The interruption came from the fortyish brunette at the next table. She beamed Sarah a friendly smile.

"Y'all are Americans, aren't you?"

"Yes, we are."

"So are we. We're the Parkers. Evelyn and Duane Parker, from Mobile."

Sarah hesitated. She hated to be rude, but Evelyn's leopard-print Versace jacket and jewel-toed boots indicated she kept up with the latest styles. If she read *Beguile,* she would probably recognize Number Three from the Sexiest Singles article. Or from the recent news coverage.

Dev solved her dilemma by gesturing to the cell phone Evelyn clutched in one hand. "I'm Dev and this is my fiancée, Sarah. Would you like me to take a picture of you and your husband?"

"Please. And I'll do one of y'all."

The accordion player began strolling the aisle while cell phones were still being exchanged and photos posed for. When he broke into a beautiful baritone, all conversation on the boat ceased and Sarah breathed easy again.

Moments later, they pulled away from the dock and glided under the first of a dozen or more bridges yet to come. Meal service began then. Sarah wasn't surprised at the quality of the food. This was Paris, after all. She and Dev sampled each of the starters: foie gras on a toasted baguette; Provençal smoked salmon and shallots; duck magret salad with cubes of crusty goat cheese; tiny vegetable egg rolls fried to a pale golden brown. Sarah chose honey-and-sesame-seed pork tenderloin for her main dish. Dev went with the veal blanquette. With each course, their server poured a different wine. Crisp, chilled whites. Medium reds. Brandy with the rum baba they each selected for dessert.

Meanwhile, Paris's most famous monuments were framed in the windows. The Louvre. La Conciergerie. Notre Dame. The Eiffel Tower.

The boat made a U-turn while Sarah and Dev lingered over coffee, sharing more of their pasts. She listened wide-eyed to the stories Dev told of his Air Force days. She suspected he edited them to minimize the danger and maximize the role played by others on his crew. Still, the wartorn countries he'd flown into and the horrific disasters he'd helped provide lifesaving relief for made her world seem frivolous by comparison.

"Grandmama took us abroad every year," she related when he insisted it was her turn. "She was determined to expose Gina and me to cultures other than our own."

"Did she ever take you to Karlenburgh?"

"No, never. That would have been too painful for her. I'd like to go someday, though. We still have cousins there, three or four times removed."

She traced a fingertip around the rim of her coffee cup.

Although it tore at her pride, she forced herself to admit the truth.

"Gina and I never knew what sacrifices Grandmama had to make to pay for those trips. Or for my year at the Sorbonne."

"I'm guessing your sister still doesn't know."

She jerked her head up, prepared to defend Gina yet again. But there was nothing judgmental in Dev's expression. Only quiet understanding.

"She has a vague idea," Sarah told him. "I never went into all the gory details, but she's not stupid."

Dev had to bite down on the inside of his lower lip. Eugenia Amalia Therése St. Sebastian hadn't impressed him with either her intelligence or her common sense. Then again, he hadn't been particularly interested in her intellectual prowess the few times they'd connected.

In his defense, few horny, heterosexual males could see beyond Gina's stunning beauty. At least not until they'd spent more than an hour or two in the bubbleheaded blonde's company. Deciding discretion was the better part of valor, he chose not to share that particular observation.

He couldn't help comparing the sisters, though. No man in his right mind would deny that he'd come out the winner in the St. Sebastian lottery. Charm, elegance, smarts, sensuality and...

He'd better stop right there! When the hell had he reached the point where the mere thought of Sarah's smooth, sleek body stretched out under his got him rock hard? Where the memory of how she'd opened her legs for him damned near steamed up the windows beside their table?

Suddenly Dev couldn't wait for the boat to pass under the last bridge. By the time they'd docked and he'd hustled Sarah up the gangplank, his turtleneck was strangling him. The look of confused concern she flashed at him as they climbed the steps to street level didn't help matters.

"Are you all right?"

He debated for all of two seconds before deciding on the truth. "Not anywhere close to all right."

"Oh, no! Was it the foie gras?" Dismayed, she rushed to the curb to flag down a cab. "You have to be careful with goose liver."

"Sarah…"

"I should have asked if it had been wrapped in grape leaves and slow cooked. That's the safest method."

"Sarah…"

A cab screeched to the curb. Forehead creased with worry, she yanked on the door handle. Dev had to wait until they were in the taxi and heading for the hotel to explain his sudden incapacitation.

"It wasn't the foie gras."

Concern darkened her eyes to deep, verdant green. "The veal, then? Was it bad?"

"No, sweetheart. It's you."

"I beg your pardon?"

Startled, she lurched back against her seat. Dev cursed his clumsiness and hauled her into his arms.

"As delicious as lunch was, all I could think about was how you taste." His mouth roamed hers. His voice dropped to a rough whisper. "How you fit against me. How you arch your back and make that little noise in your throat when you're about to climax."

She leaned back in his arms. She wanted him as much as he wanted her. He could see it in the desire that shaded her eyes to deep, dark emerald. In the way her breath had picked up speed. Fierce satisfaction knifed into him. She was rethinking the cooling-off period, Dev thought exultantly. She had to recognize how unnecessary this phase two was.

His hopes took a nosedive—and his respect for Sarah's

willpower kicked up a grudging notch—when she drew in a shuddering breath and gave him a rueful smile.

"Well, I'm glad it wasn't the goose liver."

Fourteen

As the cab rattled along the quay, Sarah wondered how she could be such a blithering idiot. One word from her, just one little word, and she could spend the rest of the afternoon and evening curled up with Dev in bed. Or on the sofa. Or on cushions tossed onto the floor in front of the fire, or in the shower, soaping his back and belly, or...

She leaned forward, her gaze suddenly snagged by the green bookstalls lining the riverside of the boulevard. And just beyond the stalls, almost directly across from the renowned bookstore known as Shakespeare and Company, was a familiar bridge.

"Stop! We'll get out here!"

The command surprised both Dev and the cabdriver, but he obediently pulled over to the curb and Dev paid him off.

"Your favorite bookstore?" he asked with a glance at the rambling, green-fronted facade of the shop that specialized in English-language books. Opened in 1951, the present store had assumed the mantle of the original Shakespeare and Company, a combination bookshop, lending library and haven for writers established in 1917 by American expatriate Sylvia Beach and frequented by the likes of Ernest Hemingway, Ezra Pound and F. Scott Fitzgerald. During her year at the Sorbonne, Sarah had loved exploring the shelves crammed floor to ceiling in the shop's small, crowded rooms. She'd never slept in one of the thirteen beds available to indigent students or visitors who just wanted to sleep in the rarified literary atmosphere, but she'd hunched for hours at the tables provided for scholars, researchers and book lovers of all ages.

It wasn't Shakespeare and Company that had snagged her eye, though. It was the bridge just across the street from it.

"That's the Archbishop's Bridge," she told Dev with a smile that tinged close to embarrassment.

She'd always considered herself the practical sister, too levelheaded to indulge in the kind of extravagant flights of fancy that grabbed Gina. Yet she'd just spent several delightful hours on a touristy, hopelessly romantic river cruise. Why not cap that experience with an equally touristy romantic gesture?

"Do you see these locks?" she asked as she and Dev crossed the street and approached the iron bridge.

"Hard to miss 'em," he drawled, eyeing the almost solid wall of brass obscuring the bridge's waist-high grillwork. "What's the story here?"

"I'm told it's a recent fad that's popping up on all the bridges of Paris. People ascribe wishes or dreams to locks and fasten them to the bridge, then throw the key in the river."

Dev stooped to examine some of the colorful ribbons, charms and printed messages dangling from various locks. "Here's a good one. This couple from Dallas wish their kids great joy, but don't plan to produce any additional offspring. Evidently seven are enough."

"Good grief! Seven would be enough for me, too."

"Really?"

He straightened and leaned a hip against the rail. The breeze ruffled his black hair and tugged at the collar of his camel-hair sport coat.

"I guess that's one of those little idiosyncrasies we should find out about each other, almost as important as whether we prefer dogs or cats. How many kids *do* you want, Sarah?"

"I don't know." She trailed a finger over the oblong hasp of a bicycle lock. "Two, at least, although I wouldn't mind three or even four."

As impulsive and thoughtless as Gina could be at times, Sarah couldn't imagine growing up without the joy of her bubbly laugh and warm, generous personality.

"How about you?" she asked Dev. "How many offspring would you like to produce?"

"Well, my sisters contend that the number of kids their husbands want is inversely proportional to how many stinky diapers they had to change. I figure I can manage a couple of rounds of diapers. Three or maybe even four if I get the hang of it."

He nodded to the entrepreneur perched on his overturned crate at the far end of the bridge. The man's pegboard full of locks gleamed dully in the afternoon sun.

"What do you think? Should we add a wish that we survive stinky diapers to the rest of these hopes and dreams?"

Still a little embarrassed by her descent into sappy sentimentality, Sarah nodded. She waited on the bridge while Dev purchased a hefty lock. Together they scouted for an open spot. She found one two-thirds of the way across the bridge, but Dev hesitated before attaching his purchase.

"We need to make it more personal." Frowning, he eyed the bright ribbons and charms dangling from so many of the other locks. "We need a token or something to scribble on."

He patted the pockets of his sport coat and came up

with the ticket stubs from their lunch cruise. "How about one of these?"

"That works. The cruise gave me a view of Paris I'd never seen before. I'm glad I got to share it with you, Dev."

Busy scribbling on the back of a ticket, he merely nodded. Sarah was a little surprised by his offhanded acceptance of her tribute until she read what he'd written.

To our two or three or four or more kids,
we promise you one cruise each on the Seine.

"And I thought *I* was being mushy and sentimental," she said, laughing.

"Mushy and sentimental is what phase two is all about." Unperturbed, he punched the hasp through the ticket stub. "Here, you attach it."

When the lock clicked into place, Sarah knew she'd always remember this moment. Rising up on tiptoe, she slid her arms around Dev's neck.

She'd remember the kiss, too. Particularly when Dev valiantly stuck to their renegotiated agreement later that evening.

After their monster lunch, they opted for supper at a pizzeria close to the Hôtel Verneuil. One glass of red wine and two mushroom-and-garlic slices later, they walked back to the hotel through a gray, soupy fog. Monsieur LeBon had gone off duty, but the receptionist on the desk relayed his shock over the news of the attack on Lady Sarah and his profound regret that she had suffered such an indignity while in Paris.

Sarah smiled her thanks and made a mental note to speak to the manager personally tomorrow. Once on her floor, she slid the key card into her room lock and slanted Dev a questioning look.

"Do you want to come in for a drink?"

"A man can only endure so much torture." His expression rueful, he traced a knuckle lightly over the bruise she'd already forgotten. "Unless you're ready to initiate phase three, we'd better call it a night."

She was ready. More than ready. But the companionship she and Dev had shared after leaving Inspector Delacroix's office had delivered as much punch as the hours they'd spent tangled up in the sheets. A different kind of punch, admittedly. Emotional rather than physical, but every bit as potent.

Although she knew she'd regret it the moment she closed the door, Sarah nodded. "Let's give phase two a little more time."

She was right. She did regret it. But she decided the additional hours she spent curled up on the sofa watching very boring TV were appropriate punishment for being so stupid. She loved Dev. He obviously loved her. Why couldn't she just trust her instincts and...

The buzz of her cell phone cut into her disgusted thoughts. She reached for the instrument, half hoping it was Alexis trying to reach her again. Sarah was in the mood to really, really unload on her ex-boss. When her sister's picture flashed up on the screen, she almost dropped the phone in her excitement and relief.

"Gina! Where are you?"

"Lucerne. I...I waited until morning in New York to call you but..."

"I'm not in New York. I'm in Paris, as you would know if you'd bothered to answer any of my calls."

"Thank God!"

The moaned exclamation startled her, but not as much as the sobs her sister suddenly broke into. Sarah lurched upright on the sofa, the angry tirade she'd intended to deliver instantly forgotten.

"What's wrong? Gina! What's happened?"

A dozen different disasters flooded into her mind. Gina had taken a tumble on the ski slopes. Broken a leg or an arm. Or her neck. She could be paralyzed. Breathing by machine.

"Are you hurt?" she demanded, fear icing her heart. "Gina, are you in the hospital?"

"Nooo."

The low wail left her limp with relief. In almost the next heartbeat, panic once again fluttered like a trapped bird inside her chest. She could count on the fingers of one hand the times she'd heard her always-upbeat, always-sunny sister cry.

"Sweetie, talk to me. Tell me what's wrong."

"I can't. Not…not over the phone. Please come, Sarah. *Please!* I need you."

It didn't even occur to her to say no. "I'll catch the next flight to Lucerne. Tell me where you're staying."

"The Rebstock."

"The hotel Grandmama took us to the summer you turned fourteen?"

That set off another bout of noisy, hiccuping sobs. "Don't…don't tell Grandmama about this."

About *what?* Somehow, Sarah choked back the shout and offered a soothing promise.

"I won't. Just keep your phone on, Gina. I'll call you as soon as I know when I can get there."

She cut the connection, switched to the phone's internet browser and pulled up a schedule of flights from Paris to Lucerne. Her pulse jumped when she found a late-night shuttle to Zurich that departed Charles de Gaulle Airport at 11:50 p.m. From there she'd have to rent a car and drive the sixty-five kilometers to Lake Lucerne.

She could make the flight. She had to make it. Her heart racing, she reserved a seat and scrambled off the sofa. She started for the bedroom to throw some things together but made a quick detour to the sitting room desk and snatched up the house phone.

"Come on, Dev. Answer!"

Her quivering nerves stretched tighter as it rang six times, then cut to the hotel operator.

"May I help you, Lady Sarah?"

"I'm trying to reach Monsieur Hunter, but he doesn't answer."

"May I take a message for you?"

"Yes, please. Tell him to call me as soon as possible."

Hell! Where was he?

Slamming the phone down, she dashed into the bedroom. She didn't have time to pack. Just shove her laptop in her shoulder tote, grab her sweater coat, make sure her purse held her passport and credit cards and run.

While the elevator made its descent, she tried to reach Dev by cell phone. She'd just burst into the lobby when he answered on a husky, teasing note.

"Please tell me you've decided to put me out of my misery."

"Where are you?" The phone jammed to her ear, she rushed through the lobby. "I called your room but there wasn't any answer."

"I couldn't sleep. I went out for a walk." He caught the tension in her voice. The teasing note dropped out of his. "Why? What's up?"

"Gina just called."

"It's about time."

She pushed through the front door. The fog had cleared, thank God, and several taxis still cruised the streets. She waved a frantic arm to flag one down, the phone clutched in her other fist.

"She's in some kind of trouble, Dev."

"So what else is new?"

If she hadn't been so worried, the sarcastic comment might not have fired her up as hot and fast as it did.

"Spare me the editorial," she snapped back angrily. "My sister needs me. I'm on my way to Switzerland."

"Whoa! Hold on a minute…"

The taxi rolled up to the curb. She jumped in and issued a terse order. "De Gaulle Airport. Hurry, please."

"Dammit, Sarah, I can't be more than ten or fifteen minutes from the hotel. Wait until I get back and we'll sort this out together."

"She's *my* sister. I'll sort it out." She was too rushed and too torqued by his sarcasm to measure her words. "I'll call you as soon as I know what's what."

"Yeah," he bit out, as pissed off now as she was. "You do that."

In no mood to soothe his ruffled feathers, she cut the connection and leaned into the Plexiglas divider.

"I need to catch an eleven-fifty flight," she told the cabdriver. "There's an extra hundred francs in it for you if I make it."

The Swiss Air flight was only half-full. Most of the passengers looked like businessmen who wanted to be on scene when Zurich's hundreds of banks opened for business in the morning. There were a few tourists scattered among them, and several students with crammed backpacks getting a jump start on spring break in the Alps.

Sarah stared out the window through most of the ninety-minute flight. The inky darkness beyond the strobe lights on the wing provided no answers to the worried questions tumbling through her mind.

Was it the ski instructor? Had he left Gina stranded in Lucerne? Or Dev's Byzantine medallion? Had she tried to sell it and smacked up against some law against peddling antiquities on the black market?

Her stomach was twisted into knots by the time they landed in Zurich, and she rushed to the airport's Europcar desk. Fifteen minutes later she was behind the wheel of a rented Peugeot and zipping out of the airport. Once she hit the main motorway, she fumbled her phone out of her purse and speed-dialed her sister.

"I just landed in Zurich," Sarah informed her. "I'm in a rental car and should be there within an hour."

"Okay. Thanks for coming, Sarah. I'll call down to reception and tell them to expect you."

To her profound relief, Gina sounded much calmer. Probably because she knew the cavalry was on the way.

"I'll see you shortly."

Once Sarah left the lights of Zurich behind, she zoomed south on the six-lane E41. Speed limits in Switzerland didn't approach the insanity of those in Germany, but the 120 kilometers per hour max got her to the shores of Lake Lucerne in a little over forty minutes.

The city of Lucerne sat on the western arm of the lake. A modern metropolis with an ancient center, its proximity to the Alps had made it a favorite destination for tourists from the earliest days of the Hapsburg Empire. The Duchy of Karlenburgh had once constituted a minuscule part of that vast Hapsburg empire. As the lights of the city glowed in the distance, Sarah remembered that Grandmama had shared some of the less painful stories from the St. Sebastians' past during their stay in Lucerne.

She wasn't thinking of the past as she wound through the narrow streets of the Old Town. Only of her sister and whether whatever trouble Gina was in might impact their grandmother's health. The old worries she'd carried for so long—the worries she'd let herself slough off when she'd gotten so tangled up with Dev—came crashing back.

It was almost 3:00 a.m. when she pulled up at the entrance to the Hotel zum Rebstock. Subdued lighting illuminated its half-timbered red-and-white exterior. Three stories tall, with a turreted tower anchoring one end of the building, the hotel had a history dating back to the 1300s.

Even this early in the season, geraniums filled its window boxes and ivy-covered trellises defined the tiny terrace that served as an outdoor restaurant and *biergarten*.

Weary beyond words, Sarah grabbed her tote and purse and left the car parked on the street. She'd have a valet move it to the public garage on the next block tomorrow. Right now all she cared about was getting to her sister.

As promised, Gina had notified reception of a late arrival. Good thing, since a sign on the entrance informed guests that for safety purposes a key card was required for entry after midnight. A sleepy attendant answered Sarah's knock and welcomed her to the Rebstock.

"Lady Eugenia asked that we give you a key. She is in room 212. The elevator is just down the hall. Or you may take the stairs."

"Thank you."

She decided the stairs would be quicker and would also work out the kinks in her back from the flight and the drive. The ancient wooden stairs creaked beneath their carpeted runner. So did the boards of the second-floor hallway as Sarah counted room numbers until she reached the one at the far end of the hall. A corner turret room, judging by the way its door was wedged between two others.

She slid the key card into the lock and let herself into a narrow, dimly lit entryway.

"Gina?"

The door whooshed shut behind her. Sarah rounded the corner of the entryway, found herself in a charming bedroom with a sitting area occupying the octagonal turret and came to a dead stop. Her sister was tucked under the double bed's downy duvet, sound asleep.

A rueful smile curved Sarah's lips. She'd raced halfway across Europe in response to a desperate plea. Yet whatever was troubling Gina didn't appear to be giving her nightmares. She lay on one side, curled in a tight ball with a hand under her cheek and her blond curls spilling across the pillow.

Shaking her head in amused affection, Sarah dropped her tote and purse on the sofa in the sitting area and plunked down on the side of the bed.

"Hey!" She poked her sister in the shoulder. "Wake up!"

"Huh?" Gina raised her head and blinked open blurry eyes. "Oh, good," she muttered, her voice thick with sleep. "You made it."

"Finally."

"You've got to be totally wiped," she mumbled. Scooting over a few inches, she dragged up a corner of the comforter. "Crawl in."

"Oh, for…!"

Sarah swallowed the rest of the exasperated exclamation. Gina's head had already plopped back to the pillow. Her lids fluttered shut and her raised arm sank like a stone.

The elder sister sat on the edge of the bed for a few moments longer, caught in a wash of relief and bone-deep love for the younger. Then she got up long enough to kick off her boots and unbelt the cherry-red sweater coat. Shrugging it off, she slid under the comforter.

As exhausted as she was from her frantic dash across Europe, it took Sarah longer than she would have believed possible to fall asleep. She lay in the half darkness, listening to her sister's steady breathing, trying yet again to guess what had sparked her panic. Gradually, her thoughts shifted to Dev and their last exchange.

She'd overreacted to his criticism of Gina. She knew that now. At the time, though, her one driving thought had been to get to the airport. She'd apologize tomorrow. He had sisters of his own. Surely he'd understand.

Fifteen

Sarah came awake to blinding sunshine and the fuzziness that results from too little sleep. She rolled over, grimacing at the scratchy pull of her slept-in slacks and turtleneck, and squinted at the empty spot beside her.

No Gina.

And no note, she discovered when she crawled out of bed and checked the sunny sitting room. More than a little annoyed, she padded into the bathroom. Face scrubbed, she appropriated her sister's hairbrush and found a complimentary toothbrush in the basket of amenities provided by the hotel.

Luckily, she and Gina wore the same size, if not the same style. While she was content to adapt her grandmother's vintage classics, her sister preferred a trendier, splashier look. Sarah raided Gina's underwear for a pair of silky black hipsters and matching demibra, then wiggled into a chartreuse leotard patterned in a wild Alice In Wonderland motif. She topped them with a long-sleeved, thigh-skimming wool jumper in electric blue and a three-inch-wide elaborately studded belt that rode low on her hips.

No way was she wearing her red sweater coat with these

eye-popping colors. She'd look like a clown-school dropout. She flicked a denim jacket off a hangar instead, hitched her purse over her shoulder and went in search of her sister.

She found Gina outside on the terrace, chatting with an elderly couple at the next table. She'd gathered her blond curls into a one-sided cascade and looked impossibly chic in pencil-legged jeans, a shimmering metallic tank and a fur-trimmed Michael Kors blazer. When she spotted Sarah, she jumped up and rushed over with her arms outstretched.

"You're finally up! You got in so late last night I… Omigod! What happened to your face?"

Sarah was more anxious to hear her sister's story than tell her own. "I got crosswise of a metal strut."

"I'm so sorry! Does it hurt?"

"Not anymore."

"Thank goodness. We'll have to cover it with foundation when we go back upstairs. Do you want some coffee?"

"God, yes!"

Sarah followed her back to the table and smiled politely when Gina introduced her to the elderly couple. They were from Düsseldorf, were both retired schoolteachers and had three children, all grown now.

"They've been coming to Lake Lucerne every spring for forty-seven years to celebrate their anniversary," Gina related as she filled a cup from the carafe on her table. "Isn't that sweet?"

"Very sweet."

Sarah splashed milk into the cup and took two, quick lifesaving gulps while Gina carried on a cheerful conversation with the teachers. As she listened to the chatter, Sarah began to feel much like the tumbling, upside-down Alices on the leotard. Had she fallen down some rabbit hole? Imagined the panic in her sister's voice last night? Dreamed the sobs?

The unreal feeling persisted until Gina saw that she'd downed most of her coffee. "I told the chambermaid to wait until you were up to do the room. She's probably in there now. Why don't we take a walk and...and talk?"

The small stutter and flicker of nervousness told Sarah she hadn't entered some alternate universe. With a smile for the older couple, Gina pushed her chair back. Sarah did the same.

"Let's go down to Chapel Bridge," she suggested. "We can talk there."

The Rebstock sat directly across the street from Lucerne's centuries-old Church of Leodegar, named for the city's patron saint. Just beyond the needle-spired church, the cobbled street angled downward, following the Reuss River as it flowed into the impossibly blue lake. Since the Reuss bisected the city, Lucerne could claim almost as many bridges as Venice. The most famous of them was the Chapel Bridge, or *Kapellbrücke*. Reputed to be the oldest covered wooden bridge in Europe, it was constructed in the early 1300s. Some sections had to be rebuilt after a 1993 fire supposedly sparked by a discarded cigarette. But the octagonal watchtower halfway across was original, and the window boxes filled with spring flowers made it a favorite meandering spot for locals and tourists alike.

Zigzagging for more than six hundred feet across the river, it was decorated with paintings inside that depicted Lucerne's history and offered wooden benches with stunning views of the town, the lake and the snowcapped Alps. Gina sank onto a bench some yards from the watchtower. Sarah settled beside her and waited while her sister gnawed on her lower lip and stared at the snowy peaks in uncharacteristic silence.

"You might as well tell me," she said gently after several moments. "Whatever's happened, we'll find a way to fix it."

Gina exhaled a long, shuddering breath. Twisting around on the bench, she reached for Sarah's hands.

"That's the problem. I came here to fix it. But at the last minute, I couldn't go through with it."

"Go through with what?"

"Terminating the pregnancy."

Sarah managed not to gasp or groan or mangle the fingers entwined with hers, but it took a fierce struggle.

"You're pregnant?"

"Barely. I peed on the stick even before I missed my period. I thought... I was sure we were safe. He wore a condom." She gave a short, dry laugh. "Actually, we went through a whole box of condoms that weekend."

"For God's sake, I don't need the details. Except maybe his name. I assume we're talking about your ski instructor."

"Who?"

"The cuddly ski instructor you texted me about."

"Oh. There isn't any ski instructor. I just needed an excuse for my sudden trip to Switzerland."

That arrowed straight to Sarah's heart. Never, *ever* would she have imagined that her sister would keep a secret like this from her.

"Oh, Gina, why did you need an excuse? Why didn't you just tell me about the baby?"

"I couldn't. You've been so worried about Grandmama and the doctor bills. I couldn't dump this problem on you, too."

She crunched Sarah's fingers, tears shimmering in her eyes.

"But last night... After I canceled my appointment at the clinic...it all sort of came down on me. I had to call you, had to talk to you. Then, when I heard your voice, I just lost it."

When she burst into wrenching sobs, Sarah wiggled a hand free of her bone-crushing grip and threw an arm around her.

"I'm *glad* you lost it," she said fiercely as Gina cried into her shoulder. "I'm *glad* I was close enough to come when you needed me."

They rocked together, letting the tears flow, until Gina finally raised a tear-streaked face.

"You okay?" Sarah asked, fishing a tissue out of her purse.

"No, but...but I will be."

Thank God. She heard the old Gina in that defiant sniff. She handed her the tissue and hid a grin when her sister honked like a Canadian goose.

"I meant to ask you about that, Sarah."

"About what?"

"How you could get here so fast. What were you doing in Paris?"

"I'll tell you later. Let's focus on you right now. And the baby. Who's the father, Gina, and does he know he is one?"

"Yes, to the second part. I was so wigged-out last night, I called him before I called you." She scrunched up her nose. "He didn't take it well."

"Bastard!"

"And then some." Her tears completely gone now, Gina gave an indignant sniff. "You wouldn't believe how obnoxious and overbearing he is. And I can't believe I fell for him, even for one weekend. Although in my defense, he gives new meaning to the phrase sex on the hoof."

"Who *is* this character?"

"No one you know. I met him in L.A. My company catered a party for him."

The bottom dropped out of Sarah's stomach. She could have sworn she heard it splat into the weathered boards. She stared at the snow-covered peaks in the distance, but all she could see was the surveillance video of Gina. At Dev's house in L.A. Catering a private party.

"What's...?" She dragged her tongue over suddenly dry lips. Her voice sounded hollow in her ears, as though it came from the bottom of a well. "What's his name?"

"Jack Mason." Gina's lip curled. "Excuse me, John Harris Mason, the third."

For a dizzying moment, Sarah couldn't catch her breath. She only half heard the diatribe her sister proceeded to pour out concerning the man. She caught that he was some kind of ambassador, however, and that he worked out of the State Department.

"How in the world did you hook up with someone from the State Department?"

"He was in L.A. for a benefit. A friend introduced us."

"Oh. Well…"

Since Gina seemed to have finally run out of steam, Sarah asked if she'd eaten breakfast.

"No, I was waiting for you to wake up."

"The baby…" She gestured at her sister's still-flat stomach. "You need to eat, and I'm starved. Why don't you go back to the hotel and order us a gargantuan breakfast? I'll join you after I make a few calls."

"You're not going to call Grandmama?" Alarm put a squeak in Gina's voice. "We can't drop this on her long-distance."

"Good Lord, no! I need to call Paris. I raced out so fast last night, I didn't pack my things or check out of the hotel."

Or wait for Dev to hotfoot it back to the Hôtel Verneuil. Sarah didn't regret that hasty decision. She wouldn't have made the Swiss Air flight if she'd waited. But she did regret the anger that had flared between them.

No need to tell Gina about Dev right now. Not when she and Sarah were both still dealing with the emotional whammy of her pregnancy. She'd tell her later, after things had calmed down a bit.

Which was why she waited until her sister was almost to the exit of the wooden tunnel to whip out her phone. And why frustration put a scowl on her face when Dev didn't answer his cell.

She left a brief message. Just a quick apology for her spurt of temper last night and a request for him to return her call as soon as possible. She started to slip the phone back into her purse, but decided to try his hotel room. The house phone rang six times before switching to the hotel operator, as it had last night.

"May I help you?"

"This is Sarah St. Sebastian. I'm trying to reach Monsieur Hunter."

"I'm sorry, Lady Sarah. Monsieur Hunter has checked out."

"What! When?"

"Early this morning. He told Monsieur LeBon an urgent business matter had come up at home that required his immediate attention. He also instructed us to hold your room for you until you return."

For the second time in less than ten minutes, Sarah's stomach took a dive.

"Did he...? Did he leave a message for me?"

"No, ma'am."

"Are you sure?"

"Quite sure, ma'am."

"I see. Thank you."

The hand holding the phone dropped to her lap. Once again she stared blindly at the dazzling white peak. Long moments later, she gave her head a little shake and pushed off the bench.

Gina needed her. They'd work on her problem first. Then, maybe, work on Sarah's. When she was calmer and could put this business with Dev in some kind of perspective.

The scene that greeted her when she walked into the Rebstock's lobby did nothing to promote a sense of calm. If anything, she was jolted into instant outrage by the sight of a tawny-haired stranger brutally gripping one of Gina's wrists. She was hammering at him with her free fist. The receptionist dithered ineffectually behind the counter.

"What are you doing?"

Sarah flew across the lobby, her hands curled into talons. She attacked from the side while Gina continued to assault the front. Between them, they forced the stranger to hunch his shoulders and shield his face from fifteen painted, raking fingernails.

"Hey! Back off, lady."

"Let her go!"

Sarah got in a vicious swipe that drew blood. The man, whom she now suspected was the overbearing, obnoxious ambassador, cursed.

"Jesus! Back off, I said!"

"Not until you let Gina go."

"The hell I will! She's got some explaining to do, and I'm not letting her out of my sight until…"

He broke off, as startled as Sarah when she was thrust aside by 180 pounds of savage male.

"What the…?"

That was all Mason got out before a fist slammed into his jaw. He stumbled back a few steps, dragging Gina with him, then took a vicious blow to the midsection that sent him to his knees.

Still, he wouldn't release Gina's wrist. But instead of fighting and twisting, she was now on her knees beside him and waving her free hand frantically.

"Dev! Stop!"

Sarah was terrified her sister might be hurt in the melee. Or the baby. Dear God, the baby. She leaped forward and hung like a monkey from Dev's arm.

"For God's sake, be careful! She's pregnant!"

The frantic shout backed Dev off but produced the opposite reaction in Mason. His brown eyes blazing, he wrenched Gina around to face him.

"Pregnant? What the hell is this? When you called me last night, all weepy and hysterical, you said you'd just come back from the clinic."

"I *had* just come back from the clinic!"

"Then what…?" His glance shot to her stomach, ripped back to her face. "You didn't do it?"

"I…I couldn't."

"But you couldn't be bothered to mention that little fact before I walked out on a critical floor vote, jumped a plane and flew all night to help you through a crisis you *also* didn't bother to tell me about until last night."

"So I didn't choose my words well," Gina threw back. "I was upset."

"Upset? You were damned near incoherent."

"And you were your usual arrogant self. Let me go, dammit."

She wrenched her wrist free and scrambled to her feet. Mason followed her up, his angry glance going from her to their small but intensely interested audience. His eyes narrowed on Sarah.

"You must be the sister."

"I… Yes."

His jaw working, he shifted to Dev. "Who the hell are you?"

"The sister's fiancé."

"What!" Gina's shriek ricocheted off the walls. "Since when?"

"It's a long story," Sarah said weakly. "Why don't we, uh, go someplace a little more private and I'll explain."

"Let's go." Gina hooked an arm through Sarah's, then whirled to glare at the two men. "Not you. Not either of you. This is between me and my sister."

It wasn't, but Dev yielded ground. Mason was forced to follow suit, although he had to vent his feelings first.

"You, Eugenia Amalia Therése St. Sebastian, are the most irresponsible, irritating, thickheaded female I've ever met."

Her nostrils flaring, Gina tilted her chin in a way that would have made the duchess proud. "Then aren't you fortunate, Ambassador, that I refused to marry you."

* * *

Her regal hauteur carried her as far as the stairwell. Abandoning it on the first step, she yanked on Sarah's arm to hurry her up to their room. Once inside, she let the door slam and thrust her sister toward the sofa wedged into the turret sitting room.

"Sit." She pointed a stern finger. "Talk. Now."

Sarah sat, but talking didn't come easy. "It's a little difficult to explain."

"No, it's not. Start at the beginning. When and where did you meet Dev?"

"In New York. At my office. When he came to show me the surveillance video of you lifting his Byzantine medallion."

Gina's jaw sagged. "What Byzantine...? Oh! Wait! Do you mean that little gold-and-blue thingy?"

"That little gold-and-blue thingy is worth more than a hundred thousand pounds."

"You're kidding!"

"I wish I was. What did you do with it, Gina?"

"I didn't do anything with it."

"Dev's surveillance video shows the medallion sitting on its stand when you sashay up to the display shelves. When you sashay away, the medallion's gone."

"Good grief, Sarah, you don't think I stole it, do you?"

"No, and that's what I told him from day one."

"*He* thinks I stole it?"

The fury that flashed in her eyes didn't bode well for Devon Hunter.

"It doesn't matter what he thinks," Sarah lied. "What matters is that the medallion's missing. Think, sweetie, think. Did you lift it off its stand? Or knock it off by accident, so it fell behind the shelves, maybe?"

"I did lift it, but I just wanted to feel the surface. You know, rub a thumb over that deep blue enamel." Her forehead creased in concentration. "Then I heard someone coming and… Oh, damn! I must have slipped it into my pocket. It's probably still there."

"Gina!" The two syllables came out on a screech. "How could you not remember slipping a twelfth-century Byzantine medallion in your pocket?"

"Hey, I didn't know it was a twelfth-century *anything*. And I'd just taken the pregnancy test that morning, okay? I was a little rattled. I'm surprised I made it to work that evening, much less managed to smile and orchestrate Hunter's damned dinner."

She whirled and headed for the door. Sarah jumped up to follow.

"I'm going to rip him a new one," Gina fumed. "How *dare* he accuse me of…" She yanked open the door and instantly switched pronouns. "How *dare* you accuse me of stealing?"

The two men in the hall returned distinctly different frowns. Jack Mason's was quick and confused. Dev's was slower and more puzzled.

"You didn't take it?"

"No, Mr. High-and-Mighty Hunter, I didn't."

"Take what?" Mason wanted to know.

"Then where is it?"

"I'm guessing it's in the pocket of the jacket I wore that evening."

"So you *did* take it?"

"Take what?"

Sarah cut in. "Gina was just running a hand over the surface when she heard footsteps. She didn't want to be caught fingering it, so she slipped it into her pocket."

"Dammit!" the ambassador exploded. "What the hell are you three talking about it?"

"Nothing that concerns you," Gina returned icily. "Why are you in my room, anyway? I have nothing more to say to you."

"Tough. I've still got plenty to say to you."

Sarah had had enough. A night of gut-wrenching worry, little sleep, no breakfast and now all this shouting was giving her a world-class headache. Before she could tell everyone to please shut up, Dev hooked her elbow and edged her out the door. With his other hand, he pushed Mason inside.

"You take care of your woman. I'll take care of mine."

"Wait a minute!" Thoroughly frustrated, Gina stamped a foot. "I still don't know how or when or why you two got engaged. You can't just…"

Dev closed the door in her face.

"Ooh," Sarah breathed. "She'll make you pay for that."

He braced both hands against the wall, caging her in. "Do I look worried?"

What he looked was unshaven, red-eyed and pissed.

"What are you doing here?" she asked a little breathlessly. "When I called the Hôtel Verneuil a while ago, they told me you had some kind of crisis in your business and had to fly home."

"I had a crisis, all right, but it was here. We need to get something straight, Lady Sarah. From now on, it's not *my* sister or *your* business. We're in this together. Forever. Or at least until we deliver on that promise to give kid number four a cruise on the Seine."

Sixteen

The prewedding dinner was held on the evening of May 3 at Avery's, where Dev had first "proposed" to Sarah. He reserved the entire restaurant for the event. The wedding ceremony and reception took place at the Plaza the following evening.

Gina, who'd emerged from a private session with the duchess white-faced and shaking, had regained both her composure and some of her effervescence. She then proceeded to astonish both her sister and her grandmother by taking charge of the dinner, the wedding ceremony and the reception.

To pull them off, she'd enlisted the assistance of Andrew at the Plaza, who'd aged with immense dignity since that long-ago day he'd discreetly taken care of an inebriated presidential aide during Grandmama's soirée for the Sultan of Oman. Gina also formed a close alliance with Patrick Donovan, Dev's incredibly capable and supremely confident executive assistant.

All Sarah had to do was draw up her guest list and select her dress. She kept the list small. She wanted to *enjoy* her wedding, not feel as though she was participating in a carefully scripted media event. Besides, she didn't have any family other than Grandmama, Gina and Maria.

She did invite a number of close friends and coworkers—including Alexis. *Beguile*'s executive editor had admitted the Paris thing was a mistake of epic proportions, but swore she'd never intended to publish a single photo without Sarah's permission. As a peace offering/wedding present, she'd had the photos printed and inserted into a beautifully inscribed, gilt-edged scrapbook. Just to be safe, Sarah had also had her hand over the disk with the complete set of JPEGs.

Dev's guest list was considerably longer than his bride's. His parents, sisters, their spouses and various offspring had flown to New York four days before the wedding. Dev had arranged a whirlwind trip to New Mexico so Sarah could meet most of them. She'd gotten to know them better while playing Big Apple tour guide. She'd also gained more insight into her complex, fascinating, handsome fiancé as more of his friends and associates arrived, some from his Air Force days, some from the years afterward.

Elise and Jean-Jacques Girault had flown in from Paris the afternoon before the wedding, just in time for dinner at the Avery. Sarah wasn't surprised that Elise and Alexis formed an instant bond, but the sight of Madame Girault snuggled against one of Dev's friends during predinner cocktails made her a tad nervous.

"Uh-oh," she murmured to Dev. "Do you think she's trying to seduce him?"

"Probably."

She searched the crowded restaurant, spotted Monsieur Girault happily chatting with Gina and relaxed.

Her wedding day dawned sunny and bright. Gina once again assumed charge. She'd accepted Dev's offer of payment without a qualm and arranged a full day at a spa for the women in the wedding party. She, Sarah, the duchess,

Maria, Dev's mother and sisters and the two little nieces who would serve as flower girls all got the works. The adults indulged in massages, facials, manicures, pedicures and hair treatments. The giggling little girls had their hair done and their fingernails and toenails painted pale lavender.

Sarah had enjoyed every moment of it, but especially treasured the half hour lying next to her sister on side-by-side massage tables while their facial masks cleaned and tightened their pores. According to the attendant, the masks were made of New Zealand Manuka honey, lavender oils and shea butter, with the additive of bee venom, which reputedly gave Kate Middleton her glowing complexion.

"At fifty-five thousand dollars per bottle, the venom better produce results," Gina muttered.

Only the fact that their masks contained a single drop of venom each, thus reducing the treatment price to just a little over a hundred dollars, kept Sarah from having a heart attack. Reaching across the space between the tables, she took Gina's hand.

"Thanks for doing all this."

"You're welcome." Her sister's mouth turned up in one of her irrepressible grins. "It's easy to throw great parties when you're spending someone else's money."

"You're good at it."

"Yes," she said smugly, "I am."

Her grin slowly faded and her fingers tightened around Sarah's.

"It's one of the few things I *am* good at. I'm going to get serious about it, Sarah. I intend to learn everything I can about the event-planning business before the baby's born. That way, I can support us both."

"What about Jack Mason? How does he figure in this plan?"

"He doesn't."

"It's his child, too, Gina."

"He'll have as much involvement in the baby's life as he wants," she said stubbornly, "but not mine. It's time—past time—I took responsibility for myself."

Sarah couldn't argue with that, but she had to suppress a few doubts as she squeezed Gina's hand. "You know I'll help you any way I can. Dev, too."

"I know, but I've got to do this on my own. And you're going to have your hands full figuring how to meld your life with his. Have you decided yet where you're going to live?"

"In L.A., if we can convince Grandmama to move out there with us. Maria, too."

"They'll hate leaving New York."

"I know."

Sarah's joy in her special day dimmed. She'd had several conversations with the duchess about a possible move. None of them had ended satisfactorily. As an alternative, Dev had offered to temporarily move his base of operations to New York and commute to L.A.

"I just can't bear to think of Grandmama alone in that huge apartment."

"Well…" Gina hesitated, indecision written all over her face. "I know I just made a big speech about standing on my own two feet, but I hate the thought of her being alone, too. I could…I could move in with her until I land a job. Or maybe until the baby's born. If she'll have me, that is, which isn't a sure thing after the scathing lecture she delivered when I got back from Switzerland."

"Oh, Gina, she'll have you! You know she will. She loves you." Sarah's eyes misted. "Almost as much as I do."

"Stop," Gina pleaded, her own tears spouting. "You can't walk down the aisle with your eyes all swollen and red. Dev'll strangle me."

As Dev took his place under the arch of gauzy netting lit by a thousand tiny, sparkling lights, strangling his soon-to-be sister-in-law was the furthest thing from his mind.

He was as surprised as Sarah and the duchess at the way
Gina had pulled everything together. So when the maid of
honor followed two giggling flower girls down the aisle,
he gave Gina a warm smile.

She returned it, but Dev could tell the sight of the unexpected, uninvited guest at the back of the room had shaken
her. Mason stood with his arms folded and an expression on
his face that suggested he didn't intend to return to Wash-
ington until he'd sorted some things out with the mother
of his child.

Then the music swelled and Dev's gaze locked on the
two women coming down the aisle arm in arm. Sarah
matched her step to that of the duchess, who'd stated bluntly
she did *not* require a cane to walk a few yards and give her
granddaughter away. Spine straight, chin high, eyes glowing with pride, she did just that.

"I hope you understand what a gift I'm giving you,
Devon."

"Yes, ma'am, I do."

With a small harrumph, the duchess kissed her granddaughter's cheek and took her seat. Then Sarah turned to
Dev, and he felt himself fall into her smile. She was so lu-
minous, so elegant. So gut-wrenchingly beautiful.

He still couldn't claim to know anything about haute
couture, but she'd told him she would be wearing a Dior
gown her grandmother had bought in Paris in the '60s.
The body-clinging sheath of cream-colored satin gave Dev
a whole new appreciation of what Sarah termed vintage.
The neckline fell in a soft drape and was caught at each
shoulder by a clasp adorned with soft, floating feathers.
The same downy feathers circled her tiny pillbox cap with
its short veil.

Taking the hand she held out to him, he tucked it close
to his heart and grinned down at her.

"Are you ready for phase three, Lady Sarah?"

"I am," she laughed. "So very, very ready."

Epilogue

I must admit I approve of Sarah's choice of husband. I should, since I decided Devon Hunter was right for her even before he blackmailed her into posing as his fiancée. How absurd that they still think I don't know about the deception.

Almost as absurd as Eugenia's stubborn refusal to marry the father of her child. I would respect her decision except, to borrow the Bard's immortal words, the lady doth protest too much. I do so dislike the sordid, steaming cauldron of modern politics, but I shall have to learn more about this Jack Mason. In the meantime, I'll have the inestimable joy of watching Eugenia mature into motherhood—hopefully!

From the diary of Charlotte,
Grand Duchess of Karlenburgh

* * * * *

FALLING FOR HER
FAKE FIANCÉ

SARAH M. ANDERSON

To Jennifer Porter, who took me under her wing before I was published and helped give me a platform to talk about heroes in cowboy hats. Thank you so much for supporting me! We'll always have dessert at Junior's together!

One

"*Mis*-ter Logan," the old-fashioned intercom rasped on Ethan's desk.

He scowled at the thing and at the way his current secretary insisted on hissing his name. "Yes, Delores?" He'd never been in an office that required an intercom. It felt as if he'd walked into the 1970s.

Of course, that was probably how old the intercom was. After all, Ethan was sitting in the headquarters of the Beaumont Brewery. This room—complete with hand-carved everything—probably hadn't been redecorated since, well...

A very long time ago. The Beaumont Brewery was 160 years old, after all.

"*Mis*-ter Logan," Delores rasped again, her dislike for him palatable. "We're going to have to stop production on the Mountain Cold and Mountain Cold Light lines."

"What? Why?" Logan demanded. The last thing he could afford was another shutdown.

Ethan had been running this company for almost three months now. His firm, Corporate Restructuring Services, had beat out some heavy hitters for the right to handle the reorganization of the Beaumont Brewery, and Ethan had to make this count. If he—and, by extension, CRS—could turn this aging, antique company into a modern-day business, their reputation in the business world would be cemented.

Ethan had expected some resistance. It was only natural. He'd restructured thirteen companies before taking the helm of Beaumont Brewery. Each company had emerged from the reorganization process leaner, meaner and more competitive in a global economy. Everyone won when that happened.

Yes, thirteen success stories.

Yet nothing had prepared him for the Beaumont Brewery.

"There's a flu going around," Delores said. "Sixty-five workers are home sick, the poor dears."

A flu. Wasn't that just a laugh and a half? Last week, it'd been a cold that had knocked out forty-seven employees. And the week before, after a mass food poisoning, fifty-four people hadn't been able to make it in.

Ethan was no idiot. He'd cut the employees a little slack the first two times, trying to earn their trust. But now it was time to lay down the law.

"Fire every single person who called in sick today."

There was a satisfying pause on the other end of the intercom, and, for a moment, Ethan felt a surge of victory.

The victorious surge was short-lived, however.

"*Mis*-ter Logan," Delores began. "Regretfully, it seems that the HR personnel in charge of processing terminations are out sick today."

"Of course they are," he snapped. He fought the urge to throw the intercom across the room, but that was an impulsive, juvenile thing to do, and Ethan was not impulsive or juvenile. Not anymore.

So, as unsatisfying as it was, he merely shut off the intercom and glared at his office door.

He needed a better plan.

He always had a plan when he went into a business.

His method was proven. He could turn a flailing business around in as little as six months.

But this? The Beaumont freaking Brewery?

That was the problem, he decided. Everyone—the press, the public, their customers and especially the employees—still thought of this as the Beaumont Brewery. Sure, the business had been under Beaumont management for a good century and a half. That was the reason All-Bev, the conglomerate that had hired CRS to handle this reorganization, had chosen to keep the Beaumont name a part of the Brewery—the name-recognition value was through the roof.

But it wasn't the Beaumont family's brewery anymore. They had been forced out months ago. And the sooner the employees realized that, the better.

He looked around the office. It was beautiful, heavy with history and power.

He'd heard that the conference table had been custom-made. It was so big and heavy that it'd been built in the actual office—they might have to take a wall out to remove it. Tucked in the far corner by a large coffee table was a grouping of two leather club chairs and a matching leather love seat. The coffee table was supposedly made of one of the original wagon wheels that Phillipe Beaumont had used when he'd crossed the Great Plains with a team of Percheron draft horses back in the 1880s.

The only signs of the current decade were the flat-screen television that hung over the sitting area and the electronics on the desk, which had been made to match the conference table.

The entire room screamed Beaumont so loudly he was practically deafened by it.

He flipped on the hated intercom again. "Delores."

"Yes, *Mis*—"

He cut her off before she could mangle his name again.

"I want to redo the office. I want all this stuff gone. The curtains, the woodwork—and the conference table. All of it." Some of these pieces—hand carved and well cared for, like the bar—would probably fetch a pretty penny. "Sell it off."

There was another satisfying pause.

"Yes, sir." For a moment, he thought she sounded sub-dued—cowed. As if she couldn't believe he would really dismantle the heart of the Beaumont Brewery. But then she added, "I know just the appraiser to call," in a tone that sounded...smug?

He ignored her and went back to his computer. Two lines shut down was not acceptable. If either line didn't pull double shifts tomorrow, he wouldn't wait for HR to terminate employees. He'd do it himself.

After all, he was the boss here. What he said went.

And that included the furniture.

Frances Beaumont slammed her bedroom door behind her and flopped down on her bed. Another rejection—she couldn't fall much lower.

She was tired of this. She'd been forced to move back into the Beaumont mansion after her last project had failed so spectacularly that she'd had to give up her luxury condo in downtown Denver. She'd even been forced to sell most of her designer wardrobe.

The idea—digital art ownership and crowdsourcing art patronage online by having buyers buy stock in digital art—had been fundamentally sound. Art might be time-less, but art production and collection had to evolve. She'd sunk a considerable portion of her fortune into Art Digi-tale, as well as every single penny she'd gotten from the sale of the Beaumont Brewery.

What an epic, crushing mistake. After months of delays and false starts—and huge bills—Art Digitale had been live for three weeks before the funds ran out. Not a single transaction had taken place on the website. In her gilded life, she'd never experienced such complete failure. How could she? She was a Beaumont.

Her business failure was bad enough. But worse? She couldn't get a job. It was as if being a Beaumont suddenly counted for nothing. Her first employer, the owner of Galerie Solaria, hadn't exactly jumped at the chance to have Frances come back, even though Frances knew how to flatter the wealthy, art-focused patrons and massage the delicate egos of artists. She knew how to sell art—didn't that count for something?

Plus, she was a *Beaumont*. A few years ago, people would have jumped at the chance to be associated with one of the founding families of Denver. Frances had been an in-demand woman.

"Where did I go wrong?" she asked her ceiling.

Unsurprisingly, it didn't have an answer.

She'd just turned thirty. She was broke and had moved back in with her family—her brother Chadwick and his family, plus assorted Beaumonts from her father's other marriages.

She shuddered in horror.

When the family still owned the Brewery, the Beaumont name had meant something. *Frances* had meant something. But ever since that part of her life had been sold, she'd been…adrift.

If only there was some way to go back, to put the Brewery under the family's control again.

Yes, she thought bitterly, that was definitely an option. Her older brothers Chadwick and Matthew had walked away and started their own brewery, Percheron Drafts. Phillip, her favorite older brother, the one who had gotten her into parties and helped her build her reputation as the Cool Girl of Denver high society, had ensconced himself out on the Beaumont Farm and gotten sober. No more parties with him. And her twin brother, Byron, was starting a new restaurant.

Everyone else was moving forward, pairing off. And Frances was stuck back in her childhood room, alone.

Not that she believed a man would solve any of her problems. She'd grown up watching her father burn through marriage after unhappy marriage. No, she knew love didn't exist. Or if it did, it wasn't in the cards for her.

She was on her own here.

She opened up a message from her friend Becky and stared at the picture of a shuttered storefront. She and Becky had worked together at Galerie Solaria. Becky had no famous last name and no social connections, but she knew art and had a snarky sense of humor that cut through the bull. More to the point, Becky treated Frances like she was a real person, not just a special Beaumont snowflake. They had been friends ever since.

Becky had a proposition. She wanted to open a new gallery, one that would merge the new-media art forms with the standard classics that wealthy patrons preferred. It wasn't as avant-garde as Frances's digital art business had been, but it was a good bridge between the two worlds.

The only problem was Frances did not have the money to invest. She wished to God she did. She could co-own and comanage the gallery. It wouldn't bring in big bucks, but it could get her out of the mansion. It could get her back to being a somebody. And not just any somebody. She could go back to being Frances Beaumont—popular, respected, *envied*.

She dropped her phone onto the bed in defeat. *Right*. Another fortune was just going to fall into her lap and she'd be in demand. *Sure*. And she would also sprout wings.

True despair was sinking in when her phone rang. She

answered it without even looking at the screen. "Hello?" she said morosely.

"Frances? Frannie," the woman said. "I know you may not remember me—I'm Delores Hahn. I used to work in accounting at—"

The name rang a bell, an older woman who wore her hair in a tight bun. "Oh! Delores! Yes, you were at the Brewery. How are you?"

The only people besides her siblings who called her Frannie were the longtime employees of the Beaumont Brewery. They were her second family—or at least, they had been.

"We've been better," Delores said. "Listen, I have a proposal for you. I know you've got those fancy art degrees."

In the safety of her room, Frances blushed. After today's rejections, she didn't feel particularly fancy. "What kind of proposal?" Maybe her luck was about to change. Maybe this proposal would come with a paycheck.

"Well," Delores went on in a whisper, "the new CEO that AllBev brought in?"

Frances scowled. "What about him? Failing miserably, I hope."

"Sadly," Delores said in a not-sad-at-all voice, "there's been an epidemic of Brew Flu going around. We had to halt production on two lines today."

Frances couldn't hold back the laugh that burst forth from her. "Oh, that's fabulous."

"It was," Delores agreed. "But it made Logan—that's the new CEO—so mad that he decided to rip out your father's office."

Frances would have laughed again, except for one little detail. "He's going to destroy Daddy's office? He wouldn't dare!"

"He told me to sell it off. All of it—the table, the bar,

everything. I think he'd even perform an exorcism, if he thought it'd help," she added.

Her father's office. Technically, it had most recently been Chadwick's office. But Frances had never stopped thinking of her father and that office together. "So what's your proposal?"

"Well," Delores said, her voice dropping past whisper and straight into conspirator. "I thought you could come do the appraisals. Who knows—you might be able to line up buyers for some of it."

"And…" Frances swallowed. The following was a crass question, but desperate times and all that. "And would this Logan fellow pay for the appraisal? If I sold the furniture myself—" say, to a certain sentimental older brother who'd been the CEO for almost ten years "—would I get a commission?"

"I don't see why not."

Frances tried to see the downside of this situation, but nothing popped up. Delores was right—if anyone had the connections to sell off her family's furniture, it'd be Frances.

Plus, if she could get a foothold back in the Brewery, she might be able to help all those poor, flu-stricken workers. She wasn't so naive to think that she could get a conglomerate like AllBev to sell the company back to the family, but…

She might be able to make this Logan's life a little more difficult. She might be able to exact a little revenge. After all—the sale of the Brewery had been when her luck had turned sour. And if she could get paid to do all of that?

"Let's say Friday, shall we?" That was only two days away, but that would give her plenty of time to plan and execute her trap. "I'll bring the donuts."

Delores actually giggled. "I was hoping you'd say that."

Oh, yes. This was going to be great.

* * *

"*Mis*-ter Logan, the appraiser is here."

Ethan set down the head count rolls he'd been studying. Next week, he was reducing the workforce by 15 percent. People with one or more "illness absences" were going to be the first to find themselves out on the sidewalk with nothing more than a box of their possessions.

"Good. Send him in."

But no nerdy-looking art geek walked into the office. Ethan waited and then switched the intercom back on. Before he could ask Delores the question, though, he heard a lot of people talking—and laughing?

It sounded as though someone was having a party in the reception area.

What the hell?

He strode across the room and threw open his office door. There was, point of fact, a party going on outside. Workers he'd only caught glimpses of before were all crowded around Delores's desk, donuts in their hands and sappy smiles on their faces.

"What's going on out here?" he thundered. "This is a business, people, not a—"

Then the crowd parted, and he saw her.

God, how had he missed her? A woman with a stunning mane of flame-red hair sat on the edge of Delores's desk. Her body was covered by an emerald-green gown that clung to every curve like a lover's hands. His fingers itched to trace the line of her bare shoulders.

She was not an employee. That much was clear.

She was, however, holding a box of donuts.

The good-natured hum he'd heard on the intercom died away. The smiles disappeared, and people edged away from him.

"What is this?" he demanded. The color drained out

of several employees' faces, but his tone didn't appear to have the slightest impact on the woman in the green gown.

His eyes were drawn to her back, to the way her ass looked sitting on the edge of the desk. Slowly—so slowly it almost hurt him—she turned and looked at him over her shoulder.

He might have intimidated the workers. He clearly had not intimidated her.

She batted her eyelashes as a cryptic smile danced across her deep red lips. "Why, it's Donut Friday."

Ethan glared at her. "What?"

She pivoted, bringing more of her profile into view. *Dear God, that dress—that body.* The strapless dress came to a deep V over her chest, doing everything in its power to highlight the pale, creamy skin of her décolletage.

He shouldn't stare. He *wasn't* staring. Really.

Her posture shifted. It was like watching a dancer arrange herself before launching into a series of gravity-defying pirouettes. "You must be new here," the woman said in a pitying tone. "It's Friday. That's the day I bring donuts."

Individually, he understood each word and every implication of her tone and movement. But together? "Donut Friday?" He'd been here for months, and this was the first time he'd heard anything about donuts.

"Yes," she said. She held out the box. "I bring everyone a donut. Would you like the last one? I'm afraid all I have left is a plain."

"And who are you, if I may ask?"

"Oh, you may." She lowered her chin and looked up at him through her lashes. She was simply the most beautiful woman he'd ever seen, which was more than enough to turn his head. But the fact that she was playing him for the fool—and they both knew it?

There were snickers from the far-too-large audience as

she held out her hand for him—not to shake, no. She held it out as though she expected him to kiss it, as if she were the queen or something.

"I'm Frances Beaumont. I'm here to appraise the antiques."

Two

Oh, this *was* fun.

"Donut?" she asked again, holding out the box. She kept as much innocence as she could physically manage on her face.

"You're the *appraiser*?"

She let the donut box hang in the space between them a few more moments before she slowly lowered the box back to her lap.

She'd been bringing donuts in on Fridays since—well, since as long as she could remember. It'd been her favorite part of the week, mostly because it was the only time she ever got to be with her father, just the two of them. For a few glorious hours every Friday morning, she was Daddy's Little Girl. No older brothers taking up all his time. No new wives or babies demanding his attention. Just Hardwick Beaumont and his little girl, Frannie.

And what was more, she got to visit all the grown-ups—including many of the same employees who were watching this exchange between her and Logan with rapt fascination—and hear how nice she was, how pretty she looked in that dress, what a sweetheart she was. The people who'd been working for the Brewery for the past thirty years had made her feel special and loved. They'd been her second family. Even after Hardwick had died and regular Donut

Fridays had faded away, she'd still taken the time to stop in at least once a month. Donuts—hand-delivered with a smile and a compliment—made the world a better place.

If she could repay her family's loyal employees by humiliating a tyrant of an outsider, then that was the very least she could do.

Logan's mouth opened and closed before he ordered, "Get back to work."

No one moved.

She turned back to the crowd to hide her victorious smile. They weren't listening to him. They were waiting on her.

"Well," she said graciously, unable to keep the wicked glint out of her eye. Just so long as Logan didn't see it. "It has been simply wonderful to see everyone again. I know I've missed you—we all have in the Beaumont family. I do hope that I can come back for another Donut Friday again soon?"

Behind her, Logan made a choking noise.

But in front of her, the employees nodded and grinned. A few of them winked in silent support.

"Have a wonderful day, everyone," she cooed as she waved.

The crowd began to break up. A few people dared to brave what was no doubt Logan's murderous glare to come close enough to murmur their thanks or ask that she pass along their greetings to Chadwick or Matthew. She smiled and beamed and patted shoulders and promised that she'd tell her brothers exactly what everyone had said, word for word.

The whole time she felt Logan's rage rolling off him in waves, buffeting against her back. He was no doubt trying to kill her with looks alone. It wouldn't work. She had the upper hand here, and they both knew it.

Finally, there was only one employee left. "Delores,"

Frances said in her nicest voice, "if Mr. Logan doesn't want his donut—" She pivoted and held the box out to him again.

Oh, yes—she had the advantage here. He could go right on trying to glare her to death, but it wouldn't change the fact that the entire administrative staff of the Brewery had ignored his direct order and listened to hers. That feeling of power—of importance—coursed through her body. God, it felt *good*.

"I do not," he snarled.

"Would you be a dear and take care of this for me?" Frances finished, handing the box to Delores.

"Of course, Ms. Frances." Delores gave Frances a look that was at least as good as—if not better than—an actual hug, then shuffled off in the direction of the break room, leaving Frances alone with one deeply pissed-off CEO. She crossed her legs at the ankle and leaned toward him, but she didn't say anything else. The ball was firmly in his court now. The only question was did he know how to play the game?

The moment stretched. Frances took advantage of the silence to appraise her prey. This Logan fellow was *quite* an attractive specimen. He was maybe only a few inches taller than Frances, but he had the kind of rock-solid build that suggested he'd once been a defensive linebacker—and an effective one at that. His suit—a very good suit, with conservative lines—had been tailored to accommodate his wide shoulders. Given the girth of his neck, she'd put money on his shirts being made-to-order. Bespoke shirts and suits were not cheap.

He had a square jaw—all the squarer right now, given how he was grinding his teeth—and light brown hair that was close cut. He was probably incredibly good-looking when he wasn't scowling.

He was attempting to regain his composure, she realized. Couldn't have that.

Back when she'd been a little girl, she'd sat on this very desk, kicking her little legs as she held the donut box for everyone. Back then, it'd been cute to hop down off the desk when all the donuts were gone and twirl in her pretty dress.

But what was cute at five didn't cut it at thirty. No hopping. Still, she had to get off this desk.

So she extended her left leg—which conveniently was the side where one of the few designer dresses she'd hung on to was slit up to her thigh—and slowly shifted her weight onto it.

Logan's gaze cut to her bare leg as the fabric fell away.

She leaned forward as she brought her other foot down. The slit in the dress closed back over her leg, but Logan's eyes went right where she expected them to—her generous cleavage.

In no great hurry, she stood, her shoulders back and her chin up. "Shall we?" she asked in a regal tone. "My cloak," she added, motioning with her chin toward where she'd removed the matching cape that went with this dress.

Without waiting for an answer from him, she strode into his office as if she owned it. Which she once had, sort of.

The room looked exactly as she remembered it. Frances sighed in relief—it was all still here. She used to color on the wagon wheel table while she waited for the rest of the workers to get in so she could hand out the donuts. She'd played dolls on the big conference table. And her father's desk…

The only time her daddy hugged her was in this room. Hardwick Beaumont had not been a hard-driven, ruthless executive in those small moments with her. He'd told her things he'd never told anyone else, like how his father, Frances's grandfather John, had let Hardwick pick out the color of the drapes and the rug. How John had let Hardwick try a new beer fresh off the line, and then made him tell the older man why it was good and what the brewers should do better.

"This office," her daddy used to say, "made me who I am." And then he'd give her a brief, rare hug and say, "And it'll make you who you are, too, my girl."

Ridiculous how the thought of a simple hug from her father could make her all misty-eyed.

She couldn't bear the thought of all this history—all *her* memories—being sold off to the highest bidder. Even if that would result in a tidy commission for her.

If she couldn't stop the sale, the best she could do was convince Chadwick to buy as much of his old office as possible. Her brother had fought to keep this company in the family. He'd understand that some things just couldn't be sold away.

But that wasn't plan A.

She tucked her tenderness away. In matters such as this one, tenderness was a liability, and God knew she couldn't afford any more of those.

So she stopped in the middle of the office and waited for Logan to catch up. She did not fold herself gracefully into one of the guest chairs in front of the desk, nor did she arrange herself seductively on the available love seat. She didn't even think of sprawling herself out on the conference table.

She stood in the middle of the room as though she was ruler of all she saw. And no one—not even a temporary CEO built like a linebacker—could convince her otherwise.

She was surprised when he did not slam the door shut. Instead, she heard the gentle whisper of it clicking closed. *Head up, shoulders back*, she reminded herself as she stood, waiting for him to make the next move. She would show him no mercy. She expected nothing but the same returned in kind.

She saw him move toward the conference table, where he draped her cape over the nearest chair. She felt his eyes on her. No doubt he was admiring her body even as he debated wringing her neck.

Men were so easy to confuse.

He was the kind of man, she decided, who would need to reassert his control over the situation. Now that the audience had dispersed, he would feel it a moral imperative to put her back in her place.

She could not let him get comfortable. It was just that simple.

Ah, she'd guessed right. He made a wide circle around her, not bothering to hide how he was checking out her best dress as he headed for the desk. Frances held her pose until he was almost seated. Then she reached into her small handbag—emerald-green silk, made to match the dress, of course—and pulled out a small mirror and lipstick. Ignoring Logan entirely, she fixed her lips, making sure to exaggerate her pouts.

Was she hearing things or had a nearly imperceptible groan come from the area behind the desk?

This was almost too easy, really.

She put the lipstick and mirror away and pulled out her phone. Logan opened his mouth to say something, but she interrupted him by taking a picture of the desk. And of him.

He snapped his mouth shut. "Frances *Beaumont*, huh?"

"The one and only," she purred, taking a close-up of the carved details on the corner of the desk. And if she had to bend over to do so—well, she couldn't help it if this dress was exceptionally low-cut.

"I suppose," Logan said in a strangled-sounding voice, "that there's no such thing as a coincidence?"

"I certainly don't believe in them." She shifted her angle and took another shot. "Do you?"

"Not anymore." Instead of sounding flummoxed or even angry, she detected a hint of humor in his voice. "I suppose you know your way around, then?"

"I do," she cheerfully agreed. Then she paused, as if she'd just remembered that she'd forgotten her manners. "I'm so sorry—I don't believe I caught your name?"

My, *that* was a look. But if he thought he could intimidate her, he had no idea who he was dealing with. "My apologies." He stood and held out his hand. "I'm Ethan Logan. I'm the CEO of the Beaumont Brewery."

She let his hand hang for a beat before she wrapped her fingers around his. He had hands that matched his shoulders—thick and strong. This Ethan Logan certainly didn't look a thing like the bean-counting lackey she'd pictured.

"Ethan," she said, dropping her gaze and looking up at him through her lashes.

His hand was warm as his fingers curled around her smaller hand. Strong, oh yes—he could easily break her hand. But he didn't. All the raw power he projected was clearly—and safely—locked down.

Instead, he turned her hand over and kissed the back of it. The very thing she'd implied he should do earlier, when they'd had an audience. It'd seemed like a safe move then, an action she knew he'd never take her up on.

But here? In the enclosed space of the office, with no one to witness his chivalrous gesture? She couldn't tell if the kiss was a threat or a seduction. Or both.

Then he raised his gaze and looked her in the eyes. Suddenly, the room was much warmer, the air much thinner. Frances had to use every ounce of her self-control not to take huge gulping breaths just to get some oxygen into her body. Oh, but he had nice eyes, warm and determined and completely focused on her.

She might have underestimated him.

Not that he needed to know that. She allowed herself an

innocent blush, which took some work. She hadn't been innocent for a long time. "A pleasure," she murmured, wondering how long he planned to kiss her hand.

"It's all mine," he assured her, straightening up and taking a step back. She noted with interest that he didn't sit back down. "So you're the appraiser Delores hired?"

"I hope you won't be too hard on her," she simpered, taking this moment to put another few steps between his body and hers.

"And why shouldn't I be? Are you even qualified to do this? Or did she just bring you in to needle me?"

He said it in far too casual a tone. *Damn.* His equilibrium was almost restored. She couldn't have that.

And what's more, she couldn't let him impinge on her ability to do this job.

Then she realized that his lips—which had, to this point, only been compressed into a thin line of anger or dropped open in shock—were curving into a far-too-cocky grin. He'd scored a hit on her, and he knew it.

She quickly schooled her face into the appropriate demureness, using the excuse of taking more pictures to do so.

"I am, in fact, highly qualified to appraise the contents of this office. I have a bachelor's degree in art history and a master's of fine art. I was the manager at Galerie Solaria for several years. I have extensive connections with the local arts scene."

She stated her qualifications in a light, matter-of-fact tone designed to put him at ease. Which, given the little donut stunt she'd pulled, would probably actually make him more nervous—if he had his wits about him. "And if anyone would know the true value of these objects," she added, straightening to give him her very best smile, "it'd be a Beaumont—don't you think? After all, this was ours for *so* long."

He didn't fall for the smile. Instead, he eyed her suspiciously, just as she'd suspected he would. She would have to reconsider her opinion of him. Now that the shock of her appearance was wearing off, he seemed more and more up to the task of playing this game.

Even though it shouldn't, the thought thrilled her. Ethan Logan would be a formidable opponent. This might even be fun. She could play the game with Ethan—a game she would win, without a doubt—and in the process, she could protect her family legacy and help out Delores and all the rest of the employees.

"How about you?" she asked in an offhand manner.

"What about me?" he asked.

"Are you qualified to run a company? This company?" She couldn't help it. The words came out a little sharper than she had wanted them to. But she followed up the questions with a fluttering of her eyelashes and another demure smile.

Not that they worked. "I am, in fact," he said in a mocking tone as he parroted her words, "highly qualified to run this company. I am a co-owner of my firm, Corporate Restructuring Services. I have restructured thirteen previous companies, raising stock prices and increasing productivity and efficiency. I have a bachelor's degree in economics and a master's of business administration, and I *will* turn this company around."

He said the last part with all the conviction of a man who truly believed himself to be on the right side of history.

"I'm quite sure you will." Of course she agreed with him. He was expecting her to argue. "Why, once the employees all get over that nasty flu that's been going around…" She lifted a shoulder, as if to say it was only a matter of time. "You'll have things completely under control within days." Then, just to pour a little lemon juice in the wound, she leaned forward. His gaze held—he didn't even glance at her cleavage. *Damn. Time to up the ante.*

She let her eyes drift over those massive shoulders and the broad chest. He was quite unlike the thin, pale men who populated the art world circles she moved within. She could still feel his lips on the back of her hand.

Oh, yes, she could play this game. For a short while, she could feel like Frances Beaumont again—powerful, beautiful, holding sway over everyone in her orbit. She could use Ethan Logan to get back what she'd lost in the past six months and—if she was very lucky—she might even be able to inflict some damage on AllBev through the Brewery. Corporate espionage and all that.

So she added in a confidential voice, "I have faith in your abilities."

"Do you?"

She looked him up and down again and smiled. A real smile this time, not one couched to elicit a specific response. "Oh, yes," she said, turning away from him. "I do."

Three

He needed her.

That crystal clear revelation was quickly followed by a second—and far more depressing one—Frances Beaumont would destroy him if he gave her half the chance.

As he watched Frances move around his office, taking pictures of the furniture and antiques and making completely harmless small talk about potential buyers, he knew he would have to risk the latter to get the former.

The way all those workers had been eating out of her hand—well, out of her donut box? The way not a single damn one of them had gotten back to work when he'd ordered them to—but they'd all jumped when Frances Beaumont had smiled at them?

It hurt to admit—even to himself—that the workers here would not listen to him.

But they would listen to her.

She was one of them—a Beaumont. They obviously adored her—even Delores, the old battle-ax, had bowed and scraped to this stunningly beautiful woman.

"If you wouldn't mind," she said in that delicate voice that he was completely convinced was a front. She kicked out of her shoes and lined one of the conference chairs up beneath a window. She held out her hand for him. "I'd like to get a better shot of the friezes over the windows."

"Of course," he said in his most diplomatic voice.

This woman—this stunning woman who's fingertips were light and warm against his hand as he helped her balance onto the chair, leaving her ass directly at eye level—had already ripped him to shreds several times over.

She was gorgeous. She was clearly intelligent. And she was obviously out to undermine him. That's what the donuts had been about. Announcing to the world in general and him in particular that this was still the Beaumont Brewery in every sense of the word.

"Thank you," she murmured, placing her hand on his shoulder to balance herself as she stepped down.

She didn't stick the landing, although he couldn't say if that was accidental or on purpose.

Before he could stop himself, his arm went around her waist to steady her.

Which was a mistake because electricity arced between them. She looked up at him through those lashes—he'd lost count of how many times she'd done that so far—but this time it hit him differently.

After almost a month of dealing with passive-aggressive employees terrified of being downsized he suddenly felt like a very different man altogether.

"Thank you," she said again, in a quiet whisper that somehow felt more honest, less calculated than almost every other word she'd uttered so far. Imperceptibly, she leaned into him. He could feel the heat of her breasts through his suit.

As soon as he was sure she wouldn't fall over, he stepped well clear of her. He needed her—but he could not need her like that. Not now, not ever. Because she *would* destroy him. He had no doubt about that. None.

Still…an idea was taking shape in his mind.

Maybe he'd been going about this all wrong. Instead of trying to strip the Beaumont out of the Beaumont Brewery, maybe what he needed to do was bring in a Beaumont. The moment the idea occurred to him, he latched on to it with both hands.

Yes. What he really needed was to have a Beaumont on board with the management changes he was implementing. If the workers realized their old bosses were signing off on the reorganization, there wouldn't be any more mass food poisonings or flu or whatever they'd planned for next week. Sure, there'd still be grumbling and personnel turnover, but if he had a Beaumont by his side...

"So!" Frances said brightly, just as she leaned over to adjust the strap on her shoe.

Ethan had to slam his eyes shut so he wouldn't be caught staring at her barely contained cleavage. If he was going to pull this off, he had to keep his wits about him and his pants zipped.

"How would you like to proceed? Ethan?" It was only when she said his name that he figured it was safe to look.

As safe as it got, anyway. More than any other woman he'd seen in person, Frances looked as if she'd walked right off a movie screen and into his office. Her hair fell in soft waves over her shoulders and her eyes were a light blue that took on a greenish tone that matched her dress. She was the stuff of fantasies, all luscious curves and soft skin.

"I want to hire you."

Direct was better. If he tried to dance around the subject, she'd spin him in circles.

It worked, too—at least for a second. Her eyes widened in surprise, but she quickly got herself back under control. She laughed lightly, like a chime tinkling in the wind. "Mr. Logan," she said, beaming a high-wattage smile at him. "You already have hired me. The furniture?" she reminded him, looking around the room. "My family's legacy?"

"That's not what I mean," he replied. "I want you to come work for me. Here. At the Brewery. As..." His mind spun for something that would be appropriate to a woman like her. "As executive vice president of human resources. In charge of employee relations." *There.* That sounded fancy without actually meaning anything.

A hint of confusion wrinkled her forehead. "You want me to be a…manager?" She said the word as if it left a bad taste in her mouth. "Out of the question." But she favored him with that smile he'd decided she wielded like other people might wield a knife in a street fight. "I'm so sorry, but I couldn't possibly work for the Beaumont Brewery if it wasn't owned by an actual Beaumont." With crisp efficiency, she snatched up her cape and elegantly swirled it around her shoulders, hiding her body from his eyes.

Not that he was looking at it. He felt the corners of his mouth curve up in a smile. He had her off balance for possibly the first time since she'd walked onto the Brewery property.

"I'll work up an appraisal sheet and a list of potential buyers for some of the more sentimental pieces," she announced, not even bothering to look over her shoulder as she strode toward the door.

Before he realized what he was doing, he ran after her. "Wait," he said, getting to the door just as she put her hand on the knob. He pushed the door shut.

And then realized he basically had her trapped between the door and his body.

She knew it, too. Moving with that dancer's grace, she pivoted and leaned back, her breasts thrust toward him and her smile coy. "Did you need something else?"

"Won't you at least consider it?"

"About the job offer?" She grinned. It was too victorious to be pretty. "I rather think not."

What else would she be thinking about? His blood began to pound in his veins. He couldn't admit defeat, couldn't admit that a beautiful woman had spun him around until he hadn't realized he'd lost until it was too late. He had to come up with something to at least make her keep her options open. He could not run this company without her.

"Have dinner with me, then."

If this request surprised her, it didn't show. Instead, she tilted her head to one side, sending waves of beautiful red hair cascading over her cloaked shoulders. Then she moved. A hand emerged from the folds of her cloak and she touched him. She touched the line of his jaw with the tips of her fingers and then slid them down to where his white shirt was visible beneath the V of his suit jacket.

Heat poured off her as she flattened her palm against him. He desperately wanted to close his eyes and focus on the way her touch made his body jump to full attention. He wanted to lower his head and taste her ruby-red lips. He wanted to pull her body into his and feel her skin against his.

He did none of those things.

Instead, he took it like a man. Or he tried to. But when she said, in that soft whisper of hers, "And why would I agree to *that*?" it nearly broke his resolve.

"I'd like the chance to change your mind. About the job offer." Which was not strictly true, not any longer. Not when her palm moved in the smallest of circles over his heart.

"Is that all?" she breathed. He could feel the heat from her hand burning his skin. "There's nothing else you want from me?"

"I just want what's best for the company." Damn it all; his voice had gotten deeper on him. But he couldn't help it, not with the way she was looking up at him. "Don't you?"

Something in her face changed. It wasn't resignation, not really—and it wasn't surrender.

It was engagement. It was a *yes*.

She lightly pushed on his chest. He straightened and

dropped his arm away from the door. "Dinner. For the company," she agreed. He couldn't interpret that statement, not when his ears were ringing with desire. "Where are you staying?"

"I have a suite at the Hotel Monaco."

"Shall we say seven o'clock tomorrow night? In the lobby?"

"It would be an honor."

She arched an eyebrow at him, and then, with a swirling turn, she was gone, striding into the reception area and pausing only to thank Delores again for all her help.

He had to find a way to get Frances on his side.

It had nothing to do with the way he could still feel her touch burned into his skin.

Four

In the end, it'd come down to one of two dresses. Frances only had four left after the liquidation of her closet anyway. The green one was clearly out—it would reek of desperation to wear the same dress twice, even if Ethan's eyes had bugged out of his head when he'd looked at her in it.

She also had her bridesmaid's dress from her brother Phillip's wedding, a sleek gray one with rhinestone accents. But that felt too formal for dinner, even if it did look good on her.

Which meant she had to choose between the red velvet and the little black dress for her negotiation masquerading as dinner with Ethan Logan.

The red dress would render him completely speechless; that she knew. She'd always had a fondness for it—it transformed her into a proper lady instead of what she often felt like, the black sheep of the family.

But there was nothing subtle about the red dress. And besides, if the evening went well, she might need a higher-powered dress for later.

The little black dress was really the only choice. It was a halter-top style and completely backless. The skirt twirled out, but there was no missing the cleavage. The dark color made it appear more subdued at first, which would work to her advantage. If she paired it with her cropped bolero jacket, she could project an air of seriousness, and then, when she needed to befuddle Ethan, she could slip off the jacket. *Perfect.*

She made it downtown almost twenty minutes late, which meant she was right on schedule. Ethan Logan could sit and cool his heels for a bit. The more she kept him off balance, the better her position would be.

Which did beg the question—what was her position? She'd only agreed to dinner because he'd said he wanted what was best for the company. And the way he'd said it...

Well, she also wanted what was best for the company. But for her, that word was a big umbrella, under which the employees were just as important as the bottom line.

And after all, if something continued to be named the Beaumont Brewery, shouldn't it still be connected to the Beaumonts?

So dinner was strictly about those two objectives. She would see what she could get Ethan to reveal about the long-term plan for the Brewery. And if there was something in those plans that could help her get her world back in order, so much the better.

Yes, that was it. Dinner had nothing to do with how she'd felt Ethan's chest muscles twitch under her touch, nothing to do with the simmering heat that had rolled off him. And it had even less to do with the way he'd looked down at her, like a man who'd been adrift at sea for too long and had finally spotted land.

She was Frances Beaumont. She could not be landed. For years, she'd had men look at her as if they were starving and she was a banquet. It was nothing new. Just a testament to her name and genetics. Ethan Logan would be no different. She would take what she needed from him—that feeling that she was still someone who mattered, someone who wielded power—and leave the rest.

Which did not explain why, for the first time in what felt

like years, Frances had butterflies in her stomach as she strode into the lobby of the Hotel Monaco. Was she nervous? It wasn't possible. She didn't get nervous, especially not about something like this. She'd spent her entire life navigating the shark-infested waters of wealthy and powerful men. Ethan was just another shark. And he wasn't even a great white. He was barely a dogfish.

"Good evening, Ms. Beaumont."

"Harold," she said to the doorman with a warm smile and a big tip.

"Ms. Beaumont! How wonderful to see you again!" At this rather loud pronouncement, several other guests in the immediate vicinity paused to gape at her.

Frances ignored the masses. "Thank you, Heidi," she said to the clerk at the front desk with another warm smile. The hotel had been catering to the Beaumont family for years, and Frances liked to keep the staff on her side.

"And what can we do for you tonight?" Heidi asked.

"I'm meeting someone for dinner." She scanned the crowd, but she didn't see Ethan. He wouldn't be easy to miss—a man as massively built as he was? All those muscles would stand out.

Then she saw him. And did a double take. Yes, those shoulders, that neck, were everything she remembered them being. The clothing, however? Unlike the conservative gray suit and dull tie he'd had on in the office, he was wearing a pair of artfully distressed jeans, a white button-up shirt without a tie and…a purple sports coat? A deep purple—plum, maybe. She would not have figured he was the kind of man who would stand outside a sartorial box with any great flair—or success.

When he saw her, he pushed himself off the column he was leaning against. "Frances, hello." Which was a perfectly normal thing to say. But he said it as if he couldn't quite believe his eyes—or his luck—as she strode toward him.

He should feel lucky. "Ethan." When he held out his hand, she took it and used it to pull herself up so she could kiss him on the cheek.

His free hand rested against her side, steadying her. "You look amazing," he murmured, his mouth close to her ear.

Warmth that bordered on heat started where his breath kissed her skin and flamed out over her body. That was what made her nervous. Not the man, not the musculature—not even his position as CEO of her family's company.

It was the way her body reacted to him. The way a touch, a look—a whispered word—could set her fluttering.

Ridiculous. She was not flattered by his attentions. This was not a date. This was corporate espionage in a great dress. This was her using what few resources she had left at her disposal to get her life back on track. This was about her disarming Ethan Logan, not the other way around.

So she clamped down on the shiver that threatened to race across her skin as she lowered herself away from him. "That's a great color on you. Very…" She let the word hang in the air for a beat too long. "Bold," she finished. "Not just any man could pull off that look."

He raised his eyebrows. She realized he was trying not to laugh at her. "Says the woman who showed up in an emerald evening gown to hand out donuts. Have no fear, I'm comfortable in my masculinity. Shall we? I made reservations at the restaurant." He held out his arm for her.

"We shall." She lightly placed her hand in the crook of his elbow. She didn't need his help—she could walk in these shoes just fine—but this was part of setting him up. It had nothing to do with wanting another flash of heat from where their bodies met.

The restaurant was busy, as was to be expected on a Saturday night. When they entered, the diners paused. She and Ethan must have made quite a pair, her with her red hair and him in his purple jacket.

People were already forming opinions. That was something she could use to her advantage. She placed her free hand on top of Ethan's arm and leaned into him. Not much, but just enough to create the impression that this was a date.

The maître d' led them to a small table tucked in a dim corner. They ordered—she got the lobster, just to be obnoxious about it, and he got the steak, just to be predictable—and Ethan ordered a bottle of pinot grigio.

Then they were alone. "I'm glad you came out tonight."

She demurely placed her hands in her lap. "Did you think I would cancel?"

"I wouldn't have been surprised if you'd tried to string me along a little bit. Just to watch me twist." He said it in a jovial way but she didn't miss the edge to his voice.

So he wasn't totally befuddled. And he was more than sharp enough to know they were here for something much more than dinner.

That didn't mean she had to own up to it. "Whatever do you mean?"

His smile sharpened. The silence carried, and she was in serious danger of fidgeting nervously under his direct gaze.

She was saved by the sommelier, who arrived with the wine. Frances desperately wanted to take a long drink, but she could not let Ethan know he was unsettling her. So she slowly twirled the stem of her wineglass until he said, "I propose a toast."

"Do you now?"

"To a long and productive partnership." She did not drink. Instead, she leveled a cool gaze at him over the rim of her glass and waited for him to notice. Which, admittedly, did not take long. "Yes?"

"I'm not taking that job, you know. I have 'considered' it, and I can't imagine a more boring job in the history of employment," she told him.

She would not let the world know she was so desperate as to take a job in management at a company that used to belong to her family. She might be down on her luck, but she wasn't going to give up.

Then, and only then, did she allow herself to sip her wine. She had to be careful. She needed to keep her wits about her and not let the wine—and all those muscles— go to her head.

"I figured as much," he said with a low chuckle that Frances felt right in her chest. What was it with this man's voice?

"Then why would you toast to such a thing?" Maybe now was the time to take the jacket off? He seemed entirely too self-aware. She did not have the advantage here, not like she'd had in the office.

Oh, she did not like that smile on him. Well, she did— she might actually like it a great deal, if she wasn't the one in the crosshairs.

He leaned forward, his gaze so intense that she considered removing her jacket just to cool down. "I'm sure you know why I want you," he all but growled.

It *was* getting hotter in here. She tried to look innocent. It was the only look she could pull off with the level of blush she'd probably achieved by now. "My sparkling wit?"

There was a brief crack in his serious facade, as if her sparkling wit was the correct answer. "I consider that a fringe benefit," he admitted with a tilt of his head. "But let's not play dumb, you and I. It's far too beneath a woman with your considerable talents. And your talents..." She straightened her back and thrust her chest out in a desperate attempt to throw him off balance. It didn't work. His gaze never left her face. "Your talents are considerable. I'm not sure I've ever met a woman like you before."

"Are you hitting on me?"

The corner of his mouth quirked up, making him look like a predator. She might have to revise her earlier opinion of him. He was *not* a dogfish. More like…a tiger shark, sleek and fast. Able to take her down before she even realized she was in danger.

"Of course not."

"Then why do you want me?" Because honestly—for the first time in her adult life—she wasn't sure what the answer would be.

Men wanted her. They always had. The moment her boobs had put in an appearance, she'd learned about base male lust—how to provoke it, how to manage it, how to use it for her own ends. Men wanted her for a simple, carnal reason. And after watching stepmother after stepmother come and go out of her father's life, she had resolved never to be used. Not like that.

The upside was that she'd never had her heart broken. But the downside?

She'd never been in love. Self-preservation, however vital to survival, was a lonely way to live.

"It's simple, really." He leaned back, his posture at complete ease. "Obviously, everyone at the Brewery hates me. I can't blame them—no one likes change, especially when they have to change against their will." He grinned at her, a sly thing. "I should probably be surprised that Delores hasn't spiked my coffee with arsenic by now."

"Probably," she agreed. Where was he going with this?

"But you?" He reached over and picked up her hand, rubbing his thumb along the edges of her fingertips. Against her will, she shivered—and he felt it. That smile deepened—his voice deepened. Everything deepened. *Oh, hell.*

"I saw how the workers—especially the lifers—responded to you and your donut stunt," he went on, still stroking her hand. "There's nothing they wouldn't do for you, and probably wouldn't do for any Beaumont."

"If you think this is going to convince me to take that job, you're sorely mistaken," she replied. She wanted to jerk her hand out of his—she needed to break that skin-to-skin contact—but she didn't. If this was how the game was going to go, then she needed to be all in.

So instead she curled her fingers around his and made small circles on the base of his palm with her thumb. She was justly rewarded with a little shiver from him. *Okay, good. Great.* She wasn't entirely at his mercy here. She could still have an impact even without the element of surprise. "Especially if you're going to call them 'lifers.' That's insulting. You make them sound like prisoners."

He notched an eyebrow at her. "What would you call them?"

"Family." The simple reply—which was also the truth—was out before she could stop it.

She didn't know what she expected him to do with that announcement, but lifting her hand to his lips and pressing a kiss against her skin wasn't it. "And that," he whispered against her skin, "is exactly why I need you."

This time, she did pull her hand away. She dropped it into her lap and fixed him with her best polite glare, the one that could send valets and servers scurrying for cover. Just then, the waiter appeared with their food—and did, in fact, pause when Frances turned that glare in his direction. He set their plates down with a minimum of fanfare and all but sprinted away.

She didn't touch her food. "I'm hearing an awful lot about how much you need me. So let us, as you said, dispense with the games. I do not now, nor have I ever, formally worked for the Beaumont Brewery. I do not now, nor have I ever, had sex with a man who thought he was entitled to a piece of the Beaumont Brewery and, by extension, a piece of me. I will not take a desk job to help you win the approval of people you clearly dislike."

"They disliked me first," he put in as he cut his steak.

What she really wanted to do was throw her wine in his face. It'd feel so good to let loose and let him have it. Despite his claims that he recognized her intelligence, she had the distinct feeling that he was playing her, and she did not like it. "Regardless. What do you want, Mr. Logan? Because I'm reasonably certain that it's no longer just the dismantling and sale of my family's history."

He set his knife and fork aside and leaned his elbows on the table. "I need you to help me convince the workers that joining the current century is the only way the company will survive. I need you to help me show them that it doesn't have to be me against them or them against me—that we can work together to make the Brewery something more than it was."

She snorted. "I'll be sure to pass such touching sentiments along to my brother—the man you replaced."

"By all accounts, he was quite the businessman. I'm sure that he'd agree with me. After all, he made significant changes to the management structure himself after his father passed. But he was constrained by that sense of family you so aptly described. I am not."

"All the good it's doing you." She took another sip of wine, a slightly larger one than before.

"You see my problem. If the workers fight me on this, it won't be only a few people who lose their jobs—the entire company will shut down, and we will all suffer."

She tilted her head from side to side, considering. "Perhaps it should. The Beaumont Brewery without a Beaumont isn't the same thing, no matter what the marketing department says."

"Would you really give your blessing to job losses for hundreds of workers, just for the sake of a name?"

"It's *my* name," she shot at him.

But he was right. If the company went down in flames, it'd burn the people she cared for. Her brothers would be safe—they'd already ensconced themselves in the Percheron Drafts brewery. But Bob and Delores and all the rest? The ones who'd whispered to her how nervous they were about the way the wind was blowing? Who were afraid for their families? The ones who knew they were too old to start over, who were scared that they'd be forced into early retirement without the generous pension benefits the Beaumont Brewery had always offered its loyal employees?

"Which brings us back to the heart of the matter. I need you."

"No, you don't. You need my approval." Her lobster was no doubt getting cold, but she didn't have much of an appetite at the moment.

Something that might have been a smile played over his lips. For some reason, she took it as a compliment, as if he was acknowledging her intelligence for real this time, instead of paying lip service to it. "Why didn't you go into the family business? You'd have made a hell of a negotiator."

"I find business, in general, to be beneath me." She cast a cutting look at him. "Much like many of the people who willingly choose to engage in it."

He laughed then, a real thing that she wished grated on her ears and her nerves but didn't. It was a warm sound, full of humor and honesty. It made her want to smile. She didn't. "I'm not going to take the job."

"I wasn't going to offer it to you again. You're right—it is beneath you."

Here it came—the trap he was waiting to spring. He leaned forward, his gaze intent on hers and in the space of a second, before he spoke, she realized what he was about to say. All she could think was, *Oh, hell.*

"I don't want to hire you. I want to marry you."

Five

The weight of his statement hit Frances so hard Ethan was surprised she didn't crumple in the chair.

But of course she didn't. She was too refined, too schooled to let her shock show. Even so, her eyes widened and her mouth formed a perfect O, kissable in every regard.

"You want to…what?" Her voice cracked on the last word.

Turnabout is fair play, he decided as he let her comment hang in the air. She'd caught him completely off guard in the office yesterday and had clearly thought she could keep that shock and awe going. But tonight? The advantage was his.

"I want to marry you. More specifically, I want you to marry me," he explained. Saying the words out loud made his blood hum. When he'd come up with this plan, it had seemed like a bold-yet-risky business decision. He'd quickly realized that Frances Beaumont would absolutely not take a desk job, but the unavoidable fact was he needed her approval to validate his restructuring plans.

And what better way to show that the Beaumonts were on board with the restructuring than if he were legally wed to the favored daughter?

Yes, it had all seemed cut-and-dried when he'd formulated the plan last night. A sham marriage, designed to bolster his position within the company. He'd done a little digging into her past and discovered that she had tried to launch some sort of digital art gallery recently, but it'd gone under. So she might need funding. No problem.

But he'd failed to take into account the actual woman he'd just proposed to. The fire in her eyes more than matched the fire in her hair, and all of her lit a hell of a flame in him. He had to shift in his chair to avoid discomfort as he tried not to look at her lips.

"You want to get married?" She'd recovered some, the haughty tone of her voice overcoming her surprise. "How very flattering."

He shrugged. He'd planned for this reaction. Frankly, he'd expected nothing less, not from her.

He hadn't planned for the way her hand—her skin—had felt against his. But a plan was a plan, and he was in for far more than a penny. "Of course, I'm not about to profess my undying love for you. Admiration, yes." Her cheeks colored slightly. Nope, he hadn't planned for that, either.

Suddenly, his bold plan felt like the height of foolishness.

"My," she murmured. Her voice was soft, but he didn't miss the way it sliced through the air. "How I love to hear sweet nothings. They warm a girl's heart."

He grinned again. "I'm merely proposing an…arrangement, if you will. Open to negotiation. I already know a job in management is not for you." He sat back, trying to look casual. "I'm a man of considerable influence and power. Is there something you need that I can help you with?"

"Are you trying to *buy* me?" Her fingertips curled around the stem of her wineglass. He kept one hand on the napkin in his lap, just in case he found himself wearing the wine.

"As I said, this isn't a proposal based on love. It's based on need. You're already fully aware of how much I need you. I'm just trying to ascertain what you need to make this arrangement worth your time. Above and beyond making sure that your Brewery family is well taken care of, that is." He leaned forward again. He enjoyed negotiations like this—probing and prodding to find the other party's breaking point. And a little bit of guilt never hurt anything.

"What if I don't want to marry you? Surely you can't think you're the first man who's ever proposed to me out of the blue." The dismissal was slight, but it carried weight. She was doing her level best to toy with him.

And he'd be lying if he said he didn't enjoy it. "I have no doubt you've been fending off men for years. But this proposal isn't based on want." However, that didn't stop his gaze from briefly drifting down to her chest. She had *such* an amazing body.

Her lips tightened, and she fiddled with the button on her jacket. "Then what's it based on?"

"I'm proposing a short-term arrangement. A marriage of convenience. Love doesn't need to play a role."

"Love?" she asked, batting her eyelashes. "There's more to a marriage than that."

"Point. Lust also is not a part of my proposal. A one-year marriage. We don't have to live together. We don't have to sleep together. We need to occasionally be seen in public together. That's it."

She blinked at him. "You're serious, aren't you? What kind of marriage would *that* be?"

Now it was Ethan's turn to fidget with his wineglass. He didn't want to get into the particulars of his parents' marriage at the moment. "Suffice it to say, I've seen long-distance marriages work out quite well for all parties involved."

"How delightful," she responded, disbelief dripping off every word. "Are you gay?"

"What? No!" He jolted so hard that he almost knocked

his glass over. "I mean, not that there's anything wrong with that. But I'm not."

"Pity. I might consider a loveless, sexless marriage to a gay man. Sadly," she went on in a not-sad voice, "I don't trust you to hold up your sexless end of the bargain."

"I'm not saying we couldn't have sex." In fact, given the way she'd pressed her lips to his cheek earlier, the way she'd held his hand—he'd be perfectly fine with sex with her. "I'm merely saying it's not expected. It's not a deal breaker."

She regarded him with open curiosity. "So let me see if I understand this proposal, such as it is. You'd like me to marry you and lend the weight of the Beaumont name to your destruction of the Beaumont Brewery—"

"Reconstruction, not destruction," he interrupted.

She ignored him. "In a starter marriage that has a built-in sunset at one year, no other strings attached?"

"That sums it up."

"Give me one good reason why I shouldn't stab you in the hand with my knife."

He flinched. "Actually, I was waiting for you to give me a good reason." She looked at him flatly. "I read online that your digital art gallery recently failed." He said it gently. He could sympathize with a well-thought-out project going sideways—or backward.

She rested her hand on her knife. But she didn't say anything. Her eyes—beautiful light eyes that walked the line between blue and green—bore into him.

"If there was something that I—as an investor—could help you with," he went on, keeping his voice quiet, "well, that could be part of our negotiation. It'd be venture capital—*not* an attempt to buy you," he added. She took her hand off her knife and put it in her lap, which Ethan took as a sign that he'd hit the correct nerve. He went on, "I wouldn't—and couldn't—cut you a personal check. But as an angel investor, I'm sure we could come to terms you'd find satisfactory."

"Interesting use of the word *angel* there," she said. Her voice was quiet. None of the seduction or coquettishness that she'd wielded like a weapon remained.

Finally, he was talking to the real Frances Beaumont. No more artifice, no more layers. Just a beautiful, intelligent woman. A woman he'd just proposed to.

This was for the job, he reminded himself. He was only proposing because he needed to get control of the Beaumont Brewery, and Frances Beaumont was the shortest, straightest line between where he was today and where he needed to be. It had nothing to do with the actual woman.

"Do you do this often? Propose marriage to women connected with the businesses you're stripping?"

"No, actually. This would be a first for me."

She picked up her knife, and he unwittingly tensed. One corner of her perfect rosebud mouth quirked into a smile before she began to cut into her lobster tail. "Really? I suppose I should be flattered."

He began to eat his steak. It had cooled past the optimal temperature, but he figured that was the price one paid for negotiating before the main course arrived. "I'm never in one city for more than a year, usually only for a few months. I have, on occasion, made the acquaintance of a woman with whom I enjoy doing things such as this— dining out, seeing the sights."

"Having sex?" she asked bluntly.

She was trying to unnerve him again. It might be working. "Yes, when we're both so inclined. But those were short-term, no-commitment relationships, as agreed upon by both parties."

"Just a way to pass the time?"

"That might sound harsh, but yes. If you agree to the

arrangement, we could dine out like this, maybe attend the theater or whatever it is you do for fun here in Denver."

"This isn't exactly a one-horse town anymore, you know. We have theaters and gala benefits and art openings and a football team. Maybe you've heard of them?" Her gaze drifted down to his shoulders. "You might consider trying out for the front four."

Ethan straightened his shoulders. He wasn't a particularly vain man, but he kept himself in shape, and he'd be lying if he said he wasn't flattered that she'd noticed. "I'll keep it in mind."

They ate in silence. He decided it was her play. She hadn't stabbed him, and she hadn't thrown a drink in his face. He put the odds of getting her to go along with this plan at fifty-fifty.

And if she didn't… Well, he'd need a new plan.

Her lobster tail was maybe half-eaten when she set her cutlery aside. "I've never fielded a marriage proposal like yours before."

"How many have you fielded?"

She waved the question away. "I've lost count. A quickie wedding, a one-year marriage with no sex, an irreconcilable-differences, uncontested divorce—all in exchange for an investment into a property or project of my choice?"

"Basically." He'd never proposed before. He couldn't tell if her no-nonsense tone was a good sign or not. "We'd need a prenup."

"Obviously." She took a much longer pull on her wine. "I want five million."

"I'm sorry?"

"I have a friend who wants to launch a new art gallery, with me as the co-owner. She has a business plan worked up and a space selected. All we need is the capital." She pointed a long, red-tipped nail at him. "And you did offer to invest, did you not?"

She had him there. "I did. Do we have a deal?" He stuck out his hand and waited.

She must be out of her ever-loving mind.

As Frances regarded the hand Ethan had extended toward her, she was sure she had crossed some line from desperation into insanity to even consider his offer.

Would she really agree to marry the living embodiment of her family's downfall for what, essentially, was the promise of job security after he was gone? With five million—a too-large number she'd pulled out of thin air—she and Becky could open that gallery in grand style, complete with all the exhibitions and parties it took to wine and dine wealthy art patrons.

This time, it'd be different. It was Becky's business plan, after all. Not Frances's. But even that thought stung a bit. Becky's plan had a chance of working. Unlike all of Frances's grand plans.

She needed this. She needed something to go her way, something to work out right for once. With a five-million-dollar investment, she and Becky could get the gallery operational and Frances could move out of the Beaumont mansion. Even if she only lived in the apartment over the gallery, it'd still be hers. She could go back to being Frances Beaumont. She could feel like a grown-up in control of her own life.

All it'd take would be giving up that control for a year. Not just giving it up, but giving it to Ethan.

She felt as if she was on the verge of passing out, but she refused to betray a single sign of panic. She did not breathe in deep gulps. She did not drop her head in her hands. And she absolutely did not fiddle with anything.

She kept herself serene and calm and did all her panicking on the inside, where no one could see it.

"Well?" Ethan asked. But it wasn't a gruff demand for an answer. His tone was more cautious than that.

And then there was the man himself. This was all quite noble, this talk of no sex and no emotions. But that didn't change the fact of the matter—Ethan Logan was one hell of a package. He could make her shiver and shake with the kind of heat she hadn't felt in a very long time.

Not that it mattered, because it didn't.

"I don't believe in love," she announced, mostly to see what kind of reaction it'd get.

"You don't? That seems unusually cynical for a woman of your age and beauty."

She didn't try to hide her eye roll. "I only mention it because if you're thinking about pulling one of those 'I'll make her love me over time' stunts, it's best to nip it in the bud right now."

She'd seen what people did in the name of love. How they made grand promises they had every intention of keeping until the next pretty face came along. As much as she'd loved her father, she hadn't been blind to his wandering eye or his wandering hands. She'd seen exactly what had happened to her mother, Jeannie—all because she'd believed in the power of love to tame the untamable Hardwick Beaumont.

"I wouldn't dream of it." Ethan's hand still hung in the air between them.

"I won't love you," she promised him, putting her palm in his. "I'd recommend you not love me."

Something in his eyes tightened as his fingers closed around hers. "I hope admiration is still on the table?"

She let her gaze drift over his body again. It wasn't desire, not really. She was an art connoisseur, and she was merely admiring his form. And wondering how it'd function. "I suppose."

"When do you want to get married?"

She thought it over. *Married.* The word felt weird rattling around her head. She'd never wanted to be married, never wanted to be tied to someone who could hurt her.

Of course, her brother Phillip had recently had a fairy-tale wedding that had been everything she might have ever wanted, if she'd actually wanted it. Which she didn't.

No, a big public spectacle was not the way to go here. This was, by all public appearances, a whirlwind romance, starting yesterday when she'd sashayed into his office. "I think we should cultivate the impression that we are swept up in the throes of passion."

"Agreed."

"Let's get married in two weeks."

Just saying it out loud made her want to hyperventilate. What would her brothers say to this, her latest stunt in a long line of stunts? "Frannie," she could practically hear Chadwick intone in his too-serious voice. "I don't think…" And Matthew? He was the one who always wanted everyone to line up and smile for the cameras and look like a big happy family. What would he say when she up and got herself hitched?

Then there was Byron, her twin. She'd thought she'd known Byron better than any other person in the world, and vice versa. But in the matter of a few weeks, he'd gone from her brother to a married man with a son and another baby on the way. Well, if anyone would understand her sudden change in matrimonial status, it'd be Byron.

Everyone else—especially Chadwick and Matthew—would just have to deal. This was her life. She could damn well do what she pleased with it.

Even if that meant marrying Ethan Logan.

Six

$\underline{}$

Ethan didn't know if it was the wine or the woman, but throughout the rest of dinner, he felt light-headed.

He was going to get married. To Frances Beaumont. In two weeks.

Which was great. Everything was going according to plan. He would demonstrate to the world that the Beaumonts were behind the restructuring of the Beaumont Brewery. That would buy him plenty of goodwill at the Brewery.

Yup. It was a great plan. There was just one major catch.

Frances leaned toward him and shrugged her jacket off. The sight of her bare shoulders hammered a spike of desire up his gut. He wasn't used to this sort of craving. Even when he found a lady friend to keep him company during his brief stints in cities around the country, he didn't usually succumb to this much *lust.*

His previous relationships were founded on...well, on *not* lust. Companionship was a part of it, sure. The sex was a bonus, definitely. And the women he consorted with were certainly lovely.

But the way he reacted to Frances? That was something else. Something different.

Something that threatened to break free from him.

Which was ridiculous. He was the boss. He was in control of this—all of this. The situation, his desires—

Well, maybe not his desires, not when Frances leaned forward and looked up at him coyly through her lashes. It shouldn't work, but it did.

"Well, then. Shall we get started?"

"Started?" But the word died on his lips when she reached across the table and ran her fingertips over his chin.

"Started," she agreed. She held out her hand, and he took it. He had no choice. "I happen to know a thing or two about creating a public sensation. We're already off to a great start, what with the confrontation outside your office and now this very public dinner. Kiss my hand again."

He did as he was told, pressing her skin against his lips and getting a hint of expensive perfume and the underlying taste of Frances.

He looked up to find her beaming at him, the megawatt smile probably visible from out on the sidewalk. But it wasn't real. Even he could tell that.

"So, kissing hands is on the table?" He didn't move her hand far from his mouth. He didn't want to.

When had he lost his head this much? When had he been this swamped by raw, unadulterated want? He needed to get his head back out of his pants and focus. He had explicitly promised that he would not make sex a deal breaker. He needed to keep his word, or the deal would be done before it got started.

"Oh, yes," she purred. Then she flipped her hand over in his grip and traced his lower lip with her thumb. "I'd imagine that there are several things still on the table."

Such as? His blood was beating a new, merciless rhythm in his veins, driving that spike of desire higher and higher until he was in actual pain. His mind helpfully supplied several vivid images that involved him, Frances and a table.

He caught her thumb in his mouth and sucked on it, his tongue tracing the edge of her perfectly manicured nail. Her eyes widened with desire, her pupils dilating until he could barely see any of the blue-green color at all. He swore he could see her nipples tighten through the fabric of her dress. Oh, yeah—a table, a bed—any flat surface would do. It didn't even have to be flat. Good sex could be had standing up.

He let go of her thumb and kissed her hand again. "Do you want to get out of here?"

"I'd like that," she whispered back.

It took a few minutes to settle the bill, during which every single look she shot him only made his blood pound that much harder. When had he been this overcome with lust? When had a simple business arrangement become an epic struggle?

She stood, and he realized the dress was completely backless. The wide swath of smooth, creamy skin that was Frances's back lay bare before him. His fingers itched to trace the muscles, to watch her body twitch under his touch.

He didn't want her to put her jacket back on and cover up that beautiful skin. And, thankfully, she didn't. She waited for him to assist her with her chair and then said, "Will you carry my jacket for me?"

"Of course." He folded it over one arm and then offered his other to her.

She leaned into his touch, her gorgeous red curls brushing against his shoulder. "Did you ever play football?" she asked, running her hands up and down his forearms. "Or were you just born this way?"

There was something he was supposed to be remembering, something that was important about Frances. But he couldn't think about anything but the way she'd looked in that green dress yesterday and the way she looked right now. The way he felt when she touched him.

He flexed under her hands and was rewarded with a little gasp from her. "I played. I got a scholarship to play in college, but I blew out my knee."

They were walking down the long hallway that separated the restaurant from the hotel. Then it'd be a quick turn to the left and into the elevators. A man could get into a lot of trouble in an elevator.

But they didn't even make it to the elevator. The moment they got to the middle of the lobby, Frances reached across his chest and slid her hand under his coat. Just like it had in the office yesterday, her touch burned him.

"Oh, that sounds awful," she breathed, curling her fingers around his shirt and pulling him toward her.

The noise of the lobby faded away until there was only the touch of her hand and the beating of his heart.

He turned into her, lowering his head. "Terrible," he agreed, but he no longer knew what they were talking about. All he knew was that he was going to kiss her.

Their lips met. The kiss was tentative at first as he tested her and she tested him. But then her mouth opened for him, and his control—the control he'd maintained for years and years, the control that made him a savvy businessman with millions in the bank—shattered on him.

He tangled his hands into her hair and roughly pulled her up to his mouth so he could taste her better—taste all of her. Dimly, somewhere in the back of his mind where at least three brain cells were doing their best to think about something beyond Frances's touch, Frances's taste—dimly, he realized they were standing in the middle of a crowd, although he'd forgotten exactly where they were.

There was a wolf whistle. And a second one—this one accompanied by laughter.

Frances pulled away, her impressive chest heaving and her eyes glazed with lust. "Your suite," she whispered, and then her tongue darted out, tracing a path on her lips that he needed to follow.

"Yeah. Sure." She could have suggested jumping out of an airplane at thirty thousand feet and he would have done it. Just so long as she went down with him.

Somehow, despite the tangle of arms and jackets, they made it to the elevators and then onto one. Other people were waiting, but no one joined them on the otherwise-empty lift. "Sorry," Frances said to the waiting guests as she curled up against his chest. "We'll send it back down," she added as the doors closed and shut them away from the rest of the world.

Then they were alone. Ethan slid his hands down her bare back before he cupped her bottom. "Where were we?"

"Here," she murmured, pressing her lips against his neck, right above his collar. "And here." Her teeth scraped over his skin as she pressed the full length of her body against his. "And…here."

She didn't touch him through his pants, not with her hands—but with her body? She shifted against him, and the pressure drove those last three rational brain cells out of his mind. "God, yes," he groaned, fisting his hands into her curls and tilting her head back. "How could I forget?"

He didn't give her time to reply. He crushed his mouth against hers. There wasn't any more time for testing kisses—all that existed in the safe space of this little moving room was his need for her and, given the way she was kissing him back, her need for him.

He liked sex—he always had. He prided himself on being good at it. But had he ever been this excited? This consumed with need? He couldn't remember. He couldn't think, not with Frances moaning into his mouth and arching her back, pushing her breasts into his body.

He reached up and started to undo the tie at the back of her neck, but she grabbed his hand and held it at waist height. "We're almost there," she murmured in a coy tone. "Can you wait just a little longer?"

No. "Yes."

Love and sex and, yes, marriage—that was all about waiting. There'd never been any instant gratification in it for him. He'd waited until he'd been eighteen before losing his virginity because it was a test of sorts. Everyone else was going as fast as they could, but Ethan was different. Better. He could resist the fire. He would not get burned.

Frances shifted against him again, and he groaned in the most delicious agony that had ever consumed him. Her touch—even through his clothing—seared him. For the first time in his life, he wanted to dance with the flames.

One flame—one flame-haired woman—in particular. Oh, how they would dance.

The elevator dinged. "Is this us?" Frances asked in a shaky whisper.

"This way." He grabbed her hand and strode out of the elevator. It was perhaps not the most gentlemanly way of going about it—essentially dragging her in her impossible shoes along behind him—but he couldn't help himself. If she couldn't walk, he'd carry her.

His suite was at the end of a long, quiet hall. The only noise that punctuated the silence was the sound of his blood pounding in his temples, pushing him faster until he was all but running, pulling Frances in his wake. Each step was pain and pleasure wrapped in one, his erection straining to do anything but walk. Or run.

After what felt like an hour of never-ending journeying, he reached his door. Torturous seconds passed as he tried to get the key card to work. Then the door swung open and he was pulling her inside, slamming the door shut behind them and pinning her against it. Her hands curled into his shirt, holding him close.

He must have had one lone remaining brain cell functioning, because instead of ripping that dress off her body so he could feast himself upon it, he paused to say, "Tell me what you want."

Because whatever she wanted was what he wanted.

Or maybe she wasn't holding him close. The thought occurred to him belatedly, just about the time her mouth curved up into what was a decidedly nonseductive smile. She pushed on his chest, and he had no choice but to let her. "Anything I want?"

She'd pushed him away, but her voice was still colored with craving, with a need he could feel more than hear. Maybe she wanted him to tie her up. Maybe she wanted to tie him up instead. Whatever it was, he was game.

"Yeah." He tried to lean back down to kiss her again, but she was strong for a woman her size. She held him back.

"I wonder what's on TV?"

It took every ounce of her willpower to push Ethan back, to push herself away from the door, but she did it anyway. She forced herself to stroll casually over to the dresser that held the flat-screen television and grab the remote. Then, without daring to look at Ethan, she flopped down on the bed. It was only after she'd propped herself up on her elbows and turned on the television that she hazarded a look at him.

He was leaning against the door. His jacket was half off; his shirt was a rumpled mess. He looked as though she'd mauled him. She was a little hazy on the details, but, as best she could recall, she had.

She turned her attention back to the television, randomly clicking without actually seeing what was on-screen. She'd only meant to put on a little show for the crowd. If they were going to do this sham marriage thing in two weeks, they needed to start their scandalous activities right now. Kissing in a lobby, getting into the elevator together? She was unmistakable with her red hair. And Ethan—he wasn't that hard to look up. People would make the connection. And people, being reliable, would talk.

When she'd stroked his face at dinner, she'd seen the headlines in her mind. "Whirlwind Romance between Beaumont Heir and New Brewery CEO?" That was what Ethan wanted, wasn't it? The air of Beaumont approval. This was nothing but a PR ploy.

Except...

Except for the way he'd kissed her. The way he'd kept kissing her.

At some point between when he'd sucked on her thumb and the kiss in the lobby—the first one, she mentally corrected—the game they'd been playing had changed.

It was all supposed to have been for show. But the way he had pinned her against the door in this very nice room? The way his deep voice had begged her to tell him what she wanted?

That hadn't felt like a game. That hadn't been for show.

The only thing that had kept her from spinning right over the edge was the knowledge that he didn't want her. Oh, he wanted her—naked, that was—but he didn't want *her*, Frances—complicated and crazy and more than a little lost. He'd only touched her because he wanted something, and she could not allow that to cloud her thinking.

"What—" He cleared his throat, but it didn't make his voice any stronger. "What are you doing?"

"Watching television." She kicked her heels up.

She cut another side glance at Ethan. He hadn't moved. "Why?"

It took everything Frances had to make herself sound glib and light. "What else are we going to do?"

His mouth dropped down to his chest. "I don't mean to sound crass, but...sex?"

Frances couldn't help it. Her gaze drifted down to the impressive bulge in his pants—the same bulge that had ground against her in the elevator.

Sex. The thought of undoing those pants and letting that bulge free sent an uncontrollable shiver down her back. She snapped her eyes back to the television screen. "Really," she said in a dismissive tone.

There was a moment where the only noise in the room was the sound of Ethan breathing heavily and some salesman on TV yelling about a cleaning cloth.

"Then what was that all about?" Ethan gruffly demanded.

"Creating an impression." She did not look at him.

"And who were we impressing in the elevator?"

She put on her most innocent look—which, granted, would have been a lot easier if her nipples weren't still chafing against the front of her dress. "Fine. A test, then."

Ethan was suddenly in front of the television, arms crossed as he glared down at her. "A *test*?"

"It has to be convincing, this relationship we're pretending to have," she explained, making a big show of looking around his body, rather than at the still-obvious bulge in his pants. "But part of the deal was that we don't have sex." She let that sink in before adding, "You're not going to back out of the deal, are you?"

Because that was a risk, and she knew it. There were many ways a deal could go south—especially when sex was on the line.

"You're testing *me*?" He took a step to the side, trying to block her view of the screen again.

"I won't marry just anyone, you know. I have standards."

She could feel the weight of his glare on her face, but

she refused to allow her skin to flush. She leaned the other way. Not that she had any idea of what she was watching. Her every sense was tuned into Ethan.

It'd be so easy to change her mind, to tell him that he'd passed his first test and that she had another test in mind—one that involved less clothing for everyone. She could find out what was behind that bulge and whether or not he knew how to use it.

She could have a few minutes where she wouldn't have to feel alone and adrift, where she could lose herself in Ethan. But that was all it would be. A few minutes.

And then the sex would be done, and she'd go back to being broke, unemployed Frances who was trading on her good looks even as they began to slip away. And Ethan? Well, he'd probably still marry her and fund her art gallery. But he'd know her in a way that felt too intimate, too personal.

Not that she was a shy, retiring virgin—she wasn't. But she had to keep her eye on the long game here, which was reestablishing herself and the Beaumont name and inflicting as much collateral damage on the new Brewery owners and operators as possible.

So this was her, inflicting a little collateral damage on Ethan—even if the dull throb that seemed to circle between her legs and up to her nipples felt like a punishment in its own right.

Okay, so it was a lot of collateral damage.

She realized she was holding her breath as she waited. Would he render their deal null and void? She didn't think so. She might not always be the best judge of men, but she was pretty sure Ethan wasn't going to claim sex behind tired old lines like "she led me on." There was something about him that was more honorable than that.

Funny. She hadn't thought of him as honorable before this moment.

But he was. He muttered something that sounded like a curse before he stalked out of her line of vision. She heard the bathroom door slam shut and exhaled.

The score was Frances: two and Ethan: one. She was winning.

She shifted on the bed. If only victory wasn't taking the shape of sexual frustration.

Frances had just stumbled on some sort of sporting event—basketball, maybe?—when Ethan threw the bathroom door open again. He stalked into the room in nothing but his trousers and a plain white T-shirt. He went over to the desk, set against the window, and opened his computer. "How long do you need to be here?" he asked in an almost-mean voice.

"That's open to discussion." She looked over at him. He was pointedly glaring at the computer screen. "I obviously didn't bring a change of clothing."

That got his attention. "You wouldn't stay the night, would you?"

Was she wrong, or was there a note of panic in his voice? She pushed herself into a sitting position, tucking her feet under her skirt. "Not yet, I don't think. But perhaps by next week, yes. For appearances."

He stared at her for another tight moment and then ground the heels of his palms into his eyes. "This seemed like *such* a good idea in my head," he groaned.

She almost felt bad for him. "We'll need to have dinner in public again tomorrow night. In fact, at least four or five nights a week for the next two weeks. Then I'll start sleeping over and—"

"Here?" He made a show of noticing there was only one bed and a pullout couch. "Shouldn't I come to your place?"

"Um, no." The very last thing she needed was to parade her fake intended husband through the Beaumont mansion. God only knew what Chadwick would do if he caught wind of this little scheme of hers. "No, we should stick to a more public setting. The hotel suits nicely."

"Well." He sagged back in his chair. "That's the evenings. And during the day?"

She considered. "I'll come to the office a couple of times a week. We'll say that we're discussing the sale of the antiques. On the days I don't stop by, you should have Delores order flowers for me."

At that, Ethan cocked an eyebrow. "Seriously?"

"I like flowers, and you want to look thoughtful and attentive, don't you?" she snapped. "Fake marriage or not, I expect to be courted."

"And what do I get out of this again?"

"A wife." A vein stood out on his forehead, and she swore she could see the pulse in his massive neck even at this distance. "And an art gallery." She smiled widely.

The look he shot her was hard enough that she shrank back.

"So," she said, unwilling to let the conversation drift back to sex just quite yet. "Tell me about this successful long-distance relationship that we're modeling our marriage upon."

"What?"

"You said at dinner that you've seen long-distance relationships work quite well. Personally, I've never seen any relationship work well, regardless of distance."

The silence between them grew. In the background, she heard the whistles and buzzers of the game on the TV.

"It's not important," he finally said. "So, fine. We won't exactly be long-distance for the next two weeks. Then we get married. Then what?"

"Oh, I imagine we'll have to keep up appearances for a month or so."

"A *month*?"

"Or so. Ethan," she said patiently. "Do you want this

to be convincing or not? If we stop being seen together the day after we tie the knot, no one will believe it wasn't a publicity stunt."

He jumped out of his chair and began to pace. "See— when I said long-distance, I didn't actually anticipate being in your company constantly."

"Is that a bad thing?" She batted her eyes when he shot her an incredulous look.

"Only if you keep kissing me like you did in the elevator."

"I can kiss you less, but we have to spend time together." She shifted so she was cross-legged on the bed. "Can you do that? At the very least, we have to be friends."

The look he gave her was many things—perhaps angry, horny—but "friendly" was not on the list.

"If you can't, we can still call it off. A night of wild indiscretion, we'll both 'no comment' to the press—it's not a big deal." She shrugged.

"It's a huge deal. If I roll into the Brewery after everyone thinks I had a one-night stand with you and then threw you to the curb, they'll hang me up by my toenails."

"I am rather well liked by the employees," she said, not a little smugly. "Which is why you thought up this plan in the first place, is it not?"

He looked to the ceiling and let out another muttered curse. "Such a good idea," he said again.

"Best laid plans of mice and men and all that," she agreed. "Well?"

He did a little more unproductive pacing, and she let him think. Honestly, she didn't know which way she wanted him to go.

There'd been the heat that had arced between them, heat that had melted her in places that hadn't been properly melted in a very long time. She'd kissed before, but Ethan's mouth against hers—his body against hers—

She needed the money. She needed the fresh start that an angel investor could provide. She needed to feel the power and prestige that went with the Beaumont name—or had, before Ethan had taken over. She needed her life back. And if she got to take the one man who embodied her fall from grace down a couple of pegs, all the better.

It was all at her fingertips. All she had to do was get married to a man she'd promised not to love. How hard could that be? She could probably even have sex with him—and it would be *so* good—without love ever entering into the equation.

"No more kissing in the elevator."

"Agreed." At least, that's what she said. She would be lying if she didn't admit she was enjoying the way she'd so clearly brought him to his knees with desire.

"What do people do in this town on a Sunday afternoon?"

That was a yes. She'd get her funding and make a few headlines and be back on top of the world for a while.

"I'll take it easy on you tomorrow—we need to give the gossip time to develop."

He shot her a look and, for the first time since dinner, smiled. It appeared to be a genuine smile even. It set off his strong chin and deep eyes nicely. Not that she wanted him to know that. "Should I be worried that you know this much about manipulating the press?"

She brushed that comment aside. "It comes with the territory of being a Beaumont. I'll leave after this game is over, and then I'll stop by the office on Monday. Deal?"

"Deal."

They didn't shake on it. Neither of them, it seemed, wanted to tempt fate by touching again.

Seven

"Becky? You're not going to believe this," Frances said as she stood in front of her closet, weighing the red evening gown versus something more…restrained. She hated being restrained, but on her current budget, it was a necessary concession.

"What? Something good?"

Frances grinned. Becky was easily excitable. Frances was pretty sure she could hear her friend bouncing up and down. "Something great. I found an investor."

There was some screaming. Frances held the phone as far away from her face as she could until the noise died down. She flicked through the hangers. She needed something sexy that didn't look as if she was trying too hard. The red gown would definitely be trying too hard for a Monday at the office. "Still with me?"

"Ohmygosh—this is so exciting! How much were they willing to invest?"

Frances braced herself for more screaming. "Up to five."

"Thousand?"

"Million." She immediately jerked the phone away from her head, but there was no sound. She cautiously put it back to her ear. "Becky?"

"I—it—what? I heard you wrong," she said with a nervous laugh. "I thought you said…"

"Million. Five million," Frances repeated, her fingers landing on her one good suit—the Escada. It was a conservative cut—at least by her standards—with a formfitting pencil skirt that went below her knee and a close-cropped jacket with only a little peplum at the waist.

It was the color, however—a warm hot pink—that made her impossible to miss.

Oh—this would be perfect. All business but still dramatic. She pulled it out.

"What—how? *How?*" Frances had never heard Becky this speechless before. "Your brothers?"

Frances laughed. "Oh no—you know Chadwick cut me off after the last debacle. This is a new investor."

There was a pause. "Is he cute?"

Frances scowled—not that Becky could see it, but she did anyway. She did not like being predictable. "No." And that wasn't a lie.

Ethan was *not* cute. He existed in the space between handsome and gorgeous. He wasn't pretty enough to be gorgeous—his features were too rough, too masculine. But handsome—that wasn't right, either. He exuded too much raw sexuality to be handsome.

"Well?" Becky demanded.

"He's…nice."

"Are you sleeping with him?"

"No, it's not like that. In fact, sex isn't even on the table." Her mind oh so helpfully provided a mental picture that completely contradicted that statement. She could see it now—Ethan bending her over a table, yanking her skirt up and her panties down and—

Becky interrupted that thought. "Frannie, I just don't want you to do something stupid."

"I won't," she promised. "But I have a meeting with

him tomorrow morning. How quickly can you revise the business plan to accommodate a five-million-dollar investment?"

"Uh… Let me call you back," Becky said.

"Thanks, Becks." Frances ended the call and fingered the fine wool of her suit. This wasn't stupid, really. This was…marriage with a purpose. And that purpose went far beyond funding an art gallery, although that was one part of it.

This was about putting the Beaumonts back in control of their own destiny. Okay, this was about putting one Beaumont—Frances—back in control of her destiny. But that still counted for a lot. She needed to get over this slump she was in. She needed her name to mean something again. She needed to feel as if she'd done something for the family honor instead of being a deadweight.

Marrying Ethan was the means to a bunch of different ends. That was all.

Those other men who'd proposed, they'd wanted what she represented, too—the Beaumont name, the Beaumont fortune—but they'd never wanted her. Not the real her. They had wanted the illusion of perfection she projected. They wanted her to look good on their arm.

What was different about Ethan? Well, he got points for being up front about his motivations. Nothing couched in sweet words about how special she was or anything. Just a straight-up negotiation. It was refreshing. Really. She didn't want anything sweet that was nothing but a lie. She didn't want him to try and make her love him.

She had not lied. She would not love him.

That was how it had to be.

"Delores," Frances said as she swept into the reception area. "Is Ethan—I mean, Mr. Logan—in?" She tried to blush at the calculated name screw-up, but she wasn't sure she could pull it off.

Delores shot her an unreadable glance over the edge of her glasses. "Had a good weekend, did we?"

Well. That was all the confirmation Frances needed that the stunt she'd pulled back in the hotel had done exactly as she'd intended. People had noticed, and those people were talking. Of course, there'd been some online chatter, but Delores wasn't the kind of woman who existed on social media. If she'd heard about the "date," then it was a safe bet the whole company knew all the gritty details.

"It was lovely." And that part was not calculated at all. Kissing Ethan had, in fact, been quite nice. "He's not all bad, I don't think."

Delores snorted. "Just bad enough?"

"Delores!" This time, her blush was more unplanned. Who knew the older lady had it in her?

"Yes, he's in." Delores's hand hovered near the intercom.

"Oh, don't—I want to surprise him," Frances said.

As she swept open the massive oak door, she heard Delores say, "Oh, we're all surprised," under her breath.

Ethan was sitting at her father's desk, his head bent over his computer. He was in his shirtsleeves, his tie loosened. When she flung the door open, his head popped up. But instead of looking surprised, he looked pleased to see her. "Ah, Frances," he said, rising to his feet.

None of the strain that she'd inflicted on him two days ago showed on his face now. He smiled warmly as he came around the desk to greet her. He did not, she noticed, touch her. Not even a handshake. "I was expecting you at some point today."

Despite the lack of physical contact, his eyes took in her hot-pink suit. She did a little twirl for him, as if she needed his approval when they both knew she didn't. Still, when he murmured, "I'm beginning to think the black dress is the most conservative look you have," she felt her cheeks warm.

For a second, she thought he was going to lean forward and kiss her on the cheek. He didn't. "You would not be wrong." She waltzed over to the leather love seats and spread herself out on one. "So? Heard any of the chatter?"

"I've been working. Is there chatter?"

Frances laughed. "You can be adorably naive. Of course there's chatter. Or did Delores not give you the same look she gave me?"

"Well…" He tugged at his shirt collar, as if it'd suddenly grown a half size too small. "She was almost polite to me this morning. But I didn't know if that was because of us or something else. Maybe she got lucky this weekend."

Unlike some of us. It was the unspoken phrase on the end of that statement that was as loud as if he'd pronounced the words.

She grinned and crossed her legs as best she could in a skirt that tight. "Regardless of Delores's private life, she's aware that we had an intimate dinner. And if Delores is aware of it, the rest of the company is, as well. There were several mentions on the various social media sites and even a teaser in the *Denver Post* online."

His eyes widened. "All of that from one dinner, huh? I am impressed."

She shrugged, as if this were all just another day at the office. Well, for her, it sort of was. "Now we're here."

He notched an eyebrow at her. "And we should be doing…what?"

She slipped the computer out of her bag. "You have a choice. We can discuss art or we can discuss art galleries. I've worked up a prospectus for potential investors."

Ethan let out a bark of laughter. "I've got to stop being surprised by you, don't I?"

"You really do," she agreed demurely. "In all honesty, I'm not that shocking. Not compared to some of my siblings."

"Tell me about them," he said, taking a perfectly safe seat to her right—not within touching distance. "Since we'll be in-laws and all that. Will I get to meet them?"

"It does seem unavoidable." She hadn't really considered the scene where the Beaumonts welcomed Ethan into the family fold with open arms. "I have nine half siblings from my father's four marriages. My older brothers are aware of other illegitimate siblings, but it's not unreasonable that there are more out there." She shrugged, as if that were normal.

Well, it was for her, anyway. Marriages, children, more children—and love had nothing to do with it.

Maybe there'd been a time, back when she was still a little girl who'd twirled in this office, when she'd been naive and innocent and had thought that her father loved her—and her brothers, their mother. That they were a family.

But then there'd been the day... She'd known her parents weren't happy. It was impossible to miss, what with all the screaming, fights, thrown dishes and slammed doors.

And it'd been Donut Friday and she'd been driven to the office with all those boxes and had bounced into the office to see her daddy and found him kissing someone who wasn't her mommy.

She'd stood there, afraid to yell, afraid to not yell—or cry or scream or do something that gave voice to the angry pain that started in her chest and threatened to leak out of her eyes. In the end, she'd done nothing, just like Owen, the driver who'd brought her and was carrying the donuts. Nothing to let her father know how much it hurt to see his betrayal. Nothing to let her mother know that Frances knew now what the fights were about.

But she knew. She couldn't un-know it, either. And

if she called her daddy on it—asked why he was kissing the secretary who'd always been so nice to Frances—she knew her father might put her aside like he'd put her mother aside.

So she said nothing. She showed nothing. She handed out donuts on that day with the biggest, best smile she could manage. Because that's what a Beaumont did. They went on, no matter what.

Just like now. So what if Ethan would eventually have to meet the family? So what if her siblings would react to this marriage with the same mix of shock and horror she'd felt when she'd walked in on her father that cold gray morning so long ago? She would go on—head up, shoulders back, a smile on her face. Her business failed? She couldn't get a job? She'd lost her condo? She'd been reduced to accepting the proposal of a man who only wanted her for her last name?

Didn't matter. Head up, shoulders back, a smile on her face. Just like right now. She called up the prospectus that Becky had put together yesterday in a flurry of excited phone calls and emails. Becky was the brains of the operation, after all—Frances was the one with the connections. And if she could deliver Ethan gift wrapped...

An image of him in nothing but a strategically placed bow popped before her. Christmas might be long gone, but there'd be something special about unwrapping *him* as a present.

She shook that image from her mind and handed the computer over to Ethan. "Our business plan."

He scrolled through it, but she got the distinct feeling he was barely looking at it. "Four wives?"

"Indeed. As you can see, my partner, Rebecca Rosenthal, has mocked up the design for the space as well as a cost-benefit analysis." She leaned over to click on the next tab. "Here's a sampling of the promotion we have planned."

"Ten siblings? Where do you fall in that?"

"I'm fifth." For some reason, she didn't want to talk about her family.

Detailing her father's affairs and indiscretions in this, his former office, felt wrong. This was where he'd been a good father to her. Even after she'd walked in on him cheating with his secretary, when she hadn't thrown a fit and hadn't tattled on him, he'd still doted on her when she was here. The next Donut Friday, she remembered, he'd had a pretty necklace waiting for her, and once again she'd been Daddy's girl for a few special minutes each week.

She didn't want to sully those memories. "Chadwick and Phillip with my father's first wife, Matthew and then Byron and me—we're twins—with his second wife." She hated referring to her mother by that number, as if that's all Jeannie had contributed. Wife number two, children three, four and five.

"You have a twin?" Ethan cut in.

"Yes." She gave him humorous look. "He's very protective of me." She did not mention that Byron was busy with his new wife and son. Better to let him worry about how her four older brothers would deal with him if he crossed a line.

Ethan's eyebrows jumped up. "And there were five more?"

"Yup. Lucy and Harry with my father's third wife. Johnny, Toni and Mark with his fourth. The younger ones are in their early twenties, for the most part. Toni and Mark are still in college and, along with Johnny, they all still live at the Beaumont mansion with Chadwick and his family." She rattled off her younger siblings' names as if they were items to be checked off a list.

"That must have been…interesting, growing up in that household."

"You have no idea." She made light of it, but *interesting* didn't begin to cover it.

She and Byron had been in an odd position in the household, straddling the line between the first generation of Hardwick Beaumont's sons and the last. Being five years older than she and Byron, Matthew was Chadwick and Phillip's contemporary. And since Matthew was their full brother, Byron and Frances had grown closer to the two older Beaumont brothers.

But then, her first stepmother—May, the not-evil one— had harbored delusional fantasies about how Frances and May's daughter, Lucy, would be the very best of friends, a period of time that painfully involved matching outfits for ten-year-old Frances and three-year-old Lucy. Which had done the exact opposite of what May intended—Lucy couldn't stand the sight of Frances. The feeling was mutual.

And the youngest ones—well, they'd been practically babies when Frances was a teenager. She barely knew them.

They were all Beaumonts, and, by default, that meant they were all family.

"What about you? Any strings of siblings floating around?"

Ethan shook his head. "One younger brother. No stepparents. It was a pretty normal life." Something in the way he said it didn't ring true, though.

No stepparents? What an odd way to phrase it. "Are you close? With your family, I mean." He didn't answer right away, so she added, "Since they'll be my in-laws, too."

"We keep in touch. I imagine the worst-case scenario is that my mother shows up to visit."

We keep in touch. What was it he'd said, about long-distance relationships working?

It was his turn to change the subject before she could

drill for more information. "You weren't kidding about an art gallery, were you?"

"I am *highly* qualified," she repeated. This time, her smile was more genuine. "We envision a grand space with enough room to highlight sculpture and nontraditional media, as well as hosting parties. As you can see, a five-million-dollar investment will practically guarantee success. I think that, as a grand opening, it would be ideal to host a showing of the antiques in this room. I don't want to auction off these pieces. Too impersonal."

He ignored the last part and focused instead on the one part Frances would have preferred to gloss over. "Practically?" He glanced at her. "What kind of track record do you have with these types of ventures?"

Frances cleared her throat as she uncrossed and recrossed her legs before leaning toward Ethan. Her distraction didn't work this time. At least, not as well. His gaze only lingered on her legs for a few seconds. "This is a more conservative investment than my last ventures," she said smoothly. "Plus, Rebecca is going to be handling more of the business side of the gallery—that's her strong suit."

"You're saying you won't be in charge? That doesn't seem like you."

"Any good businesswoman knows her limitations and how to compensate for them."

His lips quirked up into a smile. "Indeed."

There was a knock at the door. "Come in," Ethan said. Frances didn't change her position. She wasn't exactly sitting in Ethan's lap, but her posture indicated that they were engaged in a personal discussion.

The door opened and what looked like two-dozen red roses walked into the room. "The flowers you ordered, Mr. Logan." Delores's voice came from behind the blooms. "Where should I put them?"

"On the table here." He motioned toward the coffee

table, but Delores couldn't see through that many blooms, so she put them on the conference table instead.

"That's a lot of roses," Frances said in shock.

Delores fished the card out of the arrangement and carried it over to her. "For you, dear," she said with a knowing smile.

"That'll be all, Delores. Thank you," Ethan said. But he was looking at Frances as he said it.

Delores smirked and was gone. Ethan stood and carried the roses over to the coffee table while Frances read the note.

Fran—here's to more beautiful evenings with a beautiful woman—E.

It hadn't been in an envelope. Delores had read it, no doubt. It was thoughtful and sweet, and Frances hadn't expected it at all.

With a sinking feeling in her stomach, Frances realized she might have underestimated Ethan.

"Well?" Ethan said. He sounded pleased with himself.

"Don't call me Fran," she snapped. Or she tried to. It came out more as a breathless whisper.

"What should I call you? It seems like a pet name would be the thing. Snoogums?"

She shot him a look. "I thought I said you should send me flowers when I didn't come to the office. Not when I was already here."

"I always send flowers after a great first date with a beautiful woman," he replied. He sounded sincere about it, which did not entirely jibe with the way he'd acted after she'd left him hanging.

In all honesty, it did sound sweet, as if the time they'd spent together had been a real date. But did that matter?

So what if this was a thoughtful gesture? So what if it

meant he'd been paying attention to her when she'd said she liked flowers and she expected to be courted? So what if the roses were gorgeous? It didn't change the fact that, at its core, this was still a business transaction. "It wasn't a great date. You didn't even get lucky."

He didn't look offended at this statement. "I'm going to marry you. Isn't that lucky enough?"

"Save it for when we're in public." But as she said it, she buried her nose in the roses. The heady fragrance was her favorite.

It'd been a while since anyone had sent her flowers. There was a small part of her that was more than a little flattered. It was a grand gesture—or it would have been, if it'd been sincere.

Honest? Yes. Ethan was being honest with her. He'd been totally up front about the reasons behind his interest in her.

But his attention wasn't sincere. These were, if possible, the most insincere roses ever. Just all part of the game—and she had to admit, he was playing his part well.

The thought made her sadder than she'd thought it might. Which was ridiculous. Sincerity was just another form of weakness that people could use to exploit you. Her mother had sincerely loved her father, and see where that had gotten her? Nowhere good.

The corners of Ethan's eyes crinkled, as if her less-than-gracious response amused him. "Fine. Speaking of, when would you like to be seen together in public again?"

"Tomorrow night. Mondays are not the most social day of the week. I think the roses today will accomplish everything we want them to."

"Dinner? Or did you have something else in mind?"

Did he sound hopeful? "Dinner is good for now. I'm keeping my eyes open for an appropriate activity this weekend."

He nodded, as if she'd announced that the sales projections for the quarter were on target. But then he stood and handed her computer back to her. As he did so, he leaned down and whispered, "I'm glad you liked the roses," in her ear. And, damn it all, heat flushed her body.

She tilted her head up to him. "They're beautiful," she murmured. There was no audience for this, no crowd to guess and gossip. Here, in the safety of this office, there was only him and her and dozens of honest roses.

He was close enough to kiss—more than close enough. She could see the golden tint to his brown eyes that made them lighter, warmer. He had a faint scar on the edge of his nose and another one on his chin. Football injuries or brawls? He had the body of a brawler. She'd felt that for herself the other night.

Ethan Logan was a big, strong man with big, strong muscles. And he'd sent her flowers.

She could kiss him. Not for show but for herself. She was going to marry him, after all. Shouldn't she get something out of it? Something beyond an art gallery and a restored sense of family pride?

His fingers slid under her chin, lifting her face to his. His breath was warm on her cheeks. Many things were warm at this point.

Not for the Beaumonts. Not for the gallery. Just for her. Ethan was just for *her*.

They held that pose as Frances danced right up to the line of kissing Ethan because she wanted to. But she didn't cross it. And after a moment, he relinquished his hold on her. But the warmth in his eyes didn't dim. He didn't act as if she'd rejected him.

Instead, he said, "You're welcome."

And that?

That was sincere.

Oh, hell.

Eight

First thing Tuesday morning, Ethan had Delores order lilies and send them to Frances. Roses every day felt too clichéd and he'd always liked lilies, anyway.

"Any message?" the old battle-ax asked. She sounded smug.

Ethan considered. The message, he knew, was as much for Delores's loose lips as it was for Frances. And no matter what Frances said, they needed pet names for each other. "Red—until tonight. E."

Delores snorted. "Will do, boss. By the way…"

Ethan paused, his hand on the intercom switch. *Boss?* That was the most receptionist-like thing Delores had said to him yet. "Yes?"

"The latest attendance reports are in. We're operating at full capacity today."

A sense of victory flowed through him. After four days, the implied Beaumont Seal of Approval was already working its magic. "I'm glad to hear it."

He switched off the intercom and stared at it for a moment. But instead of thinking about his next restructuring move, his thoughts drifted back to Frances.

She was going to kill him for the Red bit; he was reasonably confident about that. But there'd been that moment yesterday where he'd thought all her pretense had fallen away. She'd been well and truly stunned that he'd had flowers delivered for her. And in that moment, she'd seemed…vulnerable. All of her cynical world-weariness had fallen away, and she'd been a beautiful woman who'd appreciated a small gesture he'd made for her.

Marriage notwithstanding, she wasn't looking for anything long term. Neither was he. But that didn't mean the short term couldn't mean *something*, did it? He didn't need the fire to burn for long. He just needed it to burn bright.

He flipped the intercom back on. "Delores? Did you place that order yet?"

He heard her murmur something that sounded like, "One moment," before she said more clearly, "in process. Why?"

"I want to change the message. Red—" Then he faltered. "Looking forward to tonight. Yours, E." Which was not exactly a big change and he felt a little foolish for making it. He switched off the intercom again.

His phone rang. It was his partner at CRS, Finn Jackson. Finn was the one who pitched CRS to conglomerates. He was a hell of a salesman. "What's up?"

"Just wanted to let you know—there's activity," Finn began without any further introduction. "A private holding company is making noise about AllBev's handling of the Beaumont Brewery purchase."

Ethan frowned. "Link?"

"On its way." Seconds later, the email with the link popped up. Ethan scanned the article. Thankfully, it wasn't an attack on CRS's handling of the transition. However, this private holdings company, ZOLA, had written a letter stating that the Brewery was a poor strategic purchase for AllBev and they should dump the company—preferably on the cheap, no doubt.

"What is this?" he asked Finn. "A takeover bid? Is it the Beaumonts?"

"I don't think so," Finn replied, but he didn't sound convinced. "It's owned by someone named Zeb Richards—ring any bells for you?"

"None. How does this impact us?"

"This mostly appears to be an activist shareholder making noise. I'll keep tabs on AllBev's reaction, but I don't think this impacts you at the moment. I just wanted to keep you aware of the situation." Finn cleared his throat, which was his great tell. "You could ask your father if he knows anything."

Ethan didn't say a damned thing. His father? *Hell no.* He would never show the slightest sign of weakness to his old man because, unlike the Beaumonts, family meant nothing to Troy Logan. It never had, it never would.

"Or," Finn finally said, dragging out the word, "you could maybe see if anyone on the ground knows anything about this Zeb character?"

Frances. "Yeah, I can ask around. If you hear anything else, let me know. I'd prefer for the company not to be resold until we've fulfilled our contract. It'd look like a failure on the behalf of CRS—that we couldn't turn the company around fast enough."

"Agreed." With that, Finn hung up.

Ethan stared at his computer without seeing the files. He was just starting to get a grip on this company, thanks to Frances.

This ZOLA, whatever the hell it was, *felt* like it had something to do with the Beaumonts. Who else cared about this beer company? Ethan did a quick search. Privately held firm located in New York, a list of their successful investments—but not much else. Not even a picture of Zeb Richards. Something about it was off. This could easily be a shell corporation set up with the express purpose of wrestling the Brewery away from AllBev and back into Beaumont hands.

Luckily, Ethan happened to have excellent connections here on the ground. He'd have to tread carefully, though.

He needed Frances Beaumont. The production lines at full capacity today? That wasn't his keen management skills in action, as painful as it was to admit. That was all Frances.

But on the other hand...her sudden appearance happening so closely to this ZOLA business? It couldn't be a coincidence, could it?

Maybe it was; maybe it wasn't. One thing was for sure. He was going to find out *before* he married her and *before* he cut her a huge investment check.

He sent a follow-up message to his lawyers about protecting his assets and then glanced over Frances's art gallery plans again. He knew nothing about art, which was surprising, considering his mother was the living embodiment of "artsy-fartsy." So as an art space, it didn't mean much to him. But as a business investment?

It wasn't that he couldn't spot her the five million. He had that and much more in the bank—and that didn't count his golden-parachute bonuses and stock options. Restructuring corporations was a job that paid extremely well. It just felt...

Too familiar. Like he was hell-bent on replicating his parents' unorthodox marriage. And that wasn't what he wanted.

He pushed the thoughts of his all-business father and flighty mother out of his brain. He had a company to run, a private equity firm to investigate and a woman to woo, if people still did that. And above all that, tonight he had a date.

This really wasn't that different from what he normally did, Ethan told himself as he waited at the bar of some hip restaurant. He rolled into a new town, met a woman and did the wining-and-dining thing. He saw the sights, had a little fun and then, when it was time, he moved on. This was standard stuff for him.

Which did not explain why he was sipping his gin and tonic with a little more enthusiasm than the drink required. He was just…bracing himself for another evening of sexual frustration, that was all. Because he knew that, no matter what she was wearing tonight, he wouldn't be able to take his eyes off Frances.

Maybe it wouldn't be so bad if she were just another pretty face. But she wasn't. He'd have to sit there and look at her and then also be verbally pummeled by her sharp wit as she ran circles around him. She challenged him and pushed him to his very limits of self-control, and that was something he could honestly say didn't happen much. Oh, the women he'd seen in the past were all perfectly intelligent ladies, but they didn't see their role of temporary companion as one that included the kind of conversation that bordered on warfare.

But Frances? She was armed like a Sherman tank, and she had excellent aim. She knew how to take him out with a few well-chosen words and a tilt of her head. He was practically defenseless against her.

His only consolation—aside from her company—was that he'd managed to slip past her armor a few times.

Then Frances was there, framed by the doorway. She had on a thick white coat with a fur collar that was belted tightly at the waist and a pair of calf-high boots in supple brown leather. Her hair was swept into an elegant updo and—Ethan blinked. Did she have flowers in her hair? Lilies?

Perhaps the rest of the restaurant was pondering the same question because he would have sworn the whole place paused to note her arrival.

She spotted him and favored him with a small personal

smile. Then she undid the belt of her coat and let it fall off her shoulders.

This wasn't normal, the way he reacted to what had to be the calculated revelation of her body. Hell, it wasn't even that much of a reveal—she had on a slim brown skirt and a cream-colored sweater. The sweater had a sweetheart neckline and long sleeves. Nothing overtly sexual about her appearance tonight.

She was just a gorgeous woman. And she was headed right for him. The restaurant was so quiet he could hear the click of her heels on the parquet flooring as she crossed to the bar.

He couldn't take his eyes off her.

What if things were different? What if they'd met on different terms—him not trying to reconstruct her family's former company, her not desperate for an angel investor? Would he have pursued her? Well, that was a stupid question—of course he would have. She was not just a feast for the eyes. She was quite possibly the smartest woman he'd ever gone head-to-head with. He couldn't believe it, but he was actually looking forward to being demolished by her again tonight. Blue balls be damned.

He rose and greeted her. "Frances."

She leaned up on her tiptoes and kissed his cheek. "What," she murmured against his skin. "Not Red?"

He turned his head slightly to respond but just kissed her instead. He kissed her like he'd wanted to kiss her in his office the other day. The taste of her lips burned his mouth like those cinnamon candies his mother preferred—hot but sweet. And good. *So* good. He couldn't get enough of her.

And that was a problem. It was quickly becoming *the* problem. He was having trouble going a day or two without touching her. How was he supposed to make it a year in a sexless marriage?

She pulled away, and he let her. "Still trying to find the right name for you," he replied, hoping that how much she affected him didn't show.

"Keep trying." She cocked her head to one side. "Shall we?"

Ethan signaled for the hostess, who led them back to their private table. "How was your day, darling?" Frances asked in an offhand way as she accepted the menu.

The casual nature of the question—or, more specifically, the lack of sexual innuendo—caught him off guard. "Fine, actually. The production lines were producing today." She looked at him over the edge of her menu, one eyebrow raised. "And, yes," he said, answering the unspoken question. "I give you all the credit for that."

He wanted to ask about ZOLA and Zeb Richards, but he didn't. Maybe after they'd eaten—and shared a bottle of wine. "How about you?"

They were interrupted by the waitress, so it wasn't until after they'd placed their orders that she answered. "Good. We met with the Realtors about the space. Becky's very excited about owning the space instead of renting."

Ah, yes. The money he owed her. "Have you been monitoring the chatter, as you put it?"

At that, she leaned forward, a winning smile on her face. Ethan didn't like it. It wasn't real or true. It was a piece of armor, a shield in this game they were playing. She wasn't smiling for him. She was smiling for everyone else. "So far, so good," she purred, even though there was no one else who could have heard her. "I think this weekend, we should attend a Nuggets game."

He dimly remembered her watching a basketball game on Saturday when she'd been pointedly not sleeping with him. "Big fan?"

"Not really," she replied with a casual shrug. "But sports

fans drink a lot of beer. It'd signal our involvement to a different crowd and boost the chatter significantly."

All of that sounded fine in a cold, calculated kind of way. He found he didn't much care for the cold right now. He craved her heat.

It was his turn to lean forward. "And after that? I seem to recall you saying something about how you were going to start sleeping over this weekend. Of course, you're always welcome to do so sooner."

That shield of a smile fell away, and he knew he'd slipped past her defenses again. But the moment was short. She tilted her head to one side and gave him an appraising look. "Trying to change the terms of our deal again? For shame, Ethan."

"Are you coming back to the room with me tonight?"

"Of course." Her voice didn't change, but he thought he saw her cheeks pink up ever so slightly.

"Are you going to kiss me in the lobby again?"

Yes, she was definitely blushing. But it was her only tell. "I suppose you could always kiss me first. Just for a little variety."

Oh, he'd love to show her some variety. "And the elevator?"

"You *are* trying to change the terms," she murmured as she dropped her gaze. "We discussed that—at your request. There's no kissing in elevators."

He didn't respond. At the time, it'd seemed like the shortest path to self-preservation. But now? Now he wanted to push the envelope. He wanted to see if he could get to her like she was getting to him. "I like what you've done with the lily," he said, nodding toward where she'd worked the bloom into her hair. Because thus far, the flowers were by far the best way to get to her.

There was always a chance that she wasn't all that attracted to him—that the heat he felt when he was around her was a one-way street.

Damn, that was a depressing thought.

"They were beautiful," she said. And it could have easily been another too-smooth line.

But it wasn't.

"Not as beautiful as you are."

Before she could respond to that their food arrived. They ate and drank and made polite small talk disguised as sensual flirting.

"After the game, we'll have to deal with my family," she warned him over the lip of her second glass of wine after she'd pushed her plate away. "I'm actually surprised that my brother Matthew hasn't called to lecture me about the Beaumont family name."

Ethan was wrapped in the warm buzz of his alcohol. "Oh? That a problem?"

Frances waved her hand. "He's the micromanager of our public image. Was VP of marketing before you showed up. He did a great job, too."

She didn't say it as if she was intentionally trying to score a hit, but he felt a little wounded anyway. "I didn't fire him. He was gone before I got there."

"Oh, I know." She took another drink. "He left with Chadwick."

Ethan was pondering this information when someone said, "Frannie?"

At the name, Frances's eyes widened, and she sat bolt upright. She looked over Ethan's shoulder and said, "Phillip?"

Phillip? Oh, right. He remembered now. Phillip was one of her half brothers.

Oh, hell. Ethan was one sheet to the wind and about to meet a Beaumont.

Frances stood as a strikingly blond man came around

the table. He was holding the hand of a tall, athletic woman wearing blue jeans. "Phillip! Jo! I didn't expect to see you guys here."

Phillip kissed his sister on the cheek. "We decided it was time for our once-a-month dinner date." As the woman named Jo hugged Frances, Phillip turned a gaze that was surprisingly friendly toward Ethan. "I'm Phillip Beaumont. And you are?" He stuck out his hand.

Ethan glanced at Frances, only to find that both she and Jo were watching this interaction with curiosity. "I'm Ethan Logan," Ethan said, giving Phillip's hand a firm shake.

He tried to pull his hand back, but it didn't go anywhere. "Ah," Phillip said. His smile grew—at the same time he clamped down on Ethan's hand. "You're running the Brewery these days."

The strength with which Phillip had a hold on him was more than Ethan would have given him credit for. Ethan would have anticipated her brother to be someone pampered and posh and not particularly physically intimidating. But Phillip's grip spoke of a man who worked with his hands for a living—and wasn't afraid to use them for other purposes.

"Phillip manages the Beaumont Farm," Frances said, her voice slightly louder than necessary. Ah, that explained it. "He raises the Percherons. And this is Jo, his wife. She trains horses."

It was only then that Phillip let go of Ethan so Ethan could give Jo's hand a quick shake. "A pleasure, Ms. Beaumont."

To his surprise, Jo said, "Is it?" with the kind of smile that made no pretense of being polite. But she linked arms with Phillip and physically pulled him a step away.

"Would you like to join us?" Ethan offered, because it seemed like the sociable thing to do and also because he absolutely did not want Phillip Beaumont to catch a hint of fear. Ethan would act as though having his hot date with Frances suddenly crashed by an obviously overprotective older brother was the highlight of his night if it killed him.

And given the look on Phillip's face, it just might.

"No," Jo said. "That's all right. You both look like you're finishing up, anyway."

Phillip said, "Frannie, can I talk with you—in private?"

That was a dismissal if Ethan had ever heard one. "I'll be right back," he genially offered. This called for a tactical retreat to the men's room. "If you'll excuse me," he added to Frances.

"Of course," she murmured, nodding her head in appreciation.

As Ethan walked away, he heard nothing but chilly silence.

"What are you doing?" Phillip didn't so much say the words as hiss them. His fun-times smile never wavered, though.

In that moment Phillip sounded more like stuck-up Matthew than her formerly wild older brother. "I'm on a date. Same as you."

Beside her, Jo snorted. But she didn't say anything. She just watched. Sometimes—and not that Frances would ever tell her sister-in-law this—Jo kind of freaked her out. She was so quiet, so watchful. Not at all the kind of woman Frances had envisioned with Phillip.

Which was not a complaint. Phillip was sober now and, with Jo beside him, almost a new man.

A new man who'd tasked himself with making sure Frances toed the family line. *Ugh.*

"With the man who's running the Brewery? Are you drunk?"

"That is *such* a laugh riot, coming from you," she stiffly

replied. She felt Jo tense beside her. "Sorry." But she said it to Jo. Not to Phillip. "But no, thanks for asking, I'm not drunk. I'm not insane, and, just to head you off at the pass, I'm not stupid. I know exactly who he is, and I know exactly what I'm doing."

Phillip glared at her. "Which is *what*, exactly?"

"None of your business." She made damn sure to say it with her very best smile.

Phillip was not swayed. "Frannie, I don't know what you think you're doing here—either you're completely clueless and setting yourself up for yet another failure or—"

"And thank you for that overwhelming vote of confidence," she hissed at him, her best smile cracking unnaturally. "I liked you better when you were drunk. At least then you didn't assume I was an idiot like everyone else does."

"Or," Phillip went on, refusing to be sidetracked by her attack, "you think you're going to accomplish something at the Brewery." He paused, and when Frances didn't respond immediately to that spot-on accusation, his eyes widened. "What on earth do you think you're doing?"

"I don't see what it matters to you. You don't drink beer. You don't work at any brewery, old or new. You've got the farm, and you've got Jo. You don't need anything." He had his happy life now. He couldn't begrudge her this.

Phillip did grab her then, wrapping his hand around her upper arm. "Frannie—corporate espionage?"

"I'm just trying to restore the Beaumont name. You may not remember it, but our name used to mean something. And we lost that."

Unexpectedly, Phillip's face softened. "We didn't lose anything. We're still Beaumonts. You can't go back—why would you even want to? Things are better now."

If that wasn't the most condescending thing Phillip had

ever said to her, she didn't know what was. "Better for who? Not for me."

He was undaunted, damn him. "We've moved on—we *all* have. Chadwick and Matthew have their new business. Byron's back and happy. Even the younger kids are doing okay. None of us want the Brewery back, honey. If that's what you're trying to do here..."

A rush of emotions Frances couldn't name threatened to swamp her. It was what she wanted, but it wasn't. This was about *her*. She wanted Frances Beaumont back.

She turned to Jo, who'd been watching the entire exchange with unblinking eyes. "I'm sorry if this interrupted your night out. Ethan and I were almost done anyway."

"It's not a problem," Jo said. Frances couldn't tell if Jo was saying it to her husband or to Frances. Jo then slid her arm through Phillip's. "Let it be, babe."

Phillip gave his wife an apologetic look. "My apologies. I'm just surprised. I'd have thought..."

She knew what Phillip would have thought—and she knew what Chadwick and Matthew and even Byron would all be thinking, just as fast as Phillip could text them. Another Frances misadventure. "Trust me, okay?"

Phillip's gaze cut back over her shoulder. Even without looking, Frances could tell Ethan had returned. She could *feel* his presence. Warm prickles raised the hairs on the back of her neck as he approached.

Then his arm slid around her waist in an act that could only be described as possessive. Phillip didn't miss it, curse his clean-and-sober eyes. "Well. Logan, a pleasure to meet you. Frances..."

She could hear the unspoken *be careful* in his tone. She gave Jo another quick hug and Phillip a kiss on the cheek. Ethan's hand stayed on her lower back. "I'll come out soon," she promised, as if that was what their little chat had been about.

Phillip smirked at the dodge. But he didn't say anything else. He and Jo moved off to their own table.

"Everything okay?" Ethan said. His arm was firmly back around her waist and she wanted nothing more than to lean into him.

"Oh, sure." It wasn't a lie, but it wasn't the whole truth. For someone who'd been playing a game calculated on public recognition, Frances suddenly felt overexposed.

Ethan's fingertips tightened against her side, pulling her closer against his chest. "Do you want to go?"

"Yes."

Ethan let go of her long enough to fish several hundred-dollar bills out of his wallet, and then they were walking toward the front. He held her coat for her before he slid his own back on. Frances could feel the weight of Phillip's gaze from all the way across the room.

Why did she feel so…weird? It wasn't what Phillip thought. She wasn't being naive about this. She wasn't betraying the family name—she was rescuing it, damn it. She was keeping her friends—and family—close and her enemies closer, by God. That's all this was. There was nothing else to it.

Except…except for the way Ethan wrapped his strong arm around her and hugged her close as they walked out of the restaurant and into the bitterly cold night air. As they walked from the not-crowded sidewalk to the nearly empty parking lot, where he had parked a sleek Jaguar, he held her tighter still. He opened her door for her and then started the car.

But he didn't press. He didn't have to. All he did was reach over and take her hand in his.

When they arrived at the hotel, Ethan gave the keys to the valet, who greeted them both by name. They walked into the lobby, and this time, she did rest her head on his shoulder.

She shouldn't feel weird, now that someone in the family was aware of her...independent interests. Especially since it was Phillip, the former playboy of the family. She didn't need their approval, and she didn't want it.

But...she felt suddenly adrift. And what made it worse? Ethan could tell.

They didn't stop in the middle of the lobby and engage in heavy petting as planned. Instead, he walked her over to the elevator. While they waited, he lifted her chin with one gloved hand and kissed her.

Damn him, she thought even as she sighed into his arms. Damn Ethan all to hell for being exactly who he was—strong and tough and good at the game, but also honest and sincere and thoughtful.

She did not believe in love. She struggled with believing in *like*. Infatuation, yes—she knew that existed. And lust. Those entanglements that burned hot and fast and then fizzled out.

So no, this was not love. Not now, not ever. This was merely...fondness. She could be fond of Ethan, and he could return the sentiment. Perhaps they could even be friends. Wouldn't that be novel, being friends with her soon-to-be-ex husband?

The elevator doors pinged open, and he broke the kiss. "Shall we go up?" he whispered, his gaze never leaving hers as his fingers stroked her cheek. Why did he have to be like this? Why did he have to make her think he could care for her?

Why did he make her want to care for him?

"Yes," she said, her voice shaky. "Yes, let's."

They stepped onto the elevator.

The doors closed behind them.

Nine

Before she could sag back against the wall of the elevator, Ethan had folded her into his arms in what could only be described as a hug.

She sank into his broad and warm and firm chest. When was the last time she'd been hugged? Not counting when she went to visit her mother. Men wanted many things from her—sex, notoriety, sex, a crack at the Beaumont fortune and, finally, sex. But never something as simple as a hug, especially one seemingly without conditions or expectations.

"I'm fine," she tried to say, but her words were muffled by all his muscles.

His chest moved, as if he'd chuckled. "I'm sure you are. You are, without a doubt, the toughest woman I know."

Against her wishes, she relaxed into his embrace as they rode up and up and up. "You're just saying that."

"No, I'm not." He loosened his hold on her enough to look her in the eyes. "I'm serious. You've got some of the toughest, most effective armor I've ever seen a woman wear, and you hardly ever expose a chink."

Something stung at her eyes. She ignored it. "Save it for when we have an audience, Ethan."

Something hard flashed over his eyes. "I'm not saying this for the general public, Frances. I'm saying it because it's the truth." He traced his fingertips—still gloved—down the side of her face. "This isn't part of the game."

Her breath caught in her throat.

"But every so often," he went on, as if stunning her speechless was just par for the course, "something slips past that armor." She was not going to lean into his touch. Any more than she already had, that was. "It's subtle, but I can tell. You weren't ready for your brother just then. God knows I wasn't, either." His lips—lips she'd kissed—quirked into a smile. "I'd have loved to see what you'd done with him if you'd been primed for the battle."

"It's different when it's family," she managed to get out in a breathy whisper. "You have to love them even when they think you're making a huge fool of yourself."

She felt his body tense against hers. "Is that what he told you?"

"No, no—Phillip has far more tact than that," she told him. "But I don't think he approves."

The elevator slowed, and then the doors opened on Ethan's floor. Ethan didn't make a move to exit. "Does that bother you?"

She sighed. "Come on." It took more effort than she might have guessed to pull herself out of his arms, but when she held out her hand, he took it. They walked down the long hall like that, hand in hand. She waited while he got the door unlocked, and then they stepped inside.

This time, though, she didn't make a move for the remote. She just stood in the middle of his suite—the suite that she would be spending more and more time in. Spending the night in—until they got married. Then what? They'd have to get an apartment, wouldn't they? She couldn't live in a hotel suite. Not for a year. And she couldn't see moving Ethan into the Beaumont mansion with her. Just trying to picture that made her shudder in horror.

Good God, she was going to marry this man. In…a week and a half.

Ethan stepped up behind her and slid his hands around her waist. He'd shucked his gloves and coat, she saw as his fingers undid the belt at her waist. Then he removed her coat for her.

This wasn't an act. Or was it? He could still be working an angle, one in which his interests would best be served by making her think he was really a decent man, a good human being. It was possible. He could be looking to pump more information out of her. Looking to take another big chunk of power or money away from the Beaumonts. He could be building her up to drop her like a rock and put her in her place—especially after the stunt she'd pulled with Donut Friday.

Then his arms were around her again, pulling her back into him. "Does it bother you?" he asked again. "That they won't approve of this. Of us."

"They rarely approve of anything I do—but don't worry," she hurried to add, trying to speak over the catch in her voice. "The feeling is often mutual. Disapproval is the glue that holds the Beaumonts together." She tried to say it as if it were just a comical fact of nature—because it was.

But she felt so odd, so not normal, that it didn't come out that way.

"Is he your favorite brother? Other than your twin, I mean."

"Yes. Phillip threw the best parties and snuck me beers and…we were friends, I guess. We could do anything together, and he never judged me. But he's been sober for a while now. His wife helps."

"So he's not the same brother you knew." Ethan pulled the lily out of her hair and set it on the side table. Half of her hair fell out of the twist, and he used his fingers to unravel the rest.

"No, I guess not. But then, nothing stays the same. The only thing that never changes is change itself, right?"

She knew that better than anyone. Wasn't that how she'd been raised? There were no constants, no guarantees. Only the family name would endure.

Right up until it, too, had stopped meaning what it always had.

Unexpectedly, Ethan pressed his lips against her neck. "Take off your shoes," he ordered against her skin.

She did as he said, although she didn't know why. The old Frances wouldn't have followed an order from an admirer.

Maybe, an insidious little voice in the back of her head whispered, *maybe you aren't the same old Frances anymore.* And this quest, or whatever she wanted to call it, to undermine Ethan and strike a blow against the new owners of her family's brewery—all of that was to make her feel like the old Frances again. Even the art gallery was a step back to a place where she'd been more secure.

What if she couldn't go back there? What if she would never again be the redheaded golden girl of Denver? Of the Brewery? Of her family?

Ethan relinquished his hold on her long enough to peel back the comforter from the bed. Then he guided her down. "Scoot," he told her, climbing in after her.

She would have never done so, not back when she was at the top of her form. She would have demanded high seduction or nothing at all. Champagne. Wild promises. Diamonds and gems. Not this *fondness*, for God's sake.

He pulled the covers over them and wrapped his arm around her shoulder. She curled into his side, feeling warmer and safer by the moment. For some reason, it was what she needed. To feel safe from the winds of change that had blown away her prospects and her personal fortune. In Ethan's arms, she could almost pretend none of it had happened. She could almost pretend this was normal.

"What about you?" she asked, pressing her hand against his chest.

He covered her hand with his. Warm. Safe. "What about me?"

"You must be used to change. A new company and a new hotel in a new city every other month?" She curled her fingers into the crisp cotton of his shirt. "I guess change doesn't bother you at all."

"It doesn't feel like that," he said. "It's the same thing every time, with slightly different scenery. Hotel rooms all blend together, executive offices all look the same..."

"Even the women?"

The pause was long. "Yes, I guess you could say that. Even the women were all very similar. Beautiful, good conversationalists, cultured." He began to stroke her hair. "Until this time."

"This time?" Something sparked in her chest, something that didn't feel cynical or calculated. She didn't recognize what it was.

"The hotel is basically the same. But the company? I usually spend three to six months restructuring. I've already been here for three months and I've barely made any headway. The executive office—hell, the whole Brewery—is unlike any place I've ever worked before. It's not a sterile office building that's got the same carpeting and the same crappy furniture as every other office. It's like it's this...*thing* that lives and breathes on its own. It's not just real estate. It's alive."

"It's always been that way," she agreed, but she wasn't thinking about the Brewery or the antique furniture or the people who'd made it a second home to her.

She was thinking about the man next to her, the one

who'd just told her that women were as interchangeable as hotel rooms. Which was a cold, soulless thing to admit and also totally didn't match up with the way he was holding her.

"And?"

"And…" His voice trailed off as he wrapped his fingers more tightly around hers.

She swallowed. "The woman?"

For some reason, she needed to know that she wasn't like all the rest.

Please, she thought, *please say something I can believe. Something real and honest and sincere, even if it kills me.*

"The woman," he said, lifting her hand away from his chest and pressing a kiss to her palm, "the woman is unlike any other. Beautiful, a great conversationalist, highly cultured—but there's something else about her. Something that runs deeper."

Frances realized she was holding her breath, so she made herself breathe normally. Or as close to normal as she could get, what with her heart pounding as fast as it was. "You make her sound like a river."

"Then I'm not doing a very good job," he said with a chuckle. "I'm not used to whispering sweet nothings."

"They're not nothing." Her voice felt as if it were coming from somewhere far away.

His hand trailed down from her hair to her back, where he rubbed her in long, even strokes. "Neither are you."

She wasn't, was she? She was still Frances. Hell, in a few weeks, she wouldn't even be a Beaumont anymore. She'd be a Logan. And then after that… Well, nothing stayed the same, after all.

"We can call it off," he said, as if he'd been reading her mind.

She pushed herself up and stared down at him. *"What?"* Was he serious?

Or was this the real, honest, true thing she'd asked for? Because if this was it, she took it back.

"Nothing official has changed hands. No legal commitments have been made." She saw him swallow. He stared up at her with such seriousness that she almost panicked because the look on his face went so far beyond fond that she didn't know what to do. "If you want."

She sat all the way up, pushing herself out of what had been the safe shelter of his arms. She sat back on her heels, only vaguely aware that her skirt had twisted itself around her waist. "No. No! We can't end this!"

"Why not? Relationships end all the time. We had a couple of red-hot dates and it went nowhere." He tilted his head to the side. "We just walk away. No harm, no foul."

"*Just* walk away? We can't. *I* can't." Because that was the heart of the matter, wasn't it? She couldn't back out of this deal now. This was her ticket back to her old life, or some reasonable facsimile thereof. With Ethan's angel investment, she could get the gallery off the ground, she could get a new apartment and move out of the Beaumont mansion. She could go back to being Frances Beaumont.

He sat up, which brought their bodies into close proximity again. She didn't like being this aware of him. She didn't like the fact that she wanted to know what he'd look like without the shirt. She didn't want to like him. Not even a little.

He reached over and stroked her hair tenderly. She didn't want tenderness, damn it. She didn't want feelings. She wanted cutting commentary and wars of words and… She wanted to hate him. He was the embodiment of her family's failures. He was dismantling her second home piece by piece. He was using her for her familial connections.

And he was making it damned near impossible to hate him. Stupid tender fondness.

It only got worse when he said, "I'd like to keep seeing

you," as if he thought that would make it better when it only made everything worse. "I don't think it's an exaggeration to say that I haven't stopped thinking about you since the moment you offered me a donut. But we don't have to do this rush to the altar. We don't have to get married. Not if you'd like to change the deal. Since," he added with a wry smile, "things do change."

"But you need me," she protested, trying vainly to find some solution that would not lead to where she'd started—alone, living at the family home, broke, with no prospects. "You need *me* to make the workers like you."

His lips quirked up into a tender smile, and then he was closing the distance between them. "I need more than just that."

He was going to kiss her. He was being sweet and thoughtful and kind and he was going to kiss her and it was wrong. It was all wrong.

"Ethan," she said in warning, putting her hand on his chest and pushing lightly. "Don't do this."

He let her hold him back, but he didn't let go of her hair. He didn't let go of *her*. "Do what?"

"This—*madness*. Don't start to like me. I won't like you back." His eyes widened in shock. She dug deeper. "I won't love you."

Ever so slightly, his fingers loosened their hold on her hair. "You already said that."

"I meant it. Love is for fools, and I refuse to be one. Don't lower my opinion of you by being one, too." The words felt sharp on her tongue, as if she were chewing on glass.

Cruel to be kind, she told herself. If he got infatuated with her—if real emotions came into play—well, this whole thing would fall apart. This was not a relationship, not a real one. This was a business deal. They couldn't afford to forget that.

Well, she couldn't, anyway.

If she'd expected him to pull away, to be pissed at her blanket rejection, she was sorely disappointed. He did, in fact, lean back. And he did let his fingers fall away from her hair.

But he sat there, propped up on hotel pillows that were just like any other hotel pillows, and he smiled at her. A real smile, damn him. Honest and true.

"If you want out, that's fine," she pressed on. She would not be distracted by real emotions. "But don't take pity on me and don't like me, for God's sake. We had a deal. Don't patronize me by deciding what's best for me. If I want out of the deal, I'll tell you. In the meantime, I'll hold up my end of the bargain and you'll hold up yours—unless you've changed your mind?"

"I haven't," he said after a brief pause. His mouth was still slightly curved into a smile.

She wanted to wipe that smile off his face, but she couldn't think of a way to do it without kicking and screaming. So all she said was, "Fine."

They sat there for a few moments. Ethan continued to stare at her, as if he were trying to see into her. "Yes?" she demanded as she felt her face flush under his close scrutiny.

"The woman," he murmured in what sounded a hell of a lot like approval, "is a force unto herself."

Oh, she definitely took it back. She didn't want real or honest out of him. No tenderness and, for the love of everything holy, not a single hint of fondness.

She would not *like* him. She simply would not.

She had to nip this in the bud *fast*.

"Ethan," she said, baring her teeth in some approximation of a smile, "save it for when we're in public."

Ten

The next day, Ethan had Delores send a bird of paradise floral arrangement with a note that just read, "Yours, E." Then he sent Frances a text message telling her how much he was looking forward to seeing her again that night.

He wasn't surprised when she didn't respond. Not after the way she'd stalked out of his hotel room last night.

As hard as it was, he tried to put the events of the previous evening aside. He had work to do. The production lines were up to full speed. He checked in with his department heads and was stunned by the complete lack of pushback he got when he asked about head count and department budgets. A week ago, people would have been staring at the table or out the window and saying that the employees who had those numbers were out with the flu or on vacation or whatever lame excuse they assumed wouldn't be too transparent.

But now? After less than a week of having Frances Beaumont in his life, people were making eye contact and saying, "I've got those numbers," and smiling at him. Actually smiling! Even when a turnaround was going well, there weren't a lot of smiles in the process.

Then there was what happened at the end of the last meeting of the day. He'd been discussing the marketing budget in his office with the department managers. The men and women seated around the Beaumont conference table looked comfortable, as though they belonged there. For the briefest moment, Ethan was jealous of them. He didn't belong there, and they all knew it.

It was 4:45 and the marketing people were obviously ready to go home. Ethan wrapped things up, got the promises that he'd have the information he'd requested on his desk first thing in the morning and dismissed everyone.

"So, Mr. Logan," an older man said with a smile. Ethan thought his name was Bob. Larsen, maybe? "Are you going to get a donut on Friday?"

The room came to a brief pause, everyone listening for the answer. For what was quite possibly the first time, he grasped what Frances kept talking about when she said he should save it for the public.

Still, he had to say something. People were waiting for a reaction. More than that, they were waiting for the reaction that told them their trust in Ethan's decisions wasn't about to be misplaced. They were waiting for him to admit he was one of them.

"I hope she saves me a chocolate éclair this time," he said in a conspiratorial whisper. He didn't specify who "she" was. He didn't have to.

This comment was met with an approving noise between a chuckle and a hum. *Whew*, Ethan thought as people cleared out. At least he hadn't stuck his foot in it. Not like he had with Frances last night.

She'd been right. He *did* need her. If they walked away right now, whatever new, tenuous grip he had on this company would float away as soon as the last donut had been consumed. He'd gotten more accomplished in the past week than he had in three months, and, as much as it pained him to admit it, it had nothing to do with his keen managerial handling.

So why had he offered to let her out of their deal?

He didn't know the answer to that, except there'd been a chink in her armor and instead of looking like a worthy opponent, Frances had seemed delicate and vulnerable. There'd been this pull—a pull he wasn't sure he'd ever felt before—to take care of her. Which was patently ridiculous. She could take care of herself. Even if she hadn't seen fit to remind him of that fact, he knew it to be true.

But the look on her face after they'd left her brother behind...

Ethan hadn't lied. There were similarities between Frances and all his previous lady friends. Cultured, refined— the sort of woman who enjoyed a good meal and a little evening entertainment, both the kind that happened at the theater and in the hotel room.

So what was it about her that was so damn different?

It wasn't her name. Sure, her name was the starting point of this entire relationship, but Ethan was no sycophant. The Beaumont name was only valuable to him as long as it let him do his job at the Brewery. He had no desire to get in with the family, and Ethan had his own damn fortune, thank you very much.

Was it the fact that, for the first time in his life, he was operating with marriage in mind? Was that alone enough to merit this deeper...engagement, so to speak? He would be tied to Frances for the next calendar year. Maybe it was only natural to want to take care of the woman who would be his wife.

Not that he knew what that looked like. His father had certainly never taken care of his mother, aside from providing the funds for her to do whatever she liked. Troy Logan's involvement with the mother of his two sons was strictly limited to paying the bills. Maybe that was why his mother never stayed home for longer than a few months at a time. Troy Logan wasn't capable of deeper feeling, so

Wanda had sought out that emotional connection some-where else. Anywhere else, really.

Ethan went to the private bathroom and splashed cold water on his face. This wasn't supposed to be complicated, not like his parents' relationship. This was cut-and-dried. No messy emotions. Just playing a game with one hell of an opponent who made him want to do things that were completely out of character. No problem.

He checked his jaw in the mirror—maybe he wouldn't shave before dinner tonight. As he was debating the mer-its of facial hair, he heard his office door shut with a de-cent amount of force.

"Frances?" he called out. "Is that you?"

There was no response.

He unrolled his sleeves and slid his jacket back on. The only other person who walked into his office without being announced by Delores was Delores herself. Even if it was near quitting time, he still needed to maintain his professional image.

But as he walked back into his office, he knew it wasn't Delores. Instead, a tall, commanding man sat in one of the two chairs in front of the desk.

The man looked like Phillip Beaumont—until he gave Ethan such an imperious glare that Ethan realized it wasn't the same Beaumont.

He recognized that look. He'd seen it on the covers of business magazines and in the *Wall Street Journal*. None other than Chadwick Beaumont, the former CEO of the Beaumont Brewery, was sitting in Ethan's office. The man every single employee in this company wanted back.

Ethan went on high alert. Beaumont had, until this very moment, been more of a ghost that Ethan had to work around than an actual living man to be dealt with. Yet here he was, months after Ethan had taken over. This couldn't be a coincidence, not after the interaction with Phillip last night.

"I had heard," Beaumont began with no other introduction, "that you were going to tear this office out."

"It's my prerogative," Ethan replied, keeping his voice level. He had to give Beaumont credit—at least he hadn't said *my office*. "As I am the current CEO."

Beaumont tilted his head in acknowledgment.

"To what do I owe the honor?" Ethan asked, as if this were a social call when it was clearly anything but. He took his seat behind his desk, leaving both hands on the desktop, as if all his cards were on the table.

Beaumont did not answer immediately. He crossed his leg and adjusted the cuff of his pants. Which was to be expected, Ethan figured. Beaumont was a notoriously tough negotiator, much like his father had been.

Well, two could play at this game. Troy Logan had earned his reputation as a corporate raider during the 1980s the hard way. His name alone could make high-powered bankers turn tail and run. Ethan had learned at the feet of the master. If Beaumont thought he could gain something with this confrontation, he was going to be sorely disappointed.

While Beaumont tried to wait Ethan out, Ethan studied him.

Chadwick Beaumont—the scion of the Beaumont family—was taller and blonder than Frances or even his brother Phillip. His hair held just a shine of redness, whereas Frances's was all flame. There was enough similarity that, even if Ethan hadn't met Phillip the night before, he would have recognized the Beaumont features—the chin, the nose, the ability to command a room just by existing in it.

How had the company been sold away from this man? Ethan tried to recall. An activist shareholder had precipitated the sale. Beaumont had fought against it tooth and nail, but once the sale had been finalized, he'd packed up and moved on.

So, yeah—this wasn't about the company. This was about Frances.

Which Beaumont proved when he tried out something that was probably supposed to be a smile but didn't even come close. "You're making me look bad. Flowers every day? My wife is beginning to complain."

Ethan didn't smile back. "My apologies for that." He was not sorry. "That's not my intention."

One eyebrow lifted. "What are your intentions?"

Damn, Ethan had walked right into that one. "I'm sorry—is that any of your business?"

"I'm making it my business." The statement was made in a casual enough tone, but there was no missing the implicit threat. Beaumont tried to stare him down for a moment, but Ethan didn't buckle.

"Good luck with that."

Beaumont's eyes hardened. "I don't know what your game is, Logan, but you really don't know what you're getting into with her."

That might be a true enough observation, but Ethan wasn't about to concede an inch. "As far as I can tell, I'm getting into a relationship with a grown woman. Still don't see how that's any of your concern."

Beaumont shook his head slowly, as if Ethan had blundered into admitting he was an idiot. "Either she's using you or you're using her. It won't end well."

"Again, not your concern."

"It is my concern because this will be just another one of Frances's messes that I have to clean up after."

Ethan bristled. "You talk as if she's a wayward child."

Beaumont's glare bore into him. "You don't know her like I do. She's lost more fortunes than I can count. Keeping her out of the public eye is a challenge during the best of times. And you," he said, pointing his chin at Ethan, "are pushing her back into the public eye."

Ethan stared at Beaumont. Was he serious? But Chadwick Beaumont did not look like the kind of man who made a joke. Ever.

What had Frances said last night? "Don't patronize me by deciding what's best for me." Suddenly, that statement made sense. "Does she know you're here?"

"Of course not," Beaumont replied.

"Of course not," Ethan repeated. "Instead, you took it upon yourself to decide what was best not only for her but for me, as well." He gave his best condescending smile, which took effort. He did not feel like smiling. "You'll have to excuse me, but I'm trying to figure out what gives you the right to be such a patronizing asshole to a pair of consenting adults. Any thoughts on that?"

Beaumont gave him an even look.

"I suppose," Ethan went on, "that the only surprising thing is that you came alone to intimidate me, instead of with a herd of Beaumont brothers."

"We don't tend to travel in a pack," Beaumont said coolly.

"And I'm equally sure you didn't think you'd need any help in the intimidation department."

Beaumont's eyes crinkled a little at the corners, as if he might have actually found that observation amusing. "How's the Brewery doing?"

Ethan blinked at the subject change, but only once. "We're getting there. You cultivated an incredibly loyal staff. The ones that didn't follow you to your new company were not happy about the changes."

Beaumont tilted his head at the compliment. "I imagine not. When I took over after my father's death, there was a period of about a year where we verged on total collapse. Employee loyalty can be a double-edged sword."

Ethan didn't bother to hide his surprise. *"Really."*

Beaumont nodded. "The club of Beaumont Brewery CEOs is even more exclusive than the Presidents' Club. There are only two of us alive in the world. You're only the fifth person to helm this company." He stared down at Ethan, but the intimidation wasn't as overbearing. "It's not a position to be taken lightly."

Honest to God, Ethan had never thought about it in those terms. The companies he usually restructured had often gone through a new CEO every two or three years as part of their downhill spiral. He'd never been anything special, in terms of management. He'd waltzed in, righted the sinking ship and moved on—just another CEO in a long line of them. There'd been nothing for the other employees to be loyal to except a paycheck and benefits.

Beaumont was right. Frances was right. Everything about this place, these people—this was different.

"If you need any help with the company…"

Ethan frowned. Accepting help was not something he did, especially not when it came to his job.

Except for Frances, a silky voice in the back of his head whispered. It sounded just like her.

"Actually, I do have a question. Have you ever heard of ZOLA?"

"ZOLA?" Beaumont mouthed the word like it was foreign. "What's that?"

"A private holdings company. They're making noise about the Brewery. I think they're trying to undermine— well, I'm not sure who they're trying to undermine. Not you, obviously, since you're no longer the boss around here. But it could be my company, or it could be AllBev." He fought the urge to get up and pace. "Unless, of course, ZOLA is representing your interests."

"I have no interest in reclaiming the Brewery. I've

moved on." His gaze was level, and his hands and feet were calm. Beaumont was telling the truth, damn it.

"And the rest of your family?"

"I don't speak for the entire Beaumont family."

"I'll be sure and pass that information along to Frances."

Beaumont's eyes widened briefly in surprise at this barb. "Phillip has no interest in beer. Matthew is one of my executives. Byron has his own restaurant in our new brewery. The younger Beaumonts never had anything to do with the Brewery in the first place. And you seem to be in a position to form your own opinion of Frances's motivations."

Point. Ethan was quite proud that his ears didn't burn under that one. "I appreciate your input."

Beaumont stood and held out his hand. Ethan rose to shake it. "Good to meet you, Logan. Stop by the mansion sometime."

"Likewise. Anytime." He was pretty sure they were both lying through their teeth.

Beaumont didn't let go of his hand, though. If anything, his grip tightened down. "But be careful with Frances. She is not a woman to be trifled with."

Ethan cracked a real smile. As if anyone could trifle with Frances Beaumont and hope to escape with their dignity—or other parts—intact.

Still, this level of meddling was something new to Ethan. No wonder seeing her other brother last night had shaken her so badly. Ethan hadn't really anticipated this much peer pressure. He increased his grip right back. "I think she can take care of herself, don't you?"

He waited for Beaumont to make another thinly veiled threat, but he didn't. Instead, he dropped Ethan's hand and turned toward the door.

Ethan watched him go. If Beaumont had shown up here,

had anyone been designated to give Frances a talking-to? Hopefully she'd had her armor on.

Then Beaumont paused at the door. He turned back, his gaze sweeping the entirety of the room. Instead of another pronouncement about how they were members of the world's smallest club, he only gave Ethan a little grin that was somehow tinged with sadness before he turned and was gone.

Ethan got the feeling that Beaumont wouldn't come back to the Brewery again.

Ethan collapsed back into his chair. What the ever-loving hell was that all about, anyway? He still wasn't going to rule out Beaumont—any Beaumont—of having direct involvement with ZOLA. Including Frances. There were no such things as coincidences—she'd said so herself. Frances had waltzed into his life just as ZOLA had started making noise. There had to be a connection—didn't there? But if that connection didn't run through her brothers, what was it?

Frances. His thoughts always came back to her. He couldn't wait to see her at dinner tonight, but he got the feeling that she might need something a little more than a floral arrangement, if she'd gotten half the pushback Ethan had today.

He checked his watch. He had time to make a little side trip, if he didn't shave.

Hopefully Frances liked stubble.

Eleven

Frances was unsurprised to find Byron waiting for her when she got back to the mansion after a long day of going over real estate contracts.

"Phillip called you, didn't he?" she began, pushing past her twin brother on her way up to her room. She had a date tonight, and she was already on edge. This would be a great night to put on the red dress. That'd drive any thoughts of affection right out of Ethan's mind. He'd be nothing but a walking, talking vessel of lust, and that was something she knew how to deal with.

No more tenderness. End of discussion.

"He might have," Byron admitted as he followed her into her room.

She was about to tear Byron a new one when she saw the huge floral arrangement on her nightstand table. "Oh!"

The card read, "Yours, E." Of course it did.

Those two little words—a mere six letters—made her smile. Which was just another sign that she needed a shower and a stiff drink. Ethan was not hers any more than she was his. She would not like him.

It would be easier to hold that line if he could just stop being so damn perfect.

"George said you've gotten flowers every day this week."

Frances rolled her eyes. George was the chef at the mansion and far too close with Byron. "So?" she said, pointedly ignoring the massive arrangement of blooms. "It's not like I haven't gotten flowers before."

"From the guy running the Brewery?"

She leveled a tired look at Byron. It was not a stretch to pull it off. "Why are you here? Aren't you running a restaurant or something? It's almost dinnertime, you know."

Byron flopped down on her bed. "We haven't officially opened yet. If you're going to flounce all around town with this new guy, you could at least plan on stopping by next week when we open. We could use the boost."

Frances stalked to her closet and began wrenching the hangers from side to side. "Excuse me? I do not *flounce*, thank you very much."

"Look," Byron said, staring at her. "Phillip seemed to think you were making a fool of yourself. I'm sure Chadwick has been updated. But whatever's going on, you're more than capable of dealing with it. If you're seeing this guy because you like him, then I want to meet him. And if you're seeing him for some other reason..."

The jerk had the nerve to crack his knuckles.

"Oh, for God's sake, Byron," she huffed at him. "Ethan could break you in half. No offense."

"None taken," Byron said without a trace of insult in his voice. "All I'm saying is that Phillip asked me to talk to you, and I've done that. Consider yourself talked to."

She pulled out the red dress and hung it on the closet door. "Seriously?"

Byron looked at the dress and then whistled. "Damn, Frannie. You either really like him or..."

This was part of the game, wasn't it? Convincing other people that she did like Ethan a great deal. Even if those people were Byron. She wasn't admitting to anything, not really. Not as long as she knew the truth deep down inside.

"I do, actually." It was supposed to come out strong and powerful because she was a woman in control of the situation.

It didn't. And Byron heard the difference. He wrinkled his forehead at her.

She was suddenly talking far more than was prudent. But this was Byron, damn it. She'd been sharing with him since their time in the womb, for crying out loud. "I mean, I do like him. There's something about him that's not your typical multimillionaire CEO. But I don't like *like* him, you know?" Which did not feel like the most honest thing to say. Because she might like him, even if it were a really bad idea.

Wasn't that what had almost happened last night? She'd let her guard down, and Ethan had been right there, strong and kind and thoughtful and she almost liked him.

Byron considered her juvenile argument. "So if you don't like *like* him, you're busting out the red dress because..."

Her mouth opened, and she almost admitted to the whole plan—the sham wedding, the angel investment, how she'd originally agreed to the whole crazy plan so she could inflict a little collateral damage on the current owners of the Brewery. For the family honor. If anyone would understand, it'd be Byron. She could always trust her brother and, no matter how crazy the situation was, he'd always stand behind her. *Always*.

But...

She couldn't do it. She couldn't admit she was breaking out the red dress because this was all a game, with high-dollar, high-power stakes, and she needed to level the playing field after the disaster that had been last night.

Her gaze fell on the bird of paradise arrangement. It was beautiful and had no doubt cost Ethan a fortune. She couldn't admit to anyone that she might not be winning the game. Not to Byron. Not to herself.

She decided it was time for a subject change. "How's the family?" Byron had recently married Leona Harper, an old girlfriend who was, awkwardly, the daughter of the Beaumonts' nemesis. Leona and Byron had a baby boy and another baby on the way. "Any other news from Leon Harper?"

"No," Byron said. "I don't know what we're paying the family lawyers these days, but it's worth it. Not a peep." He dug out his phone and called up a picture. "Guess what?"

Frances squinted at the ultrasound. "It's a...baby? I already knew Leona was pregnant, you goof."

"Ah, but did you know this? It's a girl," he said, his voice brimming with love. It almost hurt Frances to hear it—and to know that was not what she had with Ethan. "We're going to name her Jeannie."

"After Mom?" Frances didn't have a lot of memories of her mother and father together—at least, not a lot of memories that didn't involve screaming or crying. But Mom had made a nice, quiet life for herself after Hardwick.

There had been times when Frances had been growing up in this mansion that she'd wanted nothing more than to move in with Mom and live a quiet life, too. Frances bore the brunt of the new wives' dislike. By then, her older brothers had been off at college or, in Byron's case, off in the kitchen. Frances was the one who'd been expected to make nice with the new wives and the new kids—and Frances was the one who was supposed to grin and bear it when those new wives felt the need to prove that Hardwick loved them more than he'd loved anyone else. Even his own daughter.

Love had always been a competition. Never anything more.

Until now, damn it. Chadwick had married his assistant,

and no matter which way Frances looked at it, the two of them seemed to be wildly in love. And Phillip—her former partner in partying—had settled down with Jo. He had never been the kind of man to stick to one woman, and yet he was devoted to Jo. Matthew had decamped to California to be with his new wife. And now this—Byron and his happy, perfect little family.

Were you winning the game if you were the only one still playing it?

Byron nodded. "Mom's going to move in with us."

Frances looked at him in surprise. "Really?"

"Dad was such a mess, and God knows Leona's parents are, too. But Mom can be a part of the family again. And we've got plenty of room," he added, as if that were the deciding factor. "A complete mother-in-law apartment. Percy adores her, and I think Leona is thrilled to have Mom around. She never had much of a relationship with her own mother, you know."

Frances, as jaded as she was, felt tears prick at her eyes. The one thing their mother had never gotten over was losing her sense of family when Hardwick Beaumont had steamrolled her in court. When she'd lost her game, she'd lost *everything*.

That wasn't going to be how Frances wound up. "Oh, Byron—Mom's going to be *so* happy."

"So," Byron said, standing and taking his phone back. "I know you. And I know that you are occasionally prone to rash decisions."

She narrowed her eyes at him. "Is this the part where I get to tell you to go to hell, so soon after that touching moment?"

But Byron held up his hands in surrender. "All I'm saying is, if you do something that some people *might* consider rash, just call Mom first, okay? She was there when

Matthew got married and when I got married. And I get dibs on walking you down the aisle."

Frances stared at him. *"What?"* Where had he gotten *that*? The impending wedding was something that she and Ethan had only discussed behind closed doors. No one else was supposed to have a clue.

No one but Byron, curse him. She'd never been able to hide anything from him for long, anyway, and he knew it. He gave her a wry smile and said, "You heard me. And come to the restaurant next week, okay? I'll save you the best table." He kissed her on the cheek and gave her shoulders a quick hug. "I've got to go. Take care, Frannie."

She stood there for several moments after Byron left. *Rash?* This wasn't rash. This was a carefully thought-out plan. A plan that did not necessarily include her mother watching her get married to Ethan Logan or having Byron—or any other brother—walk her down the aisle.

She didn't want her mother to think she'd found a happily-ever-after. Maybe she should call Mom and warn her that this whole thing wasn't real and it wouldn't last.

Frances found herself sitting on her bed, staring at the flowers. She was running out of room in here—the roses were on the dresser, the lilies on the desk. He didn't have to spend this much on flowers for her.

She plucked the card out and read it again. It didn't take long to process the two words. *Yours, E.*

She grinned as her fingertip traced the *E*. No, he was not particularly good at whispering—or writing—sweet nothings.

But he was hers, at least for the foreseeable future.

She needed to call her mom. And she would. Soon.

Right now, however, she had to get ready for a date.

Ethan knew the moment Frances walked into the restaurant. Not because he saw her do it, but because the entire place—including the busboy passing by and the bartender pouring a glass of wine—came to a screeching halt. There wasn't a sound, not even a fork scraping on a plate.

He knew before he even turned around that he wasn't going to make it. He wasn't going to be able to wall himself off from whatever fresh hell Frances had planned for him tonight. And what only made it worse? He didn't want to. God help him, he didn't want to.

While he finished his whiskey he took a moment to remind himself that part of the deal was that sex was not part of the deal. It didn't matter if she were standing there completely nude—he would give her his present and take her up to his hotel room and lock himself in the bathroom if he had to. He'd control himself. He'd never succumbed to wild passion before. Now was not the time to start.

After a long, frozen moment, everyone moved again. Ethan took a deep breath and turned around.

Oh, Jesus. She was wearing a strapless fire-engine-red dress that hugged every curve. And as good as she looked, all he wanted to do was strip that dress off her and see the real her, without armor—or anything else—on.

Even across the dim restaurant, he saw her smile when their eyes met. She did not like him, he reminded himself. That smile was for public consumption, not for him. But damned if it didn't make him smile back at her.

He got off his stool and went to meet her. He knew he needed to say things—for the diners who were all not so subtly listening in. He needed to compliment Frances's dress and tell her how glad he was to see her.

He couldn't get his stupid mouth to work. Even as part of his brain knew that was the whole point of that dress, he couldn't fight it.

He couldn't fight her.

So instead of words, he did the next best thing—he pulled her into his arms and kissed her like he'd been thinking of doing all damn day long. And it wasn't for the viewing public, either.

It was for her. All for her.

Somehow, he managed to pull away before he slid his hands down her back and cupped her bottom in the middle of the restaurant. "I missed you today," he whispered as he touched his forehead to hers.

"Did you?"

Maybe it was supposed to sound dismissive, but that's not how it hit his ears. Instead, she sounded as if she couldn't quite believe he was being sincere—but she wanted him to be.

"I did. Our table's ready." He took her hand in his and led her to the waiting table. After they were seated, he asked, "Anything interesting happen today?"

She arched an eyebrow at him. "Yes, actually. My twin, Byron, came to see me."

"Oh?" Had it been the same kind of visit he'd gotten from Chadwick?

Frances was watching him closely. "His new restaurant opens next week. He'd appreciate it if we could put in an appearance. Apparently, we're great publicity right now."

"Which was the plan," he said, more to remind himself than her. Because he had to stick to that plan, come hell or high water.

She leaned forward on her elbows, her generous cleavage on full display. He felt his pulse pick up a notch. "Indeed. You? Anything interesting today?"

"A few things," he tried to say casually. "Everyone at the Brewery is waiting to see if you bring me my very own donut this Friday."

A dazzling—and, he hoped, genuine—smile lit up her face. "Oh, really? I guess I should plan on coming, then?" Her tone was light and teasing.

This was what he'd missed today. She could talk circles

around him, and all he could do was keep up. He reached over and cupped her cheek in his hand, his thumb stroking her skin.

She leaned into his touch—a small movement that no one else could see. It was just for him, the way she let him carry a little of her weight. Just for him, the way her eyelashes fluttered. "I requested a chocolate éclair."

"Maybe I'll bring you a whole box, just to see what they say."

She would not like him. He should not like her.

But he did, damn it all. He liked her a great deal.

He didn't want to tell her the other interesting thing. He didn't want to watch her armor snap back into place at the mention of one of her brothers. Hell, for that matter, he didn't really want to be sitting in this very nice restaurant. He wanted to be someplace quiet, where they could be alone. Where her body could curl up against his and he could stroke her hair and they could talk about their days and kiss and laugh without giving a flying rat's ass what anyone else saw, much less thought.

"Chadwick came by the office today."

It was a hard thing to watch, her reaction. She sat up, pulling away from his touch. Her shoulders straightened and her eyes took on a hard look. "Did he now?"

Ethan let his hand fall away. "He did."

She considered this new development for a moment. "I suppose Phillip talked to him?"

"I got that feeling. He also said I'm making him look bad, with all the flowers."

Frances waved this excuse away as if it were nothing more than a gnat. "He can afford to buy Serena flowers—and does, frequently." Her eyes closed and, elbows back on the table, she clasped her hands in front of her. She looked as though she was concentrating very hard—or praying. "Do I even want to know what he said?"

"The usual older-brother stuff. What are my intentions, I'd better not break his little sister's heart—that sort of thing." He shrugged, as if it'd been just another day at the office.

She opened her eyes and stared at him over the tops of her hands. "What did you say? Please tell me you didn't kowtow to him. It's not good for his already-massive ego."

Ethan leaned back. "I merely informed him that what happens between two consenting adults is none of his business and for him to presume he knows best for either of us was patronizing at best. A fact I have recently been reminded of myself."

Frances's mouth opened, but then what he said registered and she closed it again. A wry smile curved her lips. He wanted to kiss that smile, those lips—but there was a table in the way. "You didn't."

"I did. I don't recall any kowtowing."

She laughed at that, which made him feel good. It wasn't as if he'd fought to the death for her honor or anything, but he'd still protected her from a repeat of what had happened last night.

She shifted and the toes of her foot came into contact with his shin. Slowly, she stroked up and down. His pulse kicked it up another notch—then two.

"I got you something," he said suddenly. He had decided it would be better to wait to give her the jewelry until after dinner, but the way she was looking at him? The way she was touching him? He'd changed his mind.

"The flowers were beautiful," she murmured. Her foot moved up and then down again, stroking his desire higher.

The room was too warm. Too hot. He was going to fall into the flames and get burned, and he couldn't think of a better way to go.

He reached into his pocket and pulled out the long, thin

velvet box. "I picked it out," he told her, holding it out to her. "I thought it suited you."

Her foot paused against his leg, and he took advantage of the break to adjust his pants. Sitting had suddenly become uncomfortable.

Her eyes were wide as she stared at the box. "What did you do?"

"I bought my future wife a gift," he said simply. The words felt right on his tongue, like they belonged there. *Wife.* "Open it."

She hesitated, as if the box might bite her. So he opened it for her.

The diamond necklace caught the light and glittered. He'd chosen the drop pendant, a square-cut diamond that hung off the end of a chain of three smaller diamonds, all set in platinum. Tiffany's had some larger solitaires, but this one seemed to fit Frances better.

"Oh, Ethan," she gasped as he held the box out toward her. "I didn't expect this."

"I like to keep you guessing," he told her. He set the box down and pulled the platinum chain out of its moorings. "Here," he said, his voice deeper than he remembered it being. "Allow me."

He stood and moved behind her, draping the necklace in front of her. She swept her mane of hair away from her neck, exposing the smooth skin. Ethan froze. He wanted nothing more than to lean down and taste her, to run his lips over the delicate curve where her neck met her shoulders—to see how she would react if he trailed kisses lower, pulling the dress down farther until...

She tilted her head down, pulling him back to the reality of standing in a crowded restaurant, holding nine thousand dollars' worth of diamonds. As he tried to fasten the clasp, his hands began to shake with need—the need to hold her, the need to stroke her bare shoulders. The need to make her *his*.

He'd had other lady friends, bought them nice gifts—usually when it was time for him to move on—but he had never felt this much need before. He didn't know what it was—only that it was because of her.

He willed his hands—and other body parts—to stand down. This was just a temporary madness; that was all. A beautiful woman in a gorgeous dress designed to inspire lust—nothing more, really.

Except it wasn't. No matter what he told himself, he knew he wasn't being honest—not with himself, not with her.

Honesty was not supposed to figure into this, after all. The whole premise of their relationship was based on a stack of lies that only got taller with each passing day and each passing floral arrangement. No, it was not supposed to be honest, their relationship. It was, however, supposed to be simple. She needed the money. He needed the Beaumont seal of approval. Everyone came out a winner.

That was possibly the biggest lie of all. Nothing about Frances Beaumont had been simple since the moment he'd laid eyes on her.

Finally, he got the clasp hooked. He managed to restrain himself enough that he did not press a kiss to her neck, did not wind her long hair into his hands.

But he was not exactly restrained. His fingertips drifted over the skin she'd exposed when she'd moved her hair and then down her bare shoulders with the lightest of touches. It shouldn't have been overtly sexual, shouldn't have been all that erotic—but unfamiliar need hammered through his gut.

It only got worse when she let go of her hair and that mass of fire-red silk brushed over the backs of his hands. Without meaning to—without meaning any of this—he dug his fingers into her skin, pulling her against him. She was soft and warm, and she leaned back and looked up at him.

Their gazes met. He supposed that, with another woman, he'd be staring down her front, looking at how his diamonds were nestled between her breasts, so large and firm and on such display at this angle.

But he was only dimly aware of her cleavage because Frances was staring up at him, her lips parted ever so slightly. Color had risen in her cheeks, and her eyes were wide. One of her hands reached up and found his. It was only when she pressed his hand flat against her skin that he realized his palms were moving along her skin, moving to feel everything about her—to learn everything about her.

He stroked his other thumb over her cheek. She gasped, a small movement that he felt more than saw. His body responded to her involuntary reaction with its own. Blood pounded in his ears as it raced from his brain to his erection as fast as it could. And, given how she was leaning against it, she knew it, too.

This was the moment, he thought dimly—as much as he could think, anyway. She could say something cutting and put him in his place, and he'd have to sit down and eat dinner with blue balls and not touch her like he meant it.

"Ethan," she whispered as she stared up at him. Her eyes seemed darker now, the pupils widening until the blue-green had almost disappeared.

Yes, he wanted to shout, to groan—yes, yes. He wanted to hear his name on her lips, over and over, in the most intimate of whispers and the loudest of passionate shouts. He wanted to push her to the point where all she could do, say—think—was his name. Was him.

His hand slipped lower, stroking the exposed skin of her throat. Lower still, tracing the outline of the necklace he'd bought for her.

Her grip on his hand tightened as his fingers traced the pendant. She didn't tell him to stop, though. She didn't lean away, didn't give a single signal that he should stop touching her. His hand started to move even lower, stroking down into the body of her dress and—

"Are we ready to order?" a too-bright, too-loud voice suddenly demanded.

Frances and Ethan both jumped. Suddenly he was aware that they were still in public, that at least half the restaurant was still watching them—that he'd been on the verge of sheer insanity in the full view of anyone with a cell phone. What the hell was wrong with him?

He tried to step away from her, to put at least a respectable three inches between their bodies—but Frances didn't let go of his hand.

Instead—incredibly—she stood and said, "Actually, I'm not hungry. Thanks, though." Then she turned to give him a look over her shoulder. "Shall we?"

"We shall," was the most intelligent thing he was capable of coming up with. The waiter smirked at them both as Ethan fished a fifty out of his wallet to cover his bar tab.

Every eye was on them as they swept up to the front together. Ethan took Frances's coat from the coat check girl and held it as Frances slipped her bare arms into it. They didn't speak as they braved the cold wind and waited for the valet to bring his car around. But Ethan put his arm around her shoulders and pulled her close. She leaned her head against his chest. Was he imagining things, or was she breathing hard—or at least, harder than normal? He wasn't sure. Maybe that was his chest, rising and falling faster than he normally breathed.

He didn't feel normal. Sex was always fun, always enjoyable—but something he could take or leave. He liked the release of it, and, yeah, sometimes he needed that release more than other times. But that's all it was. A pressure valve that sometimes needed to be depressurized a bit.

It wasn't this pain that made thinking rationally impossible—a pain that could only be erased by burying himself in her body over and over again until he was finally sated.

This wasn't about a simple release. He could achieve that with anyone. Hell, he didn't even need another person.

But this? Right now? This was about Frances and this unknown need she inspired in him. And the more he tried to name that need, the more muddled his head became. He wanted to show her what he could do for her, how he could take care of her, protect her and honor her. That they could be good together. For each other.

Finally, the car arrived. Ethan held her door for her and then got behind the wheel. He gunned it harder than he needed to, but he didn't want to waste another minute, another second, without Frances in his arms.

They weren't far from the hotel. He wouldn't have even bothered with the car if it'd been twenty degrees warmer. The drive would take five minutes, tops.

Or it would have—until Frances leaned over and placed her hand on his throbbing erection. Even through the layers of his boxers and wool trousers, her touch burned hot as she tested his length. Ethan couldn't do anything but grip the steering wheel as she made her preliminary exploration of his arousal.

It was when she squeezed him, shooting the pain that veered into pleasure through his whole body, that he forced out the words. "This isn't a game, Frances."

"No, it's not," she agreed, her voice breathy as her fingers stroked him. His body burned for her. If she stopped, he didn't know if he could take it. "Not anymore."

"Are you coming up to my room?" It came out far gruffer than he'd intended—not a request but not quite a demand.

"I don't think the hotel staff would appreciate it if we had sex in the lobby." She didn't let go of him when she said it. If anything, her hand was tighter around him.

"Is that what you really want? Sex, I mean. Not the lobby part." Because he was honor-bound to ask and more than honor-bound to accept her answer as the final word on the matter. Even if it killed him. "Because it wasn't part of the original deal."

That pushed her away from him. Her hot hand was gone, and he was left aching without her touch. "Ethan," she said in the most severe voice he'd heard her use all night long. "I don't want to talk about the damned deal. I don't want to think about it."

"Then what do you want?" he asked as they pulled up in front of the hotel.

She didn't answer. Instead, she got out, and he had no choice but to follow her, handing his keys to the valet. They walked into the hotel without touching, waited for the elevator without speaking. Ethan was thankful his coat was long enough to hide his erection.

They walked into the elevator together. Ethan waited until the doors were closed before he moved on her. "Tell me what you want, Frances," he said, pinning her against the back of the elevator. Her body was warm against his as she looked up at him through her lashes and he saw her. Not her armor, not her carefully constructed front— he saw *her*. "To hell with the deal. Tell me what you want right now. Is it sex? Is it *me*?"

"I shouldn't want you," she said, her voice soft, almost uncertain. She took his face in her hands, their mouths a whisper away. "I shouldn't."

"I shouldn't want you, either," he told her, an unfamiliar flash of anger pushing the words out of his mouth. "You drive me mad, Frances. Absolutely freaking mad. You undermine me at the Brewery and work me into a lather, and you turn my head around so fast that I get dizzy every time I see you. And, damn it all, you do it with that smile that lets me know it's easy for you. That *I'm* easy for you." He touched his thumb to her lips. She tried to kiss his thumb, and when he pulled it away, she tried to kiss him, pulling his head down to hers.

He didn't let her. He peeled her hands off his face and pinned them against the elevator walls. For some reason, he had to tell her this now before they went any further. "You *complicate* things. God help me—you make everything harder than it has to be, and I don't want you any other way."

Her eyes were wide, although he didn't know if that was because he was holding her captive or what he'd said. "You…don't?"

"No, I don't. I want you complicated and messy." He leaned against her, so she could feel exactly how much he wanted her. "I want you taunting and teasing me, and I want you with your armor up because you're the toughest woman I know. And I want you with your armor off entirely because—" Abruptly, the flash of anger that gave him all of those words was gone, and he realized that instead of telling a beautiful woman how wonderful she was, he was pretty sure he'd been telling her that she irritated him. "Because that's how I want you," he finished, unsure of himself.

Her lips parted and her mouth opened—right as the elevator did the same. They were on Ethan's floor. He held her like that for just a second longer, then released his hold in time to keep the doors from closing on them.

He held out his hand for her.

And he waited.

Twelve

"You *want* me complicated?" Frances stood there, staring at Ethan as if he'd casually announced he wore a cape in his off time while fighting crime.

No one had wanted her messy and complicated before. They wanted her simply, as an object of lust or as a step up the social ladder. It was when things got messy or complicated or—God help her—both that men disappeared from her life. When Frances dared to let her real self show through—that was when the trouble began. She was too dramatic, too high-maintenance, her tastes and ambitions too expensive. Her family life was far too complex—that was always rich, coming from the ones who wanted an association with the prestige of the Beaumont name but none of the actual work that went into maintaining it.

She'd heard it all before. *So* many times before.

The elevator beeped in warning. Ethan said, "I do," and grabbed her, hauling her past the closing doors.

She didn't know what to say to that, which was a rarity in itself. They stood in the middle of the hallway for a moment, Ethan holding on to her hand tightly. "Do you?" he asked in a gentle voice. "Want me, that is."

She felt the cool weight of the diamonds he'd laid against her skin. How many thousands of dollars had he spent on them? On her? It was not supposed to be complicated. If they had sex, then it was supposed to be this simple quid pro quo. This was the way of her world—it always had been. The man buys an expensive, extravagant gift and the woman takes her clothes off. It was not messy.

Except it was.

"You're ruining the last of my family's legacy and business," she told him. "You're everything that went wrong. When we lost the Brewery, I lost a part of my identity and I should hate you for being party to that. God, how I wanted to hate you."

Oh, Lord—were her eyes watering? No. Absolutely not. There was no crying in baseball or in affairs of the heart. At least, not in her affairs of the heart, mostly because her affairs never actually involved her heart.

She kept that locked away from everyone, and no one had ever realized it—until Ethan Logan had shown up and seen the truth of the matter. Until he'd seen the truth of her.

"You can still hate me in the morning," he told her. "I don't expect anything less from you."

"But what about tonight?" Because it was all very well and good to say that he liked her messy, but that didn't mean she wasn't still a mess. And that wore on a man after a while.

He stepped into her. His body was strong and warm, and she knew if she gave first and leaned against him, breathed in his woodsy scent, that she would be lost to him.

She'd already lost so much. Could she afford to lose anything else?

He stroked his fingers down her face, then slid them back through her hair, pulling her up to him. "Let me love you tonight, Frances. Just you and me. Nothing else."

It was real and honest and sincere, damn him to hell. It was true because he was true. None of those little lies and half glosses of compliments that hid the facts better than they illuminated them. And for a man who did not

grasp the finer points of sweet nothings, it was the sweet-
est damn something she'd ever heard.

A door behind them opened. She didn't know if it was
the elevator or another guest and she didn't much care.
She took off down the hall toward Ethan's room without
letting go of his hand.

He got the door open and pulled her inside. "I won't
like you in the morning," she told him, her voice shaking
as he undid the belt at her waist and pushed the coat from
her shoulders.

"But you like me now," he replied, shucking his own
coat in the process. "Don't you?"

She did. Oh, this was a heartache waiting to happen,
this thing between her and Ethan.

"I don't want to talk anymore," she said in as commanding a voice as she could muster. More than that, she didn't
want to think anymore. She only wanted to feel, to get lost
in the sweet freedom of surrendering to her baser lust.

She grabbed him by the suit jacket and jerked it down
his arms, trying to get him as naked as possible as fast as
possible. He let her, but he said, "Don't you dare hide behind that wall, Frances."

"I'm not hiding," she informed him, grabbing his belt
and undoing it. "I'm getting you naked. That's generally
how sex works best."

The next thing she knew, they were right back to where
they'd been in the elevator, with the full weight of his
body pinning her against the door, her wrists in his hands.
"Don't," he growled at her. "I don't want to sleep with your
armor. I want to sleep with you, damn it. I *like* you. Just
the way you are. So don't try to be some flippant, distant
princess who's above this. Above us."

Her breath caught in her throat. "You don't know what
you're asking of me." It didn't come out confident or cocky
or even flippant.

"Maybe I do." He kissed her then, with enough force to knock her head back. "Sorry," he murmured against her lips.

"It's okay," she replied because if they were getting to the sex part, they'd stop talking and she could just feel. Even the small pain in the back of her head was okay because she didn't have to talk about it, about what it really meant. "Just keep kissing me hard."

"Is that how you want it?"

She tested her wrists against his grip. There was a little give, but not much. "Yes," she said, knowing full well that he was a man who knew exactly what that meant. "That's how I want *you*." Hard and fast with no room to stop and think. None.

A deep sound came out of his chest, a growl that she felt in her bones. His hips shifted and his erection ground against her. Yes, she wanted to feel all of that.

But then he said, "Tell me if something doesn't work," and she heard his control starting to fray. "Promise me that, babe."

She blinked up at him through a haze of desire. Had anyone ever said that to her before? "Of course," she said, trying to make it sound as though all of her previous lovers had put her orgasms first—had put her first.

He raised an eyebrow at her. He didn't even have to say it—she could still hear him telling her not to pretend.

Then he moved. "Whatever else," he said as he slid her hands up over her head and put both her wrists under one of his massive hands, "I expect complete and total honesty in bed."

"We aren't currently in bed," she reminded him. She tested her wrists again, but he wasn't playing around. He had her pinned.

It wasn't that she wasn't turned on—she was. But a new kind of excitement started to build underneath the standard sexual arousal that she normally felt. Ethan had her pinned. He had a free hand. He could do anything that he wanted to her.

And he'd stop the moment she told him to.

For once in her life, she wouldn't have to think about anything except what he was going to do next.

"Turn around," he ordered as he lifted her wrists away from the door just enough that she could spin in place. Then he swept her hair away from her neck and—and— oh, God. He didn't just kiss her there, he scraped his teeth over her exposed skin, raw and hungry.

Frances sucked in air at the unexpected sensation. "Good?" he asked.

"Yeah."

"Good," he said, biting a little harder this time, then kissing the sore spot.

Frances shifted, the weight between her legs growing hotter and heavier as he worked over her skin. Then he was pulling the zipper down on her dress, and the whole thing fell to her feet, leaving her in nothing but a white lace pair of panties that left very little to the imagination.

"Oh, babe," Ethan said in undisguised appreciation. She started to turn so she could see his face when he said it, but he gave her bottom a light smack and then used his body to keep hers flat against the door. "No, don't look," he ordered. "Just feel."

"Yeah," she moaned, her skin slightly stinging from where he'd smacked her. "I want to feel you."

His hand popped against her bare bottom again—not hard. He wasn't hurting her. But the unexpected contact made her body involuntarily tighten, and the anticipation of the next touch drove everything else from her mind.

Ethan's free hand circled her waist, pushing her just far enough away from the door that he could cup one of her breasts, teasing the nipple until it was hard with desire.

Then he tugged at it with more force. "Yeah?" he asked, his breath hot against her neck. He shoved one of his knees between her legs and she sagged onto it, grinding her hips, trying to take the pressure off the one spot in her body that made standing hard.

"Yeah," she moaned, her body moving without her permission, trying to find release, that moment where there was a climax that only Ethan could bring her to.

"You want more?" he demanded, tugging at her nipple again.

"Ethan, please," she panted, for no matter how she shifted her hips, the only pressure she felt did not push her over the edge.

He pulled away from her. "Don't move," he said. Then her wrists were free and his knee was gone and she felt cold, pressed up against this impersonal hotel door. Behind her, she heard the sound of plastic tearing. The condom. *Good.*

Then Ethan put his hand on the back of her neck and pulled her away from the door. "Hard?" he asked again, as if he wanted to make absolutely sure.

"Hard," she all but begged. "Hard and fast and—"

He led her to the bed, but instead of laying her out on it, he bent her over the edge. Her panties were pulled down, and she was exposed before him.

Her body quivered with need and anticipation and excitement because this was not gentle and sweet, not when he grabbed her by the hips and lifted her bottom against his rock-hard erection. His fingers dug into her flesh in a hungry way.

"Ethan," she moaned as he smacked her bottom again, just hard enough that her muscles tightened and she almost came right then. She fisted the bedclothes in her hands and tensed, hoping and praying for the next touch. "Hard and fast and now. Now, Ethan, or I won't like you in the morning, I swear to God, I'll hate you. *Now*, Ethan, *now*."

Then he was against her, and, with a moan of pure masculine satisfaction, he was in her, thrusting hard. Frances gasped at the suddenness of him—oh, he was huge—but her body took him in as he pounded her with all the aggression she needed so badly.

She hit her peak, moaning into the sheets as the wave cascaded over her. *Thank heavens*, she thought, going soft after it'd passed. She'd wanted to come so badly and—and—

And Ethan didn't stop. He didn't sputter to a finish. Instead, he paused long enough to reach forward and tangle his hands in her hair and pull so that her head came off the bed. "Are you nice and warmed up now?" he demanded, and a shiver ran through her body. He felt it, too—she could tell by the way he twined her hair around her fingers. "That's it, babe. Ready?"

He wasn't done. Oh, he wasn't done with her. He was going to make her come again, so fast and so hard that when he began to thrust again, all she could do was take him in. He kept one hand tangled in her hair, lifting her head up and back so that she arched away from him and her bottom lifted up to his greedy demands.

All she could do was moan—she wanted to cry out, but the angle of her neck made that too hard. Everything about her tightened as Ethan gave her exactly what she wanted—him, hard and fast.

This time, when he brought his hand against her ass in time with his thrusting, she came equally as hard. She couldn't help it. Her body acted without her input at all. All she was, all she could feel, was what Ethan did to her. The climax was unlike anything she'd ever felt before, so intense she forgot to breathe even.

Ethan held her there as waves of pleasure washed her

clean of everything but satisfaction. When she sagged against the bed, spent and panting, he let go of her hair, dug his fingertips back into her hips and pumped into her three more times before groaning and falling forward onto her.

They lay there for a moment, his body pressing hers against the mattress while she tried to remember how to breathe like a normal human. She didn't feel normal anymore; that was for sure.

She didn't know how she felt. Good—oh, yes. She felt wonderful. Her body was limp and her skin tingled and everything was amazing.

But when Ethan rolled off her and then leaned down and pressed a kiss between her shoulder blades—she felt decidedly not normal. She didn't turn her head to look at him. She didn't know what to say. Her! Frances Beaumont! Speechless! That was hard enough to accomplish by itself—but to have had sex so intense and so satisfying that she had not a single snappy observation or cutting comeback?

Not that he was waiting for her to say something. He kissed her on the shoulder and said, "I'll be right back," before he hefted himself off the bed. She heard the bathroom door click shut, and then she was alone in the hotel room with only her feelings.

Now what was she going to do?

Thirteen

Ethan splashed cold water on his face, trying to get his head to clear. He felt like a jackass. That wasn't how he normally took a woman to bed. Not even close. He usually took his time, making sure the foreplay left everyone satisfied before the actual sex.

But pinning Frances against the door and then bending her over the edge of the bed? Pawing at her as if he were little more than a lust-crazed animal? That hadn't been tender and sweet.

He didn't want to be responsible for his actions. He'd smacked her bottom—more than once! That wasn't like him. He wanted that to be her fault—she'd worn the red dress, she'd been this *siren* that pushed him past sanity, past responsibility.

But that was crap, and he knew it. All she'd said was that she wanted it hard and fast. He could have still been a gentleman about it. Instead, he'd gotten rough. He'd never done that before. He didn't know...

Well, he just didn't know.

And he wasn't going to find out hiding in the bathroom.

He'd apologize; that was all there was to it. He'd gotten carried away. It wouldn't happen again.

He finished up and headed out. He hadn't even gotten undressed. He'd stripped her down, but aside from shoving his pants out of the way, he was still dressed. Yes, that was quite possibly the best sex of his life, but still. He couldn't shake the feeling that he'd gone too far.

That feeling got even stronger when he saw her. Frances had curled up on her side. She looked impossibly small against the expanse of white sheets. She watched him, her eyes wide. Was she upset? *Hell*.

Then her nose wrinkled, and he was pretty sure she smiled. "You're not naked," she said. Her voice was raw, as if she'd been shouting into the wind for hours.

"Is that a problem?" He tried to keep it casual sounding. He wasn't sure he made it.

She uncurled from the bed like a flower opening for him. "I wanted to see you. And I didn't get to."

"My apologies for the disappointment." He started to jerk open the buttons on his shirt, but she stood and closed the distance between them. His hands fell around her waist, still warm from the sex. He wanted to fold her into his arms and hold her for as long as he could.

Where was all this ridiculous sentiment coming from? He wasn't a sentimental guy.

"Let me," she said. He saw that her hands were trembling. "And it wasn't disappointing. It was wonderful. Except that I couldn't see you."

Ethan blinked twice, trying to process that. "I didn't go too far?"

"No," she said, giving him a nervous smile. "I—" She paused and took a deep breath. "Honestly?"

"Even though we're still not in bed," he said with a grin, tilting her chin up so he could look her in the eyes.

She held his gaze for a moment before forcibly turning her attention back to his buttons. "Thank you," she said quietly.

That was not quite what he'd been expecting. "For what? I think I got just as much out of that as you did."

She undid the last button and pushed the shirt off him. Then his T-shirt followed. Finally she shoved his pants down, and Ethan kicked out of them.

"Oh, my," she whispered, skimming her fingers over his chest and ruffling his hair.

He fought the urge to flex. The urge won. She giggled as his muscles moved under her hands. "Ethan!"

"Sorry," he said, walking her back toward the bed. "I can't seem to help myself around you."

This time, they actually got under the covers. Ethan pulled her on top of him. He didn't mean it in an explicitly sexual way, but her body covering his? Okay, it was more than a little sexual. "Why did you thank me?"

She laid out on him, her head tucked against his chest. "You really want me messy and complicated?"

"Seems to be working so far."

She sighed, tracing small circles against his skin. "No one's ever wanted me. Not the real me. Not like this."

"I find that hard to believe. You are a hell of a woman."

"They don't want me," she insisted. "They want the fantasy of me. Beautiful and sexy and rich and famous. They want the mystique of the Beaumont name. That's what I am to people." When he didn't have a response to that, she propped herself up on one elbow and stared down at him. "That's what I was to you, wasn't I?"

There was no point in playing games about it. "You were. But you're not anymore."

Her smile was tinged with sadness. "I'm not used to being honest, I guess."

He cupped her face in his hands and kissed her. He didn't intend for it to be a distraction, but she must have taken it that way because she pulled back. "Why did you agree to a sham marriage? And don't give me that line about the workers loving me."

"Even though they do," he put in.

"Most men do not agree to sham marriages as business deals," she went on as if he hadn't interrupted her. "I seem to recall you making quite a point of saying love wasn't a part of marriage when we came to terms. So spill it."

She had him trapped. Sure, he could throw her off him, but then she shifted and straddled him, and his body stirred at the thought of her bare legs wrapped around his waist, her body so close to his.

So, with mock exasperation, he flopped back against the bed. "My parents have an…unusual relationship," he said.

She leaned down on him, her arms crossed over her chest, her chin on her arms. "I don't want you to take this the wrong way, but so? I mean, my mom was second out of four wives for my dad. I wouldn't know a usual relationship if it bit me. Present company included."

He wrapped his arms around her body, enjoying the warmth she shared with him. No, this wasn't usual, not even close. But he was enjoying it anyway. "Have you ever heard of Troy Logan?"

"No. Brother or father?"

He wasn't surprised. Her brother Chadwick would probably recognize the name, but that wasn't Frances's world. "Father. Notorious on Wall Street for buying companies and dismantling them at a profit."

She tilted her head from side to side. "I take it the apple did not fall terribly far from the tree?"

"I don't take companies apart. I restructure them." She gave him an arch look, and he gave in. "But, yes, you're correct. We're in nearly the same line of work."

"And…" she said. "Your mother?"

"Wanda Kensington." He braced for the reaction.

He didn't have to wait long. She gasped, which made him wince. "What? You don't mean—*the* Wanda Kensington? The artist?"

"I can't tell you how rare it is that someone knows my

mother's name but not my father's," he said, stroking her hair away from her face.

"Don't change the subject," she snapped, sitting all the way up. Which left her bare breasts directly in Ethan's line of sight. The diamonds he'd bought for her glittered between those perfect breasts. "Your mother is—but Wanda's known for her art installations! Massive performance pieces that take like a year to assemble! I don't ever remember reading anything about her having a family."

"She wasn't around much. I don't know why they got married, and I don't know why they stayed married. I'm not even sure they like each other. They never made sense," he admitted. "She'd be gone for months, a year—we had nannies that my father was undoubtedly sleeping with—and then she'd walk back in like no time at all had passed and pretend to be this hands-on mother who cared."

He was surprised to hear the bitterness in his voice. He'd long ago made peace with his mother. Or so he'd thought. "And she'd try, I think. She'd stick it out for a few weeks—once she was home for almost three months. She made it to Christmas, and then she was gone again. We never knew, my brother and I. Never had a clue when she'd show up or when she'd disappear again."

"So you were—what? Another piece of performance art? The artist as a mother?"

"I suppose." Not that he'd ever thought about it in those terms. "It wasn't bad. Dad wasn't jealous of her. She wasn't jealous of him. It wasn't like there was drama. It was just... a marriage on paper."

"It was a sham," Frances corrected.

He skimmed his hands up and down her thighs, shifting her weight against him. His erection was more than interested in the shifting. "Didn't seem like it'd be hard to replicate," he agreed.

But that was before—before he'd seen past Frances's

armor, before he'd stupidly begun to like the real woman underneath.

She rocked her hips, and his body responded. He stroked her nipples—this time, without the roughness—and Frances moaned appreciatively. He shouldn't want her this much, shouldn't *like* her this much. Passion wasn't supposed to figure into his plans. It never had before.

He lifted her off long enough to roll on another condom, and then she settled her weight back onto him, taking him in with a sigh of pure pleasure. *This* was honesty. This was something real between them because she meant something more to him than just her last name.

She rode him slowly, taking her time, letting him play with her breasts and her nipples until she was panting and he was driving into her. He leaned forward enough to catch one of her breasts in his mouth and sucked her nipple hard between his teeth.

She might not like him in the morning, and she'd be well within her rights.

But he was going to like her. Hell, he already did. It was going to be a huge problem.

As she shuddered down on him, urging him to suck her nipples harder as she came apart, he didn't care. Complicated and messy and his.

She was his.

After she'd collapsed onto him and he'd taken care of the condom, they lay in each other's arms. He had things he wanted to say to her, except he didn't know what those things were, which wasn't like him. He was a decisive man. The buck stopped with him.

"Are we still going to get married next week?" she asked in a drowsy voice.

"If you want," he said, feeling even as he said it that it was not the best response. He tried again. "I thought we weren't going to talk about the deal tonight."

"We aren't," she agreed and then immediately qualified that statement. "It's just that…this changes things."

"Does it?" He leaned over and turned out the light and then pulled the covers up over them both. When was the last time he'd had a woman spend the night in his arms? He couldn't think of when. His previous relationships were not spend-the-night relationships.

He tucked his arm around her body and held her close. Something cold and metallic poked at his side—the necklace. It was all she had on.

"We were supposed to barely live together," she reminded him. "We weren't supposed to sleep together. We weren't…"

He yawned and shrugged. "So we'll be slightly more married than we planned on. The marital bed and all that."

"And you're okay with that?"

"I'm okay with you." He kissed the top of her head. "I guess… Well, when we made the deal, I didn't think I'd enjoy spending time with you."

"You mean sex. You didn't think you'd enjoy sleeping with me." She sounded hurt about that, although he couldn't tell if she was playing or actually pouting.

"No, I don't," he clarified. "I mean, I didn't think I'd want to spend time with you. I didn't think I'd like you this much."

The moment the words left his mouth, he knew that he'd said too much. Damn it, they were supposed to roll over and go to sleep and not have deep, meaningful conversations until he'd recovered from the sex and had some more.

Instead, Frances tensed and then sat up, pulling away from him. "Ethan," she said, her voice a warning. "I told you not to like me."

"You make it sound like I have a choice about it," he said.

"You do."

"No, I don't. I can't help it." She didn't reply, didn't curl back into his arms. "We don't have to rush to get married. I'm willing to wait for you."

"Jesus," she said. The bed shifted, and then she was out of it, fumbling around the room in the dark. "Jesus, you sound like you *want* to marry me."

He turned on the light. "What's wrong?"

She threw his words back at him. "What's wrong?" She grabbed her dress and started to shimmy into it. Any other time, watching Frances Beaumont get dressed would be the highlight of his day. But not now, not when she was angrily trying to jerk up the zipper.

"Frances," he said, getting out of bed. "Where are you going?"

"This was a mistake," was the short reply.

He could see her zipping into her armor as fast as the dress—if not faster. "No, it wasn't," he said defensively, trying to catch her in his arms. "This was good. Great. This was us together. This is what we could be."

"Honestly, Ethan? There is no us. Not now, not ever. My God," she said, pushing him away and snagging her coat. "I thought you were smarter than this. Good sex and you're suddenly in love—in like?" she quickly corrected. "Unacceptable."

"Like hell it is," he roared at her.

"This is causal at best, Ethan. *Casual.* Casual sex, casual marriage." She flung her coat over her barely zipped dress and hastily knotted the belt. "I warned you, but you didn't listen, did you?"

"Would you calm the hell down and tell me what's wrong?" he demanded. "I did listen. I listened when you told me you expected to be courted with flowers and gifts and thoughtfulness."

"I did not—"

But he cut her off. "I listened when you told me about

your plans for a gallery. I listened when your family caught you off guard."

"I do not like you." She bit the words off as if she were killing them, one syllable at a time.

"I don't believe you. Not anymore. I've seen the real you, damn it all."

She drew herself up to her full height, a look on her face like a reigning monarch about to deliver a death sentence. "Have you?" she said. "I thought you were better at the game than this, Ethan. How disappointing that you're like all the rest."

And then she was gone. The door to the room swung open and slammed shut behind her, leaving Ethan wondering what the holy hell had just happened.

Fourteen

When had Frances lost control? That was the question she kept asking herself on the insanely long elevator ride down to the hotel lobby. She asked it as the valet secured a cab for her, and she asked it again on the long ride out to the mansion.

Because she had. She'd lost all sorts of control.

She slipped into the mansion. The place was dark and quiet—but then, it was late. Past midnight. The staff had left hours ago. Chadwick and Serena and their little girl were no doubt asleep, as were Frances's younger siblings.

She felt very much alone.

She took off her shoes and tiptoed up to her room. She jerked her zipper down so hard she heard tearing, which was a crying shame because this dress was her best one. But she couldn't quite care.

Frances dug out her ugly flannel pajamas, bright turquoise plaid and baggy shapelessness. They were warm and soft and comforting, and far removed from the nothing she'd almost fallen asleep wearing when she'd been in bed with Ethan.

God, what a mess. And, yes, she was aware that she was probably making it messier than it had to be, just by virtue of being herself.

But was he serious? Sure, she could have believed it if

he'd said he loved being with her and she was special and wonderful before the sex. It was expected, those words of seduction. Except he hadn't said them then. He'd said things that should have been insults—that she made his life harder than he wanted her to, that she drove him mad, that she was a complicated hot mess.

Those were not the words of a man trying to get laid.

Those were the words of an honest man.

And then after? To lay there in his arms and feel as if she'd exposed so much more than her body to him and to have him tell her that he enjoyed being with her, that he liked her, that—

That he'd happily push back their agreed-on marriage because she was worth waiting for?

It was all supposed to be a game. A game she'd played before and a game she'd play again. Yes, this was the long game—a wedding, a yearlong marriage—but that didn't change the rules.

Did it?

She climbed under her own covers in her own bed, a bed that was just as large as Ethan's. It felt empty compared with what she'd left behind.

Ethan wasn't following the rules. He was changing them. She'd warned him against doing so, but he was doing so anyway. And it was all too much for Frances. Too much honesty, too much realness. Too much intimacy.

Men had proposed before. Professed their undying love and admiration for her. But no one had ever meant it. No one ever did, not in her world. Love was a bargaining chip, nothing more. Sex was calling a bluff. All a game. Just a game. If you played it right, you got diamonds and houses and money. And if you lost...you got nothing.

Nothing.

She curled up into a tight ball, just like she'd always done back when she was little and her parents were fighting. On bad nights, she'd sneak into Byron's room and curl up in his bed. He took the top half and she took the bottom, their backs touching. That's how they'd come into this world. It felt safer that way.

Once, Mom had loved Dad. And Dad must have had feelings for Mom, right? That's why he'd married her and made their illegitimate child, Matthew, legitimate.

But they couldn't live together. They couldn't share a roof. They'd have been better off like Ethan's folks, going their separate ways 85 percent of the time and only coming together when the stars aligned just so. And in the end, her father had won and her mother had lost, and that had been the game.

She almost got up and got her phone to call Byron. To tell him she might have been rash and that she needed to come hang out for a couple of days until things cooled off. Mom was out there, anyway.

It was late. Byron was probably still asleep.

And then there was Friday. Donut Friday.

She had to face Ethan again. With an audience. Just like they'd planned it.

She had nothing to wear.

Delores walked in with a stack of interoffice envelopes. Ethan glared at her, trying to get his heart to calm down.

He hadn't heard from Frances since she'd stormed out of his room two nights ago, and it was making him jumpy. He did not like being jumpy.

"Any donuts yet?" he made himself say casually.

"Haven't seen her yet, but I can check with Larry to find out if she's on the premises," Delores said in a genial manner. She handed him a rather thick envelope. It had no return address. It just said, "E. Logan."

"What's this?"

"I'm sure I don't know." When Ethan glared at her, she said, "I'll go check on those donuts."

The old battle-ax, he thought menacingly as he undid the clasp and slid out a half-inch-thick manila folder.

"Potentially of our mutual interest—C. Beaumont," proclaimed a small, otherwise benign yellow sticky note on the front of the folder.

The only feeling that Ethan did not enjoy more than jumpiness was uncertainty. And that's what the manila folder suddenly represented. What on earth would Chadwick Beaumont consider of mutual interest? The only thing that came to mind was Frances.

And what of Frances could merit a folder this thick?

The possibilities—everything from blackmail to depravities—ran together in his mind. He shoved them aside and opened the file.

And found himself staring at a dossier for one Zeb Richards, owner of ZOLA.

Ethan blinked in astonishment as he scanned the information. Zeb Richards, born in Denver in 1973, graduated from Morehouse College with a bachelor of arts degree and from the University of Georgia with a master's in business administration. Currently resided in New York. There was a small color photo of the man, the first that Ethan had seen.

Wait—had he met Zeb Richards before? There was something about the set of the man's jaw that looked familiar. He had dark hair that was cropped incredibly close to his head, the way many black men wore it.

But Ethan would remember meeting someone named Zeb, wouldn't he?

Then he flipped the page and found another document—a photocopy of a birth certificate. Well, he had to hand it to Chadwick—he was nothing if not thorough. The certificate confirmed that Zebadiah Richards was born in Denver in 1973. His mother was Emily Richards and his father was…

Oh, hell.

Under "Father" was the unmistakable name of one Hardwick James Beaumont.

Ethan flipped back to the photo. Yes, that jaw—that was like Chadwick's jaw, like Phillip's. Those two men had been unmistakably brothers—full brothers. The resemblance had been obvious. And they'd looked a fair deal like Frances. The jaw was softer on her, more feminine—more beautiful.

But if Zeb's mother had been African-American… That would account for everything else.

Oh, hell.

Suddenly, it all made sense. This agitation on behalf of ZOLA to sell the Beaumont Brewery? It wasn't a rival firm looking to discredit Ethan's company, and it wasn't an activist shareholder looking to peel the Beaumont Brewery off so it could pick it up for pennies on the dollar and sell it off, like Ethan's father did.

This was personal.

And it had nothing to do with Ethan.

Except he was, as of about two nights ago, sleeping with a Beaumont. He was probably still informally engaged to be married to said Beaumont, although he wouldn't be sure of that until the donut situation was confirmed. And, perhaps most important of all, he was currently running the Beaumont Brewery.

"Delores," he said into the intercom. "Was this envelope hand-delivered to you?"

"It was on my desk this morning, Mr. Logan."

"I need to speak to Chadwick Beaumont. Can you get me his number?"

"Of course." Ethan started to turn the intercom off, but then she added, "Oh, Ms. Beaumont is on the premises."

"Thank you," he said. He flipped the intercom off and stuffed the folder back into the envelope. It was no joke to say he was out of his league here. A bastard son coming back to wreak havoc on his half siblings? Yeah, Ethan was *way* out of his league.

Chadwick must have a sense of humor, what with that note about Zeb Richards being "potentially" a mutual interest.

But Frances—she didn't know anything about her siblings from unmarried mothers, did she? No, Ethan was certain he remembered her saying she didn't know any of them. Just that there were some.

So Zeb Richards was not, at this exact moment, something she needed to know about.

Unless...

He thought back to the way she'd stood before him last night, all of her armor fully in place while he'd been naked in every sense of the word. And she'd said—*No, be honest*, he told himself—*sneered* that she'd thought he'd be better at the game.

Was Zeb Richards part of the game?

Just because Frances said she didn't know any of the illegitimate Beaumonts didn't mean she'd been truthful about it.

She'd asked Ethan why he wanted to marry her. Had he asked why she'd agreed to marry him? Beyond the money for her art gallery?

What else was she getting out of their deal?

Why had she shown up with donuts last week?

The answer was right in front of him, a manila folder in an envelope.

Revenge.

Hadn't she told him that she'd lost part of herself when the family lost the Brewery? And hadn't she said she should hate him for his part in that loss?

What had seemed like a distant coincidence—Frances disrupting his personal life at nearly the exact same time some random investor was trying to disrupt his business—now seemed less like a coincidence and more like directly correlated events.

What if she not only knew Zeb Richards was her half brother—what if she was helping him? Getting insider information? Not from Ethan, necessarily—but from all the people here who loved and trusted her because she was their Frannie?

Did Chadwick know? Or did he suspect? Was that why he'd sent the file?

Ethan had assumed it'd been the encounter with Phillip Beaumont that had prompted Chadwick's appearance at the Brewery the other day. But what if there'd been something else? What if one of Chadwick's loyal employees had tipped him off that Frances was asking around, digging up dirt?

And if that was possible, who's side was Chadwick on? Ethan's? Frances's? Zeb Richards's?

Ethan's head began to ache. This, he realized with a half laugh, was what he was trying to marry into—a family so sprawling, so screwed up that they didn't even have a solid head count on all their relatives.

"She's here," Delores's voice interrupted his train of thought.

Ethan stood and straightened his tie. He didn't know why. He pushed the thought of bastards with an ax to grind out of his head. He had to focus on what was important here—Frances. The woman he'd taken to his bed last night and then promptly chased right out of it, all because he was stupid enough to develop feelings for her.

The woman who might be setting him up to fail because it was a game. Nothing but a game.

He had no idea which version of Frances Beaumont was on the other side of that door.

He wanted to be wrong. He wanted it to be one giant coincidence. He did not want to know that he'd misjudged her so badly, that he'd been played for such a fool.

Because if he had, he didn't know where he would go from here. He was still the CEO of this company. He still had a deal to marry her and invest in her gallery. He had his own company to protect. As soon as the Brewery was successfully restructured, he'd pull up stakes and move on to the next business that needed to be run with an iron fist and an eye to the bottom line. They'd divorce casually and go on with their lives.

And once he was gone, he'd never have to think about anything Beaumont ever again.

He opened his door. Frances was standing there in jeans and boots. She wore a thick, fuzzy cable-knit sweater, and her hair was pulled back into a modest bun. Not a sky-high heel or low-cut silk blouse in sight. She looked...plain, almost, which was something because if there was one thing Frances Beaumont wasn't, it was plain.

And despite the fact that his head felt as if an anvil had just been dropped on it, despite the fact that he was in over his head—despite the fact that, no, he was most likely not as good at the game as he'd thought he was and, no, she did not like him—he was glad to see her. He absolutely shouldn't be, but he was.

It only got worse when she lifted her head. There was no crowd today, no group of eager employees around to stroke her ego or destroy his. Just her and Delores and a box.

"Frances."

"Chocolate éclair?" she asked simply.

Even her makeup was simple today. She looked almost innocent, as if she was still trying to understand what had happened between them last night, just like he was.

But was that the truth of the matter? Or was this part of the game?

"I saved you two," she told him, holding the box out.

"Come in," he said, holding his door open for her. "Delores, hold my calls."

"Even—" she started to say.

"I'll call him back." Yes, he needed to talk to Chadwick, but he needed to talk to Frances more. He wasn't sleeping with Chadwick. Frances came first.

Frances paused, a look on her face that yesterday Ethan would have assumed to be confusion. Today? He couldn't be sure.

She walked past him, her head held high and her bearing regal. Ethan wanted to smile at her. Evening gowns or blue jeans, she could pull off imperial like nobody's business.

But he didn't smile. She did not like him. And liking her? Wanting to take care of her, to spend time with her? That had been a massive error on his part.

So the moment the door shut, he resolved that he would not care about her. He would not pull her into his arms and hold her tight and try to find the right sweet nothings to whisper in her ear to wipe that shell-shocked look off her face.

He would not comfort her. He couldn't afford to.

She carried the donut box over to the wagon-wheel coffee table and set it down. Then she sat on the love seat, tucking her feet up under her legs. "Hi," she said in what seemed like a small voice.

He didn't like it, that small voice, because it pulled at him, and he couldn't afford to let her play his emotions like that. "How are you today?" he asked politely. He went back to his desk and sat. It seemed like the safest place to be, with a good fifteen feet and a bunch of historic furniture between them.

She watched him with those big eyes of hers. "I brought you donuts," she said.

"Thank you." He realized his fingers were tapping on the envelope Chadwick had sent. He made them be still.

She said, "Oh. Okay," in such a disappointed voice that it almost broke him because he didn't want to disappoint her, damn it, and he was anyway.

But then, what was he supposed to do? He'd given her everything he had last night, and look how that had turned out. She'd cut him to shreds. She'd been disappointed that he'd liked her.

So she wasn't allowed to be disappointed that he was keeping his distance right now. End of discussion.

He stared at the envelope again. He had to know—how deep was she in this? "So," he said. "How are the plans for the art gallery going?"

"Fine. Are we..."

"Yes?"

She cleared her throat and stuck out her chin, as if she was trying to look tough and failing, miserably. "Are we still on? The deal, that is."

"Of course. Why would you think it's off?"

She took a deep breath. "I—well, I said some not-nice things last night. You've been nothing but wonderful and I... I was not gracious about it. About you."

Was she apologizing? For hurting his feelings? Not that he'd admit to having his feelings hurt.

Was it possible that, somewhere under the artifice, she actually cared for him, too?

No, probably not. This was just another test, another move. Ethan made a big show of shrugging. "At no point did I assume that this relationship—or whatever you want to call it—is based on 'niceness.'" She visibly winced. "You were right. Affection is irrelevant." This time, he did not offer to let her out of the deal or postpone the farce that would be their wedding. "And a deal's a deal, after all."

A shadow crossed her face, but only briefly. "Of course," she agreed. She wrapped her arms around her waist. She looked as though she was trying to hold herself together. "So we'll need to get engaged soon?"

"Tonight, if that's all right with you. I've made reservations for us as we continue our tour of the finer restaurants in Denver." He let his gaze flick over her outfit in what he hoped was judgment.

"Sounds good." That's what she said. But the way she said it? Anything but good.

"I did have a question," he said. "You asked me last night why I'd agreed to get married to you. To a stranger."

"Because it seems normal enough," she replied. He refused to be even the slightest bit pleased that she recalled their conversation about his parents. "And the workers love me."

He tilted his head in appreciation. "But when we were naked and sharing, I failed to ask what you were getting out of this deal. Why *you* would agree to marry a total stranger."

She paled, which made her red hair stand out that much more. "The gallery," she said in a shaky voice. "It's going to be my job, my space. Art is what I'm good at. I need the gallery."

"Oh, I'm quite sure," he agreed, swiveling his chair so he was facing her fully. His hand was tapping the envelope again. Damn that envelope. Damn Zebadiah Richards. Hell, while he was at it, damn Chadwick Beaumont, too. "But that's not all, is it?"

Slowly, her head moved from side to side, a no that she was apparently unaware she was saying. "Of course that's all. A simple deal."

"With the man who represented the loss of your family business and your family identity."

"Well, yes. That's why I need the gallery. I need a fresh start."

He leveled his stoniest glare at her, the one that produced results in business negotiations. The very look that usually had employees falling all over themselves to do what he wanted, the way he wanted it.

To her credit, she did not buckle. He would have been disappointed if she had, frankly. He watched her armor snap into place. But it didn't stop the rest of the color from draining out of her face.

He had her, and they both knew it.

"You wanted revenge."

The statement hung in the air. Frances's gaze darted from side to side as if she was looking for an escape route. When she didn't find what she wanted, she sat up straighter.

Good, Ethan thought. She was going to brazen this out. For some reason, he wanted it that way, wanted her to go down fighting. He didn't want her meek and apologetic and fragile, damn it. He wanted her biting and cutting, a warrior princess with words as weapons.

He wanted her messy and complicated, and, damn it all, he was going to get her that way. Even if it killed him.

"I don't know what you're talking about." As she said it, she uncurled on the couch. Her legs swung down and stretched out before her, long and lean, the very legs that had been wrapped around him. At the same time, she stretched up, thrusting out her breasts.

This time, he did smile. She was going to give him hell. *This* was the woman who'd walked into his office a week ago, using her body as a weapon of mass distraction.

This was the woman he could love.

He pushed that thought aside.

"How did you plan to do it?" he asked. "Did you plan on pumping me for information, or just gather some from the staff while you plied them with donuts?"

One eyebrow arched up. "*Plied?* Really, Ethan." She shifted forward, which would have worked much better to distract him if she'd been in a low-cut top instead of a sweater. "You make it sound like I was spiking the pastries with truth-telling serum."

He caught the glint of a necklace—his necklace, the one he'd given her last night. She was wearing it. For some reason, that distracted him far more than the seductive pose did.

"What I want to know," he said in a calm voice, "is if Richards contacted you first, or if you contacted him."

Her mouth had already opened to reply, but the mention of Richards's name pulled her up short. She blinked at him, her confusion obvious. Too obvious. "Who?"

"Don't play cute with me, Frances. You said so yourself, didn't you? This is all part of the game. I just didn't realize how far it went until this morning."

Her brow wrinkled. "I don't—who is Richards?"

"This innocent thing isn't working," he snapped.

Abruptly, she stood. "I don't know who Richards is. I didn't ply anyone with donuts to tell me anything they weren't willing to tell me anyway—which, for the most part, was how you were a jerk who didn't know the first thing about running the Brewery. So you can accuse me of plotting some unspecified revenge with some unspecified man named Richards, if that makes you feel better about not being able to do your own job without me smiling like an idiot by your side. But in the meantime, go to hell." She swept out of the room with all the cold grace he could have expected. She didn't even slam the door on the way out, probably because that would have been beneath her.

"Dinner tonight," he called after her, just so he could get in the last word.

"Ha!" he heard her say as she walked away from him.

Damn, that last bit had been more than loud enough that Delores would have heard. And Ethan knew that whatever Delores heard, the rest of the company heard.

The thing was, he was still no closer to an answer about Frances's level of involvement with ZOLA and Zeb Richards than he'd been before she'd shown up. He'd thought he'd learned how to read her, but last night, she'd made him question his emotional investment in her.

He had no idea how to trust anything she said or how to decide if she was telling the truth.

A phone rang. It sounded as if it came from a long way away. Delores stuck her head through the door. "I know you said to hold your calls," she said in a cautious voice, "but Chadwick's on the phone."

"I'll take it," he said because to pretend he was otherwise involved would look ridiculous.

He was going to get engaged tonight. Frances was supposed to start sleeping over. He was going to get married to her next weekend so he could maintain control over his company.

Because that was the deal.

He picked up his phone. "Who the hell is Zeb Richards?"

Fifteen

Frances found herself at the gallery—actually, at what would become the gallery. It wasn't a gallery yet. It was just an empty industrial space.

Becky was there with some contractors, discussing lighting options. "Oh, Frances—there you are," she said in a happy voice. But then she paused. "Are you okay?"

"Fine," Frances assured her. "Why would anything be wrong? Excuse me." She dodged contractors and headed back to the office. This room, at least, was suitable to hide in. It had walls, a door—and a lock.

Why would anything be wrong? She'd only screwed up. That wasn't unusual. That was practically par for the course. Ethan had been—well, he'd been wonderful. She'd spent a week with him. She'd let her guard down around him. She'd even slept with him—and he was amazing.

So of course she'd gone and opened her big mouth and insulted him, and now he was colder than a three-day-old fish.

She sat down at what would be her desk when she got moved in and stared at the bare wooden top. He'd said he liked her messy and complicated. And for a moment, she'd almost believed him.

But he hadn't meant it. Oh, he thought he had, of that she had no doubt. He'd thought he liked her all not simple.

He'd no doubt imagined he'd mastered the complexities of her extended family, besting her brothers in a show of sheer skill and Logan-based manliness.

The fool, she thought sadly. He'd gone and convinced himself that he could handle her. And he couldn't. Maybe no one could.

Then there'd been the conversation today. What the ever-loving hell had that been about? Revenge? Well, yeah—revenge had been part of it. She hadn't lied, had she? She'd told him that she'd lost part of herself when the Brewery had been sold. She just hadn't expected him to throw that back in her face.

And who the hell was this Richards she was supposed to be conspiring with?

Still, a deal was a deal. And as Ethan had made it quite clear that morning, it was nothing but a deal. She supposed she'd earned that.

It was better this way, she decided. She couldn't handle Ethan when he was being tender and sweet and saying absolutely ridiculous things like how he'd happily put the wedding off because she was worth the wait.

The sooner he figured out she wasn't worth nearly that much, the better.

The doorknob turned, but the lock held. This was followed by a soft knock. "Frances?" Becky said. "Can I come in?"

Against her better judgment, Frances got up and unlocked the door for her friend. A deal was a deal, after all—especially since Frances wasn't the only one who needed this gallery. Becky was depending on it just as much as Frances was. "Yes?"

Becky pushed her way into the office and shut the door behind her. "What's wrong?"

"Nothing," Frances lied. Too late, she remembered she

should try to look as if that statement were accurate. She attempted a lighthearted smile.

Becky's eyes widened in horror at this expression. "Ohmygosh—what happened?"

Maybe she wouldn't try to smile right now. It felt wrong, anyway. "Just a…disagreement. This doesn't change the deal. It's fine," Frances said with more force. "I just thought—well, I thought he was different. And I think he's really much the same."

That was the problem, wasn't it? For a short while, she'd believed Ethan might actually be interested in her, not her famous name or famous family.

Why hadn't she just taken him at his word? Why had she pushed and pushed and pushed, for God's sake, until whatever honest fondness he felt for her had been pushed aside under the glaring imperfection that was Frances Beaumont? Why couldn't she have just let good enough alone and accepted his flowers and his diamonds and his offers of affection and companionship?

Why did she have to ruin everything?

She'd warned him. She'd told him not to like her. She just hadn't realized that she'd do everything in her power to make sure he didn't.

She'd screwed up *so* much. She'd lost a fortune three separate times. Every endeavor she'd ever attempted outside of stringing a man along had failed miserably. She'd never had a relationship that could come close to breaking her heart because there was nothing to break.

So this relationship had been doomed from the get-go. Nothing lost, nothing gained. She was not going to let this gallery fail. She needed the steady job and the sense of purpose far more than she needed Ethan to look her in the eye and tell her that he wanted her just as complicated as she was.

Unexpectedly, Becky pulled her into a tight hug. "I'm so sorry, honey," she whispered into Frances's ear.

"Jeez, Becks—it was just a disappointing date. Not the end of the world." And the more Frances told herself that, the truer it'd become. "Now go," she said, doing her best to sound as if it was just another Friday at the office. "Contractors don't stand around for free."

She had to make this gallery work. She had to…

She had to do something to not think about Ethan.

That was going to be rather difficult when they had dinner tonight.

She wore the green dress. She felt more powerful in the green dress than she did in the bridesmaid's dress. And she'd only worn the green dress to the office, not out to dinner, so it wasn't like wearing the same outfit two days in a row.

The only person who would recognize the dress was Ethan, and, well, there was nothing to be done about that.

Frances twisted her hair up. The only jewelry she wore was the necklace. The one he'd gotten for her. It felt odd to wear it, to know he'd picked it out on his own and that, for at least a little while, she'd been swayed by something so cliché as diamonds.

But it was a beautiful piece, and it went with the dress. And, after all, she was getting engaged tonight so it only seemed right to wear the diamonds from her fiancé.

She swept into the restaurant, head up and smile firmly in place. She'd given herself a little pep talk about how this wasn't about Ethan; this was about her and she had to get what she needed out of it. And if that occasionally included mind-blowing sex, then so be it. She needed to get laid every so often. Ethan was more than up to the task. Casual sex in a casual marriage. No big whoop.

Ethan was waiting for her at the bar again. "Frances,"

he said, pulling her into a tight embrace and brushing his lips over her cheek. She didn't miss the way he avoided her lips. "Shall we?"

"Of course." She was ready for him tonight. He was not going to get to her.

"You're looking better," he said as he held her chair for her.

"Oh? Was I not up to your usual high standards this morning?"

Ethan's mouth quirked into a wry smile. "You seem better, too."

She waved away his backhanded compliment. "So," she said, not even bothering to look at the menu, "tell me about this mysterious Richards person. If I'm going to be accused of industrial espionage, I should at least get some of the details."

His smile froze and then fell right off his face. It made Frances feel good, the rush of power that went with catching him off guard.

So she'd had a rough night and a tough morning. She was not going down with a whimper. And if he thought he could steamroll her, well, he'd learn soon enough.

"Actually," he said, dropping his gaze to his menu, "I did want to talk to you about that. I owe you an apology."

He owed her an apology? This morning he'd accused her of betrayal. This evening—apologies?

No. She did not want to slide back into that space where he professed to care about her feelings because that was where she got into trouble. She pointedly stared at her menu.

"Do you know who Zeb Richards is?"

"No. I assume he is the Richards in question, however." She still didn't look at Ethan. She realized she was fiddling with the diamonds at her neck, but she couldn't quite help herself.

"He is." Out of the corner of her eye, she saw Ethan lay down his menu. "I don't feel it's my place to tell you this, but I don't want to come off as patronizing, so—"

"A tad late for that," she murmured in as disinterested a voice as possible.

"A company called ZOLA is trying to make my life harder. They're making noises that my company is failing at restructuring and that AllBev should sell off the Brewery. One presumes that they'll either buy it on the cheap or buy it for scrap. A company like the Brewery is worth almost as much for its parts as it is for its value."

"Indeed," she said. She managed to nail "faux sympathetic," if she did say so herself. "And this concerns me how?"

"ZOLA is run by Zeb Richards."

This time, she did put down her menu. "And…? Out with it, Ethan."

For the first time, Ethan looked unsure of himself. "Zeb Richards is your half brother."

She blinked a few times. "I have many half brothers. However, I don't particularly remember one of them being named Zeb."

"When I found out this morning that he was related to you, I assumed you were working with him."

She stared at him. "How do you know about any supposed half brothers of mine?"

"Chadwick," he added with an apologetic smile.

"I should have known," she murmured.

"I asked him if he knew about ZOLA, and he gave me a file on Richards. Including proof that you and Zeb are related."

"How very nice of him to tell *you* and not *me*." Oh, she was damnably tired of Chadwick meddling in her affairs.

"Hence why I'm trying not to be patronizing." Ethan

fiddled with his silverware. "I did not have all the facts this morning when you got to the office and I made a series of assumptions that were unfair to you."

She looked at him flatly. "Is that so? And what, pray tell, was this additional information that has apparently exonerated me so completely?"

He dropped his gaze and she knew. "Chadwick again?"

"Correct. He believes that you have never had contact with your other half brothers. So, I'm sorry about my actions this morning. I was concerned that you were working with Richards to undermine the Brewery and I know now that simply isn't the case."

This admission was probably supposed to make her feel better. It did not. "*That's* what you were concerned with? *That's* what this morning was about?"

And not her? Not the way she'd insulted him last night, the way she'd stormed out of the hotel room without even pausing long enough to get her dress zipped properly?

He'd been worried about the company. His job.

Not her.

It shouldn't hurt. After all, this entire relationship was built on the premise that he was doing it for the company. For the Brewery and for his private firm.

No, it shouldn't have hurt at all.

Funny how it did.

"I could see how you were trying to get your family identity back. It wasn't a difficult mental leap to make, you understand. But I apologize."

She stared at him. She'd wanted to get revenge. She'd wanted to bring him down several pegs and put him in his place. But she hadn't conspired with some half brother she didn't even know existed to take down the whole company.

She didn't want to take down the company. The people

who worked there were her friends, her second family. Destroying the company would be destroying them.

It'd mean destroying Ethan, too.

"You're serious. You're really apologizing?"

He nodded, the look in his eyes deepening as he leaned forward. "I should have had more faith in you. It's a mistake I won't make again."

As an apology went, it wasn't bad. Actually, it was pretty damned good. There was only one problem with it.

"So that's it? The moment things actually get messy, you assume I'm trying to ruin you. But now that my brother has confirmed that I've never even heard of Zeb Richards or whatever his name is, you're suddenly all back to 'I like you complicated, Frances'?" She scoffed and slouched away from the table.

It must have come out louder than she realized because his eyes hardened. "We are in public."

"So we are. Your point?"

A muscle in his jaw tensed. "This is the night when I ask you to marry me," he said in a low growl that, despite the war of words they were engaged in, sent a shiver down her spine because it was the exact same voice he'd used when he'd bent her over the bed and made her come. Twice.

"Is it?" she growled back. "Do you always ask women to marry you when you're losing an argument?"

He stared hard at her for a second and then, unbelievably, his lips curved into an almost smile, as if he enjoyed this. "No. But I'll make an exception for you."

"Don't," she said, suddenly afraid of this. Of him. Of what he could do to her if she let him.

"This was the deal."

"Don't," she whispered, terrified.

He pushed back from his chair in full view of everyone in the restaurant. He dropped to one knee, just like in the movies, and pulled a robin's-egg-blue box out of his pocket. "Frances," he said in a stage voice loud enough to carry across the whole space. "I know we haven't known each other very long, but I can't imagine life without you. Will you do me the honor of marrying me?"

It sounded rehearsed. It wasn't the fumbling failure at sweet nothings she'd come to expect from him. It was for show. All for show.

Just like they'd planned.

This was where the small part of her brain that wasn't freaking out—and it was a very small part—was supposed to say yes. Where she was publically supposed to declare her love for him, and they were supposed to ride off into the sunset—or, at the very least, his hotel room—and consummate their relationship. Again.

He was handsome and good in bed and a worthy opponent and rich—couldn't forget that. And he liked her most of the time. He liked her too much.

She was supposed to say yes. For the gallery. For Becky. For the Brewery, for all the workers.

She was supposed to say yes so she could make Frances Beaumont important again, so that the Beaumont name would mean what she wanted it to mean—fame and accolades and people wanting to be her friend.

She was supposed to say yes for *her*. This was what she wanted.

Wasn't it?

Ethan's face froze. "Well?" he demanded in a quiet voice. "Frances."

Say yes, her brain urged. *Say yes right now.*

"I…" She was horrified to hear her voice come out as a whisper. "I can't."

His eyes widened in horror or confusion or some unholy mix of the two, she didn't know. She didn't wait around to find out. She bolted out of the restaurant as fast as she could in her heels. She didn't even wait to get her coat.

She ran. It was an act of cowardice. An act of surrender.

She'd ceded the game.

She'd lost everything.

Sixteen

"Frances?"

What the hell just happened? One second, he was following the script because, yes, he damn well had planned out the proposal. It was for public consumption.

The next second, she was gone, cutting an emerald-green swath through the suddenly silent restaurant.

"Frances, wait!" he called out, painfully aware that this was not part of the plan. He lunged to his feet and took off after her. She couldn't just leave—not like that. This wasn't how it was supposed to go.

Okay, today had not been his best work. He'd acted without all the available facts this morning and clearly, that had been a bad move. There were no such things as coincidences—except, it seemed, for right now.

Yes, he should have given her the benefit of the doubt and yes, he probably should have groveled a little more. The relief Ethan had felt when Chadwick had told him the only Beaumonts who knew of Zeb's identity were him and Matthew had been no small thing. Frances hadn't been plotting to overthrow the company. In fact, she'd been apologizing to Ethan. They could reset at dinner and continue on as they had been.

But he hadn't expected her to run away from him—especially not after the way she'd dressed him down after they'd had sex.

If she didn't want to get married, he thought as he gave chase, why the hell hadn't she just said so? He'd given her an out—several outs. And she'd refused his concessions at every turn, only to leave him hanging with a diamond engagement ring in his hand.

This wasn't right, damn it.

He caught up with her trying to hail a cab. He could see her shivering in the cold wind. "For God's sake, Frances," he said, shucking his suit jacket and slinging it around her shoulders. "You'll catch your death."

"Ethan," she said in the most plaintive voice he'd ever heard.

"What are you doing?" he demanded. "This was the deal."

"I know, I know…" She didn't elucidate on that knowledge, however.

"Frances." He took her by the arm and pulled her a step back from the curb. "We agreed—we agreed this *morning*—that I was going to ask you to marry me and you were going to say yes." When she didn't look at him, he dropped her arm and cupped her face in his hands. "Babe, talk to me."

"Don't *babe* me, Ethan."

"Then talk, damn it. What the hell happened?"

"I—I can't. I thought I could, but I can't. Don't you see?" He shook his head. "I thought—I thought I didn't need love. That I could do this and it'd be no different than watching my parents fight, no different than all the other men who wanted to get close to the Beaumont name and money. You weren't supposed to be *different*, Ethan. You were supposed to be the *same*."

Then, as he watched in horror, a tear slipped past her blinking eyelid and began to trickle down her cheek.

"I wasn't supposed to like you. And you, you big idiot, you weren't supposed to like me," she said, her voice quiet and shaky as more tears followed the first.

He tried to wipe the tears away with his thumb, but they were replaced too quickly. "I don't understand how liking each other makes marrying each other a bad thing," he said.

"You're here for your company. You're not here for me," she said, cutting him off before he could protest.

An unfamiliar feeling began to push past the confusion and the frustration—a feeling that he hadn't often allowed himself to feel.

Panic.

And he wasn't sure why. It could be that, if the workers at the Brewery got it in their collective heads that he'd broken their Frannie's heart, they might draw and quarter him. He could be panicking that his foolproof method of regaining control over his business felt suddenly very foolish.

But that wasn't it. That wasn't it at all.

"See?" She sniffed. She was openly crying at this point. It was horrifying because as much as she might have berated him for being lousy at the game when he dared admit that he might have feelings for her, he knew this was not a play on her part. "How long will it last?"

His mouth opened. *A year*, he almost said, because that was the deal.

"I could love you," he told her and it was God's honest truth. "If you'll let me."

Her eyes closed, and she turned her head away. "Ethan…" she whispered, so softly he almost didn't hear it over the sound of a cab pulling up next to them. "I could love you, too." For a moment, he thought she was agreeing; she was seeing the light, and they'd get in the cab and carry on as planned.

But then she added, "I won't settle for *could*. Not anymore. I can't believe I'm saying this, but I want to be in love with the man I marry. And I want him to be in love with me, too. I want to believe I'm worth that—worth something more than a business deal. Worth more than some company."

"You are," he said, but it didn't sound convincing, not even to his own ears. "You *are*, Frances."

She gave him a sad smile full of heartache. "I want to believe that, Ethan. But I'm not a prize to be won in the game. Not anymore."

She slipped his jacket off her slim shoulders and held it out to him.

He didn't want to take it. He didn't want her to go. "Keep it. I don't want you to freeze."

She shook her head no, and the cabbie honked and shouted, "Lady, you need a ride or not?" so Frances ducked into the cab.

He stood there, freezing his ass off as he watched the cab's taillights disappear down the street.

When he'd talked to Chadwick Beaumont on the phone today, he'd barely been able to wait for Chadwick to get done explaining who the hell Zeb Richards was before asking, "Does Frances know about this?" because he'd been desperate to know if she was leading him on or if those moments he'd thought where honesty were real.

"Unless she's hired her own private investigators, the only people who know about my father's illegitimate children are me and Matthew. My mother was the one who originally tracked down the oldest three. She'd long suspected my father was cheating on her," he had added. "There are others."

"And you don't think Frances would have hired her own PI?"

"Problem?" Chadwick had said in such a genial way that

Ethan had almost confided in him that he might have just accused Chadwick's younger sister of industrial espionage.

"No," Ethan had said because, at the time, it hadn't been a problem. A little lover's quarrel, nothing that a thirty-thousand-dollar diamond ring couldn't fix. "Just trying to understand the Beaumont family tree."

"Good luck with that," was all Chadwick had said.

Ethan had thanked him for the information and promised to pass along anything new he learned. Then he'd eaten his donuts and thought about how he'd make it up to Frances.

She'd promised not to love him—not to even like him. She'd told him to do the same. He should have listened to her, but he hadn't lied. When it came to her, he couldn't quite help himself. Everything about her had been an impulse. Even his original proposal had been half impulse, driven by some basic desire to outwit Frances Beaumont.

Their entire relationship had been based on a game of one-upmanship. In that regard, she'd gotten the final word. She'd said no.

Well, hell. Now what? He'd publically proposed, been publically rejected and his whole plan had fallen apart on him. And the worst thing was that he wasn't sure *why*. Was it because he hadn't trusted her this morning when she'd said she didn't know anything about Richards?

Or was it because, despite it all, he did like her? He liked her a great deal. More than was wise, that much was sure.

This morning she'd shown up at his office with the donuts he'd requested. She hadn't had on a stitch of her armor—no designer clothes, no impenetrable attitude. She'd been a woman who'd sat down, admitted fault and apologized for her actions.

She'd been trying to show him that she liked him. Enough to be honest with him.

He'd thrown that trust back in her face. And then cavalierly assumed that a big rock was going to make it up to her.

Idiot. She wanted to know she was worth it—and she hadn't meant worth diamonds and roses.

He was in too deep to let her go. She *was* worth it.

So this was what falling in love was like.

How was he going to convince her that this wasn't part of the game?

Frances was not surprised when no extravagant floral arrangement arrived the next day. No chocolates or champagne or jewels showed up, either.

They didn't arrive the day after that. Or the third, for that matter.

And why would they? She was not bound to Ethan. She had no claim on him, nor he on her. The only thing that remained of their failed, doomed "relationship" were several vases of withering flowers and an expensive necklace.

She had taken off the necklace.

But she hadn't been able to bring herself to return it. Not to him, not to the store for cash—cash she could use, now that the gallery was dead and she had no other job prospects, aside from selling her family's heirlooms on the open market.

The necklace sat on her bedside table, mocking her as she went to sleep every night.

She called Becky but didn't feel like talking except to say, "The funding is probably not going to happen, so plan accordingly."

To which Becky had replied, "We'll get it figured out, one way or the other."

That was the sort of platitude people said when the situation was hopeless but they needed to feel better. So Frances had replied, "Sure, we'll get together for lunch soon and go over our options," because that was the sort of thing rational grown-ups said all the time.

Then she'd ended the call and crawled back under the covers.

Byron had texted, but what could she tell him? That she'd done the not-rash thing for the first time in her life and was now miserable? And why, exactly, was she miserable again? She shouldn't be hiding under the covers in her cozy jammies! She'd won! She'd stopped Ethan in his tracks with a move he couldn't anticipate and he couldn't recover from. She'd brought him firmly down to where he belonged. He wasn't good enough for the Beaumonts, and he wasn't good enough for the Brewery.

Victory was hers!

She didn't think victory was supposed to taste this sour.

She didn't believe in love. Never had, never would. So why, when the next best thing had presented itself—someone who was fond of her, who admired her, and who could still make her shiver with need, someone who had offered to generously provide for her financial future in exchange for a year of her life even—*why* had she walked away?

Because he was only here for the company. And, fool that she was, she'd suddenly realized she wanted someone who was going to be here for her.

"I could love you." She heard his words over and over again, beating against her brain like a spike. He could.

But he didn't.

What a mess.

Luckily, she was used to it.

She'd managed to drag herself to the shower on the fourth day. She had decided that she was going to stop moping. Moping didn't get jobs, and it didn't heal broken hearts. She needed to get up and, at the very least, have lunch with Becky or go see Byron. She needed to do something that would eventually get her out of the Beaumont mansion because she was *done* living under the same roof as Chadwick. She was going to tell him that the very next time she saw him, too.

She'd just buttoned her jeans when she heard the doorbell. She ignored it as she toweled her hair.

Then someone knocked on her bedroom door. "Frannie?" It was Serena, Chadwick's wife. "Flowers for you."

"Really?" Who would send her flowers? Not Ethan. Not at this late date. "Hang on." She threw on a sweater and opened the door.

Serena stood there, an odd look on her face. She was not holding any flowers. "Um… I think you need to get these yourself," Serena said before she turned and walked down the hall.

Frances stood there, all the warning bells going off in her head at once.

Her heart pounding, she walked down the hallway and peered over the edge of the railing. There, in the middle of the foyer, stood Ethan, holding a single red rose.

She must have made a noise or gasped or something because he looked up at her and smiled. A good smile, the kind of smile that made her want to do something ridiculous like kiss him when she absolutely should not be glad to see him at all.

She needed to say something witty and urbane and snarky that would put him in his place, so that for at least a minute, she could feel like Frances Beaumont again.

Instead, she said, "You're here."

Damn. Worse, it came out breathy, as if she couldn't believe he'd actually ventured into the lair of the Beaumonts.

"I am," he replied, his gaze never leaving her face. "I came for you."

Oh. That was terribly close to a sweet nothing—no, it

wasn't a nothing. It was a sweet something. But what? "I'm here. I've been here for a few days now."

There, that was a good thing to say. Something that let him know that his apology—if this even was an apology—was days late and, judging by the single flower he was holding, dollars short.

"I had some things to do," he said. "Can you come down here?"

"Why should I?"

His grin spread. "Because I don't want to shout? But I will." He cleared his throat. *"Frances!"* he shouted, his voice ringing off the marble and the high-vaulted ceilings. *"Can you come down here? Please?"*

"Okay, okay!" She didn't know who else besides Serena was home, but she didn't need to have Ethan yelling at the top of his lungs.

She hurried down the wide staircase with Ethan watching her the entire time. She slowed only when she got to the last few steps. She didn't want to be on his level, not just yet. "I'm here," she said again.

He held out the lone red rose to her. "I brought you a flower."

"Just one?"

"One seemed…fitting, somehow." He looked her over. "How have you been?"

"Oh, fine," she tried to say lightly. "Just hanging out around the house, trying to avoid social media and gossip columns—the normal stuff, really. Just another day in the life of a Beaumont."

He took a step closer to her. It made her tense. "You don't have to do that," he said, his voice soft and quiet and just for her.

"Do what?"

"Put your armor on. I didn't come here looking for a fight."

She eyed him warily. What was this? A single rose? A claim that he didn't want to fight? "Then why did you come?"

He took another step in—close enough to touch her. Which he did. He lifted his hand and brushed his fingertips down her cheek. "I wanted to tell you that you're worth it."

She froze under his touch, the rose between them. "We aren't in public, Ethan. You don't have to do this. It's over. We made a scene. It's fine. We can go on with our lives now." Her words came out in a rush.

"Do you really believe that? That it's fine?"

"Isn't it?" Her voice cracked, damn it.

"It isn't. Three days without you has almost driven me mad."

"I drive you mad when we're together. I drive you mad when we're apart—you know how to make a woman feel special." The words should have sounded flippant. They didn't. No matter how hard she tried, she couldn't convince herself that this was no big deal. Not when Ethan was staring into her eyes with this odd look of satisfaction on his face, not when his thumb was now stroking her cheek.

"Why are you here?" she whispered, desperate to hear the answer and just as desperate to not hear it.

"I came for you. I've never met anyone like you before, and I don't want to walk away from you. Not now, not ever."

"It's all just talk, Ethan." Her voice was the barest of whispers. She was doing a lousy job convincing herself. She didn't think she was convincing him at all.

"Do you know how much you're worth to me?"

She shook her head. "Some diamonds, some flowers. A rose."

He stepped in another bit, bringing her body almost into contact with his. "As of yesterday, I am no longer the CEO of the Beaumont Brewery."

"What?"

"I quit the job. For personal reasons. My second in command, Finn Jackson, flew in today to take over the restructuring project. We're still dealing with a little fallout from AllBev, but it's nothing I can't handle." He said it as if it were just a little speed bump.

"You *quit*? The Brewery?"

"It wasn't my company. It wasn't worth it to me. Not like you are."

"I don't understand." He was saying words that she understood individually. But the way he was stringing them together? It didn't make sense. Not a bit.

Something in his eyes changed—deepened. A small shiver ran down Frances's back. "I do not need to marry you to solidify my position within the company because I no longer work for the company. I do not need to worry about unknown relations trying to overthrow my position because I have given up the position. The company was never worth more than you were."

She blinked at him. All of her words failed her. She had nothing to hide behind now.

"So," he went on, his eyes full of honesty and sincerity and hope. All of those things she hadn't believed she deserved. "Here I am. I have quit the Brewery. I have taken a leave of absence from my company. I could care less if anyone's listening to what we say or watching how we say it. All I care about is you. Even when you're messy and complicated and even when I say the wrong thing at the wrong time, I care about *you*."

"You can't mean that," she whispered, because what if he did?

"I can and I do. I truly never believed I would meet anyone I could care about, much less someone who would mean more to me than the job. But I did. It's you, Frances. I want you when your armor's up because you make sarcasm and irony into high art. I want you when you're feeling vulnerable and honest because I want to be that soft place where you can land after a hard day of putting the world in its place. And I want you all the times in between, when you challenge me and call me on my mistakes and push me to be a better man—one who can keep up with you."

Unexpectedly, he dropped to his knees. "So I'm asking you again. Not for the Brewery, not for the employees, not for the public. I'm asking you for me. Because I want to spend my life with you. Not a few months, not a year— my life. Our lives. Together."

"You want to marry me? *Me?*"

"I like you," he said simply. "I shouldn't, but I do. Even worse, I love you." He gave her a crooked grin. "I love you. I'd recommend you love me, too."

Her mouth opened, but nothing came out. Not a damn thing. Because what was she going to say? That he'd gotten better at sweet nothings? That he was crazy to have fallen for her? That…

That she wanted to say yes—but she was afraid?

"I've seen the real you," he said, still on his knees. "And that's the woman I love."

"Do we get—married? Next week?" That had been the deal, hadn't it? A whirlwind courtship, married in two weeks.

"I'm not making a deal, Frances. All I'm doing right now is asking a simple question. We can wait a year, if you want. You're worth the wait. I'm not going anywhere without you."

"It won't ever be simple," she warned him. "I don't have it in me."

He stood and pulled her into his arms as if she'd said yes, when she wasn't sure she had yet. The rose, she feared, was a total loss. "I don't want you simple. I want to know that every day, I've fought for you and every day, you've chosen me again."

Was it possible, what he was saying? Could a man love her?

"I expect to be wined and dined and courted," she warned him, trying to sound stern and mostly just laughing.

He laughed with her. "And what do I get out of this again?"

"A wife. A messy, complicated wife who will love you until the end of time."

"Perfect," he said, lowering his lips to hers. "That's *exactly* what I wanted."

* * * * *

LIVING THE CHARADE

MICHELLE CONDER

To my fabulous editor, Flo, for encouraging me to try
new things, and to Paul, for his endless love.
You both make all the difference!

CHAPTER ONE

IF the world was a fair place the perfect solution to Miller Jacobs's unprecedented crisis would walk through the double-glazed doors of the hip Sydney watering hole she was in, wearing a nice suit and sporting an even nicer personality.

Unlike the self-important banker currently sitting at the small wooden table opposite her who probably should have stopped drinking at least two hours ago.

'So, sexy lady, what is this favour you need from me?'

Miller tried not to cringe at the man's inebriated state and turned to her close friend, Ruby Clarkson, with a smile that said, *How could you possibly think this loser would be in any way suitable as my fake boyfriend this coming weekend*?

Ruby arched a brow in apology and then did what only a truly beautiful woman could do—dazzled the banker with a megawatt smile and told him to take a hike. Not literally, of course. Chances were she'd have to work with him at some point in the future.

Miller breathed a sigh of relief as, without argument, he swaggered towards the packed, dimly lit bar and disappeared from view.

'Don't say it,' Ruby warned. 'On paper he seemed perfect.'

'On paper most men seem perfect,' Miller said glumly. 'It's only when you get to know them that the trouble starts.'

'That's morose. Even for you.'

Miller's eyebrows shot up. She had good reason to be feeling morose. She had just wasted an hour she didn't have, drinking white wine she wouldn't even cook with, and was no further towards solving her problem than she'd been yesterday. A problem that had started when she'd lied to her boss about having a boyfriend who would *love* to come away for a business weekend and keep a very important and very arrogant potential client in check.

TJ Lyons was overweight, overbearing and obnoxious, and had taken her 'not interested' signs as some sort of personal challenge. Apparently he had told Dexter, her boss, that he believed Miller's cool, professional image was hiding a hot-blooded woman just begging to be set free and he was determined to add her to his stable of 'fillies'.

Miller shuddered as she recalled overhearing him use that particular phrase.

The man was a chauvinistic bore and wore an Akubra hat as if he was Australia's answer to JR Ewing. But he had her rattled. And when TJ had challenged her to 'bring your hubbie' to his fiftieth birthday celebration, where she would also present her final business proposal, Miller had smiled sweetly and said that would be lovely.

Which meant she now needed a man by tomorrow afternoon. Perhaps she'd been a little hasty in giving Mr Inebriated the flick.

Ruby rested her chin in her hand. 'There's got to be someone else.'

'Why don't I just say he's sick?'

'Your boss is already suss on you. And even if he wasn't, if you give your *fake* boyfriend a *fake* illness, you still have to deal with your amorous client all weekend.'

Miller pulled a face. 'Don't mistake TJ's intentions as amorous. They're more licentious in nature.'

'Maybe so, but I'm sure Dexter's are amorous.'

Ruby was convinced Miller's boss was interested in her, but Miller didn't see it.

'Dexter's married.'

'Separated. And you know he's keen on you. That's one of the reasons you lied about having a boyfriend.'

Miller let her head fall back on her neck and made a tortured sound through her teeth.

'I was coming off the back of a week of sixteen-hour days and I was exhausted. I might have had an emotional reaction to the whole thing.'

'Emotional? You? Heaven forbid.' Ruby shivered dramatically.

It was a standing joke between them that Ruby wore her heart on her sleeve and Miller kept hers stashed in one of the many shoeboxes in her closet.

'I was after sympathy, not sarcasm,' Miller grumped.

'But Dexter did offer to go as your "protector", did he not?' Ruby probed.

Miller sighed. 'A little weird, I grant you, but we knew each other at uni. I think he was just being nice, given TJ's drunken pronouncements to him the week before.'

Ruby did her famous eye roll. 'Regardless, you faked having a boyfriend and now you have to produce one.'

'I'll give him pneumonia.'

'Miller, TJ Lyons is a business powerhouse with a shocking reputation and Dexter is an alpha male wannabe. And you've worked too hard to let either one of them decide your future. If you go away this weekend and TJ makes a move on you his wife will have a fit and you'll be reading the unemployment pages for the next twelve months. I've seen it happen before. Men of TJ Lyons's ilk are never pinned for sexual harassment the way they should be.'

Ruby took a breath and Miller thanked God that she needed air. She was one of the best discrimination lawyers in the country and when she ranted Miller took note. She had a point.

Miller had put in six hard years at the Oracle Consulting Group, which had become like a second home to her. Or maybe it *was* her home, given how much time she spent there! If she won TJ's multi-million-dollar account she'd be sure to be made partner in the next sweep—the realisation of a long-held dream and one her mother had encouraged for a long time.

'TJ hasn't actually harassed me, Rubes,' she reminded her friend.

'At your last meeting he said he'd hire Oracle in a flash if you "played nice".'

Miller blew out a breath. 'Okay, okay. I have a plan.'

Ruby raised her eyebrows. 'Let's hear it.'

'I'll hire an escort. Look at this.' The idea had come to her while Ruby had been ranting and she turned her smartphone so Ruby could see the screen. 'Madame Chloe. She says she offers discreet, professional, *sensitive* gentlemen to meet the needs of the modern-day heterosexual woman.'

'Let me see that.' Ruby took the phone. 'Oh, my God. That guy would seriously have sex with you.'

Miller looked over Ruby's shoulder at the incredibly buffed male on the screen.

'And they cater to fantasies!' Ruby continued.

'I don't *want* him to have sex with me,' Miller yelped, slightly exasperated. The last thing she needed was sex, or her hormones, to derail her from her goal at the eleventh hour. Her mother had let that happen and look where it had got her— broke and unhappy.

'You can have a policeman, a pilot, an accountant—*urgh*, seen enough of them. Oh, and this one.' Ruby giggled and lowered her voice. 'Rough but clean tradesman. Or, wait—a sports jock.'

Miller shuddered. What intelligent woman would ever fantasise over a sports jock?

'Ruby!' Miller laughed as she took the phone back. 'Be serious. This is my future we're talking about. I need a decent guy who is polite and can follow my lead. Someone who blends in.'

'Hmmm...' Ruby grinned at one of the profile photos. 'He looks like he would blend in at an all-night gay bar.'

Miller scowled. 'Not helping.' She clicked on a few more. 'They all look the same,' she said despairingly.

'Tanned, buff and hot-to-trot,' Ruby agreed. 'Where *do* they get these guys?'

Miller shook her head at Ruby's obvious enjoyment. Then she saw the price tag associated with one of the men. 'Good God, I hope that's for a month.'

'Forget the escort,' Ruby instructed. 'Most of these guys probably can't string a sentence together beyond "Is that it?" and "How hard do you want it?"' Not exactly convincing boyfriend material for an up-and-coming partner in the fastest growing management consultancy firm in Australia.'

'Then I'm cooked.'

Ruby's eyes scanned the meagre post-work crowd, and Miller thought about the sales report she still had to get through before bed that night; she was still unable to completely fathom the predicament she was in.

'Bird flu?' she suggested, smoothing her eyebrows into place as she racked her brain for a solution.

'No one will believe he has bird flu.'

'I meant me.' She sighed.

'Wait. What about him?'

'Who?' Miller glanced at her phone and saw only a blank screen.

'Cute guy at the bar. Three o'clock.'

Miller rolled her eyes. 'Five years of university, six years in a professional career and we're still using hushed military terms when stalking guys.'

Ruby laughed. 'It's been ages since we stalked a guy.'

'And, please God, let it be ages again,' Miller pleaded, glancing ever so casually in the direction Ruby indicated.

She got an impression of a tall man leaning against the edge of the curved wooden bar, one foot raised on the polished foot pole, his knee protruding from the hole in his torn jeans. Her eyes travelled upwards over long, lean legs and an even leaner waist to a broad chest covered by a worn T-shirt with a pro- vocative slogan plastered on the front in red block letters. Her lips curled in distaste at its message and she moved on to wide shoulders, a jaw that looked as if it could have used a shave three days ago, a strong blade of a nose, mussed over long chocolate-brown hair and—oh, Lord—deep-set light-coloured eyes that were staring right back at her.

His gaze was sleepy, almost indolent, and Miller's heart took off. Her breath stalled in her lungs and her face felt bitingly hot. Flustered by her physical reaction, she instantly dropped her eyes as if she was a small child who had just been caught stealing a cookie. Her senses felt muddled and off-centre—and she'd only been looking at the man for five seconds. Maybe ten.

Ignoring the fact that she felt as if he was still watching her, she turned to Ruby. 'He's got holes in his jeans and a T-shirt that says "My pace or yours?" How many glasses of this crap wine have you had?'

Ruby paused, glancing briefly back at the bar. 'Not him— although he does fill that T-shirt out like a god. I'm talking about the suit he's talking to.'

Miller turned her gaze to the suit she hadn't noticed. Similar-coloured hair, square, clean-shaven jaw, nice nose, *great* suit. Yes, thankfully he did look more her type.

'Oh, I think I know him!' Ruby exclaimed.

'You *know* Ripped Jeans?'

'No.' Ruby shook her head, openly smiling in the direction Miller dared not turn back to. 'The hotshot in the suit beside him. Sam someone. I'm pretty sure he's a lawyer out of our L.A. office. And he's just the type you need.'

Miller glanced back and noticed that tall, dark and dishevelled was no longer watching her, but still some inner instinct told her to run. *Fast.*

'No!' She dismissed the idea outright. 'I draw the line at picking up a stranger in a bar—even if you do think you know him. Let me just go to the bathroom and then we can share a taxi home. And stop looking at those guys. They'll think we want to be picked up.'

'We do!'

Miller scowled. 'Believe me, by the look of the one who

needs to become reacquainted with a razor all it would take is a look and he'd have you horizontal in seconds.'

Ruby eyed her curiously. 'That's exactly what makes him so delicious.'

'Not to me.' Miller headed for the bathroom, feeling slightly better now that she had decided to call it a night. Her problem still hovered over her like a dark cloud, but she was too tired to give it any more brainpower tonight.

'Would you stop looking at those women? We are not here to pick up,' Tino Ventura growled at his brother.

'Seems to me it might solve your problem about what to do with yourself this weekend.'

Tino snorted. 'The day I need my baby brother to sort entertainment for me is the day you can put me in a body bag.'

Sam didn't laugh, and Tino silently berated his choice of words.

'So how's the car shaping up?' Sam asked.

Tino grunted. 'The chassis still needs work and the balancing sucks.'

'Will it be ready by Sunday?'

The concern in his brother's voice set Tino's teeth on edge. He was so *over* everyone worrying about this next race as if it was to be his last—and okay, there were a couple of nasty coincidences that made for entertaining journalism, but they weren't *signs*, for God's sake.

'It'll be ready.'

'And the knee?'

Coming off the back of a long day studying engine data and time trials in his new car, Tino was too tired to humour his brother with shop-talk.

'This catch-up drink was going a lot better before you started peppering me with work questions.'

He could do without the reminder of how his stellar racing year had started to fall apart lately. All he needed was to win this next race and he'd have the naysayers who politely suggested that he would never be as good as his father off his back.

Not that he dwelt on their opinion.

He didn't.

But he'd still be happy to prove them wrong once and for all, and equalling his father's number of championship titles in the very race that had taken his life seventeen years earlier ought to do just that.

'If it were me I'd be nervous, that's all,' Sam persisted.

Maybe Tino would be too, if he stopped to think about how he felt. But emotions got you killed in his business, and he'd locked his away a long time ago. 'Which is why you're a cottonwool lawyer in a four-thousand-dollar suit.'

'Five.'

Tino tilted his beer bottle to his lips. 'You need to get your money back, junior.'

Sam snorted. 'You ought to talk. I think you bought that T-shirt in high school.'

'Hey, don't knock the lucky shirt.' Tino chuckled, much happier to be sparring with his little brother than dissecting his current career issues.

He knew his younger brother was spooked about all the problems he'd been having that so eerily echoed his father's lead-up to a date with eternity. Everyone in his family was. Which was why he was staying the hell away from Melbourne until Monday, when the countdown towards race day began.

'Excuse me, but do I know you?'

Tino glanced at the blonde who had been eyeballing them for the last ten minutes, pleasantly surprised to find her focus on his little brother instead of himself.

Well, hell, that was a first. He knew Sam would get mileage out of it for the next decade if he could.

He turned to see where her cute friend was but she seemed to have disappeared.

'Not that I know of,' Sam replied to the stunner beside him, barely managing to keep his tongue in his mouth. 'I'm Sam Ventura and this is my brother Valentino.'

Tino stared at his brother. No one called him Valentino except their mother.

Switch your brain on, Samuel.

'I do know you!' she declared confidently. 'You're at Clayton Smythe—corporate litigation, L.A. office. Am I right?'

'You are at that.' Sam smiled.

'Ruby Clarkson—discrimination law, Sydney office.' She held out her hand. 'Please tell me you're in town this weekend and as free as a bird.'

Tino willed Sam not to blow his cool. The blonde had a sensational smile and a nice rack, but she was a little too bold for his tastes. His brother, however, he could see was already halfway to her bedroom.

Some sixth sense made him turn, and his eyes alighted on the friend in the black suit with the provocative red trim at the hem. She glanced at her empty table and her mouth fell open when she scanned the room and located her friend.

Then her eyes cut to his and her mouth snapped closed with frosty precision. Tino saw her spine straighten and grinned when she glanced at the door as if she was about to bolt through it. His eyes drifted over her again. If she'd bothered to smile, and he hadn't just ended a short liaison with a woman who had lied about understanding the term 'casual sex', she was exactly his type. Polished, poised and pert—all over. Pert nose, pert breasts and a pert ass. And he liked the way she moved too. Graceful. Purposeful.

As she approached, he took in the ruler-straight chestnut-coloured hair that shone under the bar lights, and skin that was perhaps the creamiest he had ever seen. His eyes travelled over a heart-shaped mouth designed with recreational activities in mind and the bluest wide-spaced eyes he'd ever seen.

'Ruby, I'm back. Let's go.'

And a voice that could stop a bushfire in its tracks.

Tino felt amused at the dichotomy; she should be leaning

in and whispering sweet nothings in his ear, not cutting her friend to the quick.

'Hey, relax. Why don't I get you a drink?' he found himself offering.

'I'm perfectly relaxed.' Her eyes could have shredded concrete as she turned them on him, but still he felt the effect of that magnificent aquamarine gaze like a punch in the gut. 'And if I wanted a drink I'd order one.'

Well, excuse the hell out of me.

'Miller!' Her friend instantly jumped in to try and ease the lash of her words. 'This is Sam and his brother Valentino. And—good news—Sam is free for the weekend.'

The woman Miller didn't move, but the skin at the outside of her mouth pulled tight. She seemed about to set her friend on fire, but then collected herself at the last minute.

'Hello, Sam. Valentino.'

He noticed he barely rated a nod.

'I'm very pleased to meet you. But unfortunately Ruby and I have to go.'

'Miller,' her friend chided. 'This is a perfect solution for you.'

This last was said almost under her breath, and Tino directed an enquiring eyebrow at Sam.

'It seems Miller needs a partner for the weekend,' Sam provided.

Tino eased back onto the barstool. *And what? They were recruiting Sam?*

He cocked his head. 'Come again?'

'No need,' the little ray of sunshine fumed politely. 'We're sorry to disturb you and now we have to go.'

'It's fine.' Sam raised his hand in a placating gesture Tino had seen him use in court. 'I'm more than pleased to offer my services.'

Services? Did he mean sexual?

Tino felt the hairs on the back of his neck stand on end. 'Would somebody like to fill me in here?' He sounded abrupt, but clearly someone had to protect his little brother from these weird females.

'Miller has to go away on a work weekend and she needs a partner to keep a nuisance client at bay,' her friend Ruby explained helpfully.

Tino eyed Miller's stiff countenance. 'Tried telling him you're not interested?' he drawled.

She snapped her startling eyes to his and once again he found himself mesmerised by their colour and the way they kicked up slightly at the corners. 'Now, why didn't I think of that?'

'Sometimes the things right in front of us are the hardest to see,' he offered.

'I was *joking*.' She looked aghast that he might have taken her sarcastic quip seriously and it made him want to laugh. It wasn't too difficult to see why she was in need of a *fake* partner, and he revised his earlier assessment of her.

She might be pert and blessed with an angel's face, but she was also waspish, uptight and controlling. Definitely not his type after all.

'Aren't you taking a client out on Dante's yacht this weekend?' He reminded his brother of the expedition both he and Dante, their older brother, had been trying to drag him along to.

Sam groaned as if he'd just been told he needed a root canal. 'Damn, I forgot.'

'Oh, really?' Ruby sounded as if she'd been given the same news.

'Okay—well, time to go,' Miller interjected baldly.

Tino wondered if she was truly thick, or just didn't want to see what was clearly going on between her friend and his brother.

'You do it.'

Tino's eyes snapped to Sam's.

'You said you were looking for something different to do this weekend. It's a great solution all round.'

Tino looked at his brother as if he had rocks in his head. His manager and the team owner had told him to take time out this weekend and do something that would get his mind off the coming race, but he was pretty sure posing as some uptight woman's fake partner was not what they'd had in mind.

'I don't think so,' Little Miss Sunshine scoffed, as if the very idea was ludicrous.

Which it was.

But her snooty dismissal of him rankled. 'Have I done something to upset you?' His gaze narrowed on her face and he almost reached out to grip her chin and hold her elusive eyes on his.

'Not at all.' But her tone was curt and her nose wrinkled slightly when her eyes dropped to his T-shirt.

'Ah.' He exhaled. 'It's just that I'm not good enough for you. Is that it, Sunshine?'

Her eyes flashed and he knew he'd hit the nail on the head. He wanted to laugh. Not only had this chit of a woman not recognised him—which, okay, wasn't that strange in Australia, given that the sport he competed in was Europe based—but she was dismissing him out of hand because he looked a bit scruffy. That had never happened before, and the first real smile in months crossed his face.

'It's not that, I'm just not that desperate.'

She briefly closed her eyes when she realised her faux pas and Tino's smile grew wider. He knew full well that if she had recognised him she'd be pouting that sweet mouth and slipping him her phone number instead of looking at him as if he was about to give her a fatal disease.

'Yes, you are,' her friend chimed in.

Tino casually sipped his beer while Miller glowered.

'Ruby, *please*.'

'I can vouch for my brother,' Sam cut in. 'He looks like he belongs on the bottom of a pond but he scrubs up all right.'

Now it was Tino's turn to scowl. He was about to say no way in hell would he help her out when he caught her unwavering gaze and realised that was just what she expected—was actually *hoping*—he would say, and for some reason that stopped him. He wouldn't do it, of course. Why enter into a fake relationship when he had zero interest in the real deal? But something about her uppity attitude rattled his chain.

Before he could respond Sam continued. 'Go on, Valentino. Imagine Dee facing the same problem. Wouldn't you like some decent guy to help her out?'

Tino's glare deepened. Now, that was just underhand, reminding him of their baby sister all alone in New York City.

'It's fine,' the fire-eater said. 'This was a terrible idea. We'll be on our way and you can forget this conversation ever happened.' Her voice was authoritative. Calm. *Decisive*.

He took another swig of his beer and noticed how her eyes watched his throat as he swallowed. When they caught his again they were more indigo than aquamarine. Interesting. Or it was until he felt his own body stir in response.

'You don't think we'd make a cute couple?' He caught the wild flash of her eyes and his voice deepened. 'I do.'

Her tipsy friend was practically clapping with glee.

Miller held her gaze steady on his, almost in warning. 'No, I don't.'

'So what will you do if I don't help you out?' Tino prodded. 'Let the client have another crack at you?'

He ignored his brother's curious gaze and focused on Miller's pained expression at his crude terminology. Man, but she was wound tighter than his Ferrari at full speed, and damn if he didn't have the strangest desire to unravel her.

He tried to figure out his unexpected reaction, but then decided not to waste time thinking about it.

Why bother? He was about to send her packing with four easy words.

He threw her his trademark smile as he anticipated her horrified response. 'Okay, I'll do it.'

Miller sucked in a deep breath and gave the man in front of her a scathing once-over. He was boorish, uncouth and *dirty*—and he had the most amazing bone structure she had ever seen. He also had the most amazing grey-blue eyes surrounded by thick ebony lashes, and sensual lips that seemed to be permanently tilted into a knowing smirk. A *sexually* knowing smirk.

But clearly he was crazy.

She might need someone to pose as her current boyfriend, but she'd rather pay an escort the equivalent of her annual salary than accept *his* help. His brother would have been a different story, but no way in the world could she pretend to be interested in this man. He looked as if all he had to do was crook his index finger and a woman would come running. If she didn't swoon first.

Swoon?

Miller pulled in the ridiculous thought. The man had holes in his jeans and needed a shower, but all that aside he was far too big for her tastes. Too male.

The loud clink of a rack of freshly washed glasses brought her out of her headspace and Miller felt a flush creep up her neck as she realised she'd been staring at his mouth, and that both Ruby and Sam were waiting for her to respond.

Her eyes dropped to the man's tasteless T-shirt. Ruby must have be more affected by alcohol than Miller had realised if she seriously thought Miller would go along with this.

'Well, Sunshine? What's it to be?'

She hated his deep, *smug* tone.

About to blow him out of the water, she was choosing her rejection carefully when it struck her that he *wanted* her to say no. That he was *counting* on it.

Miller exhaled slowly, her mind spinning. The sarcastic sod had never intended to help her at all this weekend. That momentary soft-eyed look he'd got when his brother had mentioned their sister was just a ruse. The man was a charlatan and clearly needed to be brought down a peg or two. And she was in the mood to do it.

Pausing for effect, Miller steeled herself to let her eyes run over him. She was so going to enjoy watching him squirm out of this one. 'Do you happen to own a suit?' she asked sweetly.

CHAPTER TWO

TAPPING her foot on the hot pavement outside her Neutral Bay apartment building, Miller again checked to see if she had any missed calls on her phone. She still couldn't believe that rather than squirm out of her phony acceptance of his help last night that thug of a man had collapsed into a full belly laugh and said he'd be delighted to help.

Delighted, my foot.

It wouldn't surprise her one bit if Valentino Ventura did a no-show on her today. He seemed the type.

Something about the way his full name rolled through her mind pinged a distant memory, but she couldn't bring it up. Maybe it was just the way it sounded. Both decadent and dangerous. Or maybe it was just the sweltering afternoon sun soaking into her black long-sleeved T-shirt combined with a sense of trepidation about this situation she had inadvertently created for herself.

She'd spent years curbing the more impetuous side of her nature after her parents had divorced and her safe world had fallen apart, but it seemed she'd have to try harder. Especially if she wanted to create a life for herself that didn't feel as precarious as the house of cards she'd grown up in.

Miller sighed. She was just tired. She'd averaged four hours' sleep a night this week and woken this morning feeling as if she hadn't slept at all.

A pair of slate-coloured eyes in a hard, impossibly handsome face had completely put her off her breakfast. As had the dream she'd woken up remembering. It had been about a man who looked horribly like the one she was waiting for, trapping her on her bed with his hands either side of her face. He'd looked at her as if she was everything he'd ever wanted in a woman and licked his beautifully carved lips before lowering his face to hers, his eyes on her mouth the whole time…

Miller's lips suddenly felt fuller, dryer, and she shivered in the afternoon heat and scanned the street for some sign of him. It must have been all those images of escorts that had set off the erotic dream, because no way could it have been about someone as reckless as she felt this man could be.

Okay. Miller gave herself a mental shakedown. She wasn't waiting around any longer for Mr Ripped Jeans to turn up. He'd had no intention of helping her out—perfectly understandable, given they were strangers and would likely never see each other again—but she couldn't fathom the tiny prick of disappointment that settled in her chest at his no-show.

Feeling silly, she shook off the sensation, frowning when a growling silver sports car shot towards the kerb in front of her and nearly rear-ended her black sedan.

About to give the owner a piece of her mind for dangerous driving, she was shocked to see her nemesis peel himself out of the driver's side of the car. She crossed her arms over her chest and puffed out a breath. He sauntered towards her, a slow grin lighting his face.

The man oozed sex and confidence, and moved with a loose limbed grace that said he owned the world. Exactly the type of man she detested.

Even though she was five foot seven, Miller wished she'd worn heels—because Valentino was nearly a foot taller and those broad shoulders just seemed to add another foot.

After her dream she had been determined to find him unattractive, but that was proving impossible; in a white pressed T-shirt and low-riding denims, he was so beautifully male it was almost painful to look at him.

And by the shape of his biceps the man clearly spent a serious amount of time in a gym.

Fighting an urge to push back the thick sable hair that had a tendency to fall forward over his forehead in staged disarray, Miller rallied her scrambled brain and tried to conjure up a polite greeting that would set the weekend off on the right foot. Polite, appreciative and unshakably professional.

Before she could come up with something he spoke first. 'The suit's in the back. Promise.'

His deep, mocking tone had her eyes snapping back to his and she forgot all about being polite or professional.

'You're late.'

His lips curved into an easy smile as if her snarky comment hadn't even registered. 'Sorry. Traffic's a bitch at this time on a Friday.'

'You'll have to watch your language this weekend. I would never go out with a man who swore.'

His eyes sparkled in the sunlight. 'That wasn't in your little dossier.'

He was referring to the pre-prepared personal profile Ruby had insisted she hand over last night before she'd hightailed it out of the bar at the speed of light.

'I didn't think writing down that I had a preference for good manners would be necessary.'

'Seems like we'll have some things to iron out on the drive down.'

Miller bit her tongue.

Seems like?

Was he being deliberately thick-headed? His brother was a lawyer—a good one, according to Ruby—but perhaps nature had bestowed Valentino with extreme beauty and compensated by making him slow on the uptake.

'Did you fill out the questionnaire attached to my personal profile?' she asked, wishing she had checked what he did for a living.

'I wouldn't dare not.'

His humorous reply grated, and she flicked a glance at the shiny phallic symbol he was leaning against. Was it even his? 'I want to be on the Princes Highway before every other weekender heading out of the city, so if you'd like to fetch your bag we'll get going.'

'Ever heard of the word *please*?'

The muscles in Miller's neck tightened at his casual taunt. Of course she had, and she had no idea why this man made her lose her usual cool so completely. 'Please.' She forced a smile to her lips that grew rigid as he continued to regard her without moving.

'Are you always this bossy?'

Yes, probably she was. 'I prefer the term *decisive*.'

'I'm sure you do.' He pushed off the car and towered over her. 'But here's a newsflash for you, Sunshine. I'm driving.'

Miller stared at him, hating the fact that he made her feel so small and...out of her depth. 'Is that a rental?'

'Actually, yes.' He seemed annoyingly amused by her question.

Closing her eyes briefly, Miller wondered how she had become stuck with the fake boyfriend from hell and how she was ever going to make this work.

'We're taking my car,' she said, some instinct warning her that if she gave him an inch he'd take the proverbial country mile.

He crossed his arms over his chest and his biceps bulged beneath the short sleeves of his T-shirt. Alarmingly, a tingly sensation tightened Miller's pelvic muscles, the unexpectedness of it making her feel light-headed.

'Is this our first official argument as a couple?' he asked innocently.

Okay, enough with the amusement already. 'Look, Mr Ventura, this is a serious situation and I'd appreciate it if you could treat it as such.' She could feel her heart thumping wildly in her chest and knew her face was heating up from all the animosity she couldn't contain.

Valentino cocked an eyebrow and stepped back to open the passenger side door. 'No problem, *Miss Jacobs*. Hop in.'

Miller didn't move.

'It would flay my masculinity to let a woman drive.'

Miller hated him. That was all there was to it.

Not wanting to play to his supersized ego, and feeling entirely out of her element as he regarded her through sleepy eyes, Miller made a quick decision. 'Well, I'd hate to be accused of insulting your masculinity, Mr Ventura, so by all means take the wheel.'

His slow smile told her that he'd heard her silent *shove it* and found it amusing. Found *her* amusing. And it made her blood boil.

Hating that he thought he'd won that round, she kept her voice courteous. 'As it turns out I don't mind if you drive. It will give me a chance to work on the way down.'

'But you're not impressed?'

'Not particularly.'

'What *does* impress you?'

He folded his arms across his torso and Miller's brain zeroed in on the shifting muscles and tendons under tanned skin. What had he just asked?

She cleared her throat. 'The usual. Manners. Intellect. A sense of humour—'

'You like your cars well-mannered and funny, Miss Jacobs? Interesting.'

Miller knew she must be bright red by now, and hate turned to loathing. 'This isn't funny.' She caught and held his amused gaze. 'Are you intending to sabotage my weekend?'

It gave her some satisfaction to see an annoyed look flash across his divine face.

'Sunshine, if I was going to do that I wouldn't have shown up.'

'I don't like you calling me Sunshine.'

'All couples have nicknames. I'm sure you've thought up a few for me.'

More than a few, she mused silently, and none that could be repeated in polite company.

Desperate to break the tension between them, Miller moved to the back of her car and pulled out her overnight bag. Valentino met her halfway and stowed it in the sports car before holding the passenger door wide for her.

Miller raised an eyebrow and gripped the doorframe, steeling herself to stare into his eyes. This close, the colour was amazing: streaks of silver over blue, with a darker band of grey encircling each iris.

She sucked in a deep breath and ignored his earthy male scent. 'You need to understand that I'm in charge this weekend.' Her voice wasn't very convincing even to her own ears but she continued on regardless. 'On the drive down we'll establish some ground rules, but basically all I need you to do is to follow my lead. Do you think you can do that?'

He smiled. That all-knowing grin that crinkled the outer edges of his amazing eyes. 'I'll give it my best shot. How does that sound?'

Terrible. It sounded terrible.

He leaned closer and Miller found herself sitting on butter-soft leather before she'd meant to. Her brain once again flashing a warning to run. Taking a deep breath, she ignored it and scanned the sleek interior of the car: dark and somehow predatory—like Valentino himself. It must have cost a fortune to rent, and again she wondered what he did for a living.

She couldn't look away from the way his jeans hugged his muscular thighs as she watched as he slid into the driver's seat. 'You're not a lawyer like your brother, are you?' she asked hopefully.

'Good God, no! Do I look like a lawyer?'

Not really. 'No.' She tried not to be too disappointed. 'Do you have the questionnaire I gave you?'

'No one could fault your excitement about wanting to get to know me.'

He reached into the back, his body leaning way too close to hers, and handed her the questionnaire.

Then he started the car, and Miller's senses were on such high alert that the husky growl of the engine made her want to squirm in her seat.

'You'll notice I added to it as well,' he informed her, merging into the building inner city traffic.

She glanced up, feeling completely discombobulated, and decided not to distract him by asking what he'd added. She concentrated on the questionnaire.

His favourite colour was blue, favourite food was Thai. He'd grown up in Melbourne. Hobbies: swimming, running and surfing—no wonder he looked so fit! No sign of any cerebral pursuits—no surprise there. Family: two sisters and two brothers.

'You have a big family.'

He grunted something that sounded like yes.

'Are you close?' The impetuous question was too personal, and unnecessary, but as she'd spent much of her youth longing for siblings her curiosity got the better of her.

He glanced at her briefly. 'Not particularly.'

That was a shame. Miller had always dreamed that large families were full of happy, supportive siblings who would do anything for each other.

'What does "Lives: everywhere" mean?' she asked, glancing at the questionnaire.

'I travel a lot.'

'Backpacking?'

That got a hoot of laughter. 'Sunshine, I'm thirty-three—a bit old to be a backpacker.'

He threw her a smile and Miller found her eyes riveted to his beautiful even white teeth.

'I travel for work.'

She blinked back the disturbing effect he had on her and once again scanned the questionnaire. 'Driving?' She couldn't keep the scepticism out of her voice as she read out the answer under 'Occupation'. 'Driving what?'

He threw her a quick look. 'Cars. What else?'

'I don't know. Buses? Trains?' She tried not to let her annoyance show. 'Trucks?' God, don't let him be a taxi driver; Dexter would never let her hear the end of it.

'Don't tell me you're one of those stuck-up females who only go for rich guys with white collar jobs.'

Miller sniffed. She'd been so busy working and establishing her career the last time she'd gone for any man was back at university. Not that she would be telling him that. 'Of course not.'

But she did like a man in a suit.

He snorted as if he didn't believe her, but he didn't elaborate on his answer.

Sensing he might be embarrassed about his job, she decided to let it drop for now. Maybe he wouldn't mind pretending to be an introverted actuary for the weekend. No one really knew what they did except that it involved mathematics, and not even Dexter was likely to try and engage him in that topic of conversation.

She flipped the page in front of her and found her eyes drawn to his commanding scrawl near the bottom.

Her nose wrinkled. 'I don't need to know what type of underwear you wear.' And she didn't want to imagine him in sexy boxer briefs.

'According to your little summary we've been dating for two months. I think you'd know what type of underwear I wear, wouldn't you?'

'Of course I would. But it's not relevant because I'll never need to use that information.'

He glanced at her again. 'You don't know that.'

'I could have just made something up had the need arisen.'

'Are you always this dishonest?'

Miller exhaled noisily. She was never dishonest. 'No. I loathe dishonesty. And I hate this situation. And what's more I'm sick of having men think that just because I'm single I'm available.'

'It's not just because of that?'

'No,' she agreed, thinking of TJ. 'My client isn't really attracted to me at all. He's attracted to the word *no*.'

'You think?'

'I know. It's what has made him his fortune. He's bullish, arrogant and pompous.'

'Not having met the man, I'll have to trust your judgement. But if you want my opinion your client is probably more turned on by your glossy hair, killer mouth and hourglass figure than your negative response.'

'Wha—? Hey!' Miller braced her hands on the dashboard as the car swerved around a bus like a bullet, nearly fainting before Valentino swung back into the left-hand lane two seconds before hitting a mini-van.

'Relax. I do this for a living.'

'Kill your passengers?' she said weakly.

He laughed. 'Drive.'

Miller forgot all about the near miss with an oncoming vehicle as his comments about her looks replayed in her head.

Did he really think she had a killer mouth? And why was her heart beating like a tiny trapped bird?

'I don't think we can say we met at yoga,' he said.

'Why not?' She didn't believe for a minute that he could be interested in her, but if he thought he would be getting easy sex this weekend he had another thing coming.

His amused eyes connected with hers. 'Because I don't do yoga.'

Miller felt her lips pinch together as she realised he was toying with her. 'You're enjoying this, aren't you?'

'More than I thought I would,' he agreed.

Miller released a frustrated breath. No one was going to believe she was serious about this guy. Her mother had always warned her not to lie, and she mostly lived by that creed. Yesterday, she'd let blind ambition get in the way of sound judgement.

Okay, maybe not blind ambition. Possibly she was a little peeved that she'd felt so professionally hamstrung in telling TJ Lyons what she thought of his lack of business ethics.

'Maybe we just shouldn't talk,' she muttered, half to herself. 'I know enough.' And she was afraid if he said any more she'd ask him to pull over so she could get out and run away as fast as she could.

'I don't.'

She looked at him warily. 'Everything you need to know is in my dossier. Presuming you read it?'

'Oh, it was riveting. You enjoy running, Mexican cuisine, strawberry ice cream, and *cross-stitching*. Tell me, is that anything like cross-dressing?'

Miller willed herself not to blow up at him. 'No.'

'That's a relief. You also like reading and visiting art galleries. No mention of what type of underwear you prefer, though.'

Miller channelled the monks of *wherever*. 'Because it's irrelevant.'

'You know mine.'

'Not by choice.' And she was trying very hard not to think about those sexy boxers under his snug-fitting jeans.

'So what *do* you prefer?'

'Sorry?'

'Are you a plain cotton or more of a lace girl?'

Miller stifled a cough. 'That's none of your business.'

'Believe me, it is. I'm not getting caught up in a conversation with your client not knowing my G-strings from my boy-legs.'

'*Potential* client. And I thought all men talked about was sport?'

'We've been known to deviate on occasion.' He threw her a mischievous grin. 'Since you won't tell me, I'll have to use my imagination.'

'Imagine away,' she said blithely, and then wished she hadn't when his eyes settled on her breasts.

'Now, there's an invitation a man doesn't get every day.'

Miller shot him a fulminating glare, alarmed to feel her nipples tightening inside her lace bra.

Striving to steady her nerves, she made the mistake of reading out the next item he'd added to the questionnaire. '"Favourite sexual position."'

'I haven't finished imagining your lingerie,' he complained. 'Though I'm heading towards sheer little lacy numbers over cotton. Am I right?'

Miller faked a yawn, wondering how on earth he had guessed her little secret and determined that he wouldn't know that he was getting to her. 'You've written down "all".'

He threw her a wolfish grin. 'I might have exaggerated slightly. It was getting late when I wrote that. Probably if I had to name one… Nope. I pretty much like them all equally.'

'I wasn't asking.'

'Although on top is always fun,' he continued as if she hadn't spoken. 'And there's something wicked about taking a woman from behind.'

His voice had dropped and the throaty purr slid over Miller's skin like a silken caress.

'Don't you think?'

Miller released a pent-up breath. She'd had one sexual partner so far and it hadn't been nearly exciting enough for them to try variations on the missionary theme. She hated that now all she could visualise was her on top of the sublime male next to her and how it would feel to have him behind her. *Inside her.*

Her heart thudded heavily in her chest and she suddenly found her attention riveted by the way his long fingers flexed around the steering wheel. Imagining them on her body.

'What I think is that you should concentrate on driving this beast of a car so we don't run into one of those semis you're so determined to fly past.'

'Nervous, Miller?'

He said her name as if he was tasting it and Miller's stomach clenched. Oh, this man was a master at sexual repartee, and she'd do well to remember that.

Miller shook her head. 'Are you ever serious about anything?'

He threw her a bemused look. 'Plenty. Are you ever *not* serious about anything?'

'Plenty.' Which was so blatantly untrue she half expected her nose to start growing.

He passed another car and Miller absently noted that after her earlier panicked response he was driving *marginally* less like a racing car driver. That thought triggered something in her mind and her brow furrowed.

Determined to ignore him for the rest of the trip, she pulled her laptop out of her computer bag.

'What happened to the getting-to-know-you part of our trip?'

He threw her a sexy smile that shot the hazy memory she'd been trying to grab on to out of her head and replaced it with an image of the way he had insolently leant against the bar last night.

'I know you run, swim, work out, and that you take your coffee black. Your favourite colour is blue and you have four siblings—'

'I also don't mind a cuddle after sex.'

'And you don't have a serious bone in your body. I, on the other hand, take my life very seriously and I am not interested in whether you like sex straight up or hanging from a chandelier. It's not relevant. What I'm looking for this weekend is someone to melt into the background and say very little. Starting right now.'

Tino smiled as he revved the engine and manoeuvred the Aston Martin around a tourist bus. He hadn't enjoyed himself this much in…he couldn't remember.

He was in a hot car, driving down a wide country highway on a warm spring afternoon, completely free from having to answer questions about his recent spate of accidents, his car or the coming race. The experience was almost blissful.

With any luck his anonymity would hold and he'd forget the pressure of being the world's number one racing driver on an unlucky streak. Because, as he'd told Sam, it was all media hoopla and coincidence anyway, and he'd prove it Sunday week.

He glanced at the stiff woman beside him and involuntarily adjusted his jeans. He hadn't expected her to give him a hard-on but she had. Which was surprising, given that her black linen trousers and matching shirt were about as provocative as a nun's habit.

His eyes drifted over the blade-straight hair that curtained her delicate profile from his view down over her elegant neck to the gentle swell of her breasts. Was she wearing lace underneath? By the blush that had crept into her face before he'd guess yes. The thought made him smile, and his gaze lingered on her hands as they poised over her computer keys.

She had an effortless sensuality that drew him, and whenever she glared at him hot sparks of sexual arousal threatened to burn him up.

They'd be good together. He knew it. It was just a pity he had no intention of using the weekend to test his theory.

He wasn't looking for a relationship right now, sexual or otherwise, and he had very strict guidelines about how women fitted into his life. The last thing he wanted was a woman getting into his headspace and worrying about whether or not he was going to buy it on the track every time he raced. He'd seen it too many times before, and no way would anyone land him with that kind of guilty pressure.

He still remembered the day he had watched his father clip the rear wheel of another car, flip over and slam into a concrete barrier. It had been one of those races that had reinvigorated race safety procedures and it had changed Tino's life for ever. He'd still known that he would follow in his father's footsteps, but after feeling helpless in the face of his beloved mother's grief, and fighting his own pain at losing his father, he'd locked his emotions away so tight he wasn't sure he'd recognise them any more.

Which was a bonus in a sport where emotions were considered dangerous, and his cool, roguish demeanour scared the hell out of most of his rivals.

His approach was so different from his father's attitude to the sport he'd loved. His father had tried to have it all, but what he should have done was choose family or racing. Emotional attachments and their job didn't mix. Any fool knew that.

CHAPTER THREE

'THIS it?' Valentino pulled the car onto the shoulder of the road and Miller glanced up from following the GPS navigator on her smartphone.

'Yes.' Miller read the plaque on the massive brick pillar that housed a set of enormous iron gates: 'Sunset Boulevard.' *So* typical of TJ's delusions of grandeur, Miller thought tetchily.

Valentino announced them through the security speakers, and the sports car crunched over loose gravel as he pulled around the circular driveway and stopped between an imposing front portico and a burbling fountain filled with frolicking cherubs holding gilded bows and arrows.

'Who's your client?'

Miller didn't answer. She was too busy staring at the enormous pink-tinged stone mansion that looked as if it had been airlifted directly from the Amalfi Coast in Italy and set down in the middle of this arid Australian beach scrub—lime-green lawns and all.

Her car door opened and she automatically accepted Valentino's extended hand. And regretted it. A sensation not unlike an electric shock bolted up her arm and shot sparks all the way down her legs.

Her eyes flew to his in surprise, but his expression was so blank she felt slightly stupid. At least that answered her earlier unasked question. No, he *didn't* find her attractive; he'd just been enjoying himself at her expense.

She registered the opening of a high white front door in her peripheral vision and felt her world right itself when Valentino dropped her hand.

'Miller. You made good time.'

She glanced towards her boss.

'And I can see why.' Dexter stared at Valentino and then cast his appreciative eyes over the silver bullet they'd driven down in.

A bulky figure followed Dexter down the stone steps and she pasted a confident smile on her face when TJ Lyons ambled forward like a cattle tycoon straight off the station.

'Well, now, isn't this a surprise?' he boomed.

Suddenly conscious of Valentino behind her, Miller nearly jumped out of her skin when she felt his large hand settle on her hip. Both men looked at him, eyes agog, as if he was the Dalai Lama come to pay homage.

'Dexter, TJ—this is—'

'We *know* who he is, Miller.' Dexter almost blustered, sticking his hand out towards Valentino. 'Tino Ventura. It's a pleasure. Dexter Caruthers—partner at OCG. Oracle Consultancy Group.'

Valentino took his hand in a firm handshake and a cog shifted in Miller's brain.

Tino?

'Maverick,' TJ said, addressing Valentino.

Maverick?

Had TJ and Dexter mistaken Valentino for someone they knew?

Valentino smiled and accepted their greetings like an old friend.

No! He couldn't *possibly* know her client!

'Miller, you dark horse,' TJ guffawed, slapping Valentino on the back. 'You certainly play your cards close to your chest. I'm impressed.'

Impressed? Miller looked up at Valentino, and just as her boss started asking him about the injury he'd incurred in a motor race in Germany last August his name slotted into place inside Miller's head.

Tino Ventura—international racing car legend.

She would have stumbled if Valentino hadn't tightened his hand on her hip to steady her.

She swore under her breath. Valentino must have heard it because he immediately took charge. 'It's been a long drive, gents. We'll save this conversation for dinner.'

Miller smiled through clenched teeth as he took their bags from the car and handed them to a waiting butler.

'Roger, please show our esteemed guests to their room,' TJ said, turning to the formally dressed man.

'Certainly. Sir? Madam?'

Miller refused to meet Dexter's eyes even though he was burning a hole right through her with his open curiosity.

She deliberately moved out of Valentino's reach as he went to place his hand at the small of her back. Her skin was still tingling from his earlier unexpected hold on her.

Ignoring his piercing gaze, Miller concentrated on keeping her legs steady as she preceded him up the stone steps.

Tino Ventura!

How had she not put two and two together? It was true that she didn't follow sport in any capacity, but as the only Australian driver in the most prestigious motor race in the world she should have recognised him. It was being introduced to him as Valentino that had thrown her, but even then, she conceded with an audible sigh, she'd been so stressed and distracted she might not have made the connection.

None of that, however, changed the fact that he should have told her who he was. That thought fired her temper all the way up the ornate rosewood staircase, ruining any appreciation she might have had of the priceless artworks lining the vast hallways of TJ's house.

Not that she cared about TJ's house. Right now she didn't care about anything but giving Valentino Ventura a piece of her mind for deceiving her.

'Stop thinking, Miller.'

Valentino's deep voice behind her sent a shiver skittering down her spine.

'You're starting to hurt *my* head.'

'This is your room, madam. Sir.'

The butler pushed open a door and Miller followed him inside. The room was spacious, and a tasteful combination of modern and old-world. At the far end was a large bay window with sweeping ocean views encompassing paper-white sand and an ocean that shifted from the brightest turquoise to a deep navy.

'Mr Lyons and his guests are about to adjourn to the rear terrace for cocktails. Dinner is to be served in half an hour.'

'Thank you.' Valentino closed the door after the departing butler. 'Okay, out with it,' he prompted, mimicking her wide-legged stance with his arms folded across his chest.

Miller stared at him for a minute but said nothing, her mind suddenly taken up by the size of the four-poster bed that dominated the large room. She glanced around for a sofa and found an antique settee, an armchair and a curved wooden bench seat inlaid into the bay window.

She heard Valentino move and her eyes followed his easy gait as he perched on the edge of the bed, testing the mattress. 'Comfy.'

He smiled, and she fumed even more because she knew he was laughing at her discomfort. 'I'm not sleeping with you in that,' she informed him shortly.

'Oh, come on, Miller. It's big enough for six people.'

Six people *her* size, maybe… Why hadn't she thought of the sleeping arrangements before now?

Probably because her mind had been too concerned with finishing her proposal and she hadn't wanted to dwell on the fact she was even in this predicament. But she *was* in it, and it was time to face it and work out how she was going to make this farce work with her fake and *very* famous boyfriend.

'It would have been nice if you had thought to let me know who you are,' she said waspishly.

'I did tell you my name. And my job.'

Miller pressed her lips together as she took in his cavalier tone and relaxed demeanour. That was true—up to a point. 'You must have known that I didn't recognise you.' She paced away from him, unable to stand still under his disturbing grey-blue gaze.

Valentino shrugged. 'If I'd thought it was going to be an issue I would have mentioned it.'

'How could you think it *wouldn't* be?' she fumed, stopping mid-pace to stare at him. 'Everyone in the country knows who you are.'

'You didn't.'

'That's because I don't follow sport, but… Oh, never mind. I need to use the bathroom and think.'

After splashing cold water on her face Miller glanced at her pale reflection and thought about what she knew about her fake boyfriend other than the garbage he'd thrown at her in the car. Taxi driver… How he would laugh if he knew she had entertained that thought for a while.

Okay, no need to rehash *that* embarrassing notion. It was time to think. Strategise.

She knew he was a world-class athlete and a world-class womaniser with a penchant for blonde model-types—although she couldn't recall where she'd read that, or how long ago. Regardless, it still made it highly improbable that they would be seeing each other. And she knew everyone who saw them together would be thinking the same thing—including Dexter, who would not be backward in asking the question.

Of course she'd refuse to answer it—she never mixed business with her personal life—but Dexter was shrewd. And he'd be too curious about her "relationship" to take it lying down. Anyone who knew her would. Serious, ambitious Miller Jacobs and international playboy Valentino Ventura a *couple*?

God, what a mess. They had as much in common as a grass-hopper with an elephant.

'You planning to hide out in there for the rest of the week-end?'

His amused voice brought her head around to stare at the closed door. Wrenching it open, she found herself momentarily breathless when she found him filling the space, one arm raised to rest across the top of the doorjamb, making him seem impossibly tall.

She pushed past him and tried to ignore the skitters of sensation that raced through her as her body brushed his. Anger. It was only anger firing her blood.

Taking a couple of calming breaths, she turned to face him. 'No one is going to believe we're a couple.'

'Why not?'

Miller rolled her eyes. 'For one, I don't exactly mix in your circles. And for two, I'm not your type and you're not mine.'

'You're a woman. I'm a man. We share a mutual attraction we can't ignore. Happens all the time.'

To him, maybe.

Miller smoothed her brows, her mind filled with an endless list of problems. 'You're right. We can't say we met at yoga…'

'Listen, you're blowing this out of proportion. Let's keep it as close to the truth as we can. We met at a bar. Liked each other. End of story. That way you'll feel more comfortable and it's highly probable—not to mention true.'

Except for the liking part. Right now Miller couldn't recall liking anyone *less*.

Valentino opened his bag on the bed.

'Why are you here?' she asked softly.

His eyes met hers. Held. 'You know why I'm here,' he said, just as softly. 'You challenged me to be here.'

Miller arched an eyebrow. 'I thought you said you were thirty-three, not thirteen.'

A crooked grin kicked up the corners of his mouth and he

pulled his shirt up over his rippling chest. Lord, did men really look that good unairbrushed?

Last night's dream flashed before her eyes and she was relieved when he turned his back on her. Only then she got to view his impressive back, and her eyes automatically followed the line of his spine indented between lean, hard muscle. 'What exactly are you doing?'

He dropped his T-shirt on the bed and turned to face her. 'Changing my shirt for dinner. I don't want to embarrass you by coming across too casual to meet your friends.'

Ha! Now that she knew who he was she knew he'd impress everyone downstairs even in a clown suit.

Tino shrugged into his shirt and tiny pinpricks of heat glanced across his back as he felt Miller's eyes on him. A powerful surge of lust and the desire to press her up against the nearest wall and explore the attraction simmering between them completely astounded him. He'd been trying to keep things light and breezy between them—his usual *modus operandi*—but his libido was insistently arguing the toss.

'Next time I'd prefer you to use the bathroom,' she said stiffly. 'And these people aren't my friends. They're business colleagues—although as to that I doubt I'll know many of the other people in attendance.'

'How many are staying here?'

'I think six others tonight. Tomorrow night at TJ's fiftieth party I have no idea.'

'I thought this was a business weekend?'

'TJ likes to multi-task.'

Tino rolled his silk shirt sleeves and noticed her frowning at his forearms. 'Problem?'

His question galvanised her into action and she crossed to her small suitcase and started rifling through it.

'I'll be ten minutes.'

Five minutes later she reappeared in the doorway and padded over to the wardrobe. She barely looked different from the way she had when she'd gone in. Black tailored pants, a black beaded top, and a thin pink belt bissecting the two. She perched on the armchair and secured a fancy pair of stilettos on her dainty feet. The silence between them was deafening.

'Am I getting the silent treatment?'

She exhaled slowly and he noticed the way the beads on her top swayed from side to side. 'I hope you're not currently in a relationship.'

'Would I be here with you if I was?'

'I don't know. Would you?'

Her chin had come up and he was surprised he had to control irritation at her deliberate slur. She didn't know him, and he supposed, given his reputation—which wasn't half as extensive as the press made out—it was a valid question.

'Okay, I'm going to humour that question with an answer—because we don't know each other and I understand you feel compromised by the fact that I'm a known personality. I don't date more than one woman at a time and I never cheat.'

'Fine. I just…' Her hand fluttered between them. 'If we really were going out you'd know I hate surprises.'

'Why is that?'

She glanced away. 'I just do.'

Her answer was clipped and he knew there was a story behind her flat tone.

'I don't suppose there's any chance you can just fade into the background and not draw attention to yourself, is there?'

Tino nearly laughed. So much for coming on to him once she found out who he was. He shook his head at his own arrogance. But, hell, most women he met simpered and preened and asked stupid questions about how many cars he owned and how fast he drove. This gorgeous female was still treating him like a disease. And she *was* gorgeous. She'd dusted her sexy mouth with a peach-coloured gloss that made him want to lick it right off.

'We need to go downstairs.' She sounded as if she was about to face a firing squad.

She grabbed a black wrap from the back of the cream chair

and stopped suddenly, nearly colliding with him. He felt a shaft of heat spear south as he touched her elbow to steady her, and knew she felt the same buzz by the way she pulled back and went all wide-eyed with shock, just as she had by the car.

A shock he himself still felt. He hadn't anticipated being this physically attracted to her. He reminded himself of his iron-clad rule of not getting involved with a woman this close to the end of the season—particularly *this* season, which had started going pear-shaped three months ago.

So why couldn't he stop imagining how she would taste if he kissed her?

He stepped back from her, out of the danger zone. 'You might want to think about not jumping six feet in the air every time I touch you.' He sounded annoyed because he was.

'And *you* might want to think about not touching me.'

Large aquamarine eyes, alight with slivers of the purest gold, stared up at him, and the ability to think flew out of his head. Her eyes reminded him of a rare jewel.

Then she blinked, breaking the spell.

Get a grip, Ventura. Since when did you start comparing eyes to jewels?

'You really have the most extraordinary eyes,' he found himself saying appreciatively. 'A little glacial right now, but extraordinary nonetheless.'

'I don't care what you think of my eyes. This isn't real so I don't need your empty compliments.'

How about the back of my hand across your tidy tush? The thought brought a low hum of pleasure winging through his body. He did his best to ignore it. 'Are you usually this rude or do I just bring out the best in you?'

Her shoulders slumped and she stepped back to put more space between them. 'I'm sorry. I'm...uncomfortable. This weekend is important to me. I wish I'd just given you chicken pox and handled everything myself. I let Ruby convince me this would be a good idea.'

Tino felt contrite at her obvious distress. 'Everything will be fine. Just think of us as two people going away for a weekend to have some fun. You've done that in the past, surely.'

'Of course,' she said, her reply a little too quick and a little too defensive. 'It's just that I would never choose to come away for a weekend with a man like you.'

He stiffened even though he knew by her tone that she was being honest rather than deliberately insulting, but, hell, he had his limits. 'What exactly is it about me that you don't like, Sunshine?' he queried, as if her answer didn't matter. Which, in the scheme of things, it didn't.

Her lips pursed at the mocking moniker, but he didn't care. 'We really need to go down.'

Tino crossed his arms. 'I'm waiting.'

'Look, I didn't mean to offend you. But I'm hardly your type either.'

'You're female, aren't you?' He couldn't help the comment. The desire to get under her skin was riding him.

'That's all it takes?'

Her incredulous tone drew a tight smile to his lips. 'What else is there?'

She shook her head. 'See, that's why you're not my type. I like someone a little more discerning, a little more...' She stopped as if she'd realised she was about to insult him.

'Don't stop now. It's just getting interesting.'

'Okay—fine. You're arrogant, condescending, and you treat everything like it's a joke.'

Tino deliberately kept his chuckle light. 'For a minute there I thought you were going to list my faults.'

She threw up her hands and stalked away from him. 'You're impossible to talk to!'

'True, but I make up for it where it counts.'

Her sexy mouth flattened and he just managed not to laugh. 'Sunshine, you are *so* easy to rile.'

She huffed out a breath and eyed him with utter disdain. 'Please remember that we are playing by my rules this weekend, not yours. When we're in company just…' She smoothed her brows. 'Just follow my lead.'

She pinned a frozen smile on her face and sailed through the door, leaving a faint trace of summertime in her wake.

Tino breathed deep. He didn't understand how a woman so intent on behaving like a man could smell so sweet. Then he wondered if she had sex like a man as well: enjoyed herself and moved on easily.

The unexpected thought made him snort as he followed her down the hall.

He might not know the answer to that, but he was damn sure they were bound to have another argument when she learned he played by no one else's rules but his own.

And as for following her lead…

CHAPTER FOUR

'So, how did you two meet?'

Miller swallowed the piece of succulent fish she'd been chewing for five minutes on a rush and felt it stick in her throat. It was the question of the night, it seemed, as TJ's guests tried to work out how an uptight management consultant could possibly ensnare the infamous Tino Ventura.

She grabbed her water glass and stiffened as she felt Valentino's strong fingers grip the back of her chair. He'd done that constantly throughout the meal, sometimes playing with the beads on her top, and she'd felt the heat of his touch sear through her clothing and all the way into her bones. The man was like a furnace.

Fortunately he took control of the conversation, having already warned her to say very little, but she could see he was as tired of the interest as she was.

Tuning out, she wondered if she shouldn't stage a massive fight right here and end the charade before they slipped up. Or before *she* slipped up—because he seemed to be doing just fine. And maybe she would feel better if Dexter didn't keep throwing her curious glances that told her in more than words that he didn't buy the whole international-racing-driver-boyfriend thing one bit.

When they had arrived for dinner the men had immediately enclosed Valentino in a circle as if he were an old friend, and the women had raked their eyes appreciatively over his muscular frame. Most of them had looked at him as if they wouldn't say no to being another notch on his well-scarred bedpost. Something that didn't interest Miller in the slightest.

Oh, she found him just as sexy as they did, but she had a ten-year plan that she had nearly accomplished, and she wasn't about to get involved with a man and let him distract her. Especially a man who treated women like sex bunnies.

Pushing back her chair, Miller politely extricated herself to the powder room. After locking the bathroom door she leant against it, closed her eyes and felt her heartbeat start to normalise now that she was out from under Valentino's mesmeric spell.

It didn't help that he kept touching her, and she really needed to talk to him about his ability to follow her lead. He hadn't taken *any* of her subtle hints all night. And every time he touched her—whether it was a fleeting brush of his fingers across the back of her hand at the dinner table or a more encompassing arm around her waist while sipping champagne—it made her feel as if she'd been branded.

When she had envisaged having a fake boyfriend she'd imagined someone dutifully trailing in her wake and playing a low-key, almost invisible role. But there was nothing invisible about Valentino Ventura, and it annoyed her that her own eyes were constantly drawn to him, as if he really was some god who had deigned to grace them with his presence.

Deciding she couldn't hide out in the powder room any longer, Miller exited to find Dexter lounging against the opposite wall, waiting for her.

She didn't want to think about Ruby's suspicions that Dexter was interested in her as more than just a work colleague, but there was no doubt he was behaving differently towards her all of a sudden.

'So…' Dexter drawled, a beer bottle swinging back and forth between his fingers. 'Tino Ventura?'

Miller smiled enigmatically in answer.

'You *do* know he's got a reputation for being the biggest playboy in Europe?'

She knew he *had* a reputation—but the *biggest* playboy? 'You shouldn't believe everything you read,' she said, though by the way he'd charmed everyone at dinner she could well believe it. Women were always falling for bad boy types they hoped to reform, and even clean-shaven he looked like a fallen angel.

'I don't see it, you know,' Dexter added snidely.

Miller narrowed her eyes. He might be her direct superior, but he wasn't behaving like it right now. 'My personal life is none of your business, Dexter. Was there something you wanted?'

'Your part of the presentation we're supposed to give to TJ tomorrow.'

'I e-mailed it just before I left to come down here.'

'Cutting it a bit fine?'

About to ask him what his problem was, she nearly screamed when she felt a warm male hand settle on the small of her back. She tried to quell the instant leap of her heart but it was already galloping away at a mile a minute.

She knew her reaction hadn't done anything to alleviate Dexter's scepticism about her relationship, but frankly this internal sense of excitement when Valentino came close was too unfamiliar and disconcerting to deal with head-on. She would have given anything to do what she'd done as a child in uncomfortable situations: run away to her room and lose herself in her drawings.

'Hey, Sunshine, I wondered where you'd got to.' Valentino's warm breath stirred the hair at her temple, and his gaze lingered on her mouth before lifting to hers.

He was terribly good at this, Miller thought, swallowing heavily. It was just a pity that *she* wasn't.

'Just discussing work. Nothing important,' she said breathlessly.

'In that case, you won't mind if I join you?'

'Of course not.' She smiled at Dexter, as if her world couldn't be more perfect. Anything was better than gazing up into Valentino's sleepy grey gaze.

'So, by my reckoning,' Dexter said, looking from one to the other, 'you will have met around the time of Tino's near fatality earlier in the year. In Germany. Funny, I don't recall okaying any trip to Europe in—what?—August, was it? In fact, I can't recall your last holiday at *all*, Miller.'

Near fatality?

Miller's eyes flew to Valentino's calm face and too late she realised she would of *course* know about this if they really were going out. Collecting herself, she attempted fascination with the conversation.

'Miller wasn't on holiday when we met,' Valentino answered smoothly. 'It was while I was recuperating in Australia.'

Dexter frowned theatrically. 'I thought you convalesced in Paris? Your second home town?'

'Monaco is my second home town.'

Miller noticed he hadn't directly answered Dexter's question. Clever.

'So, what do you make of your run of bad luck since your recovery?'

'It's nice to know you're such a fan, Caruthers.' Valentino's voice was smooth, but Miller felt sweat break out under her armpits.

She tried to keep her expression bland, but mild sparks of panic were shooting off in her brain. She had a vague recollection of Dexter talking sport during various meetings, but she'd had no idea he was such a motor racing fan either.

'I follow real sports.' The beer bottle swung a little too vigorously in his loose hold. 'Football, rugby, boxing,' Dexter opined.

Valentino smiled in a way that made Dexter's comment seem as childish as it was.

Undeterred, her boss tilted his head. 'And you know, of course, that Miller doesn't follow *any* type of sport.'

'Something I'm hoping to change once she sees me race in Melbourne next weekend.'

Miller felt like an extra in a bad theatre production, and

wondered why they were talking over her head as if she was some sort of possession.

'Ah, the race of the decade.' Dexter's remark was as subtle as a cattle prod.

Again, Miller had no idea what he was talking about and snuck a glance up at Valentino—to find his easy smile still in place.

'So they say.'

She could feel the tension coming off him in waves, and knew he wasn't as relaxed as he wanted them to believe. She couldn't blame him. It couldn't be easy, having Dexter grill him this way.

'You'll have to wear earplugs, Miller. It gets loud at the track,' Dexter said, valiantly trying to regain a foothold in the conversation.

'I'll take care of Miller,' Valentino drawled. 'And you'd do well not to believe everything you read on the internet, Caruthers. My private life is exactly that. Private.'

There was no mistaking the warning behind his words and Miller stared up at Valentino, slightly shocked at the ruthless edge in his tone. Gone was the dishevelled rogue who had baited her so mercilessly in the car on the drive down, and in his place was a lean, dangerous male you'd have to be stupid to take on.

And what was Dexter doing, talking about her as if they had a more personal relationship than they did?

Miller was about to take him aside and ask him but TJ chose that moment to intrude.

'There's the guest of honour!' he announced, his eyes fixed on Valentino.

Guest of honour? Since when?

Miller was starting to feel like Alice down the rabbit hole, but at least she could tell that TJ had backed off in his openly male interest in her; his awe of Valentino clearly overrode his lustful advances.

Almost ignoring her completely, TJ launched into a spiel

about his newest car on order and Miller was glad of the reprieve.

Eyes gritty with tiredness, she wished herself a hundred miles away from this scene.

Then she noticed the men looking at her and realised she'd been unwittingly drawn into a conversation she hadn't been following. Turning blindly to Valentino for assistance, she immediately became lost in his heated gaze.

Her breath stalled and she had to remind herself that this was just pretend. But, *wow*, the man could go into acting when his racing career ended and win a truckload of awards.

Hearing her phone blast Ruby's unique ringtone in her evening purse, Miller latched onto the excuse like a lifeline, not quite meeting Valentino's eyes as she slipped away from the group.

Heading straight for the softly lit Japanese garden she'd glimpsed from the dinner table, she let the subtle scent of gardenias and some other richly perfumed flower wash over her as she walked.

Tino watched Miller wander down the steps and along a rocky pathway towards the infinity pool that glowed as cobalt-blue as her eyes.

Dexter laughed at something TJ had said and Tino glanced back to find that his eyes were also on Miller. As they had been most of the night. Even a blind man could tell that they had history together. And the way her boss had tried to stamp his ownership all over her had Tino wondering if Miller hadn't needed an escort this weekend for more than just a deterrent for her avaricious client. Perhaps she needed cover for an office affair as well.

He was sure he'd heard talk about Dexter being married, and as a third generation Italian from a solid family background if there was one thing Tino didn't condone it was extramarital affairs.

His brows drew together as he considered the possibility

that Miller and Dexter were lovers, and he didn't like the feeling that settled in his gut.

Was that why she flinched every time he got within spitting distance of her? She didn't want her "real" boyfriend to get jealous? If so, she'd soon learn that he wouldn't play *that* particular game. Not for another second.

Tossing back the last of his red wine, Tino placed the glass on a nearby table before heading down the steps to the garden.

Obviously hearing his quiet footfalls on the loose pebbles, Miller turned, her face half in shadow under the warm light given off by the raised lanterns that edged the narrow path.

Tino stopped just inside the wide perimeter he'd come to recognise as her personal space and her eyes turned wary. As well they might.

'I came down here to be alone,' she said, her dainty chin sticking out at him.

Tino widened his stance. 'Are you having an affair with Caruthers?'

'What?'

She seemed genuinely appalled by the question, but she needed to know this was a boundary he wouldn't cross. 'Because if you are this little ruse is over.'

Her gorgeous eyes narrowed at his blunt comment.

'Of *course* I'm not having an affair with Dexter. But even if I was it would be none of your business.'

'Wrong, Sunshine. You made it my business this weekend.'

Miller shook her head. 'That's rubbish. You were the one who *offered* to come, and I can tell you I'm not very happy with the job you're doing so far.'

Tino felt a surge of annoyance that was as much because of his attraction to her as because of her snotty attitude. 'Want to explain that?'

She leaned in towards him and he got a whiff of her sexy scent. Unconsciously, he breathed deep. 'You agreed that you would follow my lead, but despite your silver-tongued sophistication you've failed to pick up on any of my signals.'

'Silver-ton…? Sunshine, you are deluded.'

'Excuse me?'

She mirrored his incredulous tone and Valentino didn't know whether to put her over his knee or just kiss her. The woman was driving him crazy. Or her scent was. He'd never smelt anything so subtly feminine before, and on a woman who seemed determined to hide her femininity it didn't bear thinking about. Like his unusually possessive exchange with her deadbeat boss inside.

'I never promised to follow your lead. That was an assumption you made before you so imperiously waltzed out the door. And if there's nothing going on between you and Caruthers, why is he behaving like a jealous boyfriend?'

'Why are *you*?'

'Because it's my job. Apparently. Now, answer the question.'

Her gaze turned wary again. 'I don't know what's up with Dexter except that he doesn't believe you and I are a couple.'

Tino rocked back on his heels and regarded her. 'I'm not surprised.'

She flashed him an annoyed look. 'And why is that? Because I'm not your usual type?'

Since when was a ballbreaker any man's usual type?

'Because you act like a startled mouse every time I touch you.'

'I do not,' she blustered. 'But if I do it's because I don't *want* you touching me.'

'I'm your *boyfriend*. I'm supposed to touch you.'

'Not at a business function.' She frowned.

He felt completely exasperated with her. 'Anywhere.' His voice had dropped an octave because he realised just how much he had enjoyed touching her all night. How much he wanted to touch her now.

Incredible.

'That's not me,' she said on a rush.

Her tongue snaked out to moisten her heart-shaped mouth; that succulent bottom lip was now glistening invitingly.

Valentino thrust his hands into the back pockets of his jeans and locked his eyes with hers. 'If you want people to believe we're a couple you're going to have to let me take the lead, because you clearly know diddly squat about relationships.'

She looked at him as if he'd just told her the world was about to end. '*Now* who's making assumptions? For your information, if we were in a real relationship something else you would know is that I'm not the demonstrative type.'

She had thrust her chin out in that annoyingly superior way again, and Valentino couldn't resist loading her up. 'Well, that's too bad, Miller, because if we were a real couple you'd know that I *am*.'

Which wasn't strictly true. Yes, he liked to touch, but he didn't usually feel the need to grab hold of his dates and stamp his possession all over them in public—or in private come to that. The only reason he had with Miller was because she had avoided eye contact with him most of the evening, and with all the interest in their relationship he'd had to do something to make it appear genuine.

In fact she should be *thanking* him for taking his role so seriously instead of busting his balls over it.

'Listen, lady—'

'No, *you* listen.' She stabbed a finger at him as his mother used to do when he was naughty. 'I am in charge here, and your inability to read my signals is putting this whole farce in jeopardy.'

Tino thrust a hand through his hair and glanced over his shoulder as the lilting murmur of chattering guests wafted on the slight breeze. 'Is that so?' he said softly.

'Yes.' She folded her arms. 'Trust me—I know what I'm doing.'

'Good, because right now anyone watching you spit at me like an angry cat will think we're having a humdinger of an argument.'

'That's fine with me.' She gave him a cool smile that he knew was meant to put him in his place. 'It will make our relationship seem more authentic than anything else that's gone on tonight.'

Valentino saw red at her self-righteous challenge.

He stepped farther into her personal space and gripped her elbows, gratified when her eyes widened to the size of dinner plates.

'What are you doing?' she demanded in a furious whisper.

Yeah, what are *you doing, Ventura?*

Tino stared down at her, watching the pulse-point in her neck pick up speed. His body hummed with sexual need and he wondered what it was about her he found just so damned tempting.

She was more librarian than seductress, and yet she couldn't have had more effect on his body if she'd been standing in front of him naked. It was a thought that was a little disconcerting and one he instantly pushed aside.

He wasn't *that* attracted to her. But he *was* that annoyed with her, and while he might not have ever felt the need to put a woman in her place before he did now. And he'd enjoy it.

'Why, Miller, I'm just doing what you asked. I'm going to make this farce of a relationship look more authentic.'

Before she could unload on him he took full advantage of her open mouth and planted his own firmly over the top of hers in a kiss that was more about punishment than pleasure.

Or at least it was meant to be. Until she stupidly tried to wriggle away from him and he had to clamp one hand at the back of her head and the other over her butt to hold her still.

She fell into him, her soft breasts nuzzling against his chest, her nipples already diamond-hard. They both stilled; heat and uncertainty a driving force between them. Her silky hair grazed the back of his knuckles and his fingers flexed. Her eyes slid closed, her soft whimper of surrender sending a powerful surge of lust through his whole body.

Her silky hair slid over his knuckles and made his fingers flex, and then she made a tiny sound that turned him harder than stone.

Tino couldn't have stopped his tongue from plunging in and

out of the moist sweetness of her mouth if he'd had a gun to his head. All day he'd wondered if she'd taste as good as her summery scent promised, and now he had his answer.

Better.

So much better.

He was powerless to pull back, his brain as stalled as the Mercedes he'd accidentally flooded in the second race of his professional career.

He gave a deep groan of pleasure as her arms wound around his neck, and he gripped her hips to pull her pelvis in tightly against his own.

His arousal jerked as it came into contact with her soft belly, and it was all he could do not to grind himself against her.

So much for not being that *attracted to her.*

He urged her lips to open even wider and she didn't resist when he possessed her mouth in a carnal imitation of the way his body wanted to possess hers. An instantaneous fire beat flames through his body, and her low, keening moans of pleasure were making him hotter still.

He had to have her.

Here.

Now.

His hand slid to her bottom, the outside of her thighs, drawing her in and up so that he could settle more fully in the tempting vee of her body. He felt her fingers move into his hair, her feminine curves pressing closer as she rubbed against him. Tino couldn't hold back another groan—and nearly exploded when he heard someone clearing their throat behind him.

Bloody hell. He drew his mouth back and took a moment before reaching up to unwind Miller's arms from around his neck. She made a moue of protest and slowly opened passion-drugged eyes. He knew when her senses returned from the same planet where his had gone that she'd be more than pissed.

'Sunshine, we have company,' he whispered gruffly, his unsteady breath ruffling the top of her hair.

He gave her time to compose herself before turning to face

the person behind them. He was certain it was Caruthers. He also gave himself time to get his raging hard-on under control. Not that it seemed to be responding with any speed.

Miller looked up at Valentino and was aghast to realise that she had become so completely lost in his kiss that she had quite forgotten they were in a public place.

Never before had she been kissed like that, and heat filled her cheeks at the realisation that she wouldn't have stopped if Dexter hadn't turned up. That she would have had sex with Valentino in the middle of a garden like some dumb groupie.

Not wanting to dwell on how that made her feel, Miller shoved the thought away before lurching backwards.

'Dexter...' she began, trying to organise her thoughts on the hop. She was almost glad when Valentino took over.

'You wanted something, Caruthers?'

Miller closed her eyes at Valentino's rough question and wished the ground would open up and swallow her whole.

'I came to let Miller know that TJ has opened champagne in the music room. As we're here in a professional capacity to win the man's business, it might be prudent for her to join us.'

Miller smoothed her eyebrows and stepped out from behind Valentino, determined that Dexter wouldn't see how mortified she felt right now. 'Of course.' She forced herself not to defend her actions, even though she desperately wanted to.

'Good. I'll leave you to pull yourself together,' Dexter said stiffly.

He was clearly upset with her, and he had good reason to be, Miller thought. She *was* here in a professional capacity, and even if she and Valentino really were lovers it didn't excuse her poor behaviour.

Although they *had been* secluded from the other guests, Dexter had found them—which meant anyone else could have.

A small voice informed her that Valentino had probably achieved his goal and put paid to Dexter's suspicions about the genuineness of their relationship, but Miller wasn't listening.

She wouldn't have chosen to do it that way, and she was furious that Valentino hadn't given her a choice. Furious that he had used his superior height and strength to hold her against him to prove a point. A point he had clearly enjoyed.

As did you. The snide voice popped up again, reminding her of how she had wrapped her tongue around his and tried to climb his body to assuage the ache that was still beating heavily between her thighs.

God, what a mess.

Valentino moved his arm in a gesture for her to precede him up the path and Miller determinedly made the same gesture back to him. He cocked an eyebrow at her, his eyes lingering on her mouth; his trademark sexy grin was more a warning than an indication of pleasantness.

Miller narrowed her eyes and thought about stomping on his foot as she strode past, but she decided not to give him the satisfaction of letting him know he had succeeded in rattling her again.

She knew he liked to take control but, dammit, this was not his show to orchestrate. She was in charge and it was time to set some clear boundaries between them. She'd dealt with alpha males in her line of work before, and she'd deal with this one too.

CHAPTER FIVE

FEELING as if the past hour had taken a day to pass, Miller unfolded a woollen blanket and laid it on the bedroom floor.

'What are you doing?'

She glanced up to find Valentino lounging against the bathroom doorway, watching her. His face was stony, but it only highlighted the chiselled jaw that was again in need of a razor. He wasn't wearing anything other than his black jeans, unbuttoned, and his biceps bulged where he folded his hands across his superbly naked chest.

'Problem with your shirt?' she said, and could have kicked herself when his mouth curled into a knowing smile.

'Only in as much as I don't wear a shirt to bed.'

Miller raised an unconcerned eyebrow. 'Lucky you wear jeans, then.'

'I don't.'

His eyebrow rose to match hers and she turned back to unfold a second blanket she'd picked up from the end of the bed. Flicking it out, she laid it on top of the first.

'I repeat—what are you doing?'

'Making up a bed. What does it look like?'

Valentino looked bored. 'If you're worried about whether or not I'm going to jump your bones now that we're alone, I doubt I could get through that passion killer you're wearing with a blowtorch.'

Miller stood up and moved to the wardrobe, where she had seen a group of pillows on the top shelf. She was glad that he didn't like her quilt-style dressing gown. It had been a present from her late father, and although the stitching was frayed in places she'd never get rid of it.

Thinking about her father made her remember the day her parents had told her they were separating. She'd been ten at the time, and while they'd talked about it calmly and rationally Miller had felt sick and confused. Then her mother had driven her from Queensland to Victoria and Miller's world had gone from cosy and safe to unpredictable and unhappy. A bit like the steely, coiled man feigning nonchalance in the bathroom doorway.

'Or are you worried you won't be able to keep your hands to yourself after that kiss?' he asked.

Miller cast him a withering look and returned to the bed she was setting up on the floor. She wasn't going to stroke his ego by responding to his provocative comments.

He'd felt her response to his kiss and it still rankled. Afterwards she'd pretended that she'd been acting for the sake of their audience, but she hadn't been, and she needed time to process that.

In the space of a short time the solid foundations of her secure life had become decidedly rickety, and she wasn't going to add to that by letting her plans for the future be derailed by a sexy-as-sin flamboyant racing car driver who treated life like a game. Because Miller knew life *wasn't* a game, and when things went wrong you only had yourself to rely on.

It had been a tough lesson she had learned hard after being sent to an exclusive girls' boarding school, where her opinion hadn't meant half as much as her lack of money. Teenage girls could be cruel, but Miller hadn't wanted to upset her mother by telling her she was having a terrible time at school. Her mother had needed to work two jobs in order to give Miller a better start in life than she'd had, so Miller had put up with the bullying and the loneliness and made sure not to give her mother any reason to be disappointed in her.

'If you think I'm sleeping on that, Sunshine, you're mistaken.'

Valentino's arrogant assurance was astounding, and Miller stared open-mouthed as he crossed to the bed and placed his watch on the bedside table.

Fortunately she had already anticipated this problem and, she thought grumpily as she fluffed up her pillows, she hoped the bed had bugs in it.

'Good to know. At least there won't be any more arguments between us tonight.'

Tino smiled. He couldn't help it. Which was surprising since he was still irritated as hell by that kiss out in the garden and the way he had become completely lost in it. Drunk on it.

He'd told himself all day to lay off the little fantasies he'd been having about her mouth, but had he listened? No.

And what was up with that? If he ignored his instincts on the track as he had out in that garden he'd have bought the farm a long time ago.

The problem was he had made her off-limits and that had spiked his interest. Stupid. But he wasn't a man who could resist a challenge. And on top of that she was clearly not fawning over him as other women did once they knew who he was. There was nothing more likely to get a woman into his bed than giving them his job title, but this pretty little ray of sunshine was not only *not* trying to sleep with him, she was making up a bed on the floor!

She couldn't have challenged him more if she'd tried, and because he had been thwarted in racing these last couple of months, first due to injury and then because his car was under-performing and causing all sorts of problems, he was more frustrated than he normally would be. Which went a lot further towards explaining his sexual fascination with her than anything else he'd come up with so far.

It was even more of a reason to keep his distance from her.

He wasn't a slave to his hormones, and he had enough complications at the moment without adding her to the list.

He yanked off his jeans and got into the king-sized bed, letting out an exaggerated sigh of appreciation as the soft mattress gave just enough beneath his body. He might as well enjoy it since he *knew* she was about to order him to sleep on the floor. He'd do it once she said please. A word she was sorely in need of learning how to use.

He grinned. He was quite looking forward to seeing how long it would take before she caved in and used it.

He watched with some satisfaction as she stalked to the main door and hit the light switch with her open palm as if she wished it was his head. Then she did something completely unexpected. She shimmied out of her robe and got into the makeshift bed on the floor.

And made him feel like an absolute idiot.

'Ever had your testosterone levels checked out?' he grumbled.

'What's the matter, Valentino? Your masculinity being challenged because I'm not falling at your feet?'

Yes, as a matter of fact it was.

'Was the kiss that good?' he purred.

'I can't remember.'

He heard her fake a yawn and shook his head. 'Sounds like you want a reminder.'

'Not in this lifetime,' she sputtered.

Her protest was a little too vigorous, which he liked.

Tino stretched out on the bed and stared at the ceiling, his eyes starting to adjust to the grey shadows cast around the room from the moonlight seeping in around the sheer curtains.

He heard the blankets on the floor rustle and his teeth gnashed together. She was being ridiculous and taking this just a little too far. He wondered if she was wearing something lacy. Something like the freshly laundered hot-pink thong hanging on the towel rail in the bathroom. The sight of those delicate panties had knocked him for a six, and he was pretty sure she hadn't left them there deliberately.

Finding out she really *did* favour sexy lingerie was a fact he could have well done without. Ball-breaking Miss Miller Jacobs was turning out to be full of contradictions. Not least of all that fiery response to his kiss in the garden.

Acting, she had said after the event. *Yeah, right.*

Acting, my ass.

Yeah, and you're not supposed to be thinking about it.

'I like the thong you left in the bathroom,' he said, unable to help annoying her as she was annoying him.

'You can't borrow it,' she said after a slight pause.

He gave a soft chuckle. *Man*, she was sassy. And, no, he didn't want to borrow it. But he wouldn't have minded stripping it down her long legs to see what he was sure would be tawny curls underneath. His heart beat the blood a little more heavily around his body and he was unable to stop his mind from imagining her naked and spread out on the four-poster bed. Imagining her soft and wet with the same need that had compelled her to wrap her tongue around his in that garden.

He breathed deep and willed his body to relax, reminding himself that he only wanted her because he'd placed an embargo around her.

The blankets rustled again as she adjusted herself on the hard floor that not even thousand-dollar-a-metre carpet could soften.

His blood was Sicilian, and if she thought he could stay sprawled out on a comfortable bed while she lay uncomfortably at his feet she had another thing coming. But he knew offering up the bed would only play into her martyr's hands and give her a reason to make him feel even more like a heel, so he stayed quiet and devised another plan that had the double advantage of allowing him to live up to his chivalrous nature and annoy the hell out of her at the same time.

Half an hour later Tino looked down on Miller's sleeping form. Her hands were tucked under her face and her shoulder-length hair was dark against the white pillow. Deep shadows beneath her eyes attested to how tired she was.

Careful not to wake her, he leaned down and pulled the meagre blanket away from her body—and instantly stilled.

She was lying half on her stomach, one leg bent to the side in an innocently provocative pose. Her pale jersey camisole top and matching three quarter length pants stretched tight over her ripe curves. As far as night attire went it wasn't the most seductive he'd ever seen, and yet as he gazed at her slender limbs, milky in the shadowy moonlight she had his full attention.

His hand itched to curve around the firm globes of her bottom while he bit down gently on the soft-as-silk skin that covered her trapezius. Would she be sensitive there? Or would she prefer him to kiss his way down each pearl-like button of her spine? Perhaps while he was buried deep inside her.

Tino groaned and closed his eyes. He felt like a randy teenager looking at a full on girlie magazine. Lust, hot and primal, beat through his body and made his legs weak. For a moment he was gripped by an almost uncontrollable urge to roll her over and wake her with a lover's kiss. Get her to open her mouth for him as she had done earlier, cup her pert breasts, shove those stretchy pants to her ankles and thrust into her until all she could do was chant his name over and over as she came for him.

Only him.

He blinked back the unusually possessive thought, the incongruity of it burning through his sensual haze and reminding him of his initial purpose in pulling the blanket from her body.

Gently, he scooped her up off the floor and carried her to the bed. She stirred and shifted in his arms, the curtain of her hair trailing down his naked arm and her orange blossom shampoo tickling his nose. His body tightened at the allure of that clean smell and he almost tumbled her onto the bed in his haste to put her down. As soon as he did she mumbled something unintelligible and sighed deeply as she curled into the soft mattress.

Tino quickly pulled the comforter up over her near naked limbs before he could change his mind about being chivalrous.

His eyes drifted to the other side of the king-sized bed. It looked vast and empty with her only taking up one quarter of it. Tiredness invaded his body, and although he had fully intended to sleep on the floor he realised he probably didn't have to. The bed was nearly as big as the infinity pool downstairs and he was an early riser. If the gods were on his side he'd be up and running along the beach before she even knew it was a new day.

Still, he laid a row of pillows down the centre of the bed. No point in tempting fate.

'Oh, yes,' Miller moaned softly as she felt the weight of a hair roughened thigh slip between her legs while a warm, callused hand palmed her breast. Her body buzzed and her nipples tightened, forcing her to arch more firmly into that warm caress. The hand squeezed her gently and somewhere above her head she heard a rough masculine sound of appreciation. Another hand was sliding confidently over her hip toward—

Holy hell!

Miller's eyes flew open and she stared straight into Valentino Ventura's sleeping face. Within seconds her brain assimilated the fact that she was no longer on the floor, but in bed and that Valentino had one of his hands on her breast and the other curved around her bottom.

Miller yelped and pushed against his impossibly hard chest, glad when he gave a grunt of discomfort, his jet-black lashes parting to reveal slate-grey eyes still glazed with sleep.

Miller pushed at his hands and scrambled backwards, her legs colliding with one of his knees as she roughly slid her leg out from between his.

Tino let out a rough expletive and moved his legs out of the way. 'Watch the knee.'

'Watch the…?' Miller had a vague recollection of the men questioning Valentino about some racing injury but she didn't care about that right now. 'Get your hands off me, you great oaf.'

She shoved harder at his immovable arm and sucked in

her tummy muscles as his steely forearm slid across her bare stomach.

Finally, fully awake, he acquiesced.

'No need to sound the alarm, I was just sleeping.'

Miller gripped the duvet up to her chin. 'You were groping me.'

'Was I? I thought you'd just ruined a pleasant dream. Sorry about that.'

'Yes, I just bet you're sorry.' She saw his eyes sharpen on hers. 'How did I end up in bed with you anyway?'

Valentino casually slid his hands beneath his head and Miller swept her angry gaze over those powerful arms and that muscular chest. She felt her breath catch and her heartbeat speed up and berated her instant reaction.

'I don't know, Sunshine,' he answered. 'Are you prone to sleepwalking?'

Miller narrowed her gaze, her mind flashing back to last night. A vague memory of being lifted floated to the surface of her mind. 'You carried me.'

Valentino yawned and pushed up until he was leaning against the headboard. The sheet dropped down to his waist, and the morning sun fell over part of his bronzed chest and corrugated abdomen as if lighting him up for a photo shoot.

He scratched his chest and her eyes soaked him up. God, the man really did look airbrushed!

'Damn. Maybe *I'm* prone to sleepwalking,' he said.

Miller hugged the duvet closer and felt her nipples throb with awareness as her hands accidentally grazed over them. Heat immediately bloomed in her face at the memory of *why* her breasts felt so heavy and sensitive.

'This isn't funny. That's sexual harassment.'

The great oaf just rolled his eyes. 'As I recall it, it was you who cuddled up to me in your sleep—not the other way around.'

'I did not.'

'Suit yourself. But last night I put a row of pillows between us, and I know it wasn't *me* who knocked them aside. Anyway,

I disengaged my hand as soon as you asked.' He raised and lowered his knee gingerly beneath the blanket and she hoped that she *had* hurt him.

'Remind me not to do you a good deed again,' he said.

'Ha. Good deed, my foot. You wanted to…to…'

'Have my wicked way with you?' His eyes glinted. 'If that was what I wanted that's what we'd be doing.'

'You wish.'

'A challenge, Miller?'

She didn't deign to respond. Why would she? Of course it wasn't a challenge—especially when she had liked the feel of him against her a little too much.

Her breathless response reminded her of the time she'd been secretly trapped in the girls' toilets at the hideous school she'd attended while the main bullies had loitered, giggling vacuously over some boy or another.

By the time they had hit fifteen, boys had been all they could talk about. Miller had wanted to yell, *What about when it all goes wrong?* But of course she hadn't. She hadn't wanted to look more like a freak than they already thought she was. All of them had seemed content to live in the moment in a way she never could after her parents had divorced.

'There was no way I was letting you sleep on the floor. Get over it.' Valentino's gruff voice jolted her back to the present.

'Turn the other way,' she demanded, letting her painful memories slip away.

When he complied without argument she shot out of bed and snatched up her robe. Ignoring him, she grabbed her running clothes and stalked towards the bathroom.

'Just so we're clear.' She stopped in the doorway. 'This arrangement does *not* extend to sex, and even if it did you would be the last man I would choose to sleep with.'

He looked at her as if he could see right through her. 'So you keep saying.'

His intense eyes never left hers and Miller found it hard to swallow. He looked irresistible and dangerous with his untidy dark hair and overnight stubble. By contrast she was sure she looked a fright, and all of sudden it seemed imperative that she get away from him. She couldn't remember ever feeling so vulnerable.

She shook her head. 'You're too used to getting your own way. That's your problem.'

Valentino threw back the covers and stood up. He was only wearing low-riding hipster briefs and Miller quickly averted her eyes. She felt irrationally angry when he laughed. He stalked towards her and Miller deliberately held his gaze, refusing to let him see how affected she was by his potent masculinity.

He shook his head. 'Lady, you are one overwound broad. Yes, my hand was on your breast—but that little moan you exhaled before your uptight brain kicked into gear let me know that you liked it. More than liked it.'

'Well, my uptight little brain rules my body, and what you felt back there was just a physiological reaction.' Miller felt irrationally stung by his assessment, even though she had insulted him first. She couldn't help it; he just made her feel so… so…*emotional*!

'You're telling me you'd get turned on if you woke up with TJ's hand on your breast?'

Miller clamped her lips together. That was a no-win question and they both knew it. 'There's no way to answer that without stroking your mountainous ego, so I won't bother.'

'You just did.'

Oh! Miller swivelled and slammed the bathroom door in his laughing face. He was *so* arrogant and *so* full of himself.

Impossible. The most impossible and most gorgeous man she had ever come across.

She leant back against the door and sighed. No wonder he had women lining up outside his hotel rooms to get a glimpse of him. The man was sex on legs and he knew it.

Miller made a frustrated noise through her teeth and her breasts tingled with remembered pleasure as she pulled on her shorts, sports bra and top. A strenuous run would help her forget this morning before her meeting with Dexter and TJ.

Taking a fortifying breath, she decided to ignore Valentino—but that plan instantly unravelled when she opened the bathroom door and noticed him sitting on the side of the bed, tying his shoelaces and dressed as she was.

'Please tell me you're not going for a run?'

Valentino looked up. 'Is there a law against it?'

His eyes immediately dropped to her bare legs and Miller felt slightly uncoordinated as she continued across the room to the closet.

She wanted to say yes, but he would no doubt think she was being uptight again—and anyway it was petty. The man was doing her a favour by being here—albeit a reluctant one—and who was she to tell him he couldn't go for a run? She might dislike the tumultuous feelings he incited in her just from looking at him, but she was going to have to get used to it if she was going to survive the next twenty-four hours with any degree of dignity. She had already decided she wasn't going to be his weekend plaything, so how hard could it be?

'Of course not,' she said, knowing full well he was a hundred times fitter than she was and would never suggest they run together.

'You run often?' he asked.

Miller glanced his way, noting his conciliatory tone. 'A couple of times a week. You?' she added, deciding to accept his olive branch.

'Every morning except Sunday.'

She didn't want to ask what he did on Sunday mornings. She was afraid her hormones would want her to do more than just visualise it.

He tilted his head, that devilish smile playing around his lips. 'I get time off for good behaviour.'

The incongruity of that statement brought an instant grin to her face. 'Yeah, right. I'm sure you were the type of teenager who crawled out of your bedroom window when your parents were asleep and partied all night.'

'They were called study nights at our house.' His deadpan expression made her laugh.

When she realised that he was laughing too she quickly sobered. Because she didn't want to enjoy his company, and by the wary darkening of his eyes he didn't much want to enjoy hers either.

But still the light-hearted connection persisted and made her nervous. A sudden impulse to place his hand back on her breast and kiss him senseless blindsided her.

'It's a beautiful morning. Why don't we stretch on the beach first?' he suggested.

Shocked by the unfamiliar emotions driving her thoughts and desperate to break the tension that throbbed between them, Miller cleared her throat and hoped that single gesture hadn't transmitted to him just how affected she was by his presence.

'I don't think we should run together.'

Valentino eyed her dubiously. 'How will it look if you run off in one direction and I go in the other?'

Telling, probably.

Miller smoothed her eyebrows in a soothing gesture that failed dismally.

She looked down at his long muscular legs dusted with dark hair.

'Come on, Miller, what are you afraid of?'

Him, for one. Her own feelings, for two. Did he need three? 'I'll slow you down,' she mumbled.

'I'll forgive you,' he replied softly.

Miller sighed. One of her strengths was knowing when she was beaten, but still she was hardly gracious when she said. 'Okay, but don't talk to me. I hate people who run and talk at the same time.'

CHAPTER SIX

THE morning *was* beautiful. Peaceful. The air was crisp, but already warmed by the sun beating down from a royal-blue sky, and the fresh scent of saltwater was tart on the silky breeze. Seagulls flew in graceful circles, while others just squatted on the white-gold sand, unaffected by the gentle, almost lackadaisical nature of the waves sweeping towards them.

The beach arced around in a gentle curve towards a rocky outcrop, and as it was in an unpopulated area it was completely deserted at this time of the morning.

After a few quick stretches Miller set off at an easy jog along the dark, wet packed sand left behind as the tide went out, sure that Valentino would get bored and surge ahead. But he didn't. And then she remembered that he'd complained about his knee and wondered if she *had* hurt him this morning.

Feeling hot already, Miller turned her head to look at him, her ponytail swinging around her face. 'I didn't really hurt your knee, did I?' she panted between breaths.

He glanced across at her, only a light sheen of sweat lining his brow, his breathing seemingly unaffected by his exertions. 'No. The knee is fine.'

'Was the accident very bad?'

When he didn't respond, she flicked her eyes over his profile, just in time to see him tense almost imperceptibly.

'Which one?'

'There's been more than one?'

He glanced towards the ocean, and she didn't think he'd answer.

'Three this year.'

She wasn't sure if that was a lot for his profession. She imagined they must crash all the time at the speeds they drove. 'The one where you hurt your knee?'

He didn't look at her. 'Bad enough.'

His voice was gruff, blunt. Very unlike his usual casual eloquence. 'Was anyone else hurt?'

'Yes.'

'Wh—?'

'I thought you said you didn't like to talk while you ran?'

It was pretty clear he didn't want to tell her about it so she let the subject drop. But of course her curiosity was piqued. Dexter's comment about his next race being the race of the decade was making her wonder if it had anything to do with his accident. She really didn't know anything about Valentino Ventura, other than the fact that he was called Maverick and he dated legions of women, but she wouldn't mind knowing what secrets she was beginning to suspect lay behind his devil-may-care attitude to life.

Tino had never run with anyone before. Not even his personal trainer. Running was meditative, and something he liked to do alone, so he hadn't expected to enjoy Miller's company as much as he was.

Despite his large family he wasn't the type to need others to be close to him. He was a loner. Maybe not always, but certainly since his father's death. And, yeah, he knew a shrink would say the two were connected but he was happy with the way he was and saw no reason to change. If he died one day pushing the limits, as his father had, and Hamilton Jones had last August, at least he knew he wouldn't be leaving a devastated family behind him.

The image of Hamilton's wife and two young daughters—

teary and slightly accusing at the funeral, because he'd survived and their father hadn't—caused guilt to fluctuate inside him.

Survivor guilt.

The team doctor had warned him about it afterwards, and while he'd never admitted to feeling it he knew that on some level he did. But he also knew it was something that would wear off if he didn't think about it. Because the accident hadn't been his fault. Hamilton had tried to overtake on one of the easiest corners on the track, but had somehow managed to clip Tino's rear wheel and hurtle them both out of control.

Hamilton had lost his life and Tino had missed three of the following races due to injury. And he'd failed to finish the last two races due to mechanical issues.

He wasn't superstitious, and he didn't believe in bad luck, but he couldn't deny—at least to himself—that there seemed to be a black cloud, like in a damned cartoon strip, following him around at the moment.

A sudden memory of the moment his mother had returned from the bathroom and he'd had to tell her that his father—the love of her life—had just been involved in a hideous accident clamped around his heart like an iron fist. No one knew what had caused the accident that had ended his father's life—engine malfunction or human error—but the pit crew had said his father hadn't been himself that morning, and Tino remembered overhearing his mother urge his father to pull out of the race. But the old man had ignored her and gone anyway.

Tino swiped a hand through his hair. Had that been what had killed him? His mother's soft request? Tino shuddered. It was a hell of a position for a man to be put in.

Refocusing on Miller's steady rhythm, he was surprised that he didn't have to temper his speed all that much for them to remain together.

Waking up beside her, he hadn't meant to have his hands all over her, and now he decided that it would be best to play the relationship game her way. So what if Caruthers had the hots for her? It was none of his business, as she had rightly pointed out. Now that he knew he wasn't being used as a patsy to hide an affair it shouldn't mean anything to him that the other man wanted her.

Had they *ever* been lovers?

Not wanting to head down that particular track he concentrated again on the rhythmic sound of their feet hitting the sand and the crystal clear waters of the South Pacific Ocean rolling onto the beach. The coastline reminded him a little of his house on Phillip Island, near Melbourne, although he knew the water there was at least ten degrees cooler and a hundred times rougher.

Miller stopped and started walking, her hands on her hips, and Valentino joined her.

'You can keep going if you want,' she panted.

He glanced at her. He *could* keep going but he didn't want to. What he wanted was to stop thinking about the past and make her smile. Like she had back in their room. He wondered what she did for fun, and then wondered why he cared.

'You work out a lot?' he asked.

She glanced at him, and he tensed when her eyes dropped to his stomach as he used his T-shirt to wipe a line of sweat off his brow. He knew she was attracted to him, maybe even as attracted as he was to her, but he also knew it would be stupid to follow up on that attraction. Not only did *she* not want it—he didn't either. And, while his body might have ideas to the contrary, his body was just an instrument for his mind, not the other way around.

'I go to the gym three times a week and try to go for a run along the Manly foreshore on the weekend.'

She walked in a small circle to ease the lactic acid burn from her legs.

'You do weights?'

'Some. Mainly light weights. Although I missed every one of my workouts this week due to work, so no doubt when I start back Monday morning I'll be a little sore.'

'Do some now.'

She cast her eyes from the sparkling ocean to the sand dunes behind them. 'I'm sorry, but if you see a weight machine anywhere around here you're on your own.'

He laughed. 'There's a lot you can do without machines. Trust me. This is part of my day job. Why don't we start with some ab crunches?'

He lay on his back and started curling his head towards his bent knees. He'd made it to twenty when out of the corner of his eye he saw her reluctantly join him. He wasn't sure why that pleased him so much.

She kept pace for a minute, then fell back on the sand. 'I've been running for a while but I'm still pretty new at the gym thing,' she said.

'Okay, now squats.'

Miller groaned. 'I really don't like squats.'

'No one likes squats except bodybuilders.'

She laughed and the husky sound made his stomach grip.

'Come on.' His voice was gruff, unnatural sounding.

She jumped lithely to her feet and he couldn't look away from the toned muscles in her thighs as she braced her legs slightly apart.

'Raise your arms overhead as you go down. And keep your chest up.' He cleared his throat, trying to concentrate on her technique rather than recalling the feel of her peaked nipple pressing eagerly into his palm. 'Squeeze your glutes and extend through your hips as you come up.'

He'd need to dunk himself in the ocean at this rate, but at least his mind was fully focused on something other than racing again.

'Am I getting a personal training session now?' She grinned at him, but didn't stop.

'Maybe.' He returned her smile. 'I do aim to please.'

'What's next?' She breathed deep and shook out her legs.

Tino could think of a lot of 'nexts' that involved her horizontal on the soft sand without the top and shorts, but he shouldn't even be thinking like that.

He sucked in a litre of air and took her through a couple of other light exercises. 'Push-ups.'

Miller grimaced. 'Oh, great. You're hitting all my favourites.'

She got down on the sand and started pushing herself up, her knees bent.

'They're not real push-ups,' he teased.

'Yes, they are!' After twenty she collapsed and rolled onto her back. 'Okay, that's it. Those and the bench press are my weakest exercises.'

He absently noted how the sun had turned her hair to burnished copper, with some of the tendrils around her temples darkened with sweat. Her cheeks were pink from exertion, her chest heaving...

Don't even go there, Ventura.

'That just means you have to do more of them.'

Miller turned her head towards him and her eyes sparkled as blue as the ocean behind her. 'Oh, darn. No bench press. What a shame.'

Tino smiled. So she did have a sense of humour.

Lifting from his sitting position beside her, he came over the top of her, before he could talk himself out of it, his body hovering far too close to her own.

Her eyes flew wide and her hands fluttered between them, the pulse-point at the base of her throat hammering wildly. 'Valentino, what are you doing?'

He liked the way she used the full version of his name. Breathless. Husky.

'Accommodating you.' His own voice was rough again, as if he'd swallowed a mouthful of sand, and he hoped to hell she hadn't noticed that he was already fully hard. 'I'll be your bench press.'

'Don't be silly.'

He braced himself on his arms and lowered his upper body slightly over hers. 'Hands on my shoulders,' he commanded.

When she put them there he barely suppressed the shudder that ran the length of his whole body.

She shifted beneath him. Swallowed. 'This won't work,' she said, but she didn't remove her hands. 'You're too big.'

Her eyes met his and the air between them sizzled.

She was wrong. This wasn't silly. This was way beyond silly. 'Ten reps. Go.' He just wanted them out of the way now.

She pushed at his shoulders and he mentally worked his way through every component of a car engine as they moved in unison. He could feel her hot breath on his neck as she exhaled and he dared not look at anything but the sand above her head.

Of all the lame-brain things to do...

He paused when he felt her weaken, intent on pushing himself away from her, but he made the mistake of looking down into eyes that had gone indigo with desire.

The sound of seagulls squalling couldn't even distract him from the hunger that burned a hole in his belly.

Her hands slipped down his arms, shaping his muscles, and her eyes drifted to his mouth. 'Valentino...'

Her husky plea weakened him more than fifty reps with twenty-five-pound dumbbells could and, groaning deep in his chest, he lowered his head and captured her soft mouth with his own.

Miller was aware of every hard inch of Valentino's male flesh pressing her into the sand. Her own body throbbing as if it was on fire, totally drugged by his heat, his smell, his taste. She couldn't remember why this was a bad idea. No rational words remained in her head to rein in her pleasure-fuelled body. Her arousal with him in bed earlier had returned full-force.

Impatient with a need she'd never felt before, she swept her hands down his back and then smoothed them up under his sweaty shirt. He groaned approvingly and with his elbows either side of her face cradled the back of her head, angling her so that his skilful mouth could ravage her lips, his moist tongue plundering and duelling with her own in a way that made the ache between her legs become almost painful.

She felt his other hand drift over her torso, feather-light as if learning her shape, his fingertips moving closer and closer to the tip of one breast. Moaning, Miller twisted in his hold, her body begging for more of his touch. She felt him smile against her mouth, his lips drifting over her jaw and down the column of her throat.

'Please, Valentino…' she pleaded, her body craving a release she had never experienced during sex but which now seemed infinitely possible. Infinitely desirable.

Obliging her, his hand rose over her breast, cupping her, his thumb flicking back and forth over her nipple at the same time as his teeth bit down on the straining, sensitive cord of her neck.

Miller cried out, jerking beneath him. Her body was liquid with need, her hips arching towards his, her mind completely focused on one outcome.

His fingers plucked more firmly at her nipple and her fingernails unconsciously scored the tight muscles of his lower back.

He shifted sideways and she whimpered in protest. Then his hand slid lower, and she stopped breathing as he cupped between her legs.

'Miller—'

She didn't want him to speak. She just wanted to lose herself in these magic sensations. She dragged his mouth back to hers, her tongue instantly gratified by the warm wetness of his deep, soul-destroying kiss. Her body was close, so close, and she couldn't think, couldn't breathe.

'Oh!'

His hand slipped beneath the hem of her shorts and knickers and then his fingers parted her and lightly stroked her swollen flesh. He groaned into her mouth, pressed deep at the same time as Miller pressed upwards, and that was all it took for her to tumble over the edge. She gripped his shoulders and wrenched her mouth from his, gasping for oxygen as her body disintegrated into a million wonderful pieces.

For a while nothing happened, and then she became aware of the sound of Valentino's harsh breathing above her own panting breaths, the seagulls squalling overhead.

When she finally managed to open her eyes she found him looking down at her with an open hunger that made her feel instantly panicked.

Oh, God... 'What have I done?'

'I believe it's called having an orgasm,' he mocked, clearly understanding the horrified expression on her face. 'Followed closely by feeling regret.'

Regret? *Did* she regret it? She didn't even know. But all the reasons this was not a good idea rushed back like a blast of cold water from a hose.

Public beach. Playboy. Promotion.

If she could bury her head in the sand right now she would.

A seagull squawked close by and Miller jumped. 'You have to get off me.'

'I'm not actually on you.'

He was right. His body hovered beside her, shielding her from any prying eyes at TJ's house some way along the beach, but he wasn't holding her down.

Miller scrambled to a sitting position and looked over his shoulder. They were still alone. Thank God.

'I said I wasn't going to have sex with you,' she spat at him accusingly. She knew full well that she was equally responsible for what had just happened between them, but was still unable to fully take in the sensations rippling through her body. 'This never happened,' she said firmly, her emotions as brittle as an empty seashell.

His eyebrows drew together and his features were taut. 'Not part of your plan, Sunshine?'

'You know it wasn't.' She hated the sarcastic tilt to his lips.

'Believe me, it's not part of mine either.' He pushed himself to a sitting position and deftly removed his runners and socks. Then he dragged his T-shirt up over his chest and Miller's insides, still soft and pliant, clenched alarmingly.

His easy acceptance of her brush-off was slightly insulting, and the illogical nature of that thought wasn't lost on her in the heat of the moment. In fact, it only made her more irritable. But whether at him or herself she wasn't sure.

She watched him jog down to the shoreline and gracefully duck dive beneath an incoming wave. Thank God she didn't like him very much. She wasn't ready to change her life for a man, and some deep feminine instinct warned her that being with him intimately, even once, would be life-changing.

She sighed. At least for her it would be. For him life would no doubt go on as normal.

CHAPTER SEVEN

TJ TIPPED his Akubra back from his forehead and rocked forward on his chair, and Miller knew the presentation she and Dexter had just delivered hadn't gone well.

'Miller, you're a talented girl, no doubt about it,' he drawled, in a condescending tone that set Miller's teeth on edge. 'But I told Winston International I'd give their show another shot.'

What?

Miller narrowed her eyes, sensing Dexter's surprise without having to look at him.

The reason TJ had even approached Oracle was because he was disgruntled with the service he'd been receiving from Winston International.

'I was thinking about it all last night, and it doesn't seem right to trash our relationship after so many years. One of their boys is going to show me what they've got Monday morning. In the meantime why don't you fix the concerns I have with your current proposal and get it back to me ASAP?'

Miller was thankful for the years of practice she'd had at pretending she was perfectly fine when she wasn't, and schooled her features into an expression of professional blandness. Was this because she'd rejected his advances in the restaurant the week before? He might be ruthless and without morals, but he didn't strike her as the vindictive type. But he did know Oracle *was* desperate for his business, so he had them over a barrel in that regard.

She had started to hate this aspect of business. The 'anything goes' mantra Oracle had adopted as the global economic crisis had deepened. In some ways she supposed it had always been there, but she hadn't noticed it in her single-minded climb to the top.

Now that she was almost there, so close she could see her name on a corner office overlooking the famed Harbour Bridge and the soaring white waves of the Opera House, she felt unsettled. Nerves, she supposed. But also the acknowledgement that maybe she didn't have the killer instinct that was required in the upper echelons of big business. Miller cared too much about business practice, and sometimes that didn't play out very well.

'Now, if you'll both excuse me, I have guests waiting to play croquet on the south lawn.'

You could have heard a snail move as TJ pushed back his chair and ambled over to the door. 'By the way, Miller.' He stopped and held her unwavering gaze. 'Tell Maverick to quit stalling on taking the Real Sport sponsorship deal, would you? My people don't seem to be able to pin him down but I'm sure you can.'

And there it was. The real reason Winston International were *supposedly* being given a second chance.

Miller heard the door snick quietly closed but hadn't realised she was staring at it until Dexter muttered a four-letter word under his breath.

Miller swung her stunned gaze towards him.

'You didn't know?' He raised a condescending eyebrow.

Miller felt her face heat up, not wanting to add to her cache of lies. 'No,' she admitted reluctantly. She'd had no idea one of TJ's subsidiary companies was professionally courting Valentino. Why would she?

Dexter swore again. 'Some relationship you've got there. Does lover boy have any idea he's put a multi-million-dollar contract in jeopardy?'

'Valentino didn't do that.' Although she was silently spitting chips that he hadn't had the decency to inform her of TJ's overtures so she could have been more prepared. 'TJ did.'

'TJ's just doing business.'

'Unethically.'

'Stop being so precious, Miller. Business is business. Getting this account will boost Oracle's reputation—not to mention yours and mine.'

Miller's stomach felt as if it had a rock in it and she methodically stuffed her notes back into her satchel.

'So, do you think you'll be able to convince Ventura to do it?'

Miller strove for calm. 'I wouldn't even try.'

'Why not?'

'Because courting favours is not the way I do business.'

'TJ Lyons's is the biggest account in the country and you want it as much as I do. Maybe more. Why wouldn't you use your influence? It's not like it's any skin off Ventura's nose. In fact, I'm quite sure TJ is offering to pay him a pretty penny for the use of his pretty face.'

Miller tried not to let her distaste show. This was a side of Dexter she hadn't experienced before.

'Maybe you could give him a little more of what you gave him on the beach this morning. To sweeten the deal,' he said snidely.

Miller felt her whole body go rigid and knew she wouldn't be able to hide her reaction from him this time.

'You know, Miller,' he continued softly, 'I expected more from you than to see you romping on the beach with your lover in full view of the house.'

Ignoring Dexter, she slammed the lid of her laptop closed and fervently hoped she hadn't broken it.

She didn't have to explain herself to Dexter, but she knew if he repeated any of this back at the office it would jeopardise her promotion. It was hard enough being taken seriously at this level, despite the pains she took to always to appear confident and professional.

Dexter tapped his pen on TJ's antique desk. 'It won't last, you know. You and Tino.'

'Whether it does or not is none of your concern,' Miller

fumed, barely keeping a lid on her anger. 'And while we may have known each other at university, that does not give you the right to comment on my personal life. I'm here to do a job. That's all you need to think about.'

Dexter looked disgusted. 'Then do your job and remember that this isn't a school camp. And another thing.' He put his hand on her arm as she turned to leave. 'If we lose this campaign because of your lover, it will be *your* reputation that suffers, not mine.'

Glaring at him, Miller shook her head. 'You know, Dexter, earlier this week I could have sworn we were working on the same team. My mistake,' she finished coolly.

She heard something skitter across TJ's desk as she let herself out of the study—presumably the pen he'd been madly tapping the whole time.

'Miller! Dammit, we have to talk!'

Miller didn't stop. She had no idea what had gotten into Dexter, but she needed time and space to work out what to do next.

Tino was sitting on the bed when the door opened. Miller stood in the doorway like Medusa on a mission. He was on the phone to his sister Katrina, who was doing her best not to talk about Sunday's race and thereby placing it front and centre in both their minds.

Miller stepped into the room, her eyes sparking fire and brimstone in his direction.

Man, she was something else when she was riled— passionately alive—just like on the beach earlier. Not that he was thinking about that. He'd been honest when he'd told her it wasn't part of his plan, but watching her come apart underneath him had been possibly the most sensually arousing experience of his life, and as such it was damned hard to put out of his mind.

'Kat, sweetheart, I'll ring you back.' Glad of the excuse to end the conversation early, he dumped his mobile on the quilt cover beside him, reminding himself that he was supposed to be keeping his distance from Miller. 'Bad day at the office, Sunshine?'

She stalked across the room and dumped her computer bag and satchel on the small desk against the wall. Then she turned on him, hands on hips, her large aquamarine eyes shooting sparks.

Tino lounged back against the bank of pillows behind him. 'Are you going to tell me what's eating at you? Or is this one of those times when a woman tries to make a man's life truly miserable by making him play Twenty Questions?'

Her gaze narrowed. 'You've got that wrong. Women do not make men's lives miserable. People do that to each other.'

He stared at her and could see she was mentally wishing her words back. He wondered who had hurt her. It was obvious she didn't like talking about herself. Something they both shared, and that protective instinct she seemed to engender in him tightened his gut.

She drew in a breath as if preparing to go into battle, but her words were resigned when she spoke. 'It would have been nice if you'd told me that TJ was trying to recruit you to represent his Real Sport stores.'

'Ah.' *That* was where he knew TJ Lyons. TJ's people had been hassling his publicist to get him to become Real Sport's public representative for about six months now.

'First—' Miller's voice brought his eyes back to her '—you don't tell me that you're the legendary lothario Valentino Ventura and *nearly* make a fool of me. Now you neglect to tell me that my client wants your face and body for his online sports brand and *succeed* in making a fool of me.'

'Miller—'

'Don't Miller me.' She stalked towards him and stopped at the foot of the bed. 'You've been having fun with me right from the start of this silly charade and I've had enough. I am not here as your resident plaything and nor am I here to alleviate your boredom.'

Irritation blossomed inside him. 'I never said you were. And might I remind you that this is *your* silly charade and I'm actually trying to help you.'

'Some help when TJ all but told me the only way we would win his business is if you "quit stalling" and give him what he wants.'

Tino rubbed his jaw. 'Sneaky bastard.'

His response seemed to knock the wind from her sails because her shoulders slumped a little and her hands dropped from her hips.

'Quite.'

'I'm sorry, Miller. I didn't deliberately withhold that information from you. I get over a hundred requests of a similar nature every week and my publicist handles that side of my business. Yesterday, when I met TJ, I was aware that I knew him from somewhere but assumed it was a race meet since he was such a fan.'

She swore lightly and retreated to sit on the velour window seat, and Tino found himself fascinated by the play of light on her thick, glossy hair.

'What did you say to him?' he prompted when she remained silent.

She scowled and he noticed that her face was slightly paler than usual. 'Nothing yet. It was his parting volley.'

'A strategic tactic.'

She looked surprised that he would know such a thing, and he didn't like the fact that she still thought he had the IQ of an insect. 'You can stop looking at me as if you're surprised I can string a sentence together.'

'I don't think that.' She paused at his disbelieving look and had the grace to blush. 'Any more.'

He grinned at her honesty.

'Anyway.' She sighed. 'I'm not going to give him the satisfaction of acknowledging it.'

'Why not?'

'Because his weapon of choice is to ask his current consultants to re-pitch for the job, but if they had any good ideas they would have already given them to him.'

'They might have something new up their sleeve.'

'Nothing as good as mine.'

Tino chuckled. He enjoyed her superior confidence and kick-ass attitude. It reminded him of himself when a rookie tried to come up against him on the circuit.

He noticed her eyes were focused on his mouth, and when she raised them to his a spark of red-hot awareness flashed between them.

Clearly not wanting to acknowledge it any more than he did, she turned to face the window.

Silence filled the room so loudly he could hear the gentle ticking of the marble clock on the desk two feet away.

'Dexter saw us on the beach this morning.'

Her voice was soft, but he heard the disappointment edging her words.

Tino rolled his stiff neck on his shoulders and swore under his breath. That man was dogging his every step and he was getting beyond irritated with him.

'Are you telling me or the seagulls?' he asked pleasantly.

Miller swivelled her head around, a frown marring her alabaster forehead. 'I'm not in the mood for your ill-timed humour, Valentino.'

'What about my well-timed humour?'

She shook her head but a smile snuck across her face. 'How is it you can make me smile even when this is deadly serious?'

'Deadly?'

She sighed. 'Maybe I'm exaggerating slightly.'

Tino sat forward and regarded her silently for a moment. 'Relax. At least he no longer thinks we're faking it.'

Her smile disappeared. 'He's right about the fact that I should behave in a more professional manner with you.'

Tino snorted. 'Let me guess. He told you no touching?'

'He told me to keep my private life private—and he's right.'

'Of course he did,' Tino drawled, half admiring the man's

nous. He wanted Miller for himself, and he was trying to drive a wedge between them to get her.

Not that he could blame him. He'd realised this morning on the beach that Miller was one of those women who had no idea of her true appeal to men and, given similar circumstance, he might have done the same as Caruthers. Then again, he had yet to want a woman enough to actually fight for her.

'What does that mean?' Miller frowned.

'It means he wants you for himself.'

'No, he doesn't.'

She turned her face away, but he'd already seen her eyes cloud over.

'I can't work out if you're actually naive when it comes to men, or hiding your head in the sand.'

Her eyes flashed a warning. 'I do not hide my head in the sand.'

'Hit a nerve, have I?'

'If you're trying to be annoying you're succeeding beyond your wildest dreams,' she retorted pithily.

'If you're trying to avoid facing your colleague's attraction to you then so are you.'

She sighed heavily and turned away. 'I'm not naive. I just…' She stopped, looked uncertain. 'Can we talk about something else? Or, better still, not talk at all?'

Tino could sense the deep emotions rolling around inside her. He knew she would hate him to know the turmoil she was obviously experiencing. He didn't think he'd met a more self-contained woman, and it wasn't his experience that women kept such a tight lid on their emotions.

His Italian mother was a classic case in point—as were most of the females he'd dated, who had wanted more from him than he had ever been prepared to give. The fact that Miller so steadfastly *didn't* want anything from him made him feel ridiculously annoyed.

'This weekend really isn't going as you planned, is it, Miller?'

She had tucked her legs up under her chin as she gazed out of the window and now she glanced back at him as if surprised he was still in the room. Another blow to his over-inflated ego, he thought bemusedly.

'You think?'

Her eyes snagged on his and for a moment he was caught by how vulnerable she looked.

'You clearly dislike TJ's business methods so why do you want to work on his account so badly?'

'Partners are not made of people who say no to clients, no matter how distasteful they are.'

It took him a minute to decipher her meaning. 'Ah. You've got a promotion riding on this.'

'Something wrong with that?' Her voice was sharp and he realised she'd taken his words as an insult. He wondered what was behind her strong reaction.

'Only if you think so.'

'I deserve this. I've sweated blood for this company. I…' She released a long breath. 'It's not something you would understand.'

'Try me.'

He thought she would reject his offer, but she heaved a resigned sigh.

'It's not rocket science, Valentino. I grew up poor with a father who thought the grass was always greener on the other side and a mother who was uneducated. My mother had to work two jobs to put me through a private school so that I would have opportunities she never had. My making partner would mean everything to her.'

'What does it mean to *you*?'

He saw her throat move as she swallowed. 'The same.'

'So you dreamt of being a corporate dynamo when you were a little girl?'

He'd meant to sound light, friendly, but Miller didn't take it that way.

'We can't all have exciting careers like yours.'

Her sheer defensiveness made him realise she was hiding something from him. 'Interesting response.'

'I expect it was easy for you,' Miller prevaricated. 'Your father raced.'

'You think because my father was a racing champion my career choice was easy?'

'I don't know. Was it?'

'My father died on the track when I was fifteen. My mother still buys me medical textbooks for Christmas in the hope I'll change careers.'

She laughed, as he'd wanted her to do, but the pain of his father's death startled him with its intensity. It was as if the crash had just happened—as if a sticking plaster had just been peeled off a festering wound.

Ruthlessly shutting down his emotions he fell back on his raconteur style. 'Astronaut.'

'What?'

'Your childhood dream.'

'No.' She shook her head at his cajoling tone.

'Lap dancer?'

'Very funny.'

Some of the tension left her shoulders, but Tino still felt claustrophobic.

Jumping to his feet, he fetched a baseball cap from his travel bag. 'Let's go.'

'Where?'

'I don't know. A drive.' It was something that always calmed him.

She looked dubious. 'You go. I have work to do.'

'And all work and no play makes Miller a dull girl. Come on. It will refresh you.'

Miller sighed. 'You're like a steamroller when you want something. You know that?'

CHAPTER EIGHT

'SORRY, I only have one baseball cap,' Valentino said, holding the car door open for her.

'That's okay. My fame hasn't reached small seaside towns yet.'

He grinned at her lame joke and for some reason she felt better. Though she wasn't really interested in feeling better. What she wanted was TJ's signature on the bottom line of a contract and the weekend to be over. And not necessarily in that order.

She sighed, turning her mind away from work for once. 'Why do celebrities wear baseball caps to hide their identity?'

'Because Lyons bought all the Akubras?'

Miller burst out laughing, suddenly enjoying the fact that he was relaxed and casual. So much simpler than being uptight and serious. So much freer... Maybe there was something to recommend the casual approach sometimes.

She noticed people looking at the silver bullet as they drove down through the main part of the town. 'Bet you wish you'd brought my car now.'

He grinned. 'We'll park around a corner.'

'What if someone steals it?'

'Dante has insurance.'

'And Dante is...?'

'My elder brother.'

'What are your sisters' names?'

She sensed more than saw his pause. 'Katrina and Deanna.'

She was about to ask him another question when he pulled

the car into an empty car space and jumped out. Was that another topic of conversation that was out of bounds?

She wondered why he didn't like talking about his family and then decided to let it go. She had to remember that he wasn't with her because he wanted to be, and talking about their personal histories wasn't part of that. Nor was what had happened on the beach, but she didn't regret it. The way he had touched her had been indescribably good.

'Where are we going?' Better not to think about something she'd rather not dwell on.

'Window shopping.'

Miller raised an eyebrow. 'You like window shopping?'

'I'm looking for something.'

Narrow Victorian-era seaside shops overlaid with modern updates and sweetly dressed cafés advertising Devonshire teas lined the quaint street.

'Want to tell me what it is?'

'Nope. I'll know it when I see it.'

Despite the fact that her curiosity was well and truly piqued Miller decided to stem her need to know and show Valentino how well she could go with the flow when she chose to. Even if it killed her!

Glancing into tourist inspired shops displaying far too many knick-knacks no one could possibly want, she nearly walked into a small child when Valentino stopped outside an ice cream shop.

She looked at him and he raised a questioning eyebrow.

Ice cream? Really?

It was just what she needed and an ear-to-ear grin split her face.

She glanced at him, so big and handsome, standing in the queue, and her chest felt tight when he remembered her favourite flavour.

Deciding that there was absolutely nothing behind the gesture, but warmed by it nonetheless, she graciously accepted the cone and together they wandered into a small park.

By tacit agreement they veered towards a weathered picnic table and perched on it when Miller discovered the bench seat was covered in bird poop.

Valentino leant back on one hand, his T-shirt riding high enough to reveal the top button of his low-slung jeans, hinting at the line of hair bisecting his toned abs.

Miller swallowed and glanced around the pretty park, pretending rapt attention on the two toddlers shouting instructions at each other on the nearby play equipment. She really didn't want him to know that just the sight of him licking his ice cream and sprawled back like that was enough for her to instantly recall their tryst on the beach that morning in minute detail.

'Where did you grow up?'

His unexpected question brought her eyes reluctantly back to him, but she was glad of the innocuous topic to focus her attention away from the physical perfection of his body.

'Mostly in Queensland, but after my parents divorced my mother moved to Melbourne.'

He studied her and she forced herself not to squirm under his regard. 'How old were you when they divorced?'

'Ten.'

'And do you like Melbourne?'

'That's difficult to say. Whenever I came home from boarding school it seemed like my mother had moved to another suburb.'

'Why did she move so often?'

'We rented, and there's not much security in rentals. Which I found hard because I've always been the type of person who needs...' She struggled for a word that didn't make her seem boring compared to him.

'Certainty?'

'Yes.' Her lips lifted into a self-deprecating smile.

'Have you ever travelled?'

'No. I was always set on working and buying my own place. Even from a young age I knew what I wanted to achieve and set out to do it. That probably makes me boring in your eyes.'

Valentino shook his head. 'Determined. I know what that's like.'

Miller concentrated on finishing the delicious ice cream, feeling the tension ease out of her body. 'I guess you do.'

'So what was your childhood dream?'

Miller flashed him an exasperated look. So much for that fleeting moment of relaxation! 'I can see why you're going for your eighth world title,' she said sourly.

A wolfish grin split his face. 'I have been told I can be somewhat tenacious at times.'

'I think that's a polite way of saying you're pigheaded.'

He laughed and she liked the sound. Liked that he didn't take himself too seriously.

'Is it really that embarrassing?'

'No...' She scratched her head and then realised he had accurately read her body language and sighed, knowing his curiosity was well and truly piqued. And really it wasn't a huge secret, or anything to be ashamed of. 'When I was about eleven I dreamt of living on a huge country property. I always saw myself in a small circular room, overlooking a paddock full of horses and—'

'Why circular?'

'I don't know. Maybe because I loved *The Hobbit*...'

'Fair enough. Go on.'

'It's not very exciting,' she warned.

'Go on.'

'And in this dream I would divide my time between illustrating children's books and taking the horses out into the hills whenever I wanted.' She stopped, feeling silly giving voice to something she hadn't thought of in years. Of course she wouldn't tell him her ultimate dream. No one knew about that.

'Nice dream.'

She heard the smile in his voice and glanced at him reclining on the weather-beaten table, the afternoon sun gilding his features into a perfect mask of casual decadence.

Her heart caught and she cleared her throat, slightly embarrassed to have shared so much of herself. 'Yes, well, as my mother pointed out, it's almost every young girl's fantasy to own horses, and she wasn't paying for me to attend the best boarding school in the country to become an out-of-work artist.'

Miller heard the note of bitterness in her voice and wondered if Valentino did as well. It made her feel ashamed. Her mother had only ever wanted the best for her.

'So you stopped dreaming and took up a serious vocation?' he guessed accurately.

Regretting whatever tangent had got them onto this topic, Miller shifted and pulled her legs up to her chest. 'Dreams aren't real. That's why they're called dreams.'

'Following them gives you a purpose.'

'Putting food on the table gives you a purpose—as my mother found out to her detriment. She had me young and didn't complete her education. It made her vulnerable.'

He leant forward, his hands dangling over the front of his knees. 'And I can see why she wouldn't want that for her daughter. But I doubt she'd want you to give up on your dreams altogether. If we don't follow our dreams, what's the point of living?'

His voice was gentle and it annoyed her. Was he being condescending?

'You don't know my mum. She has a special bottle of champagne in the fridge for when I make partner.' And there was no way Miller could imagine disappointing her when she had sacrificed so much for her.

'But it's still *her* dream for you, not yours.'

She flashed him a sharp look but nevertheless felt compelled to answer. To explain herself. 'My mother has valid points.'

'I don't doubt she means well, Miller, but are her points really valid?'

His gentle query made her edgy, because it was the same one that had been taking up her head space since TJ had started subtly hitting on her.

Feeling slightly desperate, she jumped off the table and faced him. 'It would have been selfish of me to pursue art when my mother gave up so much for me.' She glanced in the direction of the sun and wondered about the time. 'We should probably get back.'

He cocked his head to the side and made no attempt to move. 'Maybe she shouldn't have pushed you so hard in the direction she saw as right. And what about your father? Didn't he help with the bills?'

She shook her head. 'I think he tried to help. For a while. But he lived on a commune, which meant that he didn't have the means to contribute to the private school my mother chose.'

'Lived?'

'He died when I was twenty.'

'I'm sorry.'

'Don't be. We weren't very close and…he died happy. Which I'm glad of now. But—' She stopped and let out a long breath. 'I don't know why I'm telling you my life story.' She *never* talked about herself like this.

'Because I asked. Why weren't you close to your dad?'

Miller snagged her hair behind her ears, memories of her father—fit and happy before the divorce—filling her mind. 'For years I was angry at him because I blamed him for my world falling apart. He just seemed to give up. He didn't once try to see me.' She swallowed past the lump in her throat. 'He later told me it was too painful.' And she suspected he hadn't been able to afford to visit her and had been too proud to lose face. 'But life is never that simple, and even though it took me a while I see now that it wasn't all his fault.'

She'd learned that one person always loved more in a relationship than the other; needed more than the other.

In this case it had been her father. Her mother's post-break-up comments had led Miller to believe that her mother had married her father mainly for a sense of security. Constantly disappointed when he could never hold down a job for very long.

Her parents had never been the greatest role models, and

Miller wasn't sure what she thought about love other than it seemed like a lot of trouble for very little return.

Her eyes sought out the toddlers, but they had gone. Instead, she watched a young couple strolling hand in hand with their large dog. But she wasn't thinking about them. She was thinking about the man beside her. Was he living his dreams? And what did *he* think about love? Did he hope to find someone special one day?

Miller felt the blood thicken in her veins at the thought. No doubt the woman he chose would be beautiful beyond comprehension and have the same relaxed attitude to life that he did. She could almost see them now—lazing on a yacht in the Mediterranean, gazing adoringly at each other, a half-naked Valentino leaning across her to seal his lips to—

Miller sucked in air and hoped her face hadn't transmitted anything of what she'd just been thinking.

'What about you?' she asked brightly, desperate to get the conversation onto any other topic but herself.

CHAPTER NINE

MILLER smiled and gazed around TJ's large living room. It held twice as many guests as it was intended to house, and absently she thought she felt as if she had just stepped into the pages of *The Great Gatsby*.

TJ's fiftieth birthday celebrations were in full swing and seemingly a roaring success: elegant women and debonair men were conversing and laughing with unbridled joy as if their lives were truly as beautiful as the party they were now attending. Some were already dancing to TJ's eighties-inspired music, while others had taken their beverages outside and were soaking up the balmy night, absently batting at the annoying insects that darted around as if they were trying to zap someone.

It was a crowd Valentino fitted right in with—especially dressed as he was now, in an ice-blue shirt that hugged his wide shoulders and showcased his amazing eyes, and tailored pants that hung perfectly from his lean hips.

'You look like you're at a funeral,' the man of the moment murmured wryly, his breath warm against her temple.

Miller sniffed in acknowledgement of his comment. She *felt* as if she was at a funeral. Ever since they'd returned from the park she had felt edgy and stressed at her sudden attack of blabbermouth. Trying to turn the tables on him had been a dismal failure. As soon as she'd asked about him he'd sprung up from the table as if an ant had crawled into his jeans.

'I'm boring,' he'd said, which loosely translated to *conversation closed*.

It had almost been a race to see who made it back to the car first. But he must have sensed her childish hurt at his rebuff because he'd glanced at her when they were in the car.

'Everything you could possibly want to know about me is on the internet.'

She'd scoffed. 'The internet tells me superficial stuff, like how many races you've won and how many hearts you've broken.'

He'd seemed to get annoyed at that. 'As I told Caruthers, if I had slept with as many women as the media proclaim I'd have hardly had enough time to enter a race let alone win one. In fact, I rarely take up with a woman during racing season, and if I do it's very short lived.'

Take up? Could he have used a more dissociative term?

'Why? Because you bore easily?'

'There is that. But, no, I usually don't allow a woman to hang around long enough to bore me. Basically women want more attention than I'm prepared to give them, so if I indulge it's usually only for a night or two.'

'That's pretty shallow.'

He'd shrugged. 'Not if the woman is after the same thing.'

'And how many are?'

'Not enough, it's true. Most want more—hence my moratorium on limiting those intimacies during the season.'

'To make sure you don't have to contend with any broken hearts that might wreck your concentration?' she'd said churlishly.

He'd smiled as if he hadn't heard her censure. 'Not much can wreck my concentration, Sunshine, but a whiny woman can certainly do damage to a man's eardrums.'

'No more than your whiny cars,' she'd shot back pithily. But then she'd grown curious. 'Don't you ever want more?'

'Racing gives me everything I need,' he'd said.

His unwavering confidence had pushed her to probe further. 'So have you ever been in love?'

'Sure.' He'd glanced over at her and Miller remembered holding her breath. 'My first love was a bright red 1975 Maserati Bora.'

'Be serious,' she'd said, and that had made his eyes become hooded, his expression blank.

'The love you're talking about isn't on my radar, Miller.'

'Ever?'

'Let's just say I'll never marry while I'm racing, and I've yet to meet a woman who excites me enough to make me give it up.' His flat tone had turned grim. 'Love is painful. When you lose someone...' He'd stopped, collected himself. 'I won't do that to another person.'

Another person or himself? Miller wondered now, sensing that part of his emotional aloofness was just a way of protecting himself from pain. His words hovered heavily in her mind, almost like a warning.

Determined the best thing she could do for herself was to forget the whole afternoon, Miller sipped at TJ's finest vintage champagne and focused on the tiny bubbles of heaven that spilled across her tongue.

'What did you say?' Valentino's low voice caused the champagne bubbles to disperse to other parts of her body and she opened her eyes to find him staring at her mouth.

'I didn't say anything.'

'You...' His gaze lifted to her eyes. 'You murmured something.'

Miller's mouth went dry and she was more determined than ever to crush the physical effect he had on her. 'Just remember that tonight I need you to be totally circumspect and professional. Discreet.'

What she was really saying was that she didn't want him to touch her, and he knew it.

'Like the other patsies you date?'

'I do not date patsies,' she said, wondering how it was that he managed to push all her buttons so easily.

'Sure you do. You date men who are learned, PC at all times, and...*controllable*.'

His assessment annoyed her all the more because she knew if she *did* date she'd look for someone just like that—except for the controllable bit. You didn't have to control *nice* men.

'While *you* hunt out blondes with big breasts and an IQ that wouldn't challenge a glowworm,' she replied sweetly.

He paused, and Miller was just congratulating herself on getting the last word in when he said, 'She doesn't have to be blonde.'

His slow smile was a signal for her to back off before she got sucked under again.

'And anything more—'

'Don't say it,' she admonished peevishly. 'I'll only be disappointed.'

His soft laugh confirmed that he knew he had the upper hand, and Miller determinedly faced the crowded room, searching for any distraction. She heard Valentino let out a long, slow breath and wondered if he was annoyed with her.

'How about we call a truce, Miller?'

'A truce?'

'Yeah. And I don't mean the kind of pact the settlers made with the aborigines before marching them off the edge of a cliff. I mean a proper one. Friends?'

Friends? He wanted to be friends and she couldn't stop thinking about sex. Great.

She took another fortifying gulp of champagne and could have been drinking his motor oil for all the pleasure it now gave her. 'Sure.'

'Good.'

God, this was awful, and he hadn't called her *Sunshine* in hours. What was *wrong* with her?

Miller was saved from the tumultuous nature of her thoughts when TJ, his barrel chest bedecked in a white tuxedo jacket, approached.

'Miller. You look lovely tonight.'

Miller's smile was tight. She didn't look lovely at all. She looked boring in her long sleeved black blouse and matching suit pants. She hadn't brought a single provocative item of clothing this weekend because she had no wish to encourage TJ's attention. And possibly because she didn't actually own anything remotely provocative. It had been a long time since she had spent money on clothing for anything other than work or exercise.

'Thank you.' She responded to the comment as she was expected to and, with civilities attended to, TJ turned to Valentino—the latest object of his fickle affections.

'Maverick. I have someone who's been dying to meet you.'

Miller tried to smile as the famous supermodel Janelle, clothed in a clinging nude-coloured chiffon creation, stepped out from behind TJ and extended her elegant hand.

A sort of mini-dramatic entrance, Miller thought sourly. Which was a little unfair, because by all accounts the model was not only considered the most beautiful woman on the planet, but the nicest as well. And she looked sweetly nervous as Valentino's large hand engulfed hers.

'Mr Ventura…'

Janelle's awed exhalation promised sexual antics in the bedroom Miller had only ever fantasised about—and with the man now staring at the supermodel no less.

'This is Janelle,' TJ continued. 'Latest sensation to hit the New York runways. But I don't have to tell *you* that. You probably have her photo up on your garage wall.' He guffawed at his own tasteless humour and then seemed to remember his audience. 'No disrespect, Miller.'

'None taken,' Miller lied smoothly. Because what she really wanted to say would jeopardise everything she had worked so hard for.

She felt Valentino tense beside her and wondered if he wasn't experiencing some sort of extreme physical reaction to the beautiful blonde. Every other man in the room seemed to be.

'Janelle.' Valentino smiled and slowly released her hand.

God, they looked perfect together. Her blonde to his dark.

Feeling like a poor cousin next to the stunning model Miller excused herself and left the men to ogle Janelle alone. No need to be a glutton for punishment.

She'd veered off from her decoy destination of the bathroom and made it to the glass bi-fold doors leading outside when Dexter appeared at her side.

'You know, Dexter, I don't know if I can go another round with you,' Miller said with bald honesty.

It was another balmy, star-filled night and she just wanted fresh air and peace.

He had the grace to look uncomfortable. 'I read some of the ideas you put down this afternoon. They're good.'

She raised an eyebrow. 'The only thing bothering me with that comment is that you seem to have expected something less.'

He tugged at the collar on his shirt. 'Can we talk?'

Resignation settled like a brick in her stomach and she extended her hand towards the deck. Might as well fulfil the fresh air component of her plan at least.

'By all means.'

Dexter walked ahead of her, but when he made to continue down the steps towards the more secluded Japanese garden Miller stayed him. 'Here's fine.'

She had no wish to recall the heady kiss she had shared with Valentino the night before any more than she already had. Not with Dexter around anyway.

Winding around various partygoers, Miller found a quiet part of the deck and turned to face him. 'What did you want to say?'

'Firstly, I wanted to apologise for being such an a-hole in the meeting earlier today. My intention was only to stop you from getting hurt.'

Miller felt a sense of unease prickle the skin along her cheekbones. 'I've noticed that you haven't seemed yourself lately,' she ventured. 'Is something going on with Carly again?'

'No, no. That's well and truly over.' He gripped the wooden railing and seemed absorbed by the whiteness of his knuckles.

'I'm sorry to hear that.' Even though she had never met Dexter's wife, Miller hated to hear of the end of any marriage.

Dexter jerked back and flexed his hands before catching her eye. 'Come on, Miller. Surely you know what this is about?'

Miller stared at him. Shook her head. 'No.' But she did know, didn't she? Ruby and Valentino had already warned her…

'Okay, if you want me to spell it out I will.' He seemed slightly nervous. 'Us.'

'Us?' Miller knew her voice had become shrill with alarm.

He nodded, clearly warming to his subject. 'Or more specifically the chemistry between us.'

'Chemistry?'

'I want you, Miller. There's been something between us since the moment we met.'

He held his hand up and silenced her attempt to save them both any further embarrassment.

'I know you don't want to acknowledge it because we work together, but you know I've felt like this since university. My coming to work for Oracle six months ago has just made those feelings deepen. And, yes, I know what you're going to say.' He stopped her again. 'I'm your superior and office affairs don't work. But I know of plenty that have and I'm willing to risk it.'

Miller was speechless, and barely noticed when he took her hand in his. 'I've been behaving like an idiot this weekend because I haven't wanted to accept that you're really dating that pretty boy inside. Okay, I can see the appeal. But we both know it won't last, and I'm not prepared to hold my breath and wait around for it to fizzle out.'

'That's too bad, Caruthers. I would have enjoyed seeing you atrophy.'

Miller jumped at the sound of Valentino's deep, modulated voice and so did Dexter. She glanced up and was once again taken aback by the cold glint in his eyes—a stormy-grey under the soft external lights.

He looked relaxed as he regarded Dexter: *preternaturally* relaxed. In this mode she could easily see why he was going for his eighth world championship. The shock was in the fact that other drivers had dared go up against him in the first place.

Miller saw Dexter's chest puff out in a classic testosterone-fuelled gesture and was horrified that he might cause a scene. Because right now Valentino looked as if he wanted to chew Dexter up and spit him out sideways.

'You don't have ownership rights here, Ventura.'

Ownership rights? Miller's gaze swung back to Dexter. What was she? A car?

'Let her go,' Valentino ordered quietly, his eyes never straying from Dexter's.

Miller realised Dexter was still holding her hand and tugged it free, wondering why it was that only French champagne and Valentino's touch seemed to make her insides fizz with excitement.

'Miller is her own boss,' Dexter opined.

Now, *that* was more like it.

'Miller is mine.' Valentino's soft growl was full of menace.

The immediate warmth that stole through her system at his possessive words threw Miller off-balance. How many times had she imagined her father riding in on a white charger and restoring her torn world to rights again? To have Valentino stand up for her was...disconcerting. Unnerving. *Exhilarating.*

Dexter was the first to break eye contact in the stag competition going on, and Miller couldn't blame him. Even though he was cleanly shaven, Valentino, at least in this mood, was not a man you would cross. He was like a lethal warrior of old who would not only win, but would take no prisoners either.

'Dance.'

Valentino held out his hand for her and she felt herself bristle when he didn't even glance her way. Then his steely eyes cut to hers and she forgot about being grouchy.

'Please.'

Her heart beat as fast as his silver sports car had eaten up the bitumen on their trip down as he led her onto the parquet dance floor.

'What's with the caveman antics?' she asked softly.

Valentino stared at her, his feet unmoving, his eyes intense, seemingly transfixed by hers. 'Playing the part of the jealous boyfriend. What else?'

Playing the part of the jealous boyfriend...

It took a moment for his words to register fully, and when they did Miller felt sick. *Playing the part. Pretending. Fake.*

The skin on her face felt as if it had been whipped, and she briefly closed her eyes against his handsome face.

If she thought she'd been embarrassed spilling all her secrets to him earlier, she now felt one hundred times worse.

Miller tried to understand why she felt so miserable. So he had stood up for her and she'd felt warmed by it? So he had been hurt by the loss of his father, as she had? So he had remembered her favourite ice cream flavour.

He was a nice person. That was all that amounted to. Nicer than she'd first thought. But at the end of the day he was still no one to her. A virtual stranger.

A virtual stranger who had brought her to orgasm within minutes of touching her. And if only she could stop thinking about *that*!

Steeling herself against emotions she couldn't immediately label, and determined he wouldn't know how she had momentarily forgotten this whole thing was fake, Miller breathed deeply and slowly.

'Just be thankful this thing isn't real between us,' he growled menacingly. 'I would have decked him if it was.'

For a horrifying second Miller wondered if he'd read her thoughts. 'For challenging you?'

'For staring at your breasts as if he could already imagine touching them. He hasn't, has he?'

Miller's eyebrows shot up. 'Of course not.'

He scowled. 'You don't want him to, do you?'

'No!'

Wow! He almost had her convinced he was seriously miffed about Dexter's interest.

'Good. And don't ever walk off on me in the middle of a conversation again.'

Miller frowned. 'If you're referring to TJ and Janelle...?' She rolled her eyes. 'I was hardly required.'

'When it comes to relationships you have no idea what's required.'

His words stung because they were true. Relationships scared her. But she was too tired to argue any more, so she shut up and let him guide her around the floor, focusing all her attention on the music and not on the way it felt to be held within the tight circle of his powerful arms. She reminded herself that she was a professional woman with goals and dreams that did not include this man in any shape or form. Reminded herself that her orgasm on the beach was a one-off and not to be repeated.

'What are you thinking?' His deep voice made her stumble and his hold tightened momentarily.

Miller's eyes met his. She was thinking that despite everything she knew about herself, about life, she still wanted to have sex with him with a bone-deep need that defied explanation.

'Miller?'

His husky command made her peek up at him from under her fringe. This wasn't her. She didn't *peek*. She looked. She organised. She...she was melting as her eyes drifted over his handsome face and her body brushed his.

Her heart beat much faster than it needed to and she wondered what type of man he really was. Why he lived the life he did. Why he had chosen to work in a profession that had taken his father's life—something she was sure affected him more deeply than he let on.

'How do you do what you do?' she asked, latching onto her curiosity about his racing life to distract herself from the fact that she seriously wanted to throw caution to the winds and have sex with him. Just once. To see what it would be like to do it with a man who just had to touch her to make her burn hotter than the sun.

* * *

Tino's hand tightened around Miller's as they continued to sway to the music. He had no idea what she was on about. His one-track mind was heavily mired in defending himself against the onslaught of her slender curves, her light, mouth-watering scent.

After their talk in the park earlier, when he'd felt a strong desire to comfort her and slay all her demons, his self-preservation instincts had kicked in and warned him that this time he really needed to keep his distance.

Of course dancing with her wasn't exactly conducive to that plan, but seeing Caruthers pawing her earlier had made him see red, and he knew he couldn't just drag her off to a secluded location feeling the way he did. Dancing with her was the safer of the two options.

'You're going to have to be a bit more specific than that,' he said, telling himself to ignore the way she seemed to fit so perfectly in his arms.

He was still a little shocked by the way he had nearly put his fist through Dexter's arrogant face. He had *forgotten* that this thing with Miller was fake. Of course that had more to do with male pride than the delicate, sensual woman in his arms right now.

Yeah, and pigs might fly. You want her and there's no shame in admitting it. Just don't do anything about it.

Just when he was about to end the exquisite torture of dancing with her, she answered his question.

'Race? Don't you ever get scared?'

Ah, she'd been asking him about his *job.*

Okay, that he could talk about on a superficial level. 'Motor racing is all about pushing yourself to the limit. There's no room for fear.'

Her body swayed against his in time to an eighties love song; the room too warm with the crush of similarly entwined bodies dancing together.

'But you push yourself *beyond* the limit, don't you? Isn't that why they call you an arrogant adrenalin junkie and a shock-jock? Maverick?'

'Don't believe everything you read about me, Miller. I'm happiest living on the edge, it's true. But I don't take stupid chances with my own life or anyone else's. Fear is an emotion. Controllable like any other. And while I'm not crazy, sometimes...' He paused, his mind automatically spinning back to the race that had taken the life of his good friend and caused him to question the sport he loved so much. 'Sometimes you have to squeeze the fear a little.'

And in this game you never look back, he silently added.

'Squeeze the fear?'

She said the words as if she were savouring a new taste on her tongue, and his body burned with a restless energy at the thought of tasting *her* again. But this time not just her mouth.

'You really love it don't you?' she said, a soft smile curving her lips.

Tino's mind jerked and went blank. Then he used his formidable mental control to switch off the erotic images turning his body hard. 'I get to experience life in its most heightened and intense form. Nothing else has ever come close.'

And probably right now he was too close to *her*—both mentally and physically. He couldn't remember ever having revealed so much about why he raced, and as for talking about his reasons for steering clear of relationships...

He frowned down at her. 'You're not going to repeat what I just said, are you?'

'You mean to a journalist?' Her tone was light, almost teasing.

'Yes.' His wasn't.

'Are your illustrious words worth very much?'

He scowled and she smiled.

'Relax.'

That captivating smile grew and he knew she was thinking of all the times he had told her to do the same thing.

'I don't need the money.'

Tino was jostled from behind by an exuberant dancer and his whole body came up flush against Miller's. Foreign emotions he couldn't name and a healthy dose of testosterone heightened as the arousal he'd been holding at bay flared instantly to life.

So much for that formidable mental control, Ventura.

He stopped dancing. 'I think it's time to call it a night.'

He noticed her face was flushed, and his arms tightened around her like a steel cage.

She stood still, looking up at him. 'I had no idea your job was so fascinating.'

His eyes became hooded and he saw his own desperate need reflected back at him from her over-bright eyes. Her lips parted softly in silent invitation and he had to fight the instinct to crush her mouth beneath his.

He studied her slender hands curled around his shoulders, her fingers elegant, the nails unvarnished. They suited her serious nature and reminded him that 'serious' females were best avoided at all costs.

'Valentino, are you okay?'

Her hands slid from his shoulders to rest lightly against his chest and he felt scalded.

Deliberately slowing his heart-rate, he evened out his breathing and stepped back from her. Every minute he spent in her presence eroded his self-control and he hated that. Without self-control he was nothing. He had no choice but to sever whatever bond had sprung up between them, because right now he sensed she was more dangerous to him than a hairpin turn at three hundred clicks.

He saw the moment comprehension dawned that he was rejecting what she was unconsciously offering and silently cursed as a moment of hurt flashed across her beautiful face.

It was as if he'd betrayed her. And maybe he had. The way he'd come on to her on the beach, then taken her for ice cream, grilled her about her life, his behaviour with her boss…

Feeling as if he owed her a massive apology, he didn't know where to start. Or if it would make the situation between them better or worse.

Then she took the decision out of his hands and closed down

her emotions as effectively as he had, pivoting on her sexy heels and walking away from him.

Immediately, an image of his father slotted into his brain, but rather than shake it off straight away, as he usually did, he let it settle there for a moment. The image was always the same. A smiling, larger-than-life hero in a white jumpsuit with a cerulean-blue helmet under his arm.

Miller's eyes.

His father's helmet.

His father's death hanging over him like a sword.

In this game, you never look back.

Tino felt his old rage at his father rear up and flattened it. This weekend was supposed to be light and easy. Relaxing. But Miller was drawing something out of him he had no wish to face, and it was messing with his head.

She was messing with his head.

He wasn't supposed to want her. At least not this much. And he sure as hell wasn't supposed to want to make her world a better place.

What a crapshoot.

CHAPTER TEN

STALKING into the breakfast room the next morning, Tino plastered what he hoped was an easy smile across his face.

Miller was there, as were TJ, Dexter and another female guest decked out in a Lycra leotard.

Tino hadn't returned to the bedroom he shared with Miller for a good two hours after she'd walked off the dance floor the night before, and when he had it had been to find her curled up in the middle of the huge bed.

He'd slept on the floor.

If you could call staring at the bedroom ceiling all night sleeping. Then he'd risen early and gone for a run, so he didn't know what mood Miller was in. By the look of the dark shadows beneath her eyes she hadn't slept much either.

'Maverick. You're up early.'

Valentino's gaze turned from Miller to TJ. He hated the familiarity with which TJ addressed him but it was one of those things that came with success. Men always thought he was their best friend and women always wanted to nail him. Well, except Miller, who might prefer to put an axe through his head after last night. He poured muesli from the selection of breakfast cereal arranged on the sideboard into a bowl and pulled out the dining chair beside the woman he was supposed to act as if he was in love with. He'd been chivalrous last night—truly, unselfishly chivalrous for the first time in his life—and he had no doubt she'd thank him for it later. Hopefully more than he was thanking himself right now.

'As are you.' He glanced at Miller and her grip tightened around the shiny fork she was using as a weapon against a grapefruit.

'Habit,' TJ said. 'No sleeping in when you're raised on a cattle station. So, are you up for a game of tennis later today?'

'Thank you.' Valentino accepted hot coffee from the maid who had just materialised at his side.

'As I explained before you insisted I have breakfast, TJ,' Miller interjected, 'I have to get back to the city by lunchtime.'

'What could be so important you have to rush back on a glorious day like today?'

Covering for her slight hesitation, Tino jumped in. 'Unfortunately I have to go over a new engine with my engineers today.'

Miller glanced up at him through the screen of her sooty lashes and he was disconcerted to find that he couldn't read her expression.

'And have you given any more thought to my proposal, Mav? To represent Real Sport?' TJ asked, confidence dripping from every word.

Not expecting such a direct question, Tino hesitated. He would have liked to tell TJ what he thought of his business tactics, but Miller stayed him with her hand on his.

'I've advised Valentino to set aside any final decisions about working on your campaign until after *our* business is concluded. I wouldn't want to muddy the waters by mixing the two—as I'm sure you can appreciate.'

The skin around TJ's eyes tightened briefly before the man recovered himself. He clearly hadn't been expecting Miller to turn the tables on him so neatly. And neither had Dexter, who started choking on his eggs.

Tino had actually been considering telling his publicist to accept the Real Sport deal in a bid to help Miller win the account, but perhaps he didn't need to. It really wouldn't affect him all that much, so long as TJ's company fitted the strict criteria he insisted on and was willing to pay one of his pet charity organisations an exorbitant sum of money for the privilege.

TJ scratched his ear in a dead giveaway of his mounting tension. 'Interesting decision. Not one I would have made.'

'Nevertheless, it's one *I've* made.'

Miller had her bushfire extinguishing voice in place and Tino felt his fists clench when he caught Dexter's murderous expression.

Easing his bulk back in his chair, his face flushed, TJ fixed narrowed eyes on Miller's boss. 'I thought *you* were supposed to be the senior consultant on this account, Caruthers?'

He didn't need to say anything else to indicate how he felt, and everyone in the room held their collective breaths.

A muscle in Dexter's jaw twitched, but Tino cut off any response he might have made with a single look. 'Miller's principles are admirable,' he said. He reached for an apple from the middle of the table. 'Qualities I would expect any company I endorse to emulate.'

For a moment no one seemed to know what to say.

'Then get that final proposal to me quick-smart, young lady,' TJ snapped. 'I want everything wrapped by race day.' He stared at Tino. 'Maybe we can even announce our collaboration at your mother's bash next Saturday night.'

Damn. If Lyons was going to his mother's party, he would expect to see Miller there.

Tino shook his head. 'I play a low-key role at that event. It's my mother's show.'

Miller stopped torturing her breakfast. 'I'll make sure I have the proposal to you in time for an early decision, TJ.' She dabbed at her lips with her napkin and stood up. 'Thank you for your hospitality and, again, happy birthday.' Then, acknowledging the other occupants in the room, she walked out like a queen.

Miller sat beside Valentino in the car as they headed back to Sydney, nursing a headache to end all others and a stomach that felt as if it was twisted up with her intestines.

She'd hardly slept the night before, completely mortified that Valentino had not only read how much she had wanted him on the dance floor, but that he had not wanted her in return. Her embarrassment from the whole trying day had been absolute.

It was a cliché that pride went before a fall, but right now Miller was grateful for the extra cushioning. In fact, she felt so terrible she almost felt sorry for the way Dexter must have felt when she had rejected him. One-way chemistry was not a pleasant thing to come face-to-face with for anyone.

'Are you okay?'

Valentino's quiet concern in the stuffy little car was the last thing she needed. 'No, not really.' She was too tired to pretend any more. 'Dexter is probably going to put me on performance management for overstepping hierarchical boundaries, TJ is livid, my promotion is most likely dead in the water, and I have the mother of all headaches.'

'If it's any consolation I thought you were magnificent this morning.'

This morning—but not last night... 'I was stupid.' This morning *and* last night.

'You'll win TJ's business and save the day. You'll be a hero.'

'Thanks for the pep talk.' She rubbed her forehead and grimaced as she thought of pulling her computer out of its bag. Still, it had to be done. She had 'squeezed the fear' and stood up to TJ this morning—which she didn't regret—but she didn't want to lose her job over it, and she knew she had major sucking up to do if she wanted to get her goals back on track.

'TJ and Dexter will expect to see you at my mother's charity event next weekend.'

Miller had heard of the Melbourne gala charity night, of course, but she'd had no idea it was Valentino's mother's event. 'I don't care.'

'If you need to attend I can arrange it.'

Miller glanced at him and winced as the sun reflected off the circular speakers on the dashboard. Was he kidding? She couldn't wait for *this* weekend to be over. The thought of seeing him again was just...horrifying. 'It'll be fine.'

He sped up and passed two cars at once. Miller tensed.

'Surely you're not still nervous about my driving?'

'This isn't a racetrack. It's a national highway.'

'With lots of room to pass. How are you going to explain your absence next weekend?'

'I'll have a headache.' Something she could easily envisage right now. Then she realised why she hadn't connected the event with him. 'Why does your mother have a different surname from yours?'

'She remarried.'

His response to the personal question was typically abrupt, and it stupidly hurt. Her brain slow to accept that her feelings were as one-sided as Dexter's.

Reaching down, she unzipped her computer satchel and opened her laptop. *Squeeze the fear?* What had she been thinking?

Tino knew the conversation was at an end the minute Miller pulled her computer out and, really, short of hurling the thing out of the window, there was nothing he could do about it. Certainly she wouldn't be pleased if he told her she looked as pale as a snowflake and should just close her eyes and rest.

And what did *he* care? He was a man who had never found it necessary to encourage female conversation, and right now, with the sound of four hundred and forty-three pound-feet of torque eating up the heated tar of the Pacific Highway he was in his element. If she wanted to work her life away that was her choice.

A little voice in his head piped up, asking if that wasn't also his choice, but he sent it packing. The difference between him and Miller was that he loved his work. He didn't want to do anything else. Whereas, while she was clearly good at her job, it wasn't her first love.

And what did love have to do with anything?

Shaking his head, he shifted his thoughts into neutral and the car into top gear and just enjoyed the peace of the open highway and Miller tapping on her keyboard.

More than once he found himself distracted by those killer legs encased in black cotton leggings when she shifted in her seat, but as soon as that happened he forced his eyes to the road and his mind to think about the important round of meetings he had lined up for tomorrow.

Thankfully she fell asleep soon after that and he reclined her seat and tried to ignore the way her soft scent filled the car. The way her hair glinted golden-brown in the sun. The way her deep, even breaths pulled her shirt tight across her breasts. He merged onto the Harbour Bridge and pulled into the left lane, jerking the steering wheel sharply right when a car he nearly cut off blared behind him.

What's your day job again, Ventura?

Thank God it wasn't standard procedure to drive around a racing track with a raging hard-on. He'd be dead at the first corner.

The sharp movement jolted Miller's head against the car door and she woke up and rubbed her scalp. 'What happened?'

'Lousy driving. Do I go left or right off the bridge?'

He skilfully navigated the rest of the way through the posh backstreets of Neutral Bay to her apartment.

The weekend was just about over and soon they'd go their separate ways. A fact that should make him feel better than it did.

'Thank you for the weekend.'

She held out her hand in a show of politeness as he pulled the car up to the kerb near the entrance to her apartment building. He could tell by the wary look in her eyes that she instantly regretted the overture, which only made him perversely take hold of her hand and hold it firmly enough that if she pulled away from him it would make her movement jerky.

She swallowed—hard—and his eyes dropped to her lips. For a second he contemplated yanking her forward into his arms and kissing her, but her mouth flattened and he knew it would be a mistake.

Clean break.

Still holding her hand, he let his eyes snag hers and felt decidedly unsettled at the glazed look in her eyes. 'I hope I fulfilled my purpose this weekend?'

Okay, now he sounded like Sam. Time to go.

'Yes, thank you.'

Again with the thank-yous.

'Good luck with the coming race.'

'Thanks.'

Valentino frowned. Another thank-you from either one of them and he was likely to ignore all his good intentions and kiss her anyway.

Climbing out of the car, he grabbed her bag and met her on the sidewalk.

'I can take that.'

She held her hand out for her bag but he only stared at it grimly. 'I know you can, but you're not.'

She hesitated, her eyes briefly clashing with his. 'Well, thank—'

'Don't.' He watched her sharply as she stepped away from him. She was holding herself a little too stiffly. Was that so he wouldn't touch her? Or...? 'You look like you're burning up.'

'I'm fine. I just have a headache.'

Tino wasn't convinced, but he wasn't going to argue with her on the sidewalk even if it was basically empty; most of the residents of this upper-class neighbourhood were safely behind closed doors.

'Let's go, then.'

He felt a stab of remorse at how exhausted she looked and knew he was partly responsible for her condition. Possibly he should have told her who he was *before* he had agreed to help her on Thursday night, but it was too late now and he wasn't a man who wasted time on regrets.

The lift up seemed to take a month of Sundays, but finally she unlocked her door and stepped inside, reluctantly letting him follow.

He glanced around the stylish cream interior of her apartment, surprised by the splashes of colour in the rugs and cushions. 'Nice.'

'Thank you.'

She remained stubbornly in the doorway and he set her rollaway case near her bedroom door. Then he looked around, perversely unwilling to say goodbye just yet.

'I said thank you.'

Tino glanced at a row of family photos on her bookcase. 'I heard you—and, believe me, you don't want to know what that makes me want to do.'

She made a small noise in the back of her throat and he knew she was scowling at him.

'Don't you have somewhere to be?'

Yeah, inside you.

He ground his teeth together as his thoughts veered down the wrong track.

Really, it was past time to go. Her prickly challenges turned him on, and the only risk he was up for right now was six hundred and forty kilos of carbon plastic and five point six kilometres of svelte bitumen.

He turned and noticed that she didn't seem quite steady in the doorway, although she did her best to hide it.

Frowning, he pulled a business card out of his wallet. 'If you need anything contact my publicist. His number is on here.'

'What would I need?'

'I don't know, Miller. Help changing a tyre? Just take the card and stop being so damned difficult.'

She held his card between her fingers as if it had teeth.

'You're not going to return the favour?' he asked silkily.

'I'm all out of cards.'

Sure she was.

'And you already know how to change a tyre.'

He smiled. He did enjoy her dry sense of humour on the rare occasions she unleashed it.

Like her passion.

Her voice sounded scratchy and he studied her face. Her

eyes had taken on a glossy sheen and small beads of sweat clung to her hairline. This time he didn't ignore the inclination to reach out and lay his palm along her forehead. She jumped and tried to pull away, but he'd felt enough. 'Hell, Miller, you *are* burning up.'

She stiffened and her eyes were bleak when she raised them to his. 'I'm fine.'

Like hell.

A moment passed.

Two.

She jerked her eyes from his and swayed. Tino cursed, grabbed her, and eased her over into one of the overstuffed armchairs facing the TV.

'It's just a headache.'

'Sit.' He headed into the alcove kitchen and flicked on the electric kettle.

'What are you doing?'

'Making you a cup of tea. You look shattered.'

She didn't argue, which showed him how drained she was. He located a cup and saucer in her overhead cupboard and a teabag in a canister on the bench and waited for the water to boil. 'What's your mother's number?'

'Why do you want it?'

She had her eyes closed and didn't look at him when she answered.

'I think she should stay over tonight.'

'She lives in Western Australia.'

'Your friend, then—what's-her-name.'

She peeled her eyes open and looked at him as if he was joking. 'No man ever forgets Ruby's name. She's in Thailand.'

There was a wistful note in her voice and he paused. 'Were you supposed to go with her?'

'I...had to work.'

He shook his head. 'Who else can I call to take care of you?'

She closed her eyes again, shutting him out. 'I can take care of myself.'

He poured her tea. 'Do you take milk?'

'Black is fine.'

As he handed her the hot tea a compelling bright yellow canvas dotted with tiny blue and purple fey creatures caught his attention on the far wall and he stepped closer. 'Who did this?'

'No one famous. Can you please go now?'

He looked at the indecipherable artist's scrawl in the corner of the canvas and took a stab in the dark. 'When did you do this?'

'I don't remember.'

Liar.

And she hadn't just wanted to illustrate children's books either; he'd bet his next race on it.

'You're very talented. Do you exhibit?'

'No. Thank you for the tea, but I don't want to keep you.'

He heard the cup rattle and turned to find her leaning her head against the back of the chair. She looked even worse than before.

Making one of those split-second decisions he was renowned for on the circuit, he grabbed her suitcase and stalked into her bedroom.

'What are you doing now?' she called after him.

'Packing you some fresh clothes.'

He upended the contents of her case on the bed and then opened her wardrobe door. He was confronted by a dark wall of clothing. He knew she liked black but this was ridiculous. He had no idea where to start.

'Do you own anything other than black?'

'It's a habit.'

So was hiding herself. 'Never mind.'

'Why are you packing my things?' Her voice was closer and he glanced over his shoulder to see her leaning in the doorway. She should be sitting down, but he'd take care of that in a minute.

'Because you're coming with me.'

'No, I'm not.'

He knew he was forcing his will on her, and it totally went against his usually laid-back style, but *dammit* he just wasn't prepared to leave her here. What if she got really sick?

Then she'll call a doctor, lamebrain. And since when have you taken care of anyone other than yourself anyway?

'It's stress and lack of sleep,' she murmured.

'I can see that. And you've hardly eaten all day either. You need a damned keeper.'

'I'm fine.'

'Consider this a long overdue holiday.'

'Don't you *dare* go near my underwear drawer!'

'It's too late. I know you like sexy lingerie.'

She groaned, and he smiled.

He threw a fistful of brightly coloured underwear into the case, pulled a selection of footwear from her closet and zipped the case closed.

He wheeled it towards her and deftly scooped her up with one arm.

'I don't like all this he-man stuff,' she said, leaning weakly against his chest.

'Too bad.' He grabbed her computer satchel and her hand-bag, slammed her apartment door behind them. 'My instincts tell me you need someone to take care of you, and I have track practice tomorrow morning I can't miss.'

Her head dropped against his shoulder. 'I have to go to work tomorrow. I could get fired.'

'Everyone's entitled to a sick day. If you're okay tomorrow night I'll fly you back. Anyway, you could get fired for *not* coming with me. Dexter wants TJ's business, and TJ wants me. You can tell Dexter you're working on me.'

He put her down to fish his car keys out of his pocket and then gently deposited her inside the car.

'I don't think that's going to impress him.'

But she rested her head against the car seat and closed her eyes.

CHAPTER ELEVEN

MILLER knew she should probably put up more resistance to his high-handedness but she felt too weak and light-headed. And some deeply held part of herself was insanely pleased by his gesture.

But she was being a sucker again. It was obvious that his behaviour had more to do with his overdeveloped sense of responsibility than it did with her as a person and she would do well to remember that.

He expertly pulled the silver bullet into the area of the airport reserved for private planes, and Miller gave up fighting the inevitable. She was so weak she had no choice but to lean into him and soak up some of his strength as he guided her towards the steps to his plane.

It was sleek and white, and she didn't feel so unwell that she couldn't be impressed. 'You're not the prime minister, are you?' she murmured faintly.

He smiled softly. 'Sorry. I'm not that big.'

Their eyes caught and held and his smile turned devilish.

'I meant that important.'

Keeping her sheltered against his broad shoulder, he led her past wide leather bucket seats with polished trim down a narrow corridor and into a room lit only by the up-lights in the carpet.

'You have a bed?' She couldn't keep the astonishment from her voice.

'I fly a lot. Hop in.'

'Don't I have to wear a seat belt for take-off?' As she said the words she felt the jet move slowly forward. Or backwards. It was hard to tell.

'Not on a private plane.'

'Does it have a bathroom?'

'Through there.' He gestured towards a narrow sliding door. 'If you're more than five minutes I'm going to assume you've collapsed and come in.'

'And you accuse me of being bossy?' She sniffed, but didn't argue. Her back ached, her stomach hurt, and her head felt as if it had some sort of torture device attached to the top.

When she came out he was on the phone speaking to someone in Italian. One of his family maybe?

God, their worlds were so different. She felt a pang as she recalled watching the cool kids all eating at the same cafeteria table at school every day while she pretended she needed to be alone to spread out her drawing pad.

'I've ordered you a light meal. It'll be delivered as soon as we're airborne.' He shoved his phone in his pocket and came towards her. 'You look like you're about to fall over, Miller. Please get in the bed.'

He might have said please but his tone implied he'd put her there in about three seconds if she didn't comply.

Slipping off her boots, she folded herself inside the cool, crisp sheets and laid her head on the softest pillow in the world...

'Come on, Miller, we're here.'

Groggy from sleep, Miller allowed Valentino to lift her out of the bed.

'Don't forget her boots,' he told someone, and Miller rested her head against his shoulder, unable to completely pull herself from the blissful depths of unconsciousness.

Seconds later she was placed in a car, and seconds after that she was being lifted again.

The next time she woke the nausea had passed and so had the headache. She stretched and felt the resistance of a top sheet.

Someone had made this bed with hospital corners. She wondered if she was in a hospital.

Opening her eyes, the first thing she noticed was that the room was in semi-darkness, with a set of heavy silk drapes pulled across the windows. The second thing was that the room was expensively furnished in rich country decor and definitely not in a hospital. She strained her ears but could only hear the faint sound of white noise. A washing machine, perhaps.

Pulling back the covers, she was pleased to see she was wearing her T-shirt and leggings from earlier. So it was still Sunday, then. She felt utterly displaced and wouldn't have been surprised if she'd slept for a week.

Feeling grimy and hot, she checked through a door and was relieved to see it was a bathroom.

Before going in she glanced around and spied her case in a corner. Flicking on the bedside lamp, she went to rummage through it for something else to put on and was surprised to discover it held only underwear and shoes.

Resting back on her heels, she let out a short, bemused laugh, remembering the exasperation in Valentino's voice when he'd asked her if she wore anything other than black.

'You're awake, then?'

Miller spun around, so startled by his voice she fell back on her bottom. Which only made him seem to fill the doorway even more. She tried not to think about how gorgeous he looked in his casual clothing. He hadn't shaved and his hair was still slightly damp from a recent shower. Then she noticed he was holding a steaming porcelain bowl.

He walked into the room and placed it on the bedside table. 'Chicken noodle soup.'

'You made chicken noodle soup?'

His lips twitched. 'My chef did.'

'You have a chef?'

'Team chef, to be precise.'

'Well…' Miller stood up, not sure what to say. 'That's very

nice of you but I feel fine. Great, in fact. I did tell you I wasn't sick.'

'You *should* feel great. You've slept for nearly twenty-four hours.'

'Twenty-four hours! Are you kidding?'

'No. The doctor checked your vital signs this morning but he wasn't overly concerned. He said you might have picked up a bug and if you didn't wake properly by tonight to call him again. You spoke to him while he was here. You don't remember?'

'I have a vague recollection but…I thought I was dreaming. I know I've been pushing myself lately, but—wow. I feel fine now.'

Valentino stuck his hands into his jeans pocket. 'I'll leave you to have your soup and a shower.'

'Thanks.' Miller's mind was still reeling from the fact that she'd slept for so long. 'Oh, wait. I don't have anything to change into. You only packed…underwear and— What *is* that noise?'

He stopped at the door. 'The ocean. A cold front came through this morning so the swell is up.'

'You live on the ocean?'

'Phillip Island.'

'We're not even in Melbourne?'

'Take a shower, Miller, and join me in the kitchen. Down the hall, left and then right. There are clothes in the wardrobe. They should fit.'

Curious, Miller went to the wardrobe door and gasped when she opened it to find an array of beautifully crafted women's clothes filling the cupboard—half of them black! Wondering who they belonged to, she fingered the beautiful fabrics of the shirts and dresses, the soft wool pants and denim jeans.

But whose were they? And why did Valentino have a closet full of—she checked a few of the labels—size ten clothes?

Her size.

The thought of wearing another woman's clothing wasn't exactly comforting and her stomach tightened. T-shirts, jeans and shorts lined the shelves, and there was a grey tracksuit.

Feeling as if she was stealing the pretty girl's clothing from a school locker, Miller gingerly pulled out the tracksuit pants and a T-shirt. Thank God she had her own underwear—because there was no way she was wearing somebody else's. In fact, she'd put on her own clothes again if she hadn't slept in them for so long. The thought that she'd actually been ill was still something of a shock.

Going through to the marble bathroom, Miller quickly showered under the hot spray and opened the vanity and found the basics. Deodorant, toothpaste and a new brush, a comb and moisturiser. Brushing the tangles from her hair, Miller hunted in the cupboard for a hairdryer and came up empty.

Damn.

Without a hairdryer her hair would dry wavy and look a mess. She felt vulnerable and exposed without her things, but there was nothing she could do about it. Valentino had swooped down, got her at a weak moment, and she'd just have to brave it out. It was only clothes and hair anyway. He probably wouldn't even notice.

She walked back into the bedroom and her stomach growled as the smell of cooling soup filled her nostrils. Salivating, she perched on the bed and demolished the fantastic broth in seconds, her body feeling both clean and nourished.

But, knowing she couldn't hide out in this room any longer, she picked up the empty bowl and followed Valentino's directions to the kitchen.

His home was modern and spacious, with lots of exposed wood and a raw-cut stone fireplace that dominated a living area that was furnished with large pieces of furniture built to be used as well as to look good.

When she stepped into the modern cream and steel kitchen she was assailed with the smell of sautéed garlic and her eyes became riveted to the man facing the stove. She drank in his athletic physique in a fitted red T-shirt and worn, low-riding denims that cupped his rear end to perfection.

He was without a doubt the sexiest man she had ever seen,

and he made her forget all about being self-conscious or cautious. But she wasn't here because he was attracted to her. He'd made it perfectly clear Saturday night he didn't want her in that way, so it was time to stop thinking about the way he made her feel.

There was nothing else going on here but his over-developed sense of responsibility, and if she didn't pull herself together she'd likely make a huge fool of herself again.

Something must have alerted him to her presence because he stopped pushing the wooden spoon around the pan and turned towards her.

His eyes swept over her and she felt the thrill of his smoky, heavy-lidded gaze from across the room. She wished her senses weren't so attuned to his every look and nuance because the tension she felt in his presence made it impossible for her to relax.

Miller sensed he was holding himself utterly still, almost taut, and she was definitely using someone else's legs as she moved further into the kitchen.

'The clothes fit, then?'

She remembered the dull feeling that had washed over her when she'd first seen them. 'Yes. Whose are they?'

'Yours.'

'You bought me clothes?'

He shrugged carelessly at her stunned tone and added tinned tomatoes to the pan. 'Technically Mickey bought them.'

'Mickey?'

'My Man Friday.'

He had a Man Friday? One who knew his way around women's fashion? She hated to think how many other women Mickey had clothed at Valentino's request.

'Mickey runs interference between all the people vying for my attention and makes sure my life runs smoothly. Calling up a department store and organising a few items of clothing for a woman was a first.'

'I didn't say anything.' She felt impossibly peeved that he'd read her so well.

'You didn't have to. You're very easy to read.'

'Not usually,' she muttered.

His slow smile at her revelation made breathing a conscious exercise.

'Why didn't you just pack me something other than underwear and shoes?' Realising she was still holding the empty soup bowl she set it down on the benchtop between them. 'That would have made more sense.'

'Probably,' he said. 'But I saw all that black in your wardrobe and panicked. And I have a soft spot for your lingerie and shoes. How was the soup?'

'Divine.' Miller felt flustered by his admission about her underwear. 'I'm not keeping the clothes,' she said stubbornly. 'There's enough there for ten women.'

He leaned against the lacquered cabinet beside the stove. 'Mickey's ex-army—a complete amateur when it comes to what women need.'

'Whereas you're an expert?'

His eyes studied her in such a way that goosebumps rose up on her arms. 'So I've been told.'

Miller sighed deeply, searching around in her mind for some way to change the subject and lower the tension in the room to a manageable level. It would be too embarrassing if he guessed how disturbed she was in his presence.

'I should probably get going. I've taken up enough of your time.'

'I'm cooking dinner.'

'I thought you had a chef?' She tried to make her tone light but she wasn't sure she'd pulled it off.

'He provides the food. I cook it when I'm here.'

'What is it?'

'Not poison.'

He gave a short laugh, and she realised she'd screwed up her face.

'Relax. If you want to go home after dinner I'll arrange it.'

Just like that, she thought asininely. Did nothing faze this man?

Yes. Talking about his family. His father. The accident that had claimed the life of his friend. He had his demons, she knew, he just kept them close to his chest.

Miller nodded. She felt stiff and awkward, and when she wetted her painfully dry lips his eyes locked onto her mouth with the precision of a laser. She felt the start of a delicious burn deep inside.

So much about this man stimulated her to the point that she could think of little else. Which made staying for a meal a questionable decision. Wasn't it playing with fire to spend any more time in his company?

A vague memory of him feeling her head and administering a drink of water to her some time during the day filtered into her mind. His gentleness and consideration of her needs was breaking down all of her defences against him. Something she really didn't want. Lord only knew what would happen if he showed any indication that he wanted her half as much as she wanted him. She wasn't sure she would say no. Wasn't sure she *could* say no.

Spotting his phone on the far bench, her mind drifted to work.

'Did you happen to bring my phone yesterday?' she asked, wondering if she still had a job and if it was too late to call Dexter. She'd done nothing on TJ's account all day, so chances were slim, but she'd rather know than not.

He stopped stirring the sauce on the stove. 'It wasn't in your handbag?'

'No.'

'You can borrow mine. But if you're calling work don't bother. They know you're with me.'

'Sorry?' She forced her eyes away from the muscled slopes of his arms. 'What did you tell them?'

'That you were sick.'

Miller barely suppressed a groan. 'Why did you do that?'

'I presumed you'd want your workplace to know where you were and you weren't capable of telling them.'

Miller knew he was right, but it didn't change the fact that she was irritated. 'I have to finish TJ's proposal, and I'm still not sure Dexter isn't planning to put me under a formal performance review. Now he'll just think I'm skiving in order to spend time with you and definitely do it.'

'After his own behaviour over the weekend he'd be crazy to question yours. I'm sure your job is perfectly safe. And everyone's entitled to a sick day. I bet you have almost a year's worth accumulated by now.'

Miller blushed. He made her feel like a goody-two-shoes. But his championing of her gave her a warm glow that was hard to shake.

Something she could never rely on long term, she reminded herself. Especially with a man like him.

'You have a point.' Hopefully one Dexter recognised. 'But still, I can take care of myself.' She tried to hide her irritation but it wasn't easy. Everything about her response to him—and his lack of one to her—was just debilitating.

He flicked a knob on the stove and put a lid on the saucepan, his gaze never shifting from hers as he prowled towards her. He rounded the island bench and Miller felt her breathing become choppy. She knew it wasn't just because of her rush of irritation.

He stopped just shy of touching her, his blue-grey eyes piercing, his arms folded across his chest. *'Thank you, Tino, for helping me out Sunday night when I felt like something the cat had dragged in,'* he said mockingly.

Miller felt ashamed of her stroppy behaviour. What was *wrong* with her? 'Thank you, Tino, for helping me out Sunday night when I felt like something the cat had dragged in.' And probably looked it...

'That's better.'

His smile could have melted a glacier. Then his eyes locked onto her hair and she suddenly remembered that it wasn't straight, as usual, and probably looked terrible.

She raised a self-conscious hand. 'Wavy.'

He reached out and looped a semi-dry curl around a finger. 'Pretty.'

She shook her head and his finger snagged on the curl, pulling it tight. She shivered. 'I prefer it straight.'

His hand drifted to the side of her face, his fingers following the curve of her jaw. 'That's because it gives you a sense of control. I like it either way.'

Miller's breath stalled in her lungs at the way he was looking at her. She could read desire in his eyes. Want. Intent, even. She was shocked by it because previously she had assumed his interest in her wasn't real. But now she suspected he had just been resisting the chemistry between them on Saturday night—as she had done for most of the weekend. As she should still be doing...

Only she felt powerless to look away from the banked heat in his gaze and a thrill of remembered pleasure raced through her body. A thousand reasons as to why this wasn't a good idea pinged into her mind, but overwhelming her logical thinking was a wicked, sinful sensation that refused to go away.

All her life she'd done the right thing. The proper thing. Working hard to get good grades and make her mother proud, building a reputation at work that would ensure her future was secure, shelving the more risqué side of her nature. Until now that had been enough. Satisfying, even.

But Valentino brought out a delicious craving in her that was impossible to ignore.

CHAPTER TWELVE

Tino saw the sharp rise and fall of Miller's chest as his finger lingered on the side of her jaw, felt her tremble as he deepened the caress. He hadn't intended to touch her, seduce her, but now he could think of nothing else.

Some part of him hesitated. Really, if he had any integrity he'd stop. She'd been sick. She was a guest in his house. But none of that registered with her standing in front of him looking gorgeous and tousled, her cheeks pink, her lips softly parted. God, he wanted to kiss her. He wanted—

She swayed slightly towards him, pressed the side of her face into his palm. 'Valentino…?'

Her blue eyes were huge, shining with an age-old invitation that sent every ounce of blood in his body due south. Breathing felt like an effort, and it would have taken more strength than he possessed not to lean in and kiss her.

So he did.

Lightly. Gently. Just their mouths and his hand on her face connecting them.

And maybe he would have stopped so that they could eat the dinner he'd prepared, but after the slightest of hesitations she rose onto her toes, flattened herself against his chest and he was lost.

His hands moved to span her waist and curled beneath the fabric of her T-shirt to sweep up and down the smooth skin of her back. She whimpered. He groaned, angled his head, took the kiss deeper, his mouth hardening as the hunger inside him threatened to consume them both.

Her hands found his hair; his found her breasts. Those perfect round breasts.

'Miller...' Her name was a deep rasp and she wrenched her mouth from under his as his thumbs flicked across both nipples at once. She arched into his hands, her back curving like an archer's bow, and he growled his appreciation, pushing her bra cups down to pluck at her velveteen flesh more firmly.

Her sensitivity and responsiveness completely undid him, and he lifted her and turned to place her on the stone bench.

'Valentino.'

Her desire-laden sigh stalled him. He pulled in a tanker full of air and tried to steady himself as his eyes met hers. He flicked his tongue over his lips and saw her pupils dilate as she watched him.

Forking a hand through her thick waves, he forced her eyes up to his. 'Miller, I want to be inside you more than I've wanted anything in my life. Tell me you want the same,' he ordered gruffly.

He felt the thrill of desire race through her and her lips parted, her fingernails digging into his shoulders. 'Yes. I feel... I want the same thing.'

Tino's eyes grew heavy with fierce male triumph and his hands confidently moved to the waistband of the sweats she wore. 'Lift up.'

He dragged the pants down her legs, admiring her red lace panties before they dropped to the floor. 'God, I love your lingerie.' He spread her thighs wide and pulled her forward until her bottom was balanced on the edge of the bench. 'Take off the T-shirt and bra.'

She complied, and he leaned forward to capture one pointed nipple into his mouth. He suckled her. Bit down lightly. His hands steadied her hips as she jerked under the lash of his tongue. She was perfect.

'Beautiful,' he breathed. He switched his attention to her

other breast, loving the feel of her fingers speared into his hair, holding his head hard, her small whimpers of arousal testing his self-control.

He felt her hips push against his restraining hold and knew she was seeking pressure at her core. Pressure he couldn't wait to give her. He moved one hand between her legs and urged her thighs wider, opening her, his eyes momentarily closing as he revelled in the feel of his hand sliding through her curls and over her delicate folds. She was already wet and his middle finger slipped easily inside her. She made a sound like a sob, her hands clutching at him as he stroked her sweet spot with his thumb.

His erection jerked in an agony of wanting.

Soon, he promised himself. He curved his other hand around the nape of her neck and pulled her eager mouth back to his, adding another finger into her body and setting up a steady rhythm.

She groaned, a deep, keening sound, and ground herself against his hand. He felt the urgent lift of her body that signalled she was close to coming, but as much as he wanted to feel her orgasm gripping his fingers he wanted something else more.

'Lean back on your elbows.'

He waited while she shifted the empty soup bowl out of her way and then he bent forward and nuzzled her, his tongue stroking and teasing the bundle of nerve endings at the top of her sex.

She bucked against him so hard she nearly dislodged him, and he wound his arms around her waist.

'Damn, Miller, you taste so good.'

His husky words sent her over the edge and she came like a shot around his tongue. He nearly disgraced himself in his own kitchen.

Calling on every ounce of focus, he rode her orgasm with her. Then he stood, rose above her, pulled his T-shirt up over his head and shucked his jeans around his ankles. Her head was still thrown back on her shoulders, her breasts pushed high, her body open for his viewing pleasure. His eyes drank in the sheer beauty of her for all of two seconds and then he shifted closer, positioning himself between her splayed thighs before—

Condom.

Right. *Hell.*

He reached around and pulled one out of his back pocket, sheathed himself.

'Are you always this prepared?'

Her husky words and wary gaze stayed him. His usual approach would be to make a sarcastic quip. Keep things light. But her scent was warm on his tongue and for some reason he couldn't conjure up anything light.

'No. But after touching you on the beach Saturday I've dreamt of nothing else since.'

'Nothing else?'

Her tone was teasing and it gave him permission to tease her back. 'Maybe my mother's lasagna.'

She smiled, her eyes slumberous as she took him in. His erection throbbed under her perusal and her startled eyes flew to his.

His hands tightened on her hips. 'Do you want me to stop?' The words felt as if they were ripped out of his throat with a pair of pliers, but he needed to be sure she was totally on board with this.

Her eyes held his. 'Would you?'

'Of course.' Though it might kill him.

'No, I don't want you to stop.' She leaned forward, gripped him in her palm. She closed her eyes as her fingers explored him. 'I want to feel you inside me.'

He wanted that too—so badly his legs were shaking with need. He pulled her hands from his body before he lost it. 'Open your eyes.' His voice was a husky command and it seemed for ever before she raised her sleepy gaze to his. 'I want to see your eyes as I fill you.'

Her eyes widened and her tongue touched her lips as she nodded.

'Hold on to me.' She draped her arms along the line of his

shoulders and gripped the back of his neck. Tino pulled her firm breasts against his torso and lifted her.

He'd intended to take her hard, his instinct to plough himself into her, but some sense of civility whispered that this first time he might hurt her, so instead he lowered her with as much care as he could.

Even so, he felt the hiss of air against his temple as her body encircled him.

She was tight. So tight. He stilled. 'Are you okay?' Sweat beaded his forehead as he forced himself not to jam her on top of him.

She wriggled her hips and adjusted herself around his girth and his head nearly came off.

'Now I am.' Her voice was so damned sexy. Like her smell. 'You're just...big.'

Women had told him that before, but never had those words sounded so sweet.

'You can take me,' he growled, kissing her brow.

'I think I already have.' There was laughter in her voice and then he shifted his hips and surged forward, giving her more.

'Or not.' She groaned. 'I want more.'

God, so did he.

'Hook your legs around my waist.' He could barely speak. The urge to pound into her was overwhelming but he needed a soft surface for what he was about to give her—otherwise she'd end up black and blue.

Somehow he made it to his bed, but when he fell on top of her he was so close to coming he didn't hold back. Her body clung to his as if it had been made just to please him, and when he felt another orgasm building inside her he didn't know how he managed to hold off long enough to take them both over the edge together, but he was so damned glad he had.

God, had sex ever been this good?

Miller lay still, unable to move, and yet stricken with the urge to run for her life. She had just had wild, unrestrained sex with one of the beautiful people. Someone so far removed from her real world she couldn't even leap to see the platform he lived on.

And it had been amazing. He'd filled her so completely, so powerfully, all she'd been able to do was cling to him as he'd carried her into his room and then carried them both into a miracle of erotic pleasure.

At least it had been for her. For him it was probably run of the mill. *She* was probably run of the mill. Trying not to let her old insecurities swamp her, Miller clung to what was real. Which, ironically, was that this was fake.

Her sickness, his bringing her here—none of that had changed anything between them. And would it matter if it had? She had her goals, her plans for the future, and she wasn't looking for a relationship. She wasn't looking to fall in love with anyone yet.

She understood the fundamental rule that one person always loved more than the other, and she also knew that relationships were unstable at best and downright destructive at worst.

And it wasn't as if Valentino was going to insist on having a relationship with her! He'd probably prefer to be hit by one of his fast cars. And even if he did his job took him all over the world. She knew herself well enough to know she'd never cope with the uncertainty of having a relationship with someone who left her all the time. *Would* leave her as soon as he was bored.

But that still wasn't the scariest thought churning through her right now. No, the scariest thought had been the sense of connection she had felt when Valentino had joined their bodies together. It had been as if a missing part of herself had slotted into place. A ridiculous notion, and one that made her think that the sooner she got her life back to normal the better.

Valentino shifted beside her and Miller tuned into the laboured sounds of his breathing, the only noise in the otherwise silent room.

'You're thinking again.' His low voice rumbled from deep inside his chest.

'It's what I do best.'

'I think we've just discovered another occupation you could channel your energies into.'

Miller smiled weakly, and then gasped as he rolled on top of her and lightly pinned her to the bed. He fisted a hand in her hair and tilted her face up to his. She swallowed. He was so primal, so male. His hold was both possessive and dominant, and it shouldn't have thrilled her as much as it did.

'What are you thinking about?' he persisted.

'Isn't that my line?'

'I think it's pretty clear what I'm thinking about. What I want to know is if you're regretting what just happened between us.'

No, she wasn't regretting it. She was trying to figure it out. 'No. I probably should, but I don't.'

'I'm glad.'

He laid his palm across her forehead and Miller swallowed past the lump in her throat. 'I'm fine. I told you that.'

'I'm allowed to check.' Leaning down, he ran his tongue over her lips, stroking into her mouth as she automatically opened for him.

Miller gasped as pleasure arrowed straight to her pelvis, turning her liquid. She moaned when his knees urged hers wider and he settled himself between her thighs.

'I want you again,' he murmured roughly.

'Really?' Miller felt him hard between her legs and her trepidation at being here with him evaporated as she sensed just how wrong she had been about this chemistry being one-sided. He wanted her. Badly. And the knowledge gave her a giddy sense of sensual power that amazed her.

CHAPTER THIRTEEN

TINO woke up early, as usual, and smelt the scent of sex at the same time as he registered that Miller was no longer in his bed.

Confounded, he cracked an eye open and was even more puzzled to find the room empty and silent except for a couple of magpies warbling outside his window.

He was used to a woman clinging after a night of sex. Not that he remembered ever having a night quite like that. He'd been insatiable, and a grin split his face as he recalled how she had matched him the whole way.

He stretched his hands above his head and flexed stiff muscles. Last night had been incredible—and against every one of his rules.

Sort of.

It wasn't that he'd forbidden himself to have sex this close to race day, it was getting involved emotionally that was the no-go zone. He might have thought about Miller more than he would have liked over the past couple of days, but he knew now that he'd had her in his bed his interest would start to wane. It always did.

Which was why it was good that she would be leaving this morning. He had an enormously busy week, made even more so because he'd had to cancel yesterday's round of meetings to care for Miller.

Rolling out of bed, he pulled his jeans on and went in search of her to find out what time she wanted him to get the jet ready.

He found her outside, watching the sun rising over the ocean that stretched beyond his backyard. She was completely enveloped in his black robe—so appropriate, he mused—her hair mussed and wavy, the sun's rays highlighting the gold in amongst the brown.

She turned when she heard the sliding door open and fingered her hair self-consciously. She looked adorable. And uncomfortable.

He immediately sought to put her at ease and ignored the whisper of apprehension that floated across his mind. He didn't doubt for a minute his ability to control this situation between them.

'What are you thinking?'

'I didn't know men wanted to know what women were thinking so much.'

He studied her, feeling as if he was facing down one of Dante's highly strung thoroughbreds. 'I don't want to know what women are thinking, I want to know what *you're* thinking.'

'I'm thinking that you have a beautiful home. For some reason I took you as a city type.'

'I visit too many cities as part of my job. My mother lives on the other side of the island and I bought this place when she fell ill a couple of years ago.'

'Is she okay now?'

'Fine. Fitter than I am.'

Miller's lips twisted into a faint smile. 'Well, it's lovely here. Peaceful.' She glanced out over the lawn towards the beach and he caught the nervousness in her eyes. 'But I should probably be heading back home.'

Her lips were still kiss swollen from last night, and he noticed a slight red mark from where his beard growth had grazed her neck. He'd have to be more careful of her soft skin, though some primal part of him was pleased to see his mark on her.

'It's seven in the morning. Are you sore?'

She coloured prettily. 'That's personal.'

'Sunshine, it doesn't get any more personal than my mouth between your legs.'

She gasped. 'You can't *say* that!'

She looked mortified, and for some reason her reaction pleased him. He was so used to women preening and posing in front of him that her embarrassment was refreshing. She hadn't been a virgin, he knew that, but she wasn't a practised sophisticate either, and one of the things he loved—hell, *liked*—about her was that she was so easy to tease.

He stepped closer to her and urged her stiff body into the circle of his arms. 'I've embarrassed you?'

'Yes, but I don't know how.' She gave a deep sigh. 'I should have expected you to just say what you think. It's one of the first things I noticed about you.'

She gripped his forearms as if to hold him off, but he'd have none of it, his thumbs drawing lazy circles over the thin cotton of his robe covering her lower back, gentling her until she fitted against him as naturally as his tailor-made jumpsuit.

'What else did you notice?'

'That you had ripped jeans and needed a shave.'

Tino gave a hoot of laughter. 'Sunshine, you are hell on my ego.'

'Your ego is one area I would never worry about.'

She was watching his mouth, and his laughter dried up instantly. 'I usually start the day with a run followed by a green smoothie, but this morning I'm going to make an exception.'

Her aquamarine eyes lifted to his, her pupils expanding as he watched. 'What are you replacing it with?'

He enclosed the nape of her neck with his hand, slowly bringing her mouth to his. 'That depends on the answer to my earlier question.'

She frowned, and he pressed his pelvis into her to facilitate her memory recall. She smiled, and he felt tightness in his chest.

'Only a little.'

Her answer sent the tightness lower. 'I promise to be gentle.'

Miller must have dozed, because she awoke to the feel of Valentino spooning her from behind as he had done first thing that morning. Then she had slipped out of his bed, because the sensation of waking with his protective arm draped around her waist, his fingers resting protectively over her abdomen, had been both frightening and exhilarating. And now the same feelings were back.

He just seemed to swamp her. His warmth, his scent, her desire to burrow against him and never leave. It was as instinctive to her as breathing.

Right from the beginning she'd sensed he would have this intense effect on her, and wasn't that the reason behind her fear now? Hadn't she avoided feeling such intense emotions for another person because she knew better than most how tenuous relationships were? But how could a playboy racing car driver with a reputation for having a death wish make her feel so...so safe? So secure? It had to be straight hormones because otherwise it defied logic!

As did her current feeling of wellbeing. Something she hadn't experienced since before her parents had divorced, she suddenly realised. And hot on the heels of *that* little revelation was the unwelcome understanding that she had been trying to get this same sense of belonging from her job for years.

On some level that wasn't a total surprise, because she had always treated work as a second home, but what *was* newsworthy was that even the thought of making partner didn't give her quite the same sense of safety that Valentino did right now.

Confused, and feeling slightly exasperated with her see-sawing emotions, Miller again tried to creep out from under his arm—only this time his strong fingers spread out like tentacles to cover her whole belly.

'Am I going to have to tie you to my bed to make sure you're still here when I wake up?'

His deep voice was sleep-rough, his warm breath stirring her hair.

Miller stilled, wanting to run and wanting to stay at the same time. In the end she wasn't strong enough to resist his magnetic pull and subsided back against his hard body.

'Where were you going, anyway?'

'I really need to start making tracks.'

'Now, *there's* a very Aussie expression.' He rolled her onto her back and rose up on one elbow, his gunmetal-grey eyes lazily intense between thick, dark lashes.

Feeling exposed, Miller pulled the sheet up over her breasts. His gaze lingered on the sheet and she had the vague impression that he was about to flick it off her.

Glad when he didn't, she let her breath out slowly.

'Why are you so determined to run off, anyway? You don't strike me as the one-night-stand type.'

'I'm not.'

'Then stay one more day. I have a sponsors gig tonight. You can come with me.'

Alarmed by just how much she wanted to accept what she suspected was an unplanned invitation, Miller immediately reacted in the negative. 'I can't. I have to work.'

Annoyance flickered briefly across his face. 'Work from here. You have your computer.'

Miller smoothed her eyebrows. He was doing his steamroller thing again, but what was one more day to him? And when would she go home? Later tonight or in the morning?'

He stroked a strand of hair back off her forehead. God, she must look a mess.

'I know what you're thinking. You don't like the uncertainty of it.'

Miller's eyes flashed to his. Did he really know her that well, or was she really that easy to read?

'It's not hard to figure out, Miller. I know you hate surprises so it follows that you wouldn't like half-baked plans. How about we make it the whole week?'

The whole week!

'Five days, to be exact. That way you can come to my mother's gala event, which TJ is expecting to see you at anyway, and watch me race on Sunday.'

Miller felt her brows scrunch together. 'Why would you want me to come to your mother's ball?'

Tino rolled onto his back and gave her a reprieve from his intense scrutiny. 'Honestly? My mother invites every debutante in the known universe to this thing and expects me and my brothers to meet every one of them in the hope that we'll fall in love.'

His apathetic attitude to falling in love stabbed at something inside her. 'Oh, poor you. All those single women in one room. I would have thought it was every man's dream.'

Her words were sharper than she had intended, but she was slightly insulted that he would talk about other women while he was in bed with her. Even if they were women he apparently didn't want.

The reminder that he would never want anyone permanently— not even her—struck a chord, because permanence was all she did seek! She'd just never sought it with a man before.

'Hardly.' His dramatic tone nearly made her laugh, despite her aggravation. 'Debutantes come with strings attached, stars in their eyes and pushy mothers. That's no dream any man I know has ever had.'

Suddenly, he lifted onto his elbow, looming over her again, and Miller caught her breath. His gaze roved over her face and he trailed a finger over the sensitive skin of her neck just below her ear, winding a slow, sensual path downwards.

'I did you a favour last weekend. The least you can do is protect me from women I'm not interested in on Saturday night.'

His voice had lowered with intent, and Miller's body responded like one of Pavlov's dogs. She pushed his hand away. 'Stop that. I can't think when you're this close.'

'That's only fair since you have the same effect on me.'

'I do?' For some reason, his admission startled her.

'Well, I *can* think, but it's usually about one thing.' His hand returned and his fingers circled her nipple, making her arch off the bed. 'Say you'll stay.'

She tried to organise her thoughts. 'Because of the sex?'

She was breathless, and his smile as he rolled on top of her was one of pure male triumph. 'The sex is phenomenal, but the more I think about you going to my mother's party the more I like it. With you there I can relax, and I might even enjoy it. And Caruthers will expect it.'

'Since when do you care what Dexter thinks?' Miller asked breathlessly, catching a moan between her clamped lips as his fingers traced a figure eight over first one breast and then the other, skimming over her nipple just a little bit too lightly each time.

'I don't.' His skilful touch became firmer. 'Say yes.'

Miller felt deliciously light-headed. 'You're steamrollering me again,' she accused, trying to hold her body still.

Valentino nipped the skin around her clavicle. 'Is that a good thing?'

Giving up on trying to resist him, she speared her fingers through his hair, enjoying the thick, weighty texture of it curling through her fingers.

'I don't know.' She groaned and dragged his mouth to her breast. 'Please, just stop talking.'

'You're so sexy.' His voice was rough, more a low growl, as he *finally* pulled her nipple into his mouth with just the right amount of pressure.

Miller felt as if she was levitating as her legs shifted helplessly under the onslaught of pleasure. She moaned his name. He nudged her legs apart, and even though her internal muscles ached from over-use the rush of liquid heat between her thighs was instant. She felt him fumbling in his side table, his mouth briefly leaving her breast to tear the condom packet open, and then he was back, pressing her into the bed.

'Now, where was I?'

God, he made her feel… He made her feel…

'Say you'll stay.'

His mouth teased the soft skin beneath her ear, and even though she knew she must have terrible morning breath she turned her face, searching for his kiss.

'Okay.'

What had she just agreed to?

'For five days.'

His fingers stroked between her legs, drawing moisture from her body in preparation for his possession.

'I...' She arched her hips, her body already balanced on a knife-edge of pleasure, desperate to go over.

'Say yes.'

'Yes—whatever.'

She was desperate, and his husky chuckle of dominance annoyed her. With a spurt of defiance at his formidable self-control in the face of her total lack of any, she wrapped her legs around his hips and tilted her pelvis so that he had no choice but to slide deep.

He swore as he plunged into her, and Miller smiled and buried her face against his straining neck. She clenched his shoulders and her internal muscles at the same time, and suddenly the balance of power shifted as he bucked in her arms before surging deep again.

She felt him groan against her hair, and then her mind closed down as he pounded into her with such primal force she thought she might break. And then she did. Into a whirlpool of pleasure that sucked her under and blew her mind. Dimly, she heard Valentino shout her name, and she could feel the power of his release as he spilled himself inside her.

It seemed for ever before either one of them moved, and even then it was only weakly.

'Are you okay?' he asked.

Miller gulped in air. 'Ask me in a minute.'

He chuckled and shifted onto his stomach beside her. 'Sorry. That was a bit rough.'

Miller stretched her arms above her head. 'It was fabulous. I may never move again.'

Groaning, Valentino dragged himself from the bed. 'I wish I had the same luxury. Unfortunately not working yesterday and spending half the morning in bed today has no doubt put the team incredibly behind.' He bent and gently kissed her lips. 'Why don't you stay in bed? Recover? I'll send Mickey with a car at five o'clock to bring you into the city.'

The city? It took a minute for Miller to remember their conversation. She watched through half-closed lids as Valentino strolled into the bathroom and turned on the shower.

She recognised that she'd just been steamrollered *again*, and that she had agreed to stay with him for five days and attend a party to help keep eager debutantes at bay.

What were you thinking?

She stared at the ceiling and tried to feel agitated, but instead all she felt was happy. Oh, not at the whole debutantes thing, but just at being here. Maybe it was called afterglow.

Otherwise it didn't make sense. Especially given her confused emotions and the fact that she still didn't know if she had a job or not. But, yes, she was definitely happy.

But she was also smart enough to know that she couldn't rely on those feelings. Reality would intrude and she would have to get herself back on track. In the meantime maybe she should take his suggestion. Call Dexter, finish TJ's proposal, and then treat the next five days as an impromptu holiday.

Valentino, she knew, would make sure she had fun—and would it be so wrong to soak up his hospitality for a little longer? To soak *him* up for a little longer?

She rolled onto her stomach and glanced at the digital bedside clock. Ten o'clock. If this was a normal work day she'd have been hard at it for three hours by now and staring down the barrel of another ten. And those were her hours during quieter periods.

She sighed and shifted her attention to the magpies hopping about and conversing with each other outside the full-length window that took up one whole wall of Valentino's masculine room.

She was under no illusions as to why he had asked her to stay for five days, and although she had never been the type to enter into a purely sexual relationship there was a first time for everything. She just had to keep things as light and breezy as he did. No intense emotions, no second-guessing herself at every turn. Just…fun.

Miller stepped from the car and smiled at Mickey as he held the door for her. Mickey was everything she'd expected—large, fit, and capable of lifting a small house with his bare hands. The fact that he was also capable of purchasing women's clothing didn't bear thinking about.

The pavement outside the swanky Collins Street retail outlet was lined with photographers and fans, all of whom quickly lowered their cameras as soon as they saw that she wasn't anybody special. Glad for once not to be part of the in crowd, Miller quickly turned her eyes to the burly security guards who stood either side of the short red carpet.

Swallowing hard, she was just contemplating how foolish she would feel if she gave them her name and they rejected her when a woman in a chic black suit rushed forward.

'Ms Jacobs?'

'Yes.'

Thank God. Someone knew her name.

'My name is Chrissie. Mr Ventura asked me to show you in.'

Miller smiled, ready to kiss Valentino's feet for his thoughtfulness. Straightening her spine, she followed Chrissie into the brightly lit store.

Faces turned towards her but she ignored everyone as the attractive aide wound a path between glamorous, laughing guests holding sparkling glasses of wine and champagne. The room was buzzing with energy and it grew steadily more frenetic the further she went—until Chrissie stepped aside and Miller knew why.

Valentino stood in the centre of a small circle of admirers wearing a severely cut pinstriped suit and an open-necked snowy white shirt. He looked so polished and poised, so sinfully good-looking, her mind shut down and all she could do was stare.

Having chosen black trousers and a gold designer top carefully from Mickey's inspired collection, and redone her hair in its normally sleek style, Miller still felt utterly exposed, stripped bare, when Valentino's eyes honed in on her like a radio device searching out a homing beacon.

God, she was in trouble. Big trouble. He was just so beautiful, with his dishevelled sable hair and five o'clock shadow, and her body knew his, had kissed every inch of him. The urge to bolt was overwhelming, but then he smiled and she exhaled a bucketload of air. It would be all right. She was fine.

Her toes curled in her strappy heels as he walked towards her, his eyes glittering.

'You look beautiful,' he murmured as he captured her hand and brought it to his lips in an age-old gesture.

Miller's stomach flipped and she couldn't tear her eyes from his. 'Funny, I was just thinking the same about you. Though I wasn't going to mention it on account of your ego and your current cheer squad, lapping you up like Christmas pudding.'

Valentino threw his head back and laughed and Miller felt riveted to the spot. Did he have any idea that he was so completely irresistible? Yes, of course he did. The people around them couldn't take their eyes off him.

'How did you spend your day?' he asked, smiling down at her.

'I worked—'

'Now, *there's* a newsflash,' he teased.

'Yes, well. I spoke to Dexter, and although he hasn't forgiven me for what I said to TJ I don't think he's going to do anything to jeopardise my promotion.'

'Good.' He grabbed a glass of champagne from a passing waiter and handed it to her. 'When are you going to start painting again?'

Miller was exasperated that he had discovered her most secret dream.

'Valentino, don't ask me that.'

'Why not?'

'Because it was a childish dream.'

'Not childish. Daring. A dream unhampered by adult limitations. Perhaps it's time you stopped hiding behind that wall you protect yourself with and go fot it.'

'I will if you will.'

The instant the words were out she held her breath, her heart hammering.

His eyes pierced her but there was no hostility behind them, just reluctant admiration. 'I forgot you were such a shrewd operator. Come on—I have to mingle.'

That easily he closed her down, and although it made her feel slightly hollow inside she refused to address the feeling.

With Valentino beside her she felt carefree, as if he had flicked a switch inside her, and as much as she fought against the uncertainty of her emotions she felt more like herself now than she ever had.

She watched him handle a group of business executives with ease and aplomb and for a moment envied him his sheer confidence and charisma. There was just something about him that was devastatingly attractive—and it wasn't just the way he looked. It was his sense of humour, his chivalry, his deep voice, his keen intelligence...

Miller sucked in a breath as a shot of pure terror made her chest hurt.

She was falling for him.

No. It couldn't be true. She wouldn't let it be true. But...

As if sensing her distress, Valentino turned to her, his eyes intense as they swept over her. Burned into her.

'Miller, are you okay?'

Miller stared up into his concerned gaze.

'I'm fine,' she answered automatically.

His gaze narrowed, sharpened, and Miller had a horrible feeling that he could see into her deepest self.

His hand reached for hers. 'You're sure?'

No, she was far from sure. But what could she say? That she

thought her feelings for him were deeper than his for her? She shook her head, and his frown deepened.

Realising she was behaving like a nutcase, Miller pulled herself together. She *wasn't* falling in love with him; she was too smart to do that.

CHAPTER FOURTEEN

HE really should be worried about getting himself into the mental space required to win pole position for tomorrow's race but for some reason he wasn't. The race was less than twenty-four hours away, and he wondered if he had time to make a quick detour on his way to the track.

He probably should be worried about how he felt about Miller as well, but so far he'd refused to think about it—and he was going to continue doing so until after the race.

It was true he was starting to entertain some thoughts about not finishing things with her straight away...but the jury was still out on that one.

And it wasn't just because of the sexual pleasure she brought him—though that was astounding. It was that he liked being with her. He'd even let her convince him to try Mexican food yesterday. He smiled at the memory. He hadn't planned on eating much—his team manager would have thrown a fit if he'd deviated from his strict diet this close to a race—but he hadn't needed discipline to tell her he'd pass.

'What are you thinking about?'

He glanced at her, sitting beside him in his Range Rover, her long legs curled to the side. The question had become a running joke between them since Monday night.

'That bean mixture you tried to force-feed me yesterday.'

'Enchiladas.'

He shuddered, and she rolled her eyes.

'I did not try to force-feed you. There must be something wrong with your tastebuds.'

'I promise you there's nothing wrong with my tastebuds, Sunshine.' He watched her blush and brought her fingertips to his lips.

He grinned as she smiled, and the sudden realisation that he was relaxed and happy jolted him. Often he had to force those feelings, but right now they were as genuine as she was.

'Any news from TJ?' He knew the man had agreed to part of Miller's business proposal, but the crafty old bastard was holding back on the rest until he found out his own decision about representing Real Sport.

Miller had insisted that he not do it, but he'd turned the matter over to his publicist anyway.

'Not yet. But I'm confident he'll give us the rest of his business in due course.'

Tino was too, but talking business reminded him again of one of his own little projects that he'd neglected of late.

Deciding that he had enough time, he turned the car off the next exit ramp, just before the Westgate Bridge, that led to the backstreets of Yarraville.

'This isn't the way to Albert Park,' Miller said, curiosity lighting her voice.

'I want to show you something first.'

He pulled into a large empty car park and cut the engine.

'This is a go-carting track.'

'Yep. Go Wild.'

Miller followed him out of the car, her sexy legs encased in denim jeans and cute black boots.

'Why are we here?'

'I want to check it out.'

'I think it's closed.'

'It is.' He reached the double glass doors and used a key to open it. 'I bought the place two months ago, when I was bored convalescing. I've had a lot of work done on it, but I haven't been back for a while.'

He walked into a dimly lit cavernous room, the smell of grease, sawdust and petrol making him breathe deep. A sense of wellbeing settled over him as he took in the changes since the last time he had visited.

Miller walked past him, clearly impressed by the view of a twisting track that took up most of the space.

She wrinkled her nose. 'It smells of stale chips.'

He hadn't noticed that.

'I think the kitchen is the next thing to be overhauled. This is the little kids' area,' he explained, walking towards one of the barriers. 'The bigger kids' track is out back.'

'Do we have time to see it?'

'Sure—hey, Andy?'

'Tino. I wasn't expecting you.' A tall, lanky man in a plaid shirt that had seen better days and grease-streaked jeans loped towards them.

Tino clasped his friend's hand. 'Andy, this is Miller Jacobs. Miller, this is my centre manager and fellow visionary, Andy Walker.'

'Hello.'

Miller took Andy's hand and Tino was slightly annoyed with himself for automatically stepping into her personal space when he registered Andy's very male appraisal of her.

They might be sleeping together right now, but that didn't mean she belonged to him in any way. The words he'd thrown at Caruthers at the weekend—"Miller is *mine*!"—reregistered in his mind and pulled him up short.

'Tino?'

He blanked his expression and cast off the unsettling notion that he'd well and truly crossed into a no-go zone with Miller. 'Sorry, I missed that last bit.'

'I said the main track is finished,' Andy repeated. 'Did you get my text last Wednesday?'

'I did. That's why I thought I'd stop by.'

'Come on. I'll show you.'

Clamping down on his worrying thoughts, Tino followed

Andy towards the rear of the building and out into the bright sunshine, shielding his eyes as he took in the track.

'It's huge.' Miller exclaimed behind him. 'Like a mini-racetrack.'

Tino smiled. 'That's because it is.'

'I know that,' she scoffed. 'I just wasn't expecting it to be that big.'

'Want to go out on it?'

'You mean walk around it?'

'Not walking.' He turned to Andy. 'Any chance you can pull a couple of carts out?'

'Sure.'

Andy grinned like a happy Labrador and Tino enjoyed the look of surprise on Miller's stunning face.

'I've never driven a go-cart before.'

'There's nothing to it.'

Five minutes later they were both kitted out in helmets and gloves, and once he'd fixed Miller into her cart he climbed into his own.

'We're not racing each other,' she informed him nervously.

Wondering if she would get the bug, he smiled. 'Remember it's just like driving a normal car only the gears are on the steering wheel and there's no clutch. Right foot is accelerator and left is brake. Other than that there's nothing to it.'

He watched as she revved the engine, unexpectedly distracted when her face glowed. 'One more thing,' he called above the throaty whine of the carts. 'These engines are more powerful than the usual carts, so go easy on the first few laps. I'll go first, so you can follow my line as you learn the track.'

'Ha—you're going first because you can't stand being second.'

Valentino smiled. She'd got that right.

He gunned his engine and put the cart into gear. The carts were fixed with a side mirror, so he kept his eye on her as they did a couple of laps.

Both he and Andy had designed the carts, and he was impressed at how well they handled.

After five laps he pulled his cart to a stop near the starting line and waited for Miller to pull up beside him.

'How was it?'

Her face was flushed from the light wind and her eyes were glowing with excitement. Oh, yeah, she definitely had the bug.

'I think you could turn me into a speed demon.' She grinned. 'This is *amazing*. But they seem a bit powerful for kids.'

Valentino found himself once again captivated by her smile, those eyes that shifted from aquamarine to almost indigo when she was aroused. 'They're for big kids. Teenagers, adults. This is a specialised track.'

'Great to hire out to corporations for bonding sessions.'

'Maybe.' He hadn't thought that far ahead yet.

'I have an idea.'

She leaned towards him conspiratorially and his eyes instantly fell to the deep V the movement made in her black T-shirt.

'What?'

'I'll race you!'

It took him a second to get his mind off her cleavage, and by that time she was already two cart lengths ahead of him. Valentino felt his competitor's spirit champing at the bit.

Little witch. She had deliberately distracted him.

As he followed her the feeling that he was very much in trouble with this new, more relaxed Miller returned. In fact, possibly he'd been in trouble all along.

He'd sensed this latent fire in her nature many times over the weekend at TJ Lyons's, and after listening to her story about her childhood he could see how she had locked herself down to a certain extent to achieve her goals. Which he admired. It took a lot of fortitude to achieve what she had done, and even though he felt that her reasoning had been a little skewed by her mother's fears, he couldn't fault her execution. She'd devised a plan for herself and she'd worked diligently to achieve it. A bit like himself.

Tino kept pace with her, challenging her lead on one of the easier corners but never taking over. For once he was happy to take the back seat in a competition.

He came up beside her and signalled one more lap. He saw determination set in her face and had to smile. If she but knew it he could take her in a heartbeat.

He upped the pressure as they headed towards the home straight and his heart nearly exploded in his chest as her cart veered to the side and headed full speed towards a railing that had yet to be lined with safety material.

'The brake! Dammit, Miller, hit the brake!'

He knew she couldn't hear him, and he was powerless to do anything but watch. It was like seeing his father head towards that concrete barrier all over again. The feelings of pain and loss were so powerful, so ferocious, he tasted bile in his mouth.

By some dumb stroke of luck her car pulled up an inch before the railing. Tino vaulted out of his cart and wrenched her helmet off before he'd taken his next breath.

'What were you *thinking*?' he all but bellowed as he took in her wild eyes and laughing face.

'Oh, my God. I nearly hit the rail!' Her voice was vibrating with both adrenalin and mild shock.

'That was a bloody stupid thing to do.'

'I didn't mean to,' she said indignantly. 'My heel got caught under the brake pedal.'

Her heel... Tino glanced down at her feet and noted the delicate heels on boots he'd only seen as cute. Damn, he hadn't even considered her footwear when he'd made the impromptu decision to take her out on the track.

He swore under his breath. Ironically, he'd never felt more scared of anything in his life than seeing Miller hurtle towards that railing.

'Hey, relax.' She was still smiling as she pulled herself out of the cart. 'It was just a bit of— Oh!' She threw her hand out and gripped his forearm as her legs buckled beneath her weight. 'My legs feel like jelly.' She laughed and locked her knees. 'I think that was better than sex.'

Tino shook his head, his sense of humour gone. 'Those carts top out at sixty ks an hour. You could have been seriously hurt.'

And why was he yelling at her when it was his own fault?

'I'm sorry if you were worried.' She tightened her grip, suddenly becoming aware of his over-reaction at the same time as he did.

'Of course I was worried. I don't think we have insurance on this place yet.'

'I don't know what to say.' She looked stricken. 'Are you okay?'

Tino collected the helmets. 'Fine.' He clamped down on his emotions with vicious intent, doing his best to stanch the fierce male rage that flooded him. The desire to grab her, crush her up against the nearest wall and pump himself inside her was like a savage animal riding him hard.

Instead, he shook his head, trying to clear his thoughts, and stalked off towards the equipment room. He could see Andy striding across the track and deliberately headed in the other direction. He needed to do something. *Hit* something.

'Tino!' Miller called after him, and he could hear her clipped footsteps on the concrete behind him. He lengthened his strides. 'Tino?'

Dimly he registered that she had stopped walking, and he pivoted around and stared at her. Her beautiful face was pale with concern. She approached him with the caution of a lion tamer without a whip and chair.

'Don't walk away. Please.'

Her quiet voice set off a riot of emotions, and right up there with wanting to physically take her—to physically *brand* her— was the urge to hold her and keep her safe. For ever. And that was the moment he realised he was shaking.

With the kind of lethal precision that was used to construct one of his beloved racing cars Tino shut down everything inside him.

'I have to get to the track. I've wasted enough time here.'

CHAPTER FIFTEEN

'MA'S finally got her wish, I see.'

Valentino turned at the sound of his older brother's voice and kept his irritation in check. He'd been enjoying a moment's quiet after being inundated with well-wishers and pseudo-virgins at his mother's charity extravaganza all night, but fortunately now the guests seemed to have settled—chatting, dancing and enjoying the view from one of Dante's premier hotels.

'What's that?' he asked, feigning interest.

'One of her sons has found love at her famous event.' Dante glanced towards the dance floor where Miller was dancing.

Tino glowered at him. 'I'm not even going to pretend I don't know what you're getting at.'

'That's good. We can cut straight to what you're intending to do about it instead. Should I be shining my shoes?'

'Not unless you're planning to go back to school,' Tino said lightly. 'I'm not in love with Miller,' he added dismissively. 'In case that was your next inopportune comment.'

He'd rather Dante harangue him about the big race tomorrow than a woman who was already constantly on his mind. He glanced at the dance floor where Miller was teaching his twelve-year-old nephew to waltz, and his body throbbed at the pleasurable memory of their lovemaking an hour earlier when he had returned to their penthouse suite.

Not that he'd meant it to be lovemaking. What he'd meant it to be was rough and raw sex to put them squarely back on the footing they'd started out on.

He'd spent six stressful hours at the track, secured second off the grid for tomorrow's race, and endured a gruelling press conference that had focused as much on his new "girlfriend" as it had on tomorrow's race.

All day he'd ignored his over-reaction to Miller's near accident, and the effort it had taken to keep his emotions under lock and key and be able to perform on the track had worn thin.

When he'd returned to the room and found Miller standing beside the bed in a demi-cup bra and matching thong he hadn't even bothered to say hello.

He frowned, memory turning him hard as a rock.

No, he hadn't said hello. She'd glanced up, half startled to see him as he'd prowled silently into the bedroom, and then she'd been against the wall and he'd been between her legs before he'd even thought about it.

He'd barely leashed his violent need for her, and yet once again she'd been right there with him. And, just as she had a tendency to do, she'd managed to twist the final few minutes of their coupling so that he was no longer the one in control. This time she'd insisted that he look at her with just the whisper of his name, and they'd flown over the edge together in an endless rush of pleasure.

Her sweet mouth still looked a little bruised, and as for the dress she had on... He took back his declaration that Mickey knew nothing about women's fashion. The chocolate-brown silk and froth creation clung to every curve and set off her eyes and skin to perfection. He'd never actually seen a more beautiful woman in his life, and his latent fear of tomorrow's race paled in comparison to the feelings she raised in him.

She was in his head—hell, she had been in the car with him at the track that afternoon, and that couldn't happen.

'You haven't taken your eyes off her all night and you've barely gone near her,' Dante drawled.

Tino tipped the contents of his glass of iced water down his parched throat. 'That's your definition of love?' he mocked, forcing his tone to reflect bored nonchalance. 'No wonder you struggle to keep a woman.'

Dante laughed softly. 'That's my definition of a man who's still running.'

'Let me repeat,' Tino bit out. 'I am not in love with Miller Jacobs.'

'What's the problem with it?' Dante was watching Miller now, his eyes alight with admiration. 'It was bound to happen some day. You're a lover, Tino, not a fighter. And she *is* stunning.'

'You're calling me soft?' He ignored the instinct to go for his brother's throat.

'I'm telling you I think she's great, and if you don't go get her I might.'

Valentino knew Dante was baiting him but even so his brother's soft taunt twisted the knots in his gut.

'Okay.' Dante held up his hands in mock surrender, even though Tino hadn't moved a muscle. 'I take back the not a fighter bit… But seriously, man, why fight it?'

Tino turned his back on the dance floor. 'You know why.' He sighed. 'My job.'

'So quit.'

Tino was shocked by Dante's suggestion. 'Would you give up your multi-billion dollar hotel business for a woman?'

Dante shrugged. 'I can't imagine it, but…never say never. Isn't that the adage? You've done it for fifteen years and you have an omen flapping over your head the size of an albatross. I don't think your time will be up tomorrow, if that helps, but why risk it?'

Tino knew Dante was remembering the day his father had crashed, something neither brother ever talked about, but he felt better now, knowing the reason behind Dante's topic of conversation. 'Did Ma or Katrina put you up to this?'

'You think the girls tried to get me to stop you racing? Ma would never do that. She's always been a free spirit. No.' He shook his head. 'There was just something different about you on the track today. As if you were…'

He frowned, searching for a word Tino didn't want him to find.

'Distracted.' *Yep, that was the one.* 'I thought maybe you were thinking it was time for a change.'

'In conversation, yes,' Tino bit out tersely.

The fact that his brother had noticed his earlier tension before the qualifying session was more concerning to him than if either one of the females in their family *had* sicced Dante onto him.

'Fair enough.' Dante took the heavy silence between them for what it was—disconnection. 'I won't push it. God knows I'd hate someone to push me. But I'd avoid Katrina if I were you. She's already trying to work out who will be flower girls to Toby and Dylan's pageboys.'

Miller stood to the side of the sparkling room, only half listening to Katrina's friendly chatter, her body still tingling from Valentino's earlier lovemaking when he had returned from the track. He hadn't even greeted her when he'd walked into the room—just backed her against the wall like a man possessed and taken her.

It had been fast and furious, and although he had shown her the same consideration as always she couldn't shake the feeling that he had been treating her as just another pit lane popsy— someone to use and discard straight after.

After her near accident at the go-cart track that morning his emotional withdrawal had been handled with military-like precision.

Which on some level she understood. She had been a complete bag of nerves watching him whip his car around the track during the qualifying sessions at speeds that made the go-carts look like wind-up toys, so she could only imagine how badly he had felt when she had lost control of the cart.

What she couldn't understand—what she *hated*—was the

way he politely maintained that everything was still normal between them.

It was too much like the time her parents had sat her down to tell her they were separating, pretending that they were happy with the decision while they each seethed with anger and hurt below the surface.

Their denial of how they really felt had made dealing with the separation nearly impossible, because Miller had *known* something wasn't right, and yet the one time she had been brave enough to broach the subject with her mother she had brushed her off and made her feel stupid.

Which was why, she realised, she had let Valentino give her the silent treatment. She hadn't been brave enough to open herself up to that kind of hurt again.

Unfortunately, that wasn't a failsafe plan, because without her even being aware of it the unthinkable had happened.

She had fallen in love with him.

The uncomfortable realisation had hit her when she'd been pressed deliciously against the hotel wall with his body buried deep inside hers.

At that moment when he had looked at her a spiral of emotion had caused her heart to expand, and she'd shattered around him in an agony of pleasure and longing.

She'd told herself it wasn't possible to fall in love in such a short space of time, but her heart had firmly overridden her head—as it had always done with Valentino Ventura.

And now, feeling like a liferaft set adrift, she understood why people did crazy things for love. She understood what her father had been talking about when he'd said that it was too painful to visit her after she had left with her mother. He'd had his heart broken. The sudden wave of understanding made her eyes water.

Blinking back the memories, she smiled at Katrina and pretended she'd been listening—and then at her next words she really was.

'I never thought I'd see my brother so in love. He can't stop looking at you.'

Couldn't stop looking at her? He hadn't looked at her once.

Well, okay, she had seen him glancing her way a couple of times, but she'd have called that glowering at her, not the benign version of *looking*. And he'd turned away each time before their eyes could properly connect.

Which was ironic, because she was supposedly here to prevent him from being accosted by every unattached woman at the ball, and since they weren't behaving like a couple the women had been lining up to get to him in droves. In fact, if she'd known he was going to completely ignore her, she would have brought a numbering system to help the whole process go more smoothly. Sort of like a speed dating service. Give everyone their five minutes and wait for him to choose her replacement.

Miller felt a spurt of anger take over from the intense pain that thought engendered, and latched onto it.

He might not want to continue things with her, but that didn't give him the right to treat her so poorly. It wasn't as if she would suddenly develop into a needy person who wouldn't let him go. She had known it was going to end. What she hadn't expected was that she would enjoy being part of a couple so much. She had been so fiercely independent for so long the thought hadn't occurred to her. But with Valentino… He made her feel so much. Made her want so much. Was that why he was avoiding her so thoroughly? Had he guessed her guilty secret?

The thought that he had horrified her. She might feel as if she was ready to face a lot of things she hadn't before in her professional life, but personally she was very far from ready to "squeeze the fear". Certainly not with a man who would never feel for her the same way she felt for him.

But it was one thing to deceive her workplace about her relationship with Valentino, which she had hated doing, and quite another to deceive Valentino's loving family. She didn't think Valentino would care if she corrected Katrina.

'Actually, Valentino isn't in love with me.'

'Oh, I wouldn't be so sure. He might not have said—'

Miller put her hand on Katrina's arm. 'I only met Valentino last week. The only reason I'm here with him now is because he helped me out of a bind and pretended to be my boyfriend.' She saw Katrina's eyes widen with unbridled curiosity and shook her head. 'Don't ask—it's a long story. Suffice it to say I became unwell, Valentino helped me out, and…here I am. But I'm going home tomorrow.'

Katrina turned compelling blue-grey eyes on her. 'But you have feelings for my brother?'

Miller inclined her head. No point in denying what was clearly obvious to Valentino's sister. She shrugged. 'Like every other woman on the planet.'

'So you're going to do what he does?' Katrina gently chided.

Miller's brow scrunched in confusion.

'You're going to make light of it?'

'No, you're wrong. I don't make light of anything.' She gave a self-deprecating laugh. 'I'm way too serious; it's one of my faults.'

Katrina pulled a face. 'I know my brother can be intensely brooding and unapproachable at times, but don't give up on him. He's protected himself from getting hurt for so long I think its second nature to him now. After our father's death he changed, and not—'

'Giving away family secrets again, Katrina?'

A biting voice savagely cut through his sister's passionate diatribe and Miller cringed. He stood behind her, legs braced wide and larger than life in a superbly cut tuxedo that made him look even more like a devil-may-care bad-boy than his jeans and T-shirts.

'Hello, little brother. Are you having a good time?' Katrina greeted him merrily.

'No. And I need to go. I'll see you at the track tomorrow, no doubt. Miller?'

He held out his arm for her to take and Miller did so, but

only because she didn't want to cause a scene in front of his sister. 'It was lovely to meet you, Katrina.'

'Likewise.' Katrina leant in close. 'Don't let his scowl put you off. He's harmless underneath.'

Oh, she was so wrong about that, Miller thought miserably. Valentino had the power to hurt her like no one else ever had, and she was really peeved she had given him that power over her. Because it was her own stupid fault. He'd been honest right from the start.

Halfway across the room, Miller tugged on his arm. 'I might stay on a bit longer, if that's okay?'

God, when had she been reduced to sounding like a Nervous Nelly?

'Why?'

Because I don't want to go upstairs with you in this mood and have you rip my heart to pieces.

'I'm having a good time.'

'I don't want you talking to my family about me *or* my father.'

His voice was cold and she now wondered if he really was leaving because he needed to get sleep and prepare for the race tomorrow, or because he assumed she'd keep trying to wheedle secrets out of his family about him.

'I didn't ask Katrina anything,' she denied. 'She assumed that you had feelings for me. We both know you don't and I told her this whole thing was fake.'

Valentino grabbed her elbow and pulled her to the side of the room to let a couple pass by.

'Why would you say that?'

Miller forced herself not to be intimidated by his frown. 'Because I don't like being dishonest and I like your family.'

'This thing stopped being fake the minute we had sex and you know it,' he growled.

Miller's hopeful heart skipped a beat. Did he mean that? Could his black mood be because he had strong feelings for her and just didn't know how to express them?

'What is it, then?' She knew she was holding her breath but she couldn't help it.

He raked back his hair in frustration and glowered at the glittering crowd of doyennes behind her. 'I don't know. Good fun?'

Good fun?

Stupid, desperate heart.

'Look, I'm sorry. I've had a terrible day and I don't want you talking about my father. The man died racing a car. Everyone needs to get over it and move on.'

'Like you have?'

His scowl at her quietly voiced question didn't bear thinking about. 'Don't psychoanalyse me, Miller. You don't know me.'

'Only because you hide your deepest feelings under solid cement.'

She thought he would try and make light of her comment. When he didn't she realised how stressed he really was. She also realised that her breathing had grown harsh, and the last thing she wanted to do was argue with him the night before a crucial race.

'Valentino, your sister didn't mean any harm. She was boosting me up because she thinks that you protect yourself against being hurt.' A conclusion she had also drawn after talking to him that day in the park.

'That's ridiculous.'

'Is it?' Miller asked softly, her heart going out to this wounded, gorgeous man. 'Or is it that you believe that your father didn't love you enough to quit racing? Because I know that tomorrow's race has been playing on your mind, and I've seen enough to guess that maybe you're a little angry with him.'

A flash of insight hit her as she recalled how stiff he had been in his mother's company—a woman she knew he loved dearly.

'Maybe even with your mother—although I'm not sure why that would be.'

'Don't confuse your mother issues with mine, Miller,' he snarled.

Miller gasped. 'That's a horrible thing to say. My mother

did her best and while you've helped me see that I've blindly followed her dreams instead of my own that wasn't her fault. It was mine. I didn't *have* to give up my artistic aspirations. I *chose* to because it suited me at the time.' Miller felt as if he'd torn a strip off her and left her bleeding. 'Now, I can see I've overstayed my welcome, so if you'll ex—'

'Don't leave.'

Miller's stomach was in knots and she was shaking. She *had* to leave before her runaway mouth said anything more she might regret. 'I'm tired.'

'I don't mean right now. I mean tomorrow. Quit your job and travel with me. Come to Monaco next week.'

Miller stared at him. The tinkling chatter of happy guests faded to a low hum. He didn't look completely comfortable, but was he serious?

'Why?' she blurted out.

'Why does there have to be a reason? Haven't you had fun the last few days?'

Miller smoothed her brows. 'You know I have. But it's not enough to sustain a relationship.'

'Why put a label on what's between us?'

Miller paused, taking in the offhandedness of his question, his effortless arrogance.

Oh, God, he wasn't talking about having a relationship with her. Not a real one, anyway. *She* was the only one here with long-term on the brain.

'I...can't.'

She knew if she took him up on his offer it would mean a lot more to her than it did to him, and she knew herself well enough to know that it would be hell on her self-esteem. It would also be repeating the same mistakes she had made in the past— because following him around the world would be following *his* dreams at the expense of her own.

Reluctantly, she shook her head.

'Why not?' He sounded frustrated. 'You hate your job.'

'I don't hate my job.'

He made a patronising noise and swung his arm in an arc. 'It's not what you want to do.'

'How would you know? You never ask me what it is I want— you just tell me.' She knew that was slightly unfair but she wasn't about to correct herself right now. This was about protecting herself from his clear intent to change her mind for his own selfish purposes.

'If you don't want to come just say so, Miller, but don't use your job as an excuse.'

'What has got into you?' she fumed. 'You've been like a bear with a sore head all day, you've ignored me all night, and now you're trying to steamroller me again to get what you want.'

'Because I *always* get what I want.'

Miller rolled her eyes. 'That's arrogant, even for you.'

He shoved a hand in his pocket, pulling the divinely cut tuxedo jacket wide in a casually elegant move redolent of a 1950s film. 'You didn't seem to mind it this week.'

Didn't seem to... Miller couldn't fathom his indifference. She had feelings and he was treating her as if she was here just to please him.

'I don't know how serious your offer to travel with you was, but I'm assuming you want a relationship. I have to tell you that I would never enter into something with a man who is so stubborn and selfish and *angry.*'

'And finally she lists my faults.'

'Oh, that is *so* typical of you—to make fun of something so serious.'

'And it's so typical of you to make serious that which could be fun.'

Miller drew in a fortifying breath. 'I think we've said enough. We're too different, Valentino. You want everything to be light and easy, but sometimes feelings aren't like that.'

'I know that. It's why I refuse to have them.'

'You can't just refuse to have them. They're not controllable.' But Miller had the uncomfortable realisation that she had once believed exactly that.

Valentino rocked back on his heels. 'Every emotion is controllable.'

'Well, you're lucky if that's true, because I've just discovered that mine aren't, and I can't be with someone who only connects with me during sex because he's too afraid to share how he feels.'

'It's the damned uncertainty of it you don't like.'

Miller threw up her hands. 'And now you're going to tell me how I feel in an effort to hide your own feelings.'

'Fine—you want to know how I feel? I feel that my father made a bad choice when he married my mother. He wasn't a man equipped for having a family and he was never around for us. Hell, I was his favourite because of our shared love of adrenalin highs, but even then we hardly had any time together. And when his car hit that wall—' He stopped suddenly, his voice thick. 'I won't do that to another person.'

The words *it hurts too much* hovered between them and Miller's stomach pitched.

'Valentino, I'm so sorry.' She wanted to touch him, but his stiff countenance stole her confidence.

'You're not coming with me, are you?'

Miller swallowed heavily. If he had shown any inclination that his feelings might be even close to being as strong as hers she'd stay. She'd…

No. She couldn't stay for anything less than love. She refused to fall victim to the laws of relationships. She refused to be in an unequal partnership and watch it wither and die. Because it would take her along with it.

'I can't. I—' She hesitated, fear of being ridiculed stopping her from exposing exactly how she felt, but knowing she loved him too much just to walk away without trying. 'I want more than you're prepared to give.'

He raked back his hair in frustration. 'How much more?'

'I want love. I never thought I did, and I'm still afraid of it, but you've made me see that working so hard, cutting myself off from my true passions, from my *feelings*, is living half a life. I'm sure I won't be any good at a real relationship, but I'm ready to try.'

He turned his head to the side, his expression hard. 'I can't give you that. I don't do permanence.'

Miller smiled weakly, her heart breaking. 'I know. That's why I didn't ask it of you. But thank you for last weekend. For this week. And good luck tomorrow.'

'Fine.' His voice was harsh, grating. He cleared his throat. 'Tell Mickey when you want to organise the jet.'

Miller felt her lower lip wobble and turned away before the tears in her eyes spilled over. It didn't get much more definitive than that.

CHAPTER SIXTEEN

WHEN Miller disappeared from view Tino stalked off without a clear destination in mind, burning with anger. Didn't she know what a concession he had made for her? What he had just offered her?

Tino stopped when he found himself outside on a tiered balcony, staring sightlessly at the glittering city lights.

Thank God she *hadn't* taken him up on his offer. What had he been thinking? He *never* took a woman on tour.

'I'm probably not the best person to follow you out here, but I know at least out of respect you won't walk off on me.'

Valentino turned to find his mother standing behind him.

'Want to talk about it?'

No, he didn't want to talk about it.

'Thanks, but I'm fine, Ma.'

'Don't ask me how this works.' His mother stepped closer. 'But a mother always knows when one of her children is lying. Even when they're fully grown.'

Valentino blew out a breath and tipped his head to the starry sky. He really didn't want his mother bothering him right now, and he cursed himself for not leaving when he'd had the chance.

'Ma—'

His mother held her hand up in an imperious way that reminded him of Miller. 'Don't brush me off, darling. I once let your father go into a race in turmoil, and I won't let my son do the same if I can help it.'

Valentino stared down at the tiny woman who had the

strength and fortitude of an ox, and his anger morphed into something else. Something that felt a little like despair.

She stood beside him and the silence stretched taut until he couldn't stand it any more. 'You found it hard to be married to Dad with his job. I know you did.'

'Yes.'

'Why didn't you ask him to quit?' Valentino heard the pain in his voice and did his best to mask it. 'He would have done it for you.'

She regarded him steadily. 'You're still angry with him. With me, perhaps?'

He turned back to the lights below; cars like toys were moving in a steady stream along the throughways. Miller had said he was angry and right now he *felt* angry, so what was the point in denying it?

'I never realised just how much you closed yourself off from us after your father died.' His mother's soft voice penetrated the sluggish fog of his mind. 'You were always so serious. So *controlled*. But somehow you were still able to make us laugh.'

She offered him a sad smile that held a wealth of remembered pain.

'I can see now it was your way of dealing with your pain, and I'm sorry I wasn't there more for you right after it happened.'

Valentino raked an unsteady hand through his hair. 'He always acted so bloody invincible and I...' He swallowed the sudden lump in his throat. 'I stupidly believed him.'

'Oh, darling. I'm so sorry. And I must have only made it worse by relying on you so heavily after his death because I thought you understood.'

Valentino felt something release and peel open deep inside him. Clasping his mother's shoulders, he drew her into his arms. 'I'm not angry at you, Ma.'

'Not any more, hmmm?'

He heard her sniff and tightened his embrace. 'I'm sorry. I've been an ass to you and to Tom. I treated him appallingly when he dutifully drove me to go-cart meets every month, stood in the wings of every damned race.' He stopped, unable to express his remorse at the way he had treated his mother's second husband.

His mother hugged him tight. 'He understood.'

'Then he's a better man than I am.'

'You were only sixteen when we married—a difficult age at the best of times.'

'I think I resented him because he was around when Dad just never had been.'

'Your father took his responsibilities seriously, Valentino. His problem was that he'd grown up in a cold household and didn't know how to express love. He didn't know how to show you that he loved you, but he was torn. That morning...' She stopped, swallowed. 'We'd been talking a lot about him retiring leading up to that awful race, and I think that had he survived he *would* have quit.'

'I overheard you both talking about it that morning.'

His mother closed her eyes briefly. 'Then you must blame me for his death. For putting him off his race.'

Her voice quavered and Tino rushed to reassure her. 'No. Certainly not. Honestly, I blamed Dad for trying to have it all. I think, if anything, I was just upset that you hadn't tried to stop him.'

His mother pulled back and gave him a wistful smile. 'It is what it is. We are each defined by the choices that we make for good and bad. And it wasn't an easy decision for your father to make. He had sponsors breathing down his neck, the team owner, his fans. He did his best, but fate had other ideas.' She paused. 'But life goes on, and I've been lucky enough to find love not once, but twice in my life. I hope you get to experience the same thing at least once. I hope all of my children do.'

Jamming his hands in his pockets, Tino wished he could jam a lid on the emotions swirling through his brain.

Damn Miller. She had been right. He had been angry with his mother all this time. 'I'm sorry. Thank you for telling me.'

He caught a movement in his peripheral vision and saw Tom,

his stepfather, about to head back inside, his expression clearly showing that he didn't want to interrupt.

Valentino beckoned him and Tom approached, putting his arm around his wife, love shining brightly in his eyes. 'I didn't want to interrupt.'

Tino drew in a long, unsteady breath. 'Tom...' He searched for a way to thank this man he had previously disdained for loving his mother and always being there for him and his siblings.

Tom inclined his head in a brief nod. 'We're good.'

Tino felt a parody of a smile twist his mouth. He nodded at Tom, kissed his mother's cheek and left them to admire the view.

The urge to throw down a finger of whisky was intense. So was the need to find Miller.

Tino did neither.

Instead, he took the lift to the ground floor and hailed a cab to the only place he'd ever found real peace.

His car.

The tight security team at the Albert Park raceway were surprised to see him, but no one stopped him from entering.

Not ever having been in the pits this late at night, he was surprised with how eerie it felt. Everything was deadly quiet. The monitors were off, the cars tucked away under protective cloth. The air was still, with only a faint trace of gasoline and rubber.

He threw the protective covering off his car, pulled the steering wheel out and climbed in. His body immediately relaxed into the bucket seat designed specifically to fit his shape. The scent of moulded plastic and polish was instantly soothing.

After re-fixing the steering wheel, he did an automatic pre-race check on the buttons and knobs.

Then he thought of his father and the times he'd watched him do the same thing, remembering the connection they had shared.

He released a long breath, realising that he had always felt superior to his father because *he'd* kept everyone at a safe distance. He'd believed it to be one of his great strengths, but maybe he'd been wrong.

A faint memory flickered at the edges of his mind, and he let his head fall back, stared unseeing at the high metal ceiling. What was his mind trying to tell him...? Oh, yeah—his father had once told him that when love hit you'd better watch out, because you didn't have any say in the matter. You just had to go for it.

Tino's hands tensed around the steering wheel. His father hadn't been weak, as he'd assumed, he'd been strong. He'd dared to have it all. Okay, he'd made mistakes along the way, but did that make him a bad person?

In a moment of true clarity, Tino realised that he was little more than an arrogant, egotistical shmuck. One who didn't dare love because he was afraid to open himself up to the pain he had experienced at losing his father.

For years he'd truly believed he was unable to experience deep emotion, but now he realised that was just a ruse—because Miller had cracked him open and wormed her way into his head and his heart.

Damn.

Tino banged the steering wheel as the truth of his feelings for her stared him in the face. He loved Miller. Loved her as he'd never wanted to love anyone. And ironically he was now faced with his worst nightmare. Forced to face the same decision he'd held his father to account for so many years ago.

For so long he had resented his father for refusing to quit, but he'd had no right to feel that way. No right to stand in judgement of a man who'd been driven to please everyone.

Like Miller.

Tino felt a stillness settle over him.

He could hear tomorrow's crowd already, smell the gasoline in the air, the burn of rubber on asphalt, *feel* the vibration of the car surrounding him, drawing him into a place that was almost spiritual. But despite all that he couldn't *see* himself doing it.

He could only see Miller. Miller in the bar in her black suit.

Miller tapping her toes by the car as she waited for him to pick her up. Miller completely wild for him on the beach, in his bed, staring at him with wide, hurt eyes in the ballroom as the light from the chandeliers lit sparks in her wavy hair.

God, he was more of an idiot than Caruthers. He'd had her, she'd been *his*, and he'd pushed her away. Closed her down as he'd done all week whenever the conversation had veered towards anything too personal.

Levering himself out of his car, he knew he was saying goodbye to a part of his life that had sustained him for so long, but one that he didn't need any more.

He didn't care what the naysayers would say when he pulled out of the race tomorrow. For the first time ever he had too much to lose to go out onto the track. For the first time ever he wanted something else more.

The signs had been there. Or maybe they hadn't been signs, maybe they'd just been coincidences. It didn't matter. When he closed his eyes and thought about his future he wasn't standing on a podium, holding up yet another trophy. He was with Miller.

Miller who had stalked off with tears behind her eyes.

Where *was* she?

He doubted she'd organised the jet to fly back to Sydney at this late hour; she was too considerate to disturb his pilot.

Likely she was still at the hotel. But he'd bet everything he owned she'd arranged for another room by now.

Miller felt terrible. Beyond terrible. Walking away from Valentino's offer to travel with him had felt like the hardest thing she had ever done in her life. Even harder than leaving her father behind in Queensland all those years ago.

She was in love with Valentino and she was never going to see him again, never going to touch him again. There was something fundamentally wrong with that.

Travel with me. Come to Monaco next week.

Had she made a monumental mistake?

Miller looked down, half expecting to find herself standing

on a trapdoor that would open up at any minute and put her out of her misery, but instead all that was there was designer carpet.

She sighed. This morning she had woken in Valentino's arms and felt that life couldn't get any better. TJ had signed Oracle to consult for his company *before* finding out what Valentino's decision about Real Sport was, and the powers-that-be had requested a meeting with her first thing Monday morning. Which could only mean a promotion because, as Ruby had pointed out, no one got fired on a Monday.

But the idea of a promotion didn't mean half as much as it once might have. Not only because her priorities had changed over the course of the week, but because she felt as if all the colour had been leached out of her life. Try as she might to pull herself together, it seemed her heart had taken a firm hold of her head and it was miserable. Aching.

She'd known falling in love would be a mistake, and boy had she ever been right about that. Love was terrible. Painful. *Horrible.*

She had accused Valentino of keeping himself safe from this kind of pain, but of course it was what she had always done as well. Keeping her hair straight, wearing black, hiding herself away at her work in an attempt to control her life. None of it had been real—just like her relationship with Valentino.

Only towards the end it had felt real with him. Had *become* real without her even noticing… She'd fallen in love and he hadn't. Which just went to prove the law of relationships: one person always felt more.

And now, sitting on Valentino's plane as his pilot ran through the preflight check, still wearing her beautiful, frothy dress, she felt like the heroine from a tragic novel.

She sniffed back tears and wondered if she had time to put her casual clothes on. And then she wondered what was taking so long. Surely she'd been sitting on the tarmac for over an hour now?

The whoosh of the outer doors opening brought her head

round, and she was startled to see Valentino's broad shoulders filling the doorway.

Like her, he hadn't taken the time to change, and he looked impossibly virile: his bow tie was hanging loosely around his neck and the top buttons of his dress shirt were reefed open.

Miller swallowed, her heart thumping in her chest. 'What are you doing here?'

Valentino stalked inside the small cabin. 'Looking for you. And I have to say this is the last place I tried.'

'I told Mickey not to tell you.'

'He didn't. My pilot did.'

He looked annoyed.

'I'm sorry if you're upset about me commandeering your plane at this hour. I felt terrible doing it. But all the hotel rooms were booked and Mickey insisted…'

'I don't care about the plane. And stop moving.' Miller stopped when she realised she was stepping backwards. 'Where are you going, anyway?'

'The pilot stowed my bag in the rear cupboard. I was just going to get it.'

'Leave the damn bag.' He dragged a hand through his hair and Miller realised how tired he looked.

She swallowed heavily. 'Why were you looking for me?'

Had she forgotten something? Left something in their room?

'Because I realised after you left that I loved you and I needed to tell you.'

'You…what?'

He came towards her again and Miller's back bumped the cabin wall. Her senses were stunned at his announcement.

Valentino stepped into her personal space and cupped her elbows in his hands. 'You heard right. I love you, Miller. I've spent my whole life convincing myself it was the last thing I wanted, but fortunately you came along and proved me wrong.'

Miller tried to still her galloping heart. 'You told me that racing was all you ever needed.'

'Which shows you that you need to add stupidity to my list of flaws.'

'I might have been a bit harsh earlier.'

'No, you weren't.' He hesitated. 'After my father died I was determined never to love anyone because I convinced myself that I wanted to protect them from the hurt I had experienced. But you were right. I was protecting myself.' He shook his head. 'Until you came into my life, Miller, I truly believed that I didn't have the capacity to love anyone.'

Miller felt her heart swell in her chest. She desperately wanted to believe that he loved her but her old fears wouldn't let go.

He squeezed her hands gently. 'You're thinking something. What is it?'

'I thought you always knew what I was thinking?' Miller smiled weakly at her attempt at humour.

'Usually I do, but right now…I'm too scared to guess.'

Scared? Valentino was *scared*?

His admission was raw, and unbridled hope sparked deep inside her. 'You risk your life every time you race.'

He laughed. 'That's nothing compared to this. Now tell me what you're thinking, baby.'

Miller felt as if her heart had a tractor beam of sunlight shining right at it at the softness of his tone. 'I'm thinking that I may never outgrow my need for certainty, and I don't know if I can watch you throw yourself around a track every other week without making you feel guilty. Watching you qualify today, I thought I was going to throw up.'

'You won't have to do either. I've organised a meeting first thing tomorrow morning to announce my retirement from the circuit. Effective immediately.'

Miller didn't try to hide her shock. 'Why would you do that? You love racing.'

'I love you more.'

His words made her heart leap. 'But what will you do instead?'

'Andy and I have a patent over the new go-cart designs and we have visions of taking Go Wild global. I like your idea of turning it into a venue for corporations to use and I'm also thinking we can use it as a place to give kids interested in competing some personal coaching.'

Miller nodded. 'That's a great idea.'

Valentino blew out a breath as if her opinion really mattered. 'Good. I'm glad you like it. In fact, I was hoping to convince you to consult for us. Andy and I know a lot about cars, but we know jack about running a business.'

'You want me to work for you?' Miller knew she was smiling like a loon.

'Only if you want to—God, Miller, you're beautiful.' Valentino dropped her hands and hauled her against him, kissing her so passionately she couldn't think straight.

He drew back, shuddering. 'Where was I? Oh, yeah. Marry me.'

'Marry you?'

'I'm sorry I don't have a ring yet. Honestly, I've been fighting my feelings so hard for so long I'm embarrassingly underprepared, but I promise to make it up to you.'

Remembering how everything had gone so wrong between them just hours earlier, Miller felt some of her anxiety return.

As if sensing her tumultuous emotions, Valentino tugged her in against him again. 'If you don't like the idea that's fine. I know you have your own dreams to follow and I'll support you in whatever they are.' He smiled. 'Just so long as we find a little bit of time to have a house full of kids.'

'A house full?'

'You said you didn't like being an only child.'

'I hated it.' Miller's head was reeling.

'Then we should probably try for more than one, because chances are they'll hate it too.'

Once again happiness threatened to engulf her, but a tiny niggle of doubt still prevailed. 'Wait. You're steamrollering me again.'

'But I am wearing a suit this time. Does that count?'

Miller felt both fearful and excited in the face of his un-wavering resolve. 'It does help that you look insanely hand-some in one, yes.'

Valentino clasped her face in his hands. 'Okay, you're still worried. Talk to me.'

Miller wet her dry lips and took a deep breath. He'd put his heart on the line for her, was giving up his racing career to be with her. The least she could do was confide her greatest fear.

'Valentino, you can't possibly feel the same way about me as I do about you, and that will eventually ruin everything be-tween us.'

She tried to glance away, feeling utterly miserable now, but he held her fast.

'How *do* you feel about me, Miller?'

'I love you, of course. But—'

She didn't get any further as his mouth captured hers in a blistering kiss so full of sensual passion and promise that tears stung the backs of her eyes.

'Stop.' She pushed at him weakly, her body trembling against his. 'You're too good at that, and it doesn't change the funda-mental law of relationships.'

'Which one's that?' he asked, nuzzling the side of her neck.

Miller tried to put some distance between them, but his hold was implacable. 'The one that says one person will always love more than the other.'

Her voice was so anguished Valentino stopped kissing her and stared into her eyes. 'I've never heard of that law, but you'll never love me as much as I love you. I guarantee it.'

'No.' Miller shook her head. 'Your feelings can't possibly be as strong as mine are for you.'

Valentino smiled, pressed her against the cabin wall. 'Want to argue about it for the rest of our lives?'

Miller burst out laughing, radiant happiness slowly soaking into every corner of her heart. 'You're serious!'

Valentino stayed her nervous hands in one of his. 'I've never been more serious about anything. I once told you I'd never met a woman who excited me as much as racing—but, Miller, you do. I feel exhilarated just thinking about seeing you. And when I do...' He shook his head, the depth of his emotions shining brightly in his eyes.

Miller gazed back at the only man who had ever made her heart sing. 'I love you *so* much. I didn't know it was even possible to feel like this about another person.'

'Ditto, Sunshine. Now, put me out of my misery and tell me you'll marry me.'

Completely overwhelmed by emotions no longer held at bay Miller grinned stupidly. 'I'll marry you—but with one condition.'

Valentino groaned. 'I knew you wouldn't make it easy. What's the condition?'

Miller linked her hands behind his neck, deciding to have some fun with him. 'We do it at my pace, *not* yours.'

Valentino threw back his head and laughed. 'I told Sam that was my lucky shirt. Now it will be forever known as my *life-changing* shirt.'

Wriggling closer, Miller nuzzled his neck, the last of her doubts fading into nothing. 'I love you.'

Valentino's touch became purposeful, masterful. 'And I you.'

Miller smiled. How had she ever thought love was horrible? Love was w*onderful*.

* * * * *

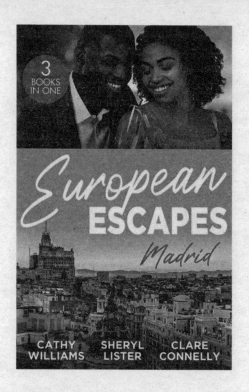

MILLS & BOON

THE HEART OF ROMANCE

A ROMANCE FOR EVERY READER

MODERN

Prepare to be swept off your feet by sophisticated, sexy and seductive heroes, in some of the world's most glamourous and romantic locations, where power and passion collide.

HISTORICAL

Escape with historical heroes from time gone by. Whether your passion is for wicked Regency Rakes, muscled Vikings or rugged Highlanders, awaken the romance of the past.

MEDICAL

Set your pulse racing with dedicated, delectable doctors in the high-pressure world of medicine, where emotions run high and passion, comfort and love are the best medicine.

True Love

Celebrate true love with tender stories of heartfelt romance, from the rush of falling in love to the joy a new baby can bring, and a focus on the emotional heart of a relationship.

Desire

Indulge in secrets and scandal, intense drama and sizzling hot action with heroes who have it all: wealth, status, good looks…everything but the right woman.

HEROES

The excitement of a gripping thriller, with intense romance at its heart. Resourceful, true-to-life women and strong, fearless men face danger and desire - a killer combination!

To see which titles are coming soon, please visit

millsandboon.co.uk/nextmonth